SKARLET

THOMAS EMSON

snowbooks

Proudly Published by Snowbooks in 2009

Snowbooks Ltd.
120 Pentonville Road
London
N1 9JN
Tel: 0790 406 2414
email: info@snowbooks.com
www.snowbooks.com

British Library Cataloguing in Publication Data
A catalogue record for this book is available from the British Library.

Paperback ISBN 978-1-905005-98-7
Library Harback ISBN 978-1-906727-01-7

SKARLET

PART ONE
OF THE
"VAMPIRE TRINITY"

AUTHOR'S NOTE

Skarlet is fiction. The characters are made up, and they're not meant to reflect real people I know or real people I don't. The Iraq War is very real, but the incident Jake Lawton was involved in is a figment of my imagination, as is the reaction to it. The locations in Skarlet are all real, but they have been fictionalized for the sake of plot. For example, the parts of London that are portrayed in the novel might not be recognizable to the residents. That's because I made them up.

Thomas Emson

PART ONE.
THE FIRST ONES.

CHAPTER 1.
BLOOD TIES.

THE stranger said, "I'll buy your children."

The father gawped. He looked at his wife. The wife put her face in her hands and whimpered.

And the stranger said, "I'll pay a good price. Do the men in the town pay a good price? I will better it and take them away from you. Your lives will improve with all that money, yes?"

The father's face tightened. He glanced across at his children. They were huddled together near the door. His daughter glared at him, and hatred shone in her purple eyes.

But we have to survive, he thought, *and your beauty sells for a good price.*

The wife looked up at him, and her face flushed with grief. She said, "What if we become poor again? We won't have them to provide for us. No one will buy me, will they."

"You'll not want," said the stranger. "What I give you will last until your old age. I will pay the highest price for your children and" – he stared down at the rags on the table – "for these."

The father shook his head. "I'll want double for these."

The stranger's face reddened. "They're not yours to barter with, sir."

"They're in my house, in my safe keeping. I'll bloody well barter if I want to." He leaned forward, elbows on the table: "Do you realize how difficult life is in Romania? They say we live well. They say we should love Ceaucescu. We're better off than the Russians, better off than the English and the Americans. We're all equal, a Socialist paradise." Sitting back, he folded his arms. "That's bollocks. We're starving. We can't work unless we suck up to the Party, unless we join the Party. We can't eat unless we sell our daughter for sex. This is our life, and if I have something to sell, then you'll have to name a price."

"I will," said the stranger. "The price is your life."

The wife gasped and clutched at her breast. The son, cowering in the corner in his sister's embrace, cried. The boy's tears ran into the blood smearing his cheeks.

The father felt a chill spread through him. He looked at the stranger and studied his eyes. The man had a Middle Eastern look to him. His brown eyes were like bottomless pits, sucking the will out of the father. The stranger had already killed two men today. And the father was sure he'd kill him and his family, too. But bartering was a way of life for him, so he had to keep his nerve.

He said, "Give me half again what you give for the kids, and you can take these rags."

The stranger slammed his fist on the table. "They are not yours. You're only their keeper. I'll take them if I want, do you understand?"

The father's throat dried out. His wife grabbed his arm and squeezed. She leaned into him, and he smelled her sweat. Whispering, she said, "Get a good price for the children, give him this shit. He'll kill us, Constantin."

The father swallowed and said, "Give me a good price for the children, and you can take this rubbish."

The stranger relaxed. His shoulders sagged, and a smile spread across his face. "Good, good." He stared over to the children.

The girl rocked her weeping brother. She stared at the adults sitting around the kitchen table – the adults who were buying and selling her flesh.

The father looked away, fixed his gaze on the slices of material spread out on the table. He said, "How much will you give? The girl, she's fifteen, she's – soiled" – his wife blew her nose and sobbed – "but the boy, he's twelve, he's – he's untouched. Apart from the wound his stupid sister gave him today."

"She gave him that to protect him from your schemes, sir," said the stranger. "To make the boy ugly to your monstrous punters. She's brave."

"She's a fool," said the father. "He's damaged, now."

"But you'll still sell him."

He stared into the stranger's eyes and the desperation flickering in his breast blazed. "We must live, we must eat. I'll sell you my children."

The stranger said, "Good, then I'll take them." He stood up and perched his trilby on his head.

"Where – where will you take them? To your country?"

"My country?"

"Yes," said the father. "You're – Egyptian? A Palestinian? Fighting for your freedoms from the Israelis?"

The stranger chuckled. "I'm not. I'm a Babylonian."

"A Babylonian?"

"An ancient culture. Which spawned you and your family, too. But you don't seem to care about culture, do you."

Anger ignited in the father's heart. "Culture doesn't feed you. Give me my money, and take these creatures with you. You've worn out your welcome." He jumped to his feet. He towered over the stranger, and for a moment he felt strong and powerful. He could steal this shrunken Arab's money and drive him out of his home. Then he'd have the children to sell to his regular customers – and he'd be laden with the Arab's stolen money. He stepped round the table with this in mind.

The stranger whipped out the gun.

The father froze, and his wife gasped.

"I'll pay you for your children, now," said the stranger.

The father tried to speak. "I – yes – I – good, good – we can – settle – the – the price – "

"The price, sir, for being willing to sell your own children is death."

The gun fired. The father ducked, and as he ducked he saw blood burst out of his wife's face. He screamed and covered his head. Silence fell. He smelled the cordite. His son whined. Rolled up into a ball, the father prayed.

The stranger said, "You're a coward, and I am ashamed of you, brother."

The barrel pressed against the back of the father's head. It was cold and sent shudders down his body. His bladder felt queasy. He started to beg for mercy. A deafening noise filled his head and the world went black and still.

CHAPTER 2.
COMING TO WORSHIP.

SOHO, LONDON — 9.15 P.M., FEBRUARY 6, 2008

JAKE Lawton, thirty-one years old with five bullet-holes in his body, watched the vampires stream into the club.

"Here they come," said Cal Milo, Lawton's partner on the door that night. "The gothed-up freaks. The bloodsuckers. The neck-biters."

Milo stared down from his six feet six as the vamps entered Religion. Some of them leered up at Milo. They weren't scared of him, showed him no respect despite his size and power. They sneered and pouted and minced as they filed past Milo and Lawton into the club.

Lawton spied for signs of drugs, booze, and weapons. His gaze flitted over the clubbers. He watched for ticks, for nervous looks, for sweaty brows. He looked at their white faces, their black-lined eyes. Chains looped from ears to noses, from eyelids to lips. Earrings clustered on lobes. Studs drilled into foreheads. Their lips were painted black or scarlet and when they bared their polished teeth, Lawton saw that a few had filed their canines into points.

"Come on, freakshows," said Milo, "or it'll be dawn and you'll turn into dust."

"Leave it," said Lawton.

"Hey, soldier boy. You do your job, I'll do mine."

"I am doing mine — and I'm doing yours as well. Keep the gob shut and the eyes open."

12

Milo scowled at Lawton over the heads of the waiting goths. He said, "Don't pull rank on me, grunt. You're not in the army, now. This is civvie street, and I'm chief bastard. I say what's what."

Lawton sighed. He didn't want trouble. He'd deal with it if it stepped up and challenged him, but better to calm situations down than stir them up.

"All right, Cal, whatever you say. Let's get them in."

"Lovers' tiff?" said a goth with blue hair, grinning up at Lawton.

Lawton saw the rage rise in Milo and decided to push his luck: he smiled at the clubber and said, "He's playing hard to get."

The goth and his mates laughed as they trooped into Religion. Lawton glanced at Milo, and Milo snarled. His hands were rolled into fists, and a pulse throbbed at his temple.

Lawton said, "You look like you're taking a shit, Cal."

"Fucking lovers' tiff. You bastard, Lawton. Soldier boys might like it up the arse, but I prefer women."

"Unfortunately, they don't prefer you."

"What kind of women did they have out there in Iraq, Lawton?"

Lawton didn't say anything. He watched the line of goths moving into the club. Wednesday night was vampire night. It was coming up to 9.30 p.m. and they were arriving for a 10.00 p.m. start. They'd be here all night, Lawton with them. The goths never caused much trouble, never any fights, and not many drugs, either. But the dealers would be here, as usual, preying on any potential customers.

The vampires who tagged along sometimes caused a bit of hassle. The staff would always find an odd couple holed up in a toilet cubicle, drinking each other's blood.

"They're sanguinarians," Jenna told him a few months ago. "They think they need blood to live. It's not much. It's consensual. They just make a little cut on a mate's arm, sup a little red."

Lawton had frowned, thought he'd seen everything. Obviously not. The hell of Iraq had not prepared him for blood-drinking, middle-class students.

Jenna laughed and said, "You've gone a bit pale. The sight of blood make you squeamish?"

"No, but the idea of drinking it does. These people need help."

She'd scowled, looked away and said, "At least they don't murder innocent Iraqi civilians."

The Army kicked him out two years ago. Lawton came back to

New Cross, where he'd been born, where his mother had died when he was a toddler. On his return he found a flat and sat in the flat all day and all night playing the incident over in his head. He drank to try and get rid of the pictures in his brain, but that didn't work. He got some unofficial security work, and that kept the wolves at bay. But he kept on drinking and he kept on staying awake.

He and Jenna had dated for a few years when they were teenagers. But Lawton joined up, and Jenna's heart broke. It healed, though, and they always got it on whenever he came home on leave.

But in 2003 they fell out over the war in Iraq. She'd gone on that march in London, that Stop The War crap.

"So you're supporting a dictator?" said Lawton.

"You're *fighting* for one – for *two* of them," said Jenna.

"Bush and Blair aren't dictators. They may be prats, but they're not dictators, you stupid cow."

"Don't patronize me, Jake. What do you know? You're just a soldier, a killing machine, trained not to think – you do what they tell you to do."

She was right: he obeyed orders. That was the job. He didn't think about the rights and wrongs of the war, just got on with the soldiering.

But once he got out there, Lawton wished Jenna and her anti-war pals could've spent some time with him on the streets of Basra, feel the gratitude of the locals, see their relief at being freed from a tyrant's yoke.

Whatever came afterwards – and what came afterwards was a fuck up on a colossal scale, Lawton and his mates knew that – seeing those faces made it all worthwhile for him.

More than a year after the Army kicked him out, he'd seen Jenna again.

He was in a pub, Wednesday night, quick pint before a cash-in-hand job. A bunch of goths came in, loud and brash, dressed up in a mix of Renaissance and Victorian gear.

And there, in black, part of this circus, was Jenna. Her short, blonde hair had gone long and dark. Her skin was pale, her lips – which looked so sexy in scarlet – were painted black.

When she saw him sitting at the bar, her smile went and her mouth opened. They held each other's eyes for a while, until she came over and said, "You're back," and he said, "What's happened to you?"

She sat next to him on a stool, and he looked down at her long legs in the leather mini skirt and black tights, boots up to her knees.

He bought her a vodka and they skirted around the issues of themselves and the war, focusing instead on a "How's your family?" and "What are you up to?" conversation.

"Are you headed out?" said Lawton, regretting his obvious question immediately.

"Yeah," said Jenna, "goth night, vampire night."

"Vampires?"

"Uh-huh. Soho. This club called Religion. Every Wednesday night" – and here she made an accent like Bela Lugosi in the original Dracula – "the children of the night rise up to drink the blood of innocents."

"You're joking."

And she said she wasn't, telling him about sanguinarians and how they took a little drop from friends, and then saying that at least they didn't kill innocent Iraqi civilians.

Lawton had furrowed his brow, glanced over at Jenna's friends, and then asked her if she drank blood.

"No, Jake, I don't. I'm in it for the clothes and the music."

"Yeah. You always liked that kind of stuff. Bauhaus, Marilyn Manson."

"The Dresden Dolls, that kind of Dark Cabaret stuff. And London After Midnight, I like. And Manson still. He's cool." She sipped her drink, then said, "You should come down. I mean, if you're doing door work and you're looking for a job. I could put in a good word. I know the guy who runs the club."

"Do you?" he said, feeling a little flare of jealousy spark in his chest.

Lawton said he'd think about it, and thanks for the suggestion. The goths were leaving, and Jenna slid off the stool, saying she'd better be off. They looked at each other like they had when she came in, and Lawton reeled through the times when things had been good between them.

"It's good to see you again," he said.

"Yeah, you too, Jake, really."

She put an arm on his shoulder and went on tiptoe to kiss his cheek. "I'll see you again," she said – a confirmation, not a question.

"That'd be good."

"Come into town. Go see Nathan Holt at Religion. Tell him I told you."

He nodded, and she waved and mouthed "bye" as she walked out of the pub after her friends.

That night, Lawton doored at an unlicensed boxing show in North London. He and two other bouncers had to fight off a dozen thugs who thought they didn't need tickets to get in. Knives and broken bottles, bricks and baseball bats, Lawton had no idea how he got out without getting badly hurt. And he thought, *Sod that*, and the next day he headed into Soho and found Religion.

Nathan, the manager, made him go on a Security Industry Authorization course – "It's all above board, Jake. All doormen, they got be authorized these days." – and a few weeks later, a regular salary dropping into his bank account, Lawton doored at Religion for the first time.

And nine months on, still there, he watched vampires wait in line.

Milo, still rabbiting on about Iraqi women, said, "All Muslims over there, ain't they. Don't do sex. Get stoned to death, don't they."

Lawton, eyes fixed on the crowd, said, "You know as much about Iraq as you do about women, Milo. And that's a little less than nothing."

"Think you're so fucking clever, Lawton. Think I don't know what you got up to out there?"

Lawton glared at the other doorman. A sweat broke out on the back of his neck, and a spark of anger ignited in his breast.

Milo, smiling, said, "Bet they're still after you, ain't they. The Army. Bet they want your head, Lawton. What happened, eh? Lost it, did you? Did some war crimes, then chickened out of the court martial?"

Lawton almost shot through the line of clubbers and smashed into Milo. But a voice saying, "Hello, soldier," stopped him. He looked down at her and smiled, but she must have noticed the fury in his eyes. "You okay?"

"I'm fine," he said, "You look great, Jen."

She rolled her eyes. "Not your thing, Jake, I know, but thanks anyway. See you later?"

He nodded, and Jenna winked at him, stroking her hand across his abdomen as she filed into the club.

"Your little bloodsucker there, Lawton. Or is she another kind of sucker?"

"That's obviously something you've never had experience of, Milo."

Lawton's anger had died away. He knew he shouldn't let Milo get to him. Being a soldier, he was used to wind-up and banter. But Milo pushed things too far. He was a bully, and bullies got Lawton's goat. He'd seen enough of that in the Army. And as a staff sergeant, he'd put a few of them in their place – officially and unofficially.

Lawton wound down. Only a few stragglers stringing into the club, now. He and Milo would move into the club at ten, a new pair replacing them on the door. A voice in his earpiece said that everything was okay inside. He relaxed, but then a familiar figure strolled around the corner.

Dressed in a black shirt, black tie, black suit, the streak of piss sneered up at Lawton. He stopped at the door, glanced at Milo, then looked at Lawton. He took a packet of fruit gums from his jacket pocket and popped one his mouth. His face creased up as he sucked. "Sharp," he said. "A bit like you, Mr. Lawton."

Lawton scowled at him.

The streak of piss said, "I'm on the guest list tonight, Jakey-wakey."

"You're banned, Fraser – for life."

"Not tonight, mate."

"For life means tonight, means every night. On your way."

"My way is that way," said Fraser Lithgow, pointing into the club, and he started up the stairs.

Lawton put an arm out to stop him, saying, "Hold your horses, golden boy. You are banned. For life. You know that, so don't be an idiot."

"He's not banned. Not tonight," said a voice.

Lawton turned. Nathan Holt, Religion's manager, stood in the reception area. Music pounded inside the club. Goths paid their fare at the ticket booth and piled into the bar.

Lawton said, "Nathan, this guy's a dealer. We banned him last month."

Holt closed his eyes and shook his head. "Misunderstanding, Jake. He's in."

Lawton looked at Lithgow, and Lithgow grinned. "Okay," said Lawton, "but you're being searched – "

"No he's not," said Holt. "Mr. Lithgow's here as a guest of the management. Let him by, Jake."

Lawton stared at Holt and kept his arm across Lithgow's chest. He glanced at Milo; and Milo shrugged. Lawton said, "Nathan, this guy's carrying drugs, I just — "

"Let him by, Jake."

Lawton blew air out of his cheeks and dropped his arm. Lithgow, still wearing that grin, brushed his jacket where Lawton's arm had pressed against the material. He popped another sweet into his mouth. His face screwed up, and then he smacked his lips. Swaggering past Lawton, he said, "Jenna in tonight, Jake?" and then he winked, adding, "I'll see her myself, find a dark corner for the both of us."

Lithgow faded into Religion's darkness and a hoard of vampires swallowed him.

CHAPTER 3.
DEALS.

LAWTON said, "I don't like this, Nathan. We caught Fraser Lithgow with pills, and we banned him for life. He's going to be a convicted drug dealer when the courts are done with him."

Holt shook his head. "No he's not."

"What do you mean, 'No he's not'?"

"Daddy Lithgow pulled a few strings."

"Who's Daddy Lithgow?"

"Barrister. Fronted up to the cops. Said his little boy hadn't been cautioned correctly — some technicality or other — I don't know. All I know is that the Fuads told me Lithgow was clear, and that if he turned up tonight, we let him in."

"He's a fucking drug dealer, Nathan."

Holt shrugged. "The Fuads said he's in, he's in."

Lawton sighed. He looked at the bank of monitors in the CCTV viewing room, trying to spot Lithgow in the crowd packed into Religion. He'd followed Holt up here to the eagle's nest to complain about Lithgow's redemption.

Lawton turned away from the monitors and gazed through the tinted window that gave him a view of the dancefloor three-storeys below.

The CCTV suite was soundproofed, so he couldn't hear the music. It was weird watching the bodies writhe and jerk in silence. Lights flashed and beamed across the crowd, highlighting faces for split seconds – but not long enough for Lawton to spot Lithgow.

He glanced across to the tinted windows on the opposite side of the dancefloor. Behind the darkened glass lay the lighting studio, where Mick and Ray directed the illuminations.

Lawton thought of going over there and asking the guys to switch on the lights for a few seconds, let him scan the crowd for Lithgow's spiked blonde hair.

His gaze skimmed across the clubbers again, trying to spot Lithgow in the splashes of ultraviolet light pulsing from the arc lamps. The white flares were powerful, and instead of enabling Lawton to see better, they momentarily blinded him. He blinked, stars dancing before his eyes.

Holt broke his thoughts, saying, "Get back downstairs, Jake. You can't hang around here. You've got a job to do – and leave Lithgow alone."

Lawton went, thinking he should find the Fuads, ask them why they'd let Lithgow into the club. But the brothers wouldn't be here. They never were, living it up in Monte Carlo to avoid paying their way in Britain.

"Moaning get you anywhere, then?" said Milo as Lawton entered the reception area. The music thumped from the behind the doors that led through to the club, and Lawton could feel the floor drum beneath his feet. The noise didn't bother him. He'd heard worse.

Vampires and goths milled around, drinking and laughing. Lawton eyed them, looking for signs of drugs. He knew that a few of them would've been stoned before coming out. You couldn't kick someone out just because you *think* they've taken something.

"Hey, man," said Milo, "don't worry about the drugs. It ain't worth it. We can't do nothing about it."

"If we've got an anti-drugs policy, we've got to operate it properly."

Milo shrugged, just like Holt had shrugged minutes before. It was a "what can you do" shrug.

"I'm going to stroll around," said Lawton.

Milo flapped a hand as if to say, "Do what you want."

Lawton slipped into the club, and the music hit him. It was deafening, a drone of flanged guitars, screeching violins, cavernous bass-lines.

Lights flared in the rafters and sliced in beams across the clubbers. The smell of booze, sweat, and incense saturated the air. The crowd moshed to the music.

Lawton narrowed his eyes and gritted his teeth. He sought Lithgow in this chaos, but didn't hold much hope.

Daddy Lithgow might have got sonny off a drugs charge, but it didn't mean Lithgow was innocent – he was probably as guilty as hell. And the let-off had given him the confidence that he could get away with anything.

Not if I can help it, thought Lawton, skirting around edge of the dancefloor, easing goths out of his way.

★ ★ ★ ★

Jenna said she wasn't interested and started to walk off, intending to leave the chill-out room and head back down to the dancefloor.

"Hey, babe, hey," he said, trotting up behind her, hand on her shoulder.

She turned to look at him, saying, "Fraser, who gave you permission to touch?"

He held his hands out in surrender, gave her a smile. Something melted in her breast, and she cocked her head. "I don't want any tonight, Fraser, that's all."

"But, babes," he said, coming up to her, "this is really cool stuff. New pills in town. Let me show you." And fishing in his pocket he took out a jewelled box, the size of a Cook's Matches box.

Jenna furrowed her brow. Fraser was close; she could smell his aftershave. A tune she didn't recognize by The Beautiful Deadly Children played downstairs. She said, "That's a nice box."

"Yeah," he said, opening it, "came with the tabs."

"Oh," said Jenna, looking at the pills.

Fraser took one out. It was red, with a "K" emblazoned on it. Fraser said, "They're called 'Skarlet', with a 'K'."

"Any good?" said Jenna.

"Lethal."

"How do you know?"

"On good authority, babes, on good authority. I trust my source. Have I ever let you down in the past?"

21

She looked up at him and grinned. "Always, sweetheart, always."

She'd known Fraser five years, dated him for a couple of months after Jake went to fight Bush's war for oil in Iraq. But she didn't trust him. He was a sneak, a layabout, and she'd really only slept with him after he sorted out her overdraft and kept her and her mates in pills.

"How much are they, Fraser?"

"Tenner."

She blew air out her cheeks.

Fraser said, "Fiver to you, lovebud."

"Gratis – then I recommend them to my mates."

He made a face, a thinking face: pouty lips and narrowed eyes.

Jenna looked around the chill-out room. Goths lazed on the red furniture, drinking, laughing, snogging. Half a dozen leaned against the barrier, moshing there as they watched the dancefloor below.

"Gratis," said Fraser, pecking a pill up between forefinger and thumb. "Open wide."

And she did, and he popped the pill on her tongue. She drew it into her mouth. It tasted sour, not the neutral taste she usually got from a tab.

"Weird taste," she said.

"Swallow it – then you'll see weird."

Jenna swallowed, gulping to make spit to carry the pill down into her stomach. She felt it slide down her throat, sensed it skimming through her gullet.

"Okay," she said, "done."

"Take these" – Fraser gave her a handful of pills – "for your mates." He winked, gave her a leer.

Jenna felt light-headed. Fraser's image swam in front of her. That was odd. If it were ecstasy, it'd take more time to hit her. Maybe it wasn't –

She shook her head, clearing the cobwebs. "Thanks, hon," she said. And she turned, moving towards the chill-out room's exit, the music and voices welding into a single sound that undulated in her head.

Weird, she thought, finding her feet on the stairs that led down to the dancefloor, *really weird*.

CHAPTER 4.
THEY WILL DIE ...

"THEY think they're vampires, these people," said Nadia Radu, glowing in a crimson gown and a scarlet choker around her throat, "but they have no idea."

Her guests, seated on leather couches, drinking brandy, laughed. Mrs. Radu's audience comprised a dozen individuals, the men in evening suits, the women wearing cocktail dresses. One, a man in his sixties, snow-white hair and 1970s sideburns, said, "They'll know soon enough, Mrs. Radu."

"They will, Your Honour," she said, "soon enough." She glanced at the grandfather Clock in the corner and said again, "Soon enough."

"These kids," said a tall man in his forties, trendy glasses perched on his nose, "think they're vampires just because they've got a cloak like Bela Lugosi, because they bought a set of fangs."

"They'll soon feel real fangs piercing their gums, Professor," said Mrs. Radu, "real fangs, and real cravings. Did you know that these so-called vampires drink blood?"

The guests chuckled, shook their heads.

Mrs. Radu said, "They refer to themselves as 'sanguine', do you know? And they drink each other's blood. They don't need it of course — "

"Yet," said the Professor.

"Yet. But they think they do. It's a lifestyle for them. A lifestyle, but not a life."

The guests hummed in agreement.

"They think that if they've read Dracula," said a red-haired woman wedged into a blue gown, "that they're committed to the faith. Put on a frilly shirt, a cape, some make-up, and" – she struck a pose, and the others laughed – "they think that's it: we're in the gang – we're vampires."

"Little do they know, Minister," said Mrs. Radu to the red-haired woman, "of the suffering and the servitude that awaits them."

The door opened and a man strode in. Tall and imposing, he wore black and had matching hair tied into a ponytail with a red knot. A scar striped his face from the corner of his eye to his jaw.

He came to Mrs. Radu, leaned into her, and whispered in her ear that "they were in". His breath brushed her bare neck, and she closed her eyes as desire swept through her.

"Thank you, Ion," she said as the man moved away, leaving the room. After he'd shut the door behind him, she said, "Everything is in place, then. They will die, they will rise, they will feed."

The guests clapped and hurrahed.

"And soon," said Mrs. Radu, raising a hand to silence the room, "the first of the three will be reborn."

They listened to her, their eyes wide and their mouths open like children hearing a story.

Mrs. Radu went on:

"And from the first, we shall raise up the second. And from the second will come the third. And the trinity will reign over London."

"London," said the snow-haired man.

"And England," said Mrs. Radu, "and all these islands."

"And from there?" said the red-haired woman.

Mrs. Radu smiled at the woman and said, "The world will be ours, Minister."

Drained of energy, Mrs. Radu slumped into a leather armchair. She watched her guests making fists, slapping backs, saying, "Yes, yes, yes," celebrating the rebirth – after three thousand years – of a vampire nation.

★ ★ ★ ★

Lawton thought he heard shrieks filtering through the cacophony, but he put it down to the partygoers going over the top, as the goths tended to do.

But fear fired up in his belly.

Something in those shrieks wasn't right.

He pushed through the crowd, using his elbows to forge a path, saying, "Let me through, let me through," as goths gave way.

Lights flashed and cast jerking shadows as the goths moshed around him.

A circle had formed on the dancefloor, and Lawton's first instinct was, *There's a fight.* But that was unusual — goths weren't violent.

But the closer he got, he saw the clubbers get down on their knees, heard screams, someone shouting, "Can't someone help him?"

He looked up at the stage. The DJ, Captain Red, squinted down at the audience. He wasn't lost in the music as he usually would be. He was focused, his forehead creased. Lawton tried to get Captain Red's attention, but there were too many people.

The music pumped through the club, and Lawton could feel it throb through him as he made his way through the crowd.

"They're — they're dying," said a voice, and Lawton looked around.

Two men convulsed on the dancefloor, as if they were performing some freakish breakdance. But Lawton knew breakdancers didn't froth at the mouth.

"Jesus," he said, changing direction, heading for the jerking pair, blood and saliva lathered at their lips.

A shriek pierced the havoc. Lawton flinched. He wheeled around. He shut his eyes, felt someone fall against him, opened his eyes and saw a girl in a spider web T-shirt.

She stumbled and slumped into his arms. He dropped to his knees, cradling her. He stared into her face. Her eyes were wide, her mouth open. Her throat jerked, as if she were struggling to breath. She was pale, her skin bleached by the make-up she wore. Her eyes were painted black. She had dark red hair.

Lawton bent forward to look into her mouth for any blockage. And the blood shot up from the girl's throat, Lawton saying, "Jesus Christ," before it gushed out, spilling over her chin, her throat, down over her T-shirt.

Clubbers screamed, but Lawton held on to her. He looked up. "Phone 999. Alert security," he said.

A couple of goths raced off – to be of some use, Lawton hoped, and not to avoid watching this girl twitch and vomit blood.

The girl jerked, Lawton trying to comfort her. Blood and spit bubbled from her lips. He laid her on the floor, turned her on her side. Blood gushed from her mouth.

Someone grabbed his shoulder, and he wheeled around. It was Milo, saying, "What the fuck's happening?" and then, "Fuck," when he saw the girl.

"Get Red to cut the music. Find Holt. Phone emergency services. They're dying, Milo, they're fucking dying."

"Oh shit, oh shit," said Milo. He dashed off, barging panicked clubbers out of his way.

Lawton looked around. Bodies jerked and twitched. People screeched and dashed about.

"Jenna," he said, "please don't take anything, please don't take anything."

And the music died and the lights came on and the screams filled Religion.

CHAPTER 5.
SLEEPLESS NIGHTS.

NEW CROSS, LONDON – FEBRUARY 7

THE 5.00 a.m. headlines said, "Police have closed off roads leading to a nightclub in Soho after dozens of clubbers are thought to have died..."

Lawton made coffee and sat at the kitchen table, listening to the LBC report. He drank the coffee and smoked a roll-up. Fatigue swept over him, but like always, sleep never came.

He'd cleared the dancefloor with the rest of the security team, then attended to the dead and dying.

Lawton shook his head, didn't want to think about the girl in his arms, blood lathering in her mouth, her eyes wide with terror, knowing that her life was ending.

He'd looked for Jenna, but couldn't find her. He'd wanted to trawl the club, check out all the bodies. But he had to help in the main hall. He tried to ring her, but she didn't answer her phone.

The police arrived and corralled the clubbers who hadn't fled Religion. They barriered off the road leading down to the club and posted a few uniforms there to keep the rest of the night's partygoers at bay. It was 3.00 a.m. by the time they got round to Lawton, a PC with tired eyes taking a witness statement.

"We'll need to speak to you again. C.I.D. will be in touch," said the PC.

"My – my ex, she was here. Jenna McCall. Have you –?"

The copper shook his head and said, "We don't have names yet. If you didn't see her among the victims, she might have left. Chances are she's okay, Mr. Langdon – "

"Lawton. It's Lawton."

"Yes. Sorry. We'll be in touch."

Lawton tried to get back inside, but scene-of-crime officers had sealed off the areas where bodies had been found: the dancefloor, the chill-out room upstairs, the toilets, the reception area.

Lawton peered into the club. White-overalled figures strolled around. They crouched over bodies. They stooped and shuffled about, looking for any piece evidence.

Lawton turned away, eyes scanning the street. He saw Holt leaning against a car having a fag. Lawton strode over.

Holt jerked when he saw him, his chubby face turning white.

Lawton said, "If this was Fraser Lithgow's doing, your head's on the block."

"Why – why d'you think it was Lithgow?"

"He's a dealer. You let him in. That smirk on his face told me he had pills on him, Nathan."

Holt shook his head. "He wouldn't have been the only one, Jake. There's dozens of dealers here every night. We wouldn't be here without them. Turn a blind eye, mate."

"Turn a blind eye, then this happens."

Holt looked at him. Lawton saw anger in the man's expression. Holt said, "We don't know if it's drugs. We don't know if it's something they took here. They could be from the same party, a bunch of freaks who took some concoction before coming out. We don't know, Jake, so don't go spreading stories."

Holt tossed the fag aside and started to walk away. Lawton grabbed his arm and forced him back against the car. Fear bleached Holt's face.

Lawton leaned into Holt's and said, "I don't spread stories, Nathan, I try to stop them spreading. We're fucked here, pal. This place is closed until further notice, and unless someone comes up with answers, you, me, the Fuads, we're going to be pulled apart by the cops."

He jolted Holt against the car, then walked away.

It was a ninety-minute trip on the night bus to get home, and all the way he was ringing Jenna's phone, and it was ringing out.

Sitting in his kitchen, sipping his coffee, he checked the time on his Nokia: 5.22 a.m. He gave it one more try, finding her name in the phone's directory. He pressed the call button, listened and waited.

Nothing.

He put the phone down and cursed. His guts churned and a finger of fear crept up his spine.

Something was wrong, he knew it.

Jenna was dead, or close to death.

He finished his coffee, took the mug to the sink and rinsed it out. He filled it with water and drank it down, then filled it again.

The bottle of Jack Daniels drew his gaze. He stared at the bottle and thought about opening it and finishing it, and then heading down to the Tesco Express for another. It was what he always did, so why break the habit of a –?

Fuck it, he thought.

Grabbing his keys and the Nokia off the table, he started for the door. He'd find her, or if he couldn't find Jenna, he'd find Lithgow. That blowjob had something to do with this; Lawton could smell it.

The phone trilled. His heart leapt. He answered it, saying, "Jenna?"

Silence at the other end, then a whimper.

"Jenna?" he said again.

"You bastard," said a man's voice, "you absolute bastard. You killed my baby."

CHAPTER 6.
QUESTIONS.

CHRISTINE Murray, forty-four, a bloodhound with blonde curls, said, "How many dead?"

Superintendent Phil Birch sneered and, checking his red clipboard, said, "Wouldn't you like to know?"

"I would, Phil, I really would. I've heard fifty, is fifty confirmed?"

Birch's face stretched into an expression of surprise and he said, "Who told you that?"

"I can't say, but I'll print it."

He scowled. "Print it, then."

"Okay, so I'm wrong. How many, Phil?"

"Can't say, Christine."

She shrugged. "Well it's mass murder, however many it is. And you've got a drugs war on your hands."

"A drugs war? How the hell do you make that out? There's no war and no mass murder. You're sniffing a story that's not there. Don't write any of that, Christine, I'm bloody warning you."

"It's drugs, isn't it? They died of an overdose." She looked at her notebook. "Frothing at the mouth – that's what one of your over-eager PCs told me."

Birch's face went red. "Who was it?"

"I can't say, but I'll print it."

"Oh, you're a bitch."

"I know, Phil, I know."

"How did you get through the cordon, anyway?"

She raised her eyebrows, and blew out her cheeks. "Cordon? I didn't see a cordon."

She glanced towards the club. Ambulances and police cars choked the street. Their flashing lights threw a glare up into the sky. Paramedics streamed in and out of Religion. It was almost 6.00 a.m., and the clubbers had gone.

"What was going on here?" she said.

Birch said, "Wednesday's goth night. The vampires come out. It's organized by" – he checked his clipboard – "The Academy of London Vampyres, but attracts goths of all kinds. Perhaps you'd like to go and harass them?"

"Perhaps I will. Anything to do with them, you think? Vampires? Some bizarre ritual gone wrong?"

"They weren't all vampires."

"Oh, that's a comfort."

"Some – most, actually – were goths. And not all goths are vampires, but all vampires are goths – that's what one of them, a goth, told me when I asked him if he drank blood."

Adrenalin flushed Murray's heart. "Drank blood?"

"Yes. They – the vampires – some of them drink blood. They're sanguine vampires."

"Blood poisoning? Is that what killed them?"

He sneered at her again. "Screws up your drugs war, Christine. Anyway, it's possible – but it wouldn't kill them straight off. Septicaemia takes time."

Murray furrowed her brow. "They drink blood? Is that legal?"

The detective shrugged. "If it's consensual. What can you do? It's a bloody shame, but we live in a free country."

"How do they –?"

"I don't know and don't bloody quote me – and this is a crime scene, so get lost." He wheeled around and strode towards the club, a red ribbon fluttering from the clamp that held a notepad to his clipboard.

Murray stared down into Old Compton Street. Dozens dead – that's what her source had said. Her heart raced at the thought, and despite the chill, she felt clammy. This *was* mass murder, no matter what Birch said.

But who killed them?

A rogue drug dealer?

Some bizarre ritual gone wrong?

That was the story she wanted:

Weird goings-on in Soho. Blood-drinkers spread poison.

The paper would love it.

Murray thought how strange the world was, and she felt a tug of fear at her heart: David and Michael, still young, still to reach the age where they could be exposed to stuff like this.

She shuddered, thinking about them at home. What was the best way to protect them?

Richard thought she should be at home, or at least in a job where she could work regular hours. He'd raged at her when the phone buzzed at 3.00 a.m., one of her police contacts tipping her off that something had "kicked off in Soho – dozens dead – drugs".

They'd had the usual argument as she left the house half-an-hour later, and her bones chilled when she walked out of the door and stared up the stairs.

David and Michael huddled together at the top of the stairs, tears streaming down David's face.

"Go to bed, babies," she tried to say, but her voice cracked.

Murray, seeing her son's faces, bit her lip.

Maybe Richard was right. Maybe twenty-five years of this was enough for anyone.

A man in a blue suit came out of the club and lit a cigarette. He headed up the road and Murray, casting thoughts of home aside, dashed after him.

"Excuse me?" she said, "excuse me?"

And he stopped and turned.

"Christine Murray," she said, offering a hand, "freelancer working for the *Daily Mail*. Could I ask who you –?"

He turned away from her, drawing on his cigarette.

"Please, sir," she said, trotting down the road after him towards the police cordon, "please give me a moment."

He turned again and canted his head to one side.

"Thank you," she said, "I'm sorry. Do you work at —?"

"You're going to have a picture of me. I saw the photographers flash away. And someone'll recognize me, no doubt. So, for the record, I'm Nathan Holt. Manager of Religion."

"You have a drugs problem here, Mr. Holt?"

He stiffened and colour flushed his cheeks. "You've got a bloody cheek."

"They say that about me, yes."

He stared at her for a moment. And then he said, "We have a very aggressive anti-drugs policy."

"So was it drugs that killed those people tonight?"

"I'm not a pathologist."

"Do you have a problem with ecstasy? Do you tolerate it, Mr. Holt?"

"Do you know how many people die from taking ecstasy? About ten a year."

"And that's all right, is it, Mr. Holt?"

He scowled. "No more 'all right' than the thousands who die from the effects of smoking."

"You should be careful, then."

"Excuse me?"

"The smoking," she said, gesturing at the fag between his fingers.

He smirked at her and said, "I've got to be going. I have to tell the owners that their club is closed until further notice."

"I suppose you're not going to have much dancing if there are dead people in your club. Who are the owners?"

He shook his head and turned, flicking his cigarette away. Murray watched him stride down the street.

★ ★ ★ ★

Lithgow shat himself. He shivered, fear like a tight band around his chest.

He'd watched Jenna stumble towards the stairs, enjoyed her arse in that tight little skirt, then she'd fucking collapsed against the wall.

He was about to go help her — *fucking honest, your honour* — but self-preservation took hold. Self-preservation and a scream from behind him.

He turned and saw a guy — a guy he'd sold a pill to moments before he'd given one to Jenna – topple over the barrier and fall twenty feet into the moshpit.

Another shriek at the chill-out room's bar, and Lithgow turned. A girl – oh, shit, he'd sold to her, too – crumpled to the floor, coughing – coughing – coughing out blood.

Move away, Fraser, he told himself, *move away, nothing to see.*

A guy with purple hair fashioned into a cockerel's comb helped Jenna to her feet. Her skin looked blanched, and blood bubbled at her lips.

The cockerel soothed her, helped her to a chair, sat her down. But Jenna jerked and choked and sprayed blood over the samaritan who still tried his best despite being spattered.

Lithgow sneaked through the crowd. His bladder turned icy. More goths were going down, their bodies jolting like someone was shooting electricity through them.

Lithgow tried to look cool, and he managed it despite the sweat pouring from his hair, down his back, despite the pulse thundering in his head, making him dizzy.

He weaved through the throng on the dancefloor, panic clutching at his heart as he saw more and more – all of them his customers – collapsing, frothing at the mouth, dying.

Okay, this is bad, he thought. *Be cool, boy, be cool.*

He made his way into the reception area. A doorman tended to a convulsing girl near the cloakroom, the cloakroom attendant saying, "Shit, shit, they're dying, there's people dying everywhere," and someone else saying, "Ring 999 – we need ambulances here, now."

Focusing on the street outside, Lithgow walked out of Religion. He waited for someone to shout at him and say, "Come back here, you're going nowhere."

But no one said a thing.

He listened to the screams behind him, and then stepped out into the rain. He walked, picking up his pace, hands in pockets looking as cool as he could – and he could look cool, could Fraser. Even when he was shitting himself.

He weaved through the crowds on Old Compton Street. He strolled past Lab, the cocktail bar where the barmen thought they were Tom Cruise. It was packed. He could pop in; disappear in the crowd.

He looked behind him. Night dwellers choked the street. No one followed him. He was okay, and slowed his pace.

In Charing Cross Road, he hailed a cab and said where he lived in Fulham. He kept cool, jabbering with the cabbie, laughing at the racist shit the guy spouted.

He threw forty quid at the driver, got inside the flat.

And then the panic burst out of him.

Shaking and sweating, he locked himself in the bog and sat on the loo.

With the lights out, he waited in the dark for − for what? What was he waiting for? A knock at the door? The cops coming to arrest him? His life totally fucked, totally over. Sent to jail for killing loads of goths.

He should've thought.

The guy, tall and powerful with a scar streaking the left side of his face, had given him the drugs for free.

"A sample," he said with a hint, maybe, of a Russian accent. "You get it for free, and you charge what you want − keep the money. There's more if you want. Lots more."

They were free. What was he supposed to do? Couldn't turn down free drugs, could he? This was capitalism, man. He had to make a profit. The free market demanded it.

Nothing Lithgow sold before had killed anyone − well, not to his knowledge. And not so many, anyway. Fuck, they dropped like flies, didn't they.

He was thirsty. He got off the loo, switched on the light, and went to the sink. Turning on the tap, he stared at his reflection in the mirror. His hair was crazy, like a mad professor's. He looked pale and scared. He poured himself a glass of water, drank it.

Lithgow thought for a moment. And then he took the jewelled box out of his pocket. He opened it and went to the toilet. He tipped the box over the loo.

Pills spilled towards the lip of the box.

Lithgow looked at the pills and thought.

Was this the right thing to do? Well, yes, but when did he ever do the right thing?

Profit, he thought − *got to make a profit*.

He levelled the box and rummaged through the pills. These might not be the ones responsible. Those goths, they might have taken something else. And Jenna − Jenna might well have had some kind of condition.

He shook his head and shut the box.

They can't pin it on me, he thought. *And if they do, Dad'll sort them out. They wouldn't dare accuse me. Not after the last time. After they fucked up and had to apologize, Dad terrorizing them.*

"It'll be okay," he said. "Stay cool, Fraize. Stay cool and it'll go away. Go to work, act like nothing's happened."

He gave the box a shake, and the pills rattled – and it almost sounded like they were cheering him on, celebrating his decision to hold on to them.

CHAPTER 7.
SOLDIER UNDER SIEGE.

SOHO – 10.24 A.M.

"NO SLEEP for the wicked," said Cal Milo as Lawton trudged up the steps into Religion.

"I never do," said Lawton, "but it's nice to see you looking like the walking dead, Cal."

Milo fiddled with wires spilling from a security panel at the front entrance. He grinned, and spite sparkled in his eyes. He said, "You look like dead man walking, Lawton."

Lawton faltered, stared up at Milo. "What d'you mean?"

The big man put his hands up in surrender, said, "Mean nothing, mate. Just saying. You look like shit, I look like shit, some of us are *in* the shit."

Lawton, his blood getting hot, stepped forward. "Say what's on your mind, Milo."

Milo's smile disappeared. "Or what, grunt?"

"Sorry, forgot. You haven't *got* anything in your mind, have you, lump."

"Piss off out of my face, Lawton."

"Or what, pondlife?"

Milo took the bait. He let go of the wires. He swung his oak-like arm around, trying to swat Lawton's head off his shoulders. Lawton raised his guard, hands resting on the top of his head, elbows flared. He blocked Milo's attack with his left forearm, and shot up his right elbow to crack Milo under the chin.

The big man grunted, and his legs buckled. He teetered, Lawton grabbing Milo's arms to prevent him from tumbling down the steps and injuring himself. With Milo finding his feet, Lawton stepped back.

Milo cradled his chin, saying, "What – the – what – did – uh – uh –?"

"You'll be all right, Milo," said Lawton. "Just don't think too much." And he turned, walked into the club.

A police constable greeted him, saying, "You are?"

"Jake Lawton. I've been told to pay Detective Superintendent Phil Birch a visit."

He'd already said this to the copper standing guard at the barricade at the bottom of the street. He was getting tired of it. The PC indicated with his chin that Lawton should go upstairs. "CCTV unit," said the policeman.

He trudged upstairs, thinking about the call he got a few hours earlier. It was Jenna's dad.

You absolute bastard. You killed my baby.

Lawton's blood had frozen, taking Mark McCall's sobs as confirmation that she was dead.

"Mark, are you sure?"

"I've just had to I.D. her dead body, you bastard, and it's all down to you, you and your fucking drug culture."

"*My* drug culture?"

"Those clubs, all that weird perverse stuff that goes on down there."

"I'm a doorman, Mark – I try to *stop* drugs getting in."

"Don't bullshit me, Jake, I know what goes on. I'm an ex-copper, so don't try to pull the wool over my eyes, son. Doormen, dealers, you all work together."

Lawton felt a knot tighten in his stomach.

He'd known McCall for years, and McCall never liked him much. Jenna's dad had left the force, disillusioned with all the red tape – "You can't give a yob a good kicking these days without having to fill in five forms beforehand, and another three after."

McCall hadn't been pleased when Lawton joined up, either. His daughter's teenaged boyfriend roaming the world, gallivanting and living it up, didn't strike McCall as a good idea. But he was glad when Lawton split with Jenna soon after, didn't care that his daughter was heartbroken. He thought Jenna would be better off without the likes of Jake Lawton: "The Army's full of layabouts, full of scum who'd be in prison if they'd not joined up. England's going down the gutter, lad, down the fucking gutter."

Lawton knew the lads he worked with weren't layabouts or scum. Some of them might be mouthy. A few got into trouble when they drank too much on R&R. But no one else did the job they did. No one else went to hell, came out, and was expected to behave normally.

No one else – not even cops like McCall – put their lives on the line like those lads did.

Things got worse when they invaded Iraq, McCall raging against Blair, against Bush, against "all the cowards who bowed down before them and let them walk into a free, independent country".

Lawton pointed out that Iraq was hardly free.

"'Course they are, Jake. Seen it on TV. Women walking around in jeans. None of this Arab nonsense. They're like us."

"Those would be the same women raped by Saddam's sons if they take a fancy to them, then. The same women whose fathers and brothers and sons are tortured if the say a word against Saddam. But that's okay. As long as they've got jeans, that's okay."

"Bollocks," said McCall. "What do you know? You're a soldier. Brainwashed."

He couldn't win, so he left it. And Jenna left him when he went to war. It wasn't that he wanted to go to war. It wasn't that he supported Blair or Bush – it was his job, that was all.

His job was soldiering and he was going off to soldier.

McCall had railed against him that morning on the phone. It was a curse Lawton came back alive from Iraq, he said, wheedling his way back into Jenna's life.

"You should've left my girl alone," he said. "She's into all that weird, vampire stuff. You could've at least got her out of that."

"She's twenty-nine, Mark. She makes her own decisions."

Silence fell. McCall breathed deep, rasping breaths. Lawton's nape prickled.

McCall said, "She *was* twenty-nine. She *made* her own decisions. Was. Made. My" – he began to cry – "baby's dead, she's dead. She'll always be 'was', now, always be past, always be gone."

Grief gouged at Lawton's guts.

"I'm sorry, Mark," he said, "I really am. If the police don't get who's responsible, I – I will. I promise."

Fraser Lithgow played on Lawton's mind: the leer, the swagger, the spiked hair.

"You're responsible, Lawton. It's you," said McCall.

Lawton listened to him weeping. And when the tears stopped, McCall cursed him again and then slammed down the phone.

* * * *

He knocked once on the CCTV monitoring room and entered.

He went to say hi to Lisa and Brian, but stopped himself. Cops filled the room. A couple of uniforms, and two suits. A balding man in his late thirties stood up and glared at Lawton. The man carried a clipboard. He'd been watching Brian reel through CCTV images, presumably from last night.

The man said, "You are?"

"Jake Lawton."

"Mr. Lawton, our doorman. I'm Superintendent Phil Birch."

"Okay." Lawton shut the door, stepped into the room.

"I understand you came up here last night."

"Here?" He glanced at Brian, who was fast-forwarding through tape. Brian's neck flushed. "Yes, I came up here to talk to Nathan Holt."

"We've met Mr. Holt."

"Good, then he explained why I came up here."

"He did, but that's not important."

"Not important?"

"No, Mr. Lawton, what's important is that the tape from last night's CCTV recording is missing."

Lawton couldn't speak, his voice trapped in his throat. And no matter how much he tried, no sound would come out.

"Mr. Holt," said Birch, "says you came up here to have a word, but he wasn't here. Neither were Mr. Smith, here" – he indicated to Brian, who had turned beetroot red – "nor his colleague Miss Lisa Dennison."

"That's a lie. Brian, that's a fucking lie."

Brian turned. Fear filled his eyes. Colour had rinsed his cheeks. His mouth open and closed.

Lawton felt his chest tightening. His mind flashed back, and he had to grab the back of a chair to steady himself.

He said, "Someone's fucking with me. I'm being set up – again."

Birch said, "Mr Smith, you can leave, now," and Brian scuttled out, head down, mumbling.

Lawton didn't look at him; he let him slip out. Brian was all right. Lawton couldn't understand why he'd lie – unless he'd been got at.

"You were here alone, Mr. Lawton," said Birch, "and the tape that could provide evidence as to who killed twenty-eight people here last night has gone missing. Any ideas?"

"I wasn't here alone. Brian was here. Lisa was here. And Holt was here. I came up to complain that a drug dealer – a *known* drug dealer – had been let into the club."

Birch tapped his teeth with the end of a pen. "Who was that, then?"

Lawton said who it was and Birch scribbled something down on his clipboard. He showed the clipboard to the other suit. The man nodded and went to a corner, where he got on the phone.

Birch said, "Why would three people give us a different story, tell us you were here alone – for long enough to snaffle that tape?"

"Why would I want to snaffle that tape?"

Birch shrugged. "You tell me."

"I can't, because I don't know."

The other suit moved back into the light. He handed Birch a scrap of paper torn from a notebook. Birch studied the piece of paper. Reading it, he said, "Fraser Lithgow was apprehended by doormen at Religion a couple of months ago, suspected of being in possession of ecstasy pills. Turned out it was all a bit of a cock up. Had nothing on him."

"That's crap," said Lawton. "I found them. Two bags of blue pills stuffed into his shoes."

Birch raised his eyebrows. "*You* found them."

"Yes I did. I found them."

Birch nodded and hummed.

"What's that mean?" said Lawton. "That humming."

"Nothing, Mr. Lawton. Interesting that you claimed to have found drugs on this gentleman, that's all. And then you claim you came up here last night to complain about him being allowed entry into Religion. Pissing on your patch was he, sir?"

Lawton glared at him, and the man's cheeks blanched.

Lawton said, "I've been here before, Superintendent Birch."

"How do you mean?"

"Being fitted up for something I didn't do."

He smiled and Lawton saw that the man knew – probably had it written down on his clipboard.

Lawton said, "If I'm not under arrest, I'm walking away. Are you going to arrest me?"

Birch shook his head. "But if you do come across that tape, you'll let me know?"

"I would bloody love to."

★ ★ ★ ★

Lawton stormed out of Religion. Milo, upgrading the club's security system, didn't see him – and that was lucky for Milo, because he'd get another smack the way Lawton felt now.

Lawton walked a little way down the street and leaned against a door. He blew air out of his cheeks and rolled a cigarette. He watched the passers-by and smelled Chinese wafting from a nearby restaurant. It got his stomach going.

He lit the cigarette and smoked, and was starting to enjoy it until a voice said, "Is it drugs or murder this time, Mr. Lawton? Or perhaps a bit of both?"

He looked up and saw her standing there, a swagger in her posture.

The rage that had been dying rose again in Lawton's breast. He stared down at his feet and smoked his cigarette, saying, "I've got nothing to say to you. I've never had anything to say to you."

"No comment, then," said Christine Murray. "That looks good in print. Implies guilt."

"I don't care what you think, I don't care what you say. You fucking lied and lied before about me, and you'll lie and lie again, I guess."

And he stepped away from the doorway, striding past her down to Old Compton Street. The rain drizzled and he pulled up the collar of his jacket.

She followed him and said, "Are you involved, Mr. Lawton? I hear the police have questioned you. Something about a tape."

He turned sharply to face her, and she stopped in her tracks. They stood like two buoys in a sea of people and the crowd washed around them.

Lawton said, "Do you want a story, Mrs. Murray —?"

"Christine, please. We're old friends."

"All right, I've got a story for you: they're setting me up. Just like I was set-up two years ago."

"You're paranoid, Jake."

"Mr. Lawton, please," he said. "We're not friends."

"What do you know about this tape?"

"I don't know anything about the tape."

"And the drugs?"

Lawton opened his mouth and then stopped himself.

"Mr. Lawton?" said Murray, canting her head to the side. "You were about to say — "

"Nothing. Nothing at all," he said, and spun away from her, then strode off.

"Come on, Mr. Lawton. You're a suspect, did you know that? They like you for this, that's what I'm hearing."

He walked and she followed, and her voice made his skin crawl. He'd heard it for months after he came home from Basra.

She pestered him by phone, harassed him at his flat, harried him in the pub.

She wrote her stories and the papers published them, but Lawton never gave them a word. And then other papers came after him, and they pestered and harassed and harried, and wrote their stories. But he didn't give them a word, either.

They went away, but Murray came back. And she kept coming back until she had nothing left to ask.

If she'd been a man, he would've killed her — he was certain of that.

And as he turned into Shaftesbury Avenue, he heard her voice filter through the noise of traffic and people.

She said, "They'll get you in the end, Mr. Lawton. I might be the only friend you'll have left — "

★ ★ ★ ★

Murray shivered and watched Lawton get swallowed by the crowds.

He chilled her, and always had. The dark hair, cropped short, and the narrow, steel-grey eyes set in a pale, sharp face, said military straight

43

off. He was lean and powerful, and she imagined he'd be like granite if you hit him. Not spongy like most men. Scars peppered his face, but he was still handsome. And she guessed that he had a soft, warm smile when he chose to smile it. He was still young, but his career was over. Not much of a future, except perhaps in the black market – drugs, protection rackets, hired killings.

She'd stalked him for months after the tape fell into her hands. It was a big story, but Lawton didn't want to play. He was still serving in Iraq.

"They still allow him to carry a weapon," she'd said to a news editor when she was trying to sell the story.

The *Mail* refused to run the tape, said it would damage the Army. The *Sun* was a bit squeamish. The *Mirror* had its fingers burnt by publishing fake images of British troops pissing on Iraqi prisoners.

But a Sunday red-top paid buckets for the story, and Murray posted the video on her website. Already well known among her peers, she became a minor celeb.

And Lawton got kicked out of the Army.

"You have your sacrifice," said Murray's Ministry of Defence mole, a sneer in his voice.

She got a lot of shit from Army types, one officer saying, "This man's been shot five times for his country, he's a hero, and you bitch of a hack destroy his career with your lies."

But commissions poured in from newspapers and magazines, and Murray became a troop-baiter.

Murray still loved the buzz of a newsroom and took on freelance shifts at all the nationals when she could. A couple of weeks ago she'd signed to do a month at the *Mail's* Kensington HQ – and the timing couldn't have been better.

Murray's vision blurred as she glared at the crowd into which Lawton had vanished.

She thought of getting a coffee and ringing the newsdesk to update them. Her phone rang, and she thought they'd got there first. But when she looked at the screen, she saw it wasn't the newsdesk and she sighed.

"Hello, Richard," she said.

A few seconds of silence filled the line, but then he said, "You said you'd be here for them."

"There are twenty-eight people dead, Richard."

"I know, I heard the news."

"Well, I've got to – "

"Your sons asked after you."

A knot of pain tugged in her belly. She flinched. "I – I know I promised but – "

"No buts anymore, Chrissie. No buts. You can't break promises you make to them, you just can't. When are you home?"

"I-I can't say."

He sighed, and she gritted her teeth, rage rising in her breast.

"Well," he said, "we'll see you when we see you. Oh, they won't, they'll be in bed, your sons. So, *I'll* see you when I see you."

He cut her off and she yanked the mobile away from her ear. She bit her lip and tried not to cry.

CHAPTER 8.
GIVING YOU EXTRA.

LAWTON said, "I'd like to make a withdrawal."

The cashier looked up and paled.

"Hello, Fraser," said Lawton.

Lithgow grimaced, trying to make a smile.

"How about it, Lithgow? A withdrawal?"

"What — what kind of withdrawal, sir?"

"Your heart, right out of your chest with my bare hands. And don't think I couldn't."

Lithgow tottered on his stool behind the counter, and the colour left his face. An Asian woman came up behind him, threw a glance at Lawton, and then spoke to Lithgow. "Everything all right, Fraser?" and then looking at Lawton said, "Sir, can we help at all?"

Lawton smiled at her and she smiled back. He said, "It's fine. My account's in a bit of a mess, and I get flustered. I may have made your colleague nervous with my outburst, but I apologize. It's my fault. I should be more careful with my money."

"All right, sir," she said. "Fraser, can you deal with this?"

"Yes, yes, it's all fine," he said, and the woman slipped away, eyeing Lawton.

"What do you want?" said Lithgow.

"I want you, in ten minutes, to have a sudden need for a cigarette and meet me in Starbucks across the road."

"I don't – I can't – "

"Or I'll put a name to the face the cops have on that CCTV tape handing out pills to kids just before they died on Wednesday night."

Lawton glared at him and hid the lie behind the steel grey of his eyes.

"Oh, fuck," said Lithgow. "Okay, okay, ten minutes."

Lawton glanced at the poster stuck on Lithgow's window. It showed the Halifax's Howard offering to give us extra.

Glaring back at Lithgow, he said, "No TV ad for you if you fuck this one up, Fraser."

Lawton strode out.

He crossed the road to Starbucks and sat in a window seat, cradling a black coffee.

He thought about Jenna and he thought about that copper trying to nail him for the missing CCTV footage. He thought about Murray, stalking him again. He blew air out of his cheeks and went into his pocket for his Rizzla and Old Holborn, but then remembered where he was.

His skin crawled, and he felt fear grind through his guts. Lawton knew he was being fitted up.

Was it Holt? And was he trying to protect Lithgow? Brian and Lisa had obviously been got at. And the copper, Birch, was being fed information.

Jenna came back into his mind, and he felt sadness well in his breast. He didn't think he'd feel like this about her. She was never the one, but he cared for her.

And if he'd let life control him, and he'd ended up falling into a marriage and babies with her, he'd have been happy enough.

He almost told Birch that he'd lost an ex in the tragedy. But he hesitated. They'd want to know why she was an ex; they'd make things up about their relationship, twist his words and give him motive. He hoped the tired looking PC he'd mentioned it to last night outside Religion would forget.

He shook the clutter out of his head and watched the traffic sweep along Kensington High Street.

He stared at the bank, waiting for Lithgow to slither out. Lawton looked at his watch. Ten minutes, he'd said. It was already fifteen. If Lithgow'd done a runner, he'd find him and wrench his neck like a chicken.

The irritation grew in Lawton. He was about to storm out of Starbucks and go find Lithgow. But then the little sneak jogged out of the bank.

Five minutes later, Lithgow cowered opposite Lawton in Starbucks with a green tea. He took a packet of sweets from his navy suit jacket and popped one in his mouth. He pouted and his face creased up.

Lawton, curling his lip, said, "Where'd you get those pills you had last night, Fraser?"

"Hey," he said, sucking the sweet, "I don't know what you're talking about. I didn't have any – "

"Don't bullshit me, you fucking insect."

"I'm telling you," Lithgow said, his gaze flitting about the coffee shop, "I was clean."

"You're about as clean as dog shit, Fraser." Lawton leaned across the table, bracing himself for the lie: "You're on tape, I told you. The cops, this morning, say, 'Who's that little shit selling pills to that girl?' Now" – he leaned back, folded his arms – "I said nothing. I thought, 'Give Fraser the benefit of the doubt, find him myself and ask him nicely.' So here I am" – he leaned forward again, frowning – "asking you nicely."

Lithgow glanced around. He swigged the tea.

Lawton said, "You know that Jenna died?"

Lithgow stared at him, his expression frozen in a look of terror. "Yeah," he said, his voice like it had been scraped off the back of his throat.

"Did you sell her a pill?"

Lithgow swallowed. "I – I did not sell Jenna a pill."

"You didn't?"

"No, no I didn't. All right, I sold pills to other people, but I did not sell to Jenna."

"So you did have drugs on you, you shit."

"Yes, yes, all right. I did. But that doesn't mean I killed them. Doesn't mean my pills killed them. There were probably loads of drugs there. Doesn't mean I killed them. No way, man." He sat back, folded his arms. "No way."

"You're a coward, Lithgow."

"Yeah, so? Big fucking deal. I do what I have to do. There's no way

I'm taking the fall for those dead people, no way. I only sell 'em on. Nothing to do with me what's in them. Not my responsibility."

Fury boiled in Lawton's belly. He wanted to drag Lithgow across the table, toss him through the window. "Okay," he said, "where'd you get them? Who sold them to you? Was it Holt? Did he have anything to do with this?"

Lithgow made a face and said, "Holt? What the fuck –? No – no way, Lawton, no fucking way. I'm not a grass."

"You are if it means saving your skin, shit for brains. Tell me about Holt. He let you in last night when you're supposed to be banned."

Customers turned, aware of Lawton's anger. He looked around, scowled at a bald man trying to look young in a Nike hoodie. The man shied away.

Lawton said, "I guess it's time to slip away. We've got ourselves an audience." Lawton stood. "I'll see you again, Fraser. I want to know where they came from, or I give you to the cops."

Lithgow stared up at him.

Lawton, lying again, said, "You're on the tape, Fraser. You're on the tape selling drugs to people who died. Think about it, mate." He straightened, pointed at Lithgow saying, "See you soon," and walked out.

CHAPTER 9.
WAR CRIMINAL.

"JAKE Lawton killed an unarmed civilian," said Murray. "Chased him down and shot him through the head."

"And he left the Army before any charges could be brought," said Commander Peter Deere. "We all saw your marvellous piece of investigative journalism, Christine." He leaned back in his chair, one hand scratching the back of his neck, the other aiming the remote control at the TV.

Murray glanced over at the TV. Sky News was broadcasting a statement from Home Office minister Jacqueline Burrows.

Murray said, "But you didn't do anything about it."

"Not a matter for British authorities. Let's listen to what Firestarter has to say," said Deere.

"Firestarter?"

"Flame red hair and fiery temper, Christine."

He turned up the volume, and Burrows's voice grew louder, saying, "... and our thoughts, today, are with the families of the twenty-eight victims. I, on behalf of the Home Secretary – "

"Who is on a jaunt in the U.S.," said Deere.

" – and the Prime Minister – "

"Same jaunt," said Deere. "While their citizens are dying."

" – want to declare the government's determination to bring the perpetrators of this crime to justice. We do not wish to pre-empt the police investigation or the forensic evidence, but it has been suggested that drugs are to blame for this tragedy. I can assure the public that this Labour government shall continue its successful campaign against – "

Deere muted the minister, saying, "These people spout such bollocks." He swivelled round to face Murray. "So your energies are directed towards this ex-soldier again, are they, Christine?"

"Where are your energies directed, Peter? I can't seem to get a straight answer from Phil Birch."

"Well, off the record Lawton is certainly someone we're looking at. It's claimed he was alone in the CCTV monitoring suite. The tape, which would probably identify the dealer, has gone missing."

"Do you really think he's the mastermind? I know he was there at the scene, but it just doesn't ring true. An organizer of such a crime" – Murray shook her head – "would be miles away, surely." A sweat broke on her back and her blood quickened. She suspected Lawton might be guilty, but wanted to hear it from the police.

Deere shrugged. "I can't tell you any more, Christine. Investigations are on-going and all that."

"What about the concern that soldiers leaving the Army are being drawn into crime? We know Lawton's worked as a doorman at some unsavoury venues – unlicensed boxing nights, illegal raves."

"I didn't know there *was* a concern."

"I've written stories about criminal incidents involving ex-Forces."

Deere smirked. "You seem to have a dislike for soldiers, Christine."

She shrugged. "Not at all. But I do think that we shouldn't regard them all as heroes when we know that individuals like Jake Lawton join up."

"Individuals like Jake Lawton?"

"Murderers. A war criminal."

Deere shook his head. "You went for the jugular, you got your reward, Christine. And you took no prisoners – even the Met got lashed – "

"You didn't charge him, Peter. You didn't even question him."

He held his hands out. "It was out of our jurisdiction. Anyway" – he sniffed and cradled the back of his head in his hands – "war's war, and nasty things happen. I know – well, I'm sorry to say this – but I know that's difficult for a woman to grasp, so – "

"It wasn't a war, Peter. The war was won, by then. This was supposedly peacetime. He murdered an innocent man. And if he's able to shoot someone in the head at point blank range, he can comfortably play a part in the distribution of drugs."

Deere leaned forward and bristled. "I shall neither confirm nor deny our interest in Jake Lawton."

Murray looked down at the notebook that rested on her knee. She said, "All right. Anyone else in the line of fire?"

"Off the record, a few drug dealers. The DJ on the night, a Captain Red – real name Steven Hammond – has convictions for possession." He turned his eyes towards to TV. Burrows still railed. "Quid pro quo, then, Christine – as usual. If you hear anything – let me in on it." He sighed up at the television. "That Jacqueline Burrows woman will be up the ACC's arse all day, and then she'll be up mine. And once the Home Secretary's back from his American junket, he'll be crawling up there with them."

"Can I quote you?"

He glared at her.

★ ★ ★ ★

Murray sat at her desk in the *Mail's* Kensington offices, pecking the currants from a scone, and thought about her conversation with Deere.

She'd known him for fifteen years. Murray worked the crime beat for the *Standard*; he worked drugs as a superintendent with the Met.

He was a known woman-doubter, a dinosaur in the multi-cultural, gay-welcoming, female-friendly Met.

But the dinosaurs still survived, and whatever picture the image-makers painted, the police would always be a man's world – like the Army; Jake Lawton's world.

She logged on to e-lib, the *Mail's* electronic library system. The database stored stories published in all the national papers. The *Mail* had installed e-lib in the past year, so this was the first time Murray had run Lawton's name through the search engine.

She waited while the system searched and thought about Lawton and how he'd come to do what he did. Murray had marched to stop the invasion of Iraq. She'd gone as a reporter and as a citizen, furious that Blair was taking Britain to war.

"Won't do any good," said Richard at the time – and he was right. He'd said, "The loudest voices are against the war, but there's a considerable majority out there who think it's right to go in – we believe in the weapons of mass destruction evidence, Christine."

"I don't want this done in my name," she'd said, screaming at her husband.

"That why you protested, went on that March – to express your outrage. Pity the Iraqis can't express their outrage against Saddam."

"Bollocks," she said, not wanting to know about Saddam. This was never about Saddam: it was about U.S. and British aggression.

But the war came, and in days it was won.

And then things started to go wrong.

Abu Ghraib sliced open the wound that had festered since the invasion, and the poison seeped out. Those images from the Baghdad prison showing U.S. troops abusing Iraqi POWs confirmed what Murray knew.

"We're all barbarians," she'd told Richard.

After Abu Ghraib, the tide, although always pushing against the war, swelled and roared in defiance. The papers chased scandals. *Mirror* chiefs made morons of themselves by publishing those hoax pictures. But the mood was clearly there for soldier baiting.

And Lawton got caught.

A friend of a friend of a friend who skulked around the anti-war movement had e-mailed Murray the footage.

The e-mail said, "Shocking video of British soldier killing an un-armed Iraqi – who's surrendering. We think the soldier's called Lawton – Jack or Jake. Not sure which regiment. There's no volume, sadly. We think the incident happened in Basra sixteen months ago, November 2004, but can only confirm this from the reading on the footage – the settings might not be correct. Leeza Dervish at *Peace Today!* said you'd want this. It's disgraceful – this is what these soldiers are doing every day in Iraq in our name."

Murray's blood boiled when she read then e-mail. But when she clicked on the RealPlayer icon attached to the message and the video played, her fury bubbled over.

This is what she saw:

The cameraman looks down into an alley. Static peppers the image. The picture shows the side of a sandstone building. Pots and pans are piled up against the wall.

Dust coughs up on the left of the screen, and a bearded man wearing combats stumbles into shot. A rucksack hangs off his shoulders. His right hand's not there, blood pulsing from his stump. He throws up dust and debris as he scuttles backwards into the alley. He falls on his backside. The sand coats his clothes and hinders the cameraman's view.

More dust belches from the earth on the left of the shot, and a soldier in full combat gear comes into view.

A rifle is jammed into his shoulder. He aims the gun at the bearded man. The soldier crouches as he shuffles forward. The gun's jerking, and the soldier's mouth opens and closes as if he's shouting at the Iraqi.

A cloud of dust swirls around the alley.

The Iraqi's jaw goes up and down – was he begging for mercy?

The soldier jabs the gun. The gun's fixed on the bearded man. The camera shakes.

In the bearded man's left hand is a mobile phone. He holds the hand up over his head, palm facing heaven, pushes it against the air. He's getting to his feet. Is he surrendering?

His wounded hand rests over on his heart. He rubs his chest, or tries to pluck something out of a breast pocket in his jacket.

Is he pleading? Trying to show his identity papers to the aggressive soldier?

Another soldier coming into shot, gun raised, barking commands by the way his mouth moves. The first soldier waves him away without drawing his eyes from the Iraqi.

The second soldier backs away. He reaches for the first soldier, but the first soldier gesticulates for his colleague to retreat.

And the second soldier reverses to the edge of the shot, drops down to one knee.

The bearded man, one hand up to heaven, the other on his heart.

Kids spill into the shot, laughing. The bearded man smiles, says something, probably telling to soldier not to shoot when there are children about.

The soldier jerks, jabbing the rifle towards the un-armed victim.

The Iraqi lunges forward, spits at the soldier. The soldier recoils. The Iraqi thrusts his left hand forward. Maybe he's saying, *Let me call my family before you kill me in cold blood*.

The soldier's mouth makes the shape of, "No, no, no."

The rifle jerks. A spark spits out of the barrel. Smoke coughs out of the rifle, clouding the image.

The bearded man jolts backwards and his head bursts in a flare of red.

He crashes to the ground, throwing up dust. His body arches, and he twitches as the soldier moves forward, gun still fixed on his victim.

The soldier stands over the body, rifle aimed at the twitching body.

More troops swarm into the shot. They crouch, they scan, they kick up a storm of sand.

The killer looks up into camera. He aims at the cameraman. His mouth makes the shape of shouting. Jake Lawton's face, creased with rage, glaring into the lens.

The picture jerks and the screen blacks out . . .

Murray, waiting for e-lib to complete its search, blew out her cheeks and let the images that had stained her mind for two years fade out.

The database came up with more than thirty pages of hits on Jake Lawton.

She flicked through the first few stories, beginning with her original piece for the Sunday tabloid. She read it, moved on to the next hit.

The Independent's piece ran stills from the video. The headline read, gazing into the abyss, and a sub-deck declared, How war makes monsters of good men.

The Sun, following up the Sunday newspaper's exclusive splash, were more to the point:

"Execution" screamed their front-page headline.

She felt a trill of excitement. I made this, she thought – this is my story. And anything to do with Jake Lawton was *still* her story.

She stared at the video grab of Lawton looming over the man in the alley that the paper used. The gun was jammed into Lawton's shoulder, ready to kill.

She said, "I've not finished with you, Mr. Lawton – by a long shot. You got away with murder in Basra, but it's not going to happen again."

CHAPTER 10.
GODS FROM DUST.

"TWENTY-EIGHT is a good number, don't you think, Professor?" said Mrs. Radu.

"I think it's an excellent number," said the Professor, wiping his glasses with a red handkerchief. He perched the spectacles on his nose, blinked, then sat back in the leather sofa. He scanned the library, taking in the shelves packed with books. The room smelled dusty, and the light was weak. "How long will it take?"

Mrs. Radu, dark hair loose over her shoulders, sat cross-legged opposite him. He glanced now and again at her legs, shapely and long in black nylon. She turned to the other man, a bent creature, short and grey-haired. "What do you say, Dr. Haddad?"

Dr. Haddad wheeled his chair over and said, "Between twenty-four and forty-eight hours is my conclusion, but that's only guesswork."

Mrs. Radu nodded, looked again at the Professor. She smiled; let her tongue slide out of her mouth.

He said, "This dealer, is he safe?"

"Oh, he's safe. He won't say a thing," she said.

"You're sure?"

"I'm sure. Firstly, he's a coward, and secondly –"The phone sitting on the glass-topped coffee table trilled. Mrs. Radu leaned forward to retrieve it. The Professor gazed down her top. She raised her eyes to his and grinned at him. She sat back up and answered the phone.

"This is Nadia Radu – ah, how are you? – Yes, it's gone well, the days will soon be with us – You will be rewarded – I see – Yes, the soldier, I see – Well, if there is to be a patsy, why not – Yes, thank you for calling – soon, then, soon."

She shut the phone.

"All good?" said the Professor.

"All good," she said. And she glanced at the elderly man in the wheelchair.

The Professor knew little about Haddad. He was from the Middle East, somewhere, but had British citizenship. A frail figure, he was deep into his nineties. He'd always lived here with the Radus, even when Nadia's husband, Viorel, was alive.

Haddad was their secret weapon, the creator of their dream.

"What are you thinking, Professor?"

"I'm thinking how fortunate we are to have Dr. Haddad."

"We are," she said. She looked at Haddad. The old man had dropped off and snored in his wheelchair. Mrs. Radu touched the choker collaring her throat. The band was her mark – the sign that she was untouchable. Watching her, the Professor fingered his own mark. Mrs. Radu went on:

"Dr. Haddad's work is coming to fruition. Once the first batch rise up, we can use them to bring in live blood for the resurrection."

The Professor's heart raced. A tight band wrapped around his belly, flushing blood into his penis. He looked at Mrs. Radu, and lust made him dizzy. "I want to fuck you, Nadia," he said.

She smiled. "I know you do, Professor, you all want to fuck me, but I can't be giving myself to everyone."

"Give yourself to me."

"After this is done, perhaps. But I must be choosy." She glanced at Haddad, trembling in his sleep.

Hot water rushed up the Professor's throat, and his guts ground. "You can't mean –?"

"I do what I must in the service of my god, Professor. You know that. My family, our family, has done the same for centuries. We do what we have to do."

She stood and the Professor heard the zip of nylon at her thighs. He got up, too, brushing down his trousers. She threw a look at his crotch and grinned.

Raising her eyes to his, she said, "Thank you for calling on me,

Professor. Pleasure to see you again. We'll be in touch soon, won't we?"

They shook hands, and he held her delicate fingers in his. He stared into her purple eyes. She mesmerized him like all the men she met. Perhaps she'd be his after this was done – after he'd washed the thought of her with Haddad from his mind.

"This is a wonderful time for us, Professor," she said. "Don't you think?"

"I do."

"We're creating gods from dust."

CHAPTER 11.
CAPTAIN RED.

HE sliced into the meat and blood bubbled from the cut.

Murray's gorge rose and she turned away and glanced around the restaurant. They were in an Aberdeen Steak House near Leicester Square, and she was paying.

"So, Steve, you organize the – the goth-stroke-vampire night at Religion through this – this Academy of London Vampyres of yours."

"That's right," said Steve Hammond, chewing on the meat, the flesh pink between his teeth.

Murray cringed, stared at her salad.

"You don't like steak?" he said.

"I'm a vegetarian. I thought you would be, too."

"Why's that?" said Hammond.

She shrugged. "Alternative culture and all that."

"Are you alternative, Christine?"

"No – I just don't like the taste of meat."

"Not a good place to be then," he said, gesturing at the tables of meat-eaters surrounding them.

"The smell is gut-wrenching, I have to admit."

"We could've gone somewhere less meaty, but since you said you'd pay and this" – he jabbed at the steak with his knife – "is my favourite meal, I thought, *Why the hell not?*"

Hammond – Captain Red, vampire-night organizer and DJ at Religion – had on a black velvet jacket and frilly white shirt. His hair was Flock Of Seagulls-style. He wore black eye makeup and lipstick. His long, clawing fingernails were painted purple.

Murray said, "Are you a vampire?"

"I am."

"Do you drink blood?"

"I don't."

"I thought vampires drank blood."

"I'm a psychic vampire. I suck the energy out of people." He leaned forward, his mouth full of flesh, and said, "That's why you feel lethargic, now: I'm drinking up your lifeforce."

"I don't feel lethargic."

Hammond shrugged and went back to his steak, saying, "Doesn't work all the time."

Murray said, "The blood-drinking. How does it work?"

"I said, I don't – "

"I know you say you don't drink blood, but some of your friends do."

"Make a little cut, drink away."

"I've read," said Murray, "that some of these sanguinarians are so convinced they need blood, they'll actually drink tomato juice, or eat black pudding, to pretend they're getting blood."

"The world is a wonderful place, Christine, full of diversity – vive la différence, eh?

"What about AIDS, HIV?"

"They don't drink from anyone they don't know. It's like sex – it's consensual. And they practise safe blood drinking."

"Do you take drugs?" she said.

He chewed and glanced up at Murray. "Sometimes. I smoke some weed. But you don't have to be a vampire or a goth or anything to take drugs – journalists take drugs, don't they. In the morning, you write a story about how terrible cocaine is, then you're off to some trendy wine bar to snort in the evening. Am I right, or am I right?"

"You're right, I'm sure – but I go home to my – family in the evening," she said, and felt a pressure in her chest.

"Nice, nice," he said, laying his knife and fork down on the blood-soaked plate.

Murray looked at the dish and took a swig of water. She put the glass down and said, "You've been charged with possession of ecstasy, Steve."

The vampire leaned back in his chair. "Few tablets," he said, "fined, that's all. And I do it for the kids, you know – it's a service."

"But a few are enough to kill, aren't they? Did you have tabs on you at Religion last night?"

He glared at her, and his face went red. "Don't write that in your fucking paper. Or I'll sue. It had nothing to do with me, no fucking way."

"I was asking, that's all, Steve – and since I'm paying for that steak, I guess I can ask pretty much anything."

He threw his hands up. He rolled his tongue around his teeth, prying out pieces of meat. He said, "Fucking ask then."

She said, "Do you know Jake Lawton?"

"Yes, I know Jake Lawton. Vaguely. He's a doorman at Religion."

"What else d'you know about him?"

Hammond shrugged. "Ex-Army. Always frowning. Tough guy. Don't mess with him." He shook his head. "I don't mix with that sort. He'd look down his nose at me."

"Is he into drugs?"

"No clue. Ask him."

"I have. He doesn't like me. I upset him once."

Hammond scratched at his teeth with a long, painted fingernail. He said, "A lot of the old-school doormen, you know, they might still be involved in drugs. But these days they're all SIA accredited – it's all legal. But you know, that means fuck all. And it wouldn't surprise me if Lawton's got his fingers in the cake. They turn a blind eye to dealers, then take a cut. But it happens everywhere, doesn't it. Cops take backhanders, don't they. And journalists."

"All the time," she said.

"So, dessert – and you can tell me how you upset Jake Lawton."

CHAPTER 12.
HASSLE.

LITHGOW, head down and watching his feet, strode through Kensington High Street towards the Tube station.

He sweated and his heart raced. He'd told the bank he was sick, could he go home, and his supervisor said it was fine. But he wasn't ill, he was scared. And it was Lawton who scared him the most. Lithgow thought about what he'd said.

Fuck, he thought *what if I am on CCTV? I'm screwed.* His mind reeled back to the early hours of the morning, him holding those pills over the toilet bowl. Should've tipped them down the loo, he thought; pulled the chain and watched them wash away.

He shook his head, cursed himself. He'd lose his job and Dad would go ballistic again.

Dad had warned him the last time: "I'm not bailing you out again, Fraser. You should've listened to me and did what I did, what your grandfather did, what your great-grandfather did – you should've gone into law. You could get yourself out of these pickles, then."

But law seemed like hard work. And Fraser was already dealing by the age of fifteen, making more money than he had fucking sense.

After scraping through his A-levels, he'd said he wasn't going to study law. "I'm doing media studies, get a job in TV or something."

Dad's face went purple and he said, "I've paid for your education, and I expect something in return."

"Well, you'll get yourself a TV-star son, won't you," said Fraser.

Dad said, "Mickey-bloody-Mouse degree."

It was – lucky for Lithgow. He scraped a Third, thought TV was too much hassle with everyone trying to get into the industry, and found himself on a bank's graduate trainee scheme.

Dad, still purple, said, "If you're going into banking, join a City bank, a proper one. Not one of these high street branches where you get all kinds of rubbish coming in and out, dealing with pennies, not pounds."

Kensington High Street's branch was hardly pondlife, but Dad still fumed. Anyway, three years down the line, a sideline in tabs, and Fraser was doing all right, thank you very much. Until he got caught by that Lawton cunt trying to sneak some pills into Religion. Dad did his purple face thing, issued his warning about not bailing Fraser out again, and got him out of trouble.

And now, Lawton was hassling him again.

Fraser stuttered to a stop outside High Street Kensington station. The *Evening Standard*'s billboard read:

Drug Deaths: 28 dead, Police Hunt Dealer.

Fraser's bladder sagged and a cold sweat made his back sticky. He whimpered, turning away from the terrible news.

And turned directly into worse news.

"Thought about what we discussed?" said Lawton, leaning against the station entrance.

"Shit." Lithgow put his head down and strode into the station. Lawton walked beside him. "You've got to give me time."

"Time to what, Fraser? Time to find a hiding place? Tell me who sold you those pills. Or I'll fuck with you for the rest of your life."

The odour of cooked pastry wafted up Fraser's nostrils from the West Country Pasties stall, and hunger carved a hole in his belly. He licked his lips, then pushed the urge for food away.

Stopping near the barriers, Fraser said, "Are you sure I'm on tape?"

"I'm sure. I've seen it."

This was all wrong. Now he'd *have* to turn to dad again. And dad would tell him to lie in his bed, since he made it.

He looked Lawton in the eye. He *could* tell this bastard bouncer everything, get him off his back. But Fraser guessed that Jake Lawton, like a dog, wouldn't let go once he got his teeth into him.

Fraser stared into Lawton's cruel face. He swallowed. Commuters swept past them. Some of them sighed because Lawton and Lithgow were in their way.

Lithgow said, "I can tell you who knows and where to find him."

"Who knows? What d'you mean, 'Who knows?' You got the pills, you know who gave them to you."

Lithgow put a hand on his head. His hair was greasy. "I can tell you who knows, Lawton, right. Who sorted this out. Who helped me."

Lawton stared at him. He didn't blink his steel-grey eyes.

Fuck, thought Fraser; *he can kill you just by looking at you.*

Lawton's glare seemed to drain the strength out of him.

Fraser said, "Steve Hammond. Captain Red. He was there with me when I got the pills. It's his local."

Lawton's eyes narrowed. "Where?"

★ ★ ★ ★

DS Phil Birch watched the grainy CCTV image showing Fraser Lithgow handing something to Jenna McCall.

The girl had died a couple of minutes later. And she wasn't the first clubber Lithgow had given drugs to that evening. He was pictured on this tape selling to a dozen – and that dozen had died, along with another sixteen of these goths or vampires or whatever the hell they were.

Birch sat in his study at home, the study illuminated by the flashes of light that came from the CCTV image playing on his PC. He'd brought the VCR in here and wired it up to the PC. He didn't want to play it at work – too risky. He didn't want to play it in the living room, Viki walking in on him, shouting that he was bringing his work home again, turning to Czech when she got agitated.

Birch curled his lip and scratched his chin.

Lawton had been telling him the truth. But why shouldn't he? Okay, he was suspected of killing a man in cold blood, got himself kicked out of the Army because of it, but Birch knew that didn't make Lawton guilty.

Who cares if he's guilty or not? he thought; that wasn't the point, was it.

Lawton was a useful diversion, that was all.

Lithgow would never be done for this. Lithgow was marked for other things.

Birch had taken the CCTV tape from the club on the night of the deaths. He'd warned the CCTV operators not to say a word. He'd told them the cops had something on Lawton. And suggesting to the doorman that the tape had gone missing was a way of getting him to make a mistake, Birch had said. If he didn't slip up, he said to the operators, then we can eliminate him from our inquiries. And he smiled at the pair, the word "eliminate" staying in his mind.

Birch stopped the tape, and the PC screen turned blue, the light shimmering in the gloomy study. He rewound the cassette and then removed it from the VCR.

He studied the photograph of Viki and the girls that was on his desk. Eyes on the picture – taken at Alton Towers last summer – Birch plucked the tape out of the cassette, spooling it around his fingers. He yanked it free of the plastic casing. Gaze still fixed on his family, Birch dropped the coil of tape into the aluminium Shrek wastepaper bin his eldest daughter had bought him for Christmas.

He reached into his pocket, took out a Zippo lighter.

He clicked the wheel. The flame flickered and he smelled the fuel.

Birch dropped the Zippo in the bin.

He stood, job done, ready to go back to work.

The tape burned.

CHAPTER 13.
INSURGENCY.

RUSTUMIYAH CANAL NEAR AL HILLAH,
MESOPOTAMIA — 8.40 P.M., JULY 24, 1920

TOM Wilson, private with the 2nd Manchester Regiment, said, "Two years ago I was covered in shit and blood in France, my mates dead or dying. Two years ago I thought I'd seen the end of war."

Lieutenant Guy Jordan, on horseback, glanced down at Wilson and said, "We'll never see an end to war, Wilson."

"You'd think, sir, that these Arabs would be grateful. We're trying to help 'em, after all."

"That's politics for you, Wilson. It's all about factions, you see, factions out to cause trouble. The nationalists, the Islamists. They all hate us, Wilson, always have and always will. Mind you, I wouldn't trust any of them, come to that."

They'd left Al Hillah at 9.15 a.m. and reached the Rustumiyah canal at 12.45 p.m. The heat lashed down, and it hit the boys badly.

"Medics," said Jordan to Wilson earlier as the whines and moans of the sick filled the air, "say sixty per cent of the lads, mostly Manchester Regiment, need complete rest for twenty-four hours. How bloody likely is that, eh?"

A group of 35th Scinde Horse rode out towards Kifl, where the relief column was headed, to scout the area. Wilson watched them go, galloping towards the minaret that rose above Kifl. Date-palm groves bordered the town, and Wilson wished he could rest in their shade.

The rest of the company made camp near the canal. Troops started to dig trenches at the north of the camp. Wilson got out of those wretched duties: he was Jordan's bagman, and had responsibility for the loot they'd captured the previous night.

Guilt still ate at Wilson for what he'd done. But Jordan flapped the soldier's remorse away, saying, "It was them or us, Wilson, and I tell you, man, they'd have gladly slit our throats. Look at what that wretch did to you."

Wilson rubbed his bandaged arm. "But lieutenant, they were youngsters – "

Jordan interrupted him, told him to be quiet. Wilson shut up and wondered about the relics wrapped up in the packs on Jordan's horse. What secrets did those artefacts hold?

In the early evening, the scouring party of Scinde horsemen returned from Kifl with the warning that ten thousand insurgents were headed their way.

Panic spread through the camp.

"Ten thousand," said Wilson. "Sir, we'll be butchered."

"Ten thousand, indeed. That's bloody Scinde Horse bullshit, my man. More likely to be three thousand. Take arms, Wilson, come along."

A dust cloud rose in the distance as the hostiles approached. Wilson heard their shouts carry across the plains. Guns barked as the 39th battery opened fire on the insurgents. Wilson hunkered down and listened to the firefight. The tribesmen were a hundred and fifty yards from the camp's perimeter.

Too close, thought Wilson, too close by half.

I'd rather them five miles away in Kifl; I'd rather be fifteen miles away from here in Hillah.

He got his wish. Senior officers ordered a retreat to Hillah.

A company of Manchesters was now ready to lead the withdrawal, Jordan and Wilson among them. The officers were on horseback and the men on foot. Fear crept through the ranks.

More troops would flank them as they marched, protecting the vehicles at the head of the column from hostiles.

July had been a bloody month. The whole country seemed to erupt. But the worst of it was down here, along the lower Euphrates. Muslims declared a jihad, a holy war, against the British in Karbala. Insurgents besieged Samawa and Rumaitha until the RAF swooped in to support ground troops. They flew over 4,000 hours and dropped 97 tons of bombs. But the rebels kept coming. And their hit-and-run tactic took its toll: the Brits lost men.

Dust peppered Wilson's eyes, and he blinked away the pain. His throat felt coarse, and he thought, *I could do with a beer in the Dog and Duck, a sing-song with my mates, a tumble with Dora the barmaid. I could do with going home.*

Jordan said, "How old are you, Wilson?"

Wilson looked up at him, "Sir? Eighteen, sir."

"Eighteen?" Jordan looked at him with narrowed eyes. "Are you, now?"

Wilson lowered his gaze and felt his cheeks redden.

"Never mind," said the lieutenant. "I don't care how old you are. If one's old enough to carry a gun, one's old enough to die for one's country."

Wilson glanced up at the officer again. Dust coated the lieutenant's skin. It made him look as if he were made of marble. His green eyes shone like emeralds, though. Despite his ashen face, he looked alive; he looked excited.

He said, "I'm going to give you an order, Wilson."

"Yes, sir, right you are, sir."

"And the order is" – the night erupted, gunfire snapping all around them – "that you must, come what may, live."

Wilson furrowed his brow. "Live, sir?"

"Survive. Get through this."

"I – that's – that's what I'd like to do, sir. I don't think I need to be ordered to do that, lieutenant."

"You do, Wilson, you do need to be ordered. You're a brave lad; I've seen that. You're all brave lads. But what I'm telling you is, I need you to be a coward if it means that you'll survive."

"A coward, sir?"

"It's most important, Wilson. By being a coward, by making sure you live, by avoiding deadly situations, you will be contributing to the survival of more than just yourself, more than a few comrades."

"Sir?"

"You'll be contributing to the survival of the human race, Wilson."

Wilson's mouth opened, but he couldn't find words. He didn't know what the lieutenant was talking about.

Jordan said, "Don't question this, Wilson. Just do it, is that clear?"

"I'm not sure I can, sir. I can't be a coward."

Jordan said, "For the sake of humankind. For your family. Your children and your children's children."

"I don't understand – I – "

"This loot," said Jordan, slapping the sack strapped to his saddle, "must get out of Mesopotamia. It must reach Britain and be destroyed. Destroyed or hidden away."

"I – I don't – "

"Those vessels we took last night, what they contain will destroy humanity, Wilson. Do you understand me?"

Wilson didn't, but he nodded.

The order came to retreat. It echoed through the darkness. Jordan spurred his horse and, as he trotted away, turned to look at Wilson.

"Do you understand, Wilson? Keep an eye on them. If I die, you must take them back to Britain" – his voice diminished, and he faded into the night – "or we are doomed, Wilson."

CHAPTER 14.
PILLS.

"DIDN'T know you were in to this kind of stuff," said Hammond, swigging at a bloody mary.

Lawton said, "My dealer got cold feet after this business at Religion. Keeping a low profile." He supped his pint and hoped he was a good liar.

Hammond nodded. "I had a chat with an old friend of yours, today."

"Oh yeah?"

"Christine Murray. Reporter."

Lawton felt his face heat up, and he said, "What did she want?"

"Your head on a plate, sounds like. Asked if you were into drugs, I said I didn't know. She told me all about that stuff in Iraq. I kind of remember the story – you know, there were so many – but I never knew it was you. Live and learn."

"Murray's rabid," said Lawton. "She gets a bone, she won't let go. I won't bore you with the truth, but what she told you was a lie."

Hammond shrugged. "Don't care. Truth, lies – don't care."

Lawton said, "So, this stuff."

"You want this stuff? The stuff that killed those people?"

"We don't know if it killed them yet."

"Something did. Twenty-eight." He shook his head. "Never known that before. Where would we be if we didn't have drugs, eh? The whole entertainment industry would shut down. But if we get this happening again – it's beer and bowls for us, Jake."

The pub was a goth spot south of the river. Thursday afternoon and it was packed, the sub-culture convalescing after last night's tragedy. Lawton, walking in, got stared at – he was the only one not wearing make-up, platform shoes, and leather gear. He could smell the sweat, smell the paint, and smell the booze. He ordered a pint and waited at the bar, scanning his surroundings. He listened to conversations and they were talking about the dead at Religion.

"Don't worry," said one, "they're vampires, they don't die."

He'd supped half his pint when he noticed Hammond shove through the crowd. His cockerel-style hair was tied back in a ponytail. His eyes were lined black, his lips a dark blue. He wore a long coat and a pair of knee-high Doc Martens. Lawton caught Hammond's eye, and when Hammond saw him there was a flash of fear in his eyes before he gave Lawton a fake smile.

"So who's the guy?" said Lawton. "Can I get some stuff?"

"What d'you want? I don't know about the pills Fraser – " and he stopped, picking up his drink, slugging it down. Tomato juice drizzled from between his lips. He looked like he'd drunk blood.

Lawton said, "What were you going to say?"

"Sorry, mate. Frog in the throat." He coughed.

Lawton wanted to grab him by the collar, flatten his face against the bar and force Fraser Lithgow's name from between those painted lips. He clenched his fists and said, "You said you didn't know about the pills, and then you said Fraser's name. Come on, Steve."

Hammond said, "No, no, I didn't say that. Not that. Fraser? I thought Fraser was banned, anyway. And I barely know him. I – " His eyes darted around the pub. "I got to go, mate."

Lawton slammed his hand down on Hammond arm. Hammond looked down at the hand and then up at Lawton's eyes.

Lawton said, "I just need some stuff, you know. Tell me about the pills."

"All I know is they're called Skarlet – with a 'K'. That's what the guy who had them said."

"And where do I get some?"

Hammond shook his head. "Can't see you getting any, now. If

they've killed someone, they'll be got rid of. Any batches left, the producer, the dealer will just flush them down the toilet. I can – can get you something else. If you're serious."

Lawton glared at him. "I'm very serious," he said.

★ ★ ★ ★

Dr. Afdal Haddad, shuffling along the cellar's flagstone floor, carried the jar over to the table.

His legs hurt, and he bared his teeth against the pain. Nadia said, "*Get an assistant*," but he couldn't trust anyone else – not even her and Ion. This was his life's work. He began it alone; he'd finish it alone.

He unplugged the plastic stopper from the jar. He took a metal jug and scooped some pills out of the washing-up bowl on the table. He poured the pills into the jar. He scooped up another jug-full, and transferred that batch into the jar. He put the stopper back into the jar. He picked up the jar, cradling it between his hands. The ancient clay felt rough on his palms. He shuffled across the cellar, his legs aching. He reached up and placed the jar next to two identical containers on the shelf, and then made his way back to the table.

He sighed and slumped into his wheelchair. He took deep breaths, and the smell of ammonia, which is a curse of methamphetamine production, filled his nostrils. He should've got used to the smell by now, but it still made him cringe. He reached into his pocket for the bottle of Aramis aftershave and squirted some into the air.

He waited for Nadia to come and get him.

CHAPTER 15.
HEIRLOOMS.

NADIA Friniuc, fifteen and sold as a whore by her father, darted across the yard towards the barn.

"Come on, Ion, come on," she said to her twelve-year-old brother. The boy panted behind her as they ran.

The cold winters gripped tightly. Food was scarce in the rural areas. You had to fight for survival. You had to sacrifice or you'd starve. But Nadia would rather go without food than see this happen to Ion.

Men had been coming from Brasov to buy her body since she'd been twelve. Papa said it was the only way, and Mama cried as she washed and prettied Nadia for the buyers.

The first year, she cried all the time. But then she got used to it and by now it was okay for her; she'd learned to bear what was happening. And the men liked her, too. They didn't slap her and spit at her like they did when it all started. They were reverent, even, thanking *domni oar* Nadia for the things she did to them. They praised her exuberance, her skills.

But she still hated them. And what she did disgusted her. But the repulsion was invigorating and addictive.

The vileness thrilled her.

But last month during dinner, Papa said they needed more money.

And his eyes moved across to Ion, beautiful Ion with his dark, dangerous eyes that sang to Nadia in a way that a brother's eyes shouldn't.

That morning, the men had arrived in a truck. Two bears, their breath billowing white in the cold morning. Papa greeted them. He bowed like a serf before lords. But they weren't lords. They were Ceaucescu puppets – local councilmen serving themselves and the regime.

They'd come for Ion.

Nadia shoved open the barn door and yanked Ion into the darkness. She slammed the door shut. She led Ion up into the haystack and they huddled into a corner. She pulled him tight into her, and she never wanted to be apart from him.

Papa yelled Ion's name from outside and then said, "*Unde este* Ion?" to Mama – Where is Ion?

Ion said, "What do they want, Nadia?"

"They want to hurt you, Ion."

He tensed in her arms, and she hugged him tighter. Her breasts pressed against him. She smelled his neck. She let her long dark hair fall over his face. She'd never let them have him, never let him be spoiled by anyone – anyone – except her.

Shouts filtered into the barn from outside. Mama and Papa calling for Ion and Nadia. They knew that she'd hidden her brother. She'd seen Papa leer at her. She'd seen his narrow, suspicious eyes on her when she stroked Ion's hair at the dinner table, when she kissed Ion's face before bed.

Ion said, "Why do they want to hurt me, Nadia?"

She said, "Mama and Papa, they – they want to sell you to these men."

He gasped and tried to pull away. But she wouldn't let go. "Nadia, Nadia, no. Why? Why would –?"

"For food, Ion, for food and fuel. They" – she leaned away, looking at him – "they sell me and the men take me. They've sold me since I was your age."

His brow creased. "Sell – I don't understand."

"To have my body. To fuck me."

He stared at her, and she knew he understood. "And – and" – his voice rasped – "and they want me for that?"

"I won't let them," she said and whipped a knife out from her coat pocket, "I'll kill them before they hurt you, Ion. I will kill them all."

He started to cry and she hugged him, feeling his body tremble against her. She pushed him down in the hay, gazing down at his tear-stained face. "You're my beautiful brother," she said. She bent her face to his and she kissed him on the mouth. "They only buy beauty, Ion," she said, tears welling in her eyes, now. "Forgive me, forgive me."

She cut Ion's face, from eye to jaw line. Blood spouted from the wound. The boy struggled in her arms, screaming. Nadia held him tight, his blood spraying over her face, warm and coppery.

The door burst open and the sun poured in.

Papa stormed in, shouting Nadia's name, calling her a bitch.

Ion's wails alerted Papa to their hideaway, and he came bounding into the haystack, shouting and cursing.

Nadia begged him not to sell Ion, not to hurt him.

Papa said, "You little whore, what have you done to his face?" The blood coloured the hay.

Papa grabbed her by the hair, dragged her off Ion. She screamed, "*Nu, nu, nu* – " – No, no, no –

Two men came into the barn and they laughed.

Papa said, "You want her, too, you want this little bitch for trying to hide?"

One of the men said, "Not today, Friniuc. We'll take your boy, bring him back tonight."

Nadia screamed, tried to scratch at Papa. But he held her by the hair, pressing her into the hay. He pulled Ion away from her. The boy's face was masked in blood.

"Take him," he said to the men, his eyes fixed on Nadia, desperation in them. "Take him now, hurry."

One of the men hauled Ion away and held him by the arm saying, "Look at his face – he's been cut. He's bleeding like a fucking pig. He's no use like this."

Papa went to them and said, "A cheaper price then. Offer me a cheaper price. Anything. We need the money or we'll starve. Please."

"Not for – "

A gun fired three times.

Nadia jerked with each shot.

The men who came for Ion fell. Blood dampened their coats.

A thin figure wearing a trilby stood at the door in the sun's glare. He pointed the gun at Papa but looked over at Nadia and Ion.

He asked them in Romanian, "Are you all right?" but Nadia barely understood him because his accent was like glue.

She said, "Who are you?"

"I'm a friend. I've come to stop this. Do you know who you are?"

Nadia didn't understand what he meant. Then he turned to Papa and said, "I've come for your heirlooms."

★ ★ ★ ★

Papa, in the house twenty minutes later, said, "You'll buy them?"

The stranger glared at Papa. "You'd sell them?"

Papa shrugged, rubbing his hands together. "If – if you'd like to pay for them."

The stranger said, "You're a terrible man."

"Don't judge me. I've sold my children before I sold these old rags." He cast a hand over what was scattered on the table. "I've been true, I've been a good brother."

The stranger looked over at Nadia and said to her, "Do you know Vlad the Impaler?"

"Yes," said Nadia. "Prince Vlad Tepes of the family Dracul."

"Castle Bran – Dracula's castle – near here," said the stranger, and then: "Transylvania. So many myths. Such nonsense written." He asked Nadia, "What have they told you about Vlad?"

"He was a Wallachian *voivode*," said Nadia. "He impaled Turks on poles to protect his kingdom."

The stranger said, "The writer Bram Stoker took Vlad as his inspiration for his fictional vampire, Dracula." He shook his head and tutted, saying, "Vlad Tepes was no vampire. Vlad Tepes was a vampire killer. The impaled Turks were not Turks. They were – "

He trailed off and breathed deeply.

Nadia saw sadness in his expression.

And then the stranger said, "They were vampires."

CHAPTER 16.
NOT SUCH A SUPER GRASS.

"SO he deals, does he?" said Superintendent Phil Birch, tapping his clipboard against the desk in the interview room.

Lithgow watched the ribbon that was tied to the clipboard flutter and said, "Yeah, totally, big time. He's Mr. Big. Number One. The Mastermind."

Birch narrowed his eyes behind the gold-framed glasses and said, "Not exaggerating are you, Fraser? I've known small-timers like you exaggerate before. You get your rocks off on being involved, don't you."

Lithgow said, "Me? No way. I tell the truth, now, Mr. Birch. I learned my lesson. You got to be careful or guys like Jake Lawton'll set you up. Luckily my dad came to the rescue, saw through the set-up." He shook his head. "I'm straight and narrow, Superintendent, straight and narrow. I work in a bank, after all."

"Oh, yes. Of course you do. Silly me," said Birch and looked at his clipboard. "Nice little flat you've got over there in Fulham."

"Yeah, it's all right."

"Aren't they expensive, flats in Fulham? The bank must pay you well."

"I save. That's what you get working at a bank, you get taught, and encouraged, to save. And – yeah, okay – my dad helped out with the deposit, but so what?"

"So what, indeed."

Lithgow looked into Birch's eyes, willing the copper to believe his story. He'd had enough of Lawton, and decided to set him up. He had a little plan, and this was Part One. Birch seemed to like the idea of Lawton as a dealer. Fraser thought he'd have more trouble convincing the detective.

"I don't know," said Fraser, "what it is with Lawton? He's like, maybe, guilty after his girlfriend died – "

Birch raised his eyebrows and said, "Girlfriend died?"

"Yeah, Jenna McCall – "

"McCall, McCall," Birch was saying as he ran a pen down the list clipped to his clipboard. "Oh, here we are – Jenna McCall, twenty-nine, assistant manager in a clothes shop in New Cross."

"That's right," said Lithgow. "She got drugs off him, you see."

"Yes, I do see," said Birch, scratching his chin.

"And, man, that stuff in Iraq – him killing that totally innocent man –"

"Yes, you're right, Fraser."

"Totally innocent," said Lithgow. "That must've fucked Lawton up. I feel sorry for him, I really do."

"I know you do," said Birch, cocking his head to one side. "You look genuinely remorseful."

"Most doormen are clean, you know," said Lithgow. "But some, like Lawton, well they need the extra cash so turn a blind eye to dealers."

"You seem to know a lot."

"Bet you know a lot about murder, Mr. Birch, but it doesn't mean you're a murderer, does it."

Birch smiled and said, "Did you know any of the victims?"

He thought for a second, then put on a sad face. "Well, to be truthful, Superintendent Birch – and I want to be – Jenna McCall."

Birch's face lit up and he said, "Oh. Same – "

Lithgow nodded and said, "I dated her for a while after Lawton, and he was really pissed off, you know. He was furious when she split with him. They went way back, apparently. Before he was in the Army, even."

"That's interesting," said Birch. "A love triangle." He leaned back in his chair and fanned his face with the clipboard. Strands of hair wafted on his balding head. "You've been very helpful, Fraser. I'd like to thank you for coming in."

"That's okay, Mr. Birch. I know that with me being arrested – *falsely* arrested – in the past, I know that some people might point the finger at me. So I wanted to, you know, clear the air. Cards on the table."

"Good cards, Fraser. Top hand."

Lithgow smiled and nodded, and said, "So, am I – would you say that – um – I'm in the clear?"

CHAPTER 17.
TAKING THE POISON.

THE headline on the website read, DOORMAN AT DEATH CLUB TRIED TO BUY PILLS NIGHT AFTER 28 DIED IN DRUGS HORROR.

Lawton felt a fire in his chest, and he clenched his fists. He'd sat down with his laptop to see what the press was saying about Religion.

And this is was what they were saying – that he'd tried to buy drugs the following night.

"Hammond," he said through his teeth, "Hammond, you bastard, I'll rip your head off," and he grabbed the phone and dialled.

"Associated Newspapers," said the voice, and Lawton said, "Christine Murray."

She answered, and he recognized her voice and, without introducing himself, he said, "Steve Hammond been gossiping about me?"

"Mr. Lawton," she said. "I tried to ring you for a comment."

"I'll sue you," he said, but knew he wouldn't.

She knew it, too, and she said that he wouldn't.

He felt the anger fade and said, "What have I done to you?"

"Nothing," she said. "It's not what you've done to me. This isn't a vendetta, Mr. Lawton. I'm doing my job."

"Bollocks. I didn't speak to you, didn't give you an interview when that video got released, and since then you've been sniffing around me like a dog sniffing shit."

"I'm not after you," she said. "I'm just after the story. Now, I'll tell you who is after you."

He narrowed his eyes. He looked at the bottle of Jim Beam. He said, "You tell me, then."

"The police."

"Oh, yeah – that's new. Hats off to you, Christine. On the fucking ball."

"And they say that an ex of yours died at Religion."

Lawton sat up. "They know I was with her?"

"Can you confirm that you and Jenna – Jenna McCall – were an item?"

Lawton said nothing.

Murray said, "And I'm also led to believe that a gentleman named Fraser Lithgow dated Jenna after you broke up with her – and that you tried to frame Mr. Lithgow for taking drugs into Religion a few months ago."

"I *will* fucking frame him when I see him. I'll make a pretty picture of his face."

"You're very aggressive, Mr. Lawton," she said.

"I'm very pissed off, Mrs. Murray," he said.

"Were you angry when Mr. Lithgow started to see Jenna?"

"Are you writing this down?"

Murray didn't say anything.

He said, "Don't write it down and I'll tell you."

She said, "All right."

Lawton took a breath. He looked at the clock on the laptop's screen. It said 6.30 p.m. And then he said, "I was in Iraq. Jenna and me, we'd not been serious for years. But I still cared for her. We'd known each other since we were kids. I wasn't worried that she was dating Lithgow, but I didn't like him. He's a snake. But I became worried when I caught him trying to smuggle tabs into Religion."

"Charges were dropped. He didn't have anything on him, he says."

"Fraser says a lot of things. Most of them come out of the back end of a male cow. He had twenty pills tucked into his shoe. That's the truth."

"But he was cleared of any suspicion."

Lawton said, "He had twenty pills – in his shoe – going into Religion. His dad, a flash harry QC, got him off."

"So you didn't set him up as revenge for him getting off with Jenna?"

Lawton blew air out his cheeks. "Doesn't matter what I say, does it. You've got me in your sights, and you don't give a shit. You know what? I've been here before – "

"I know – "

" – and it doesn't matter what other people think, as long as I know the truth. I've got no one, Christine – no mum, no dad, no family – so I can take the poison and spit it out. It doesn't hurt me, because I know it's lies. I did not set up Lithgow. I had nothing to do with those deaths at Religion. And Basra? I'll tell you about Basra, Christine. I'll tell you, I'm taking you there one day and introducing you to some families, some mums and dads and kids, and you can ask them what happened that day. And you know why you'll be able to ask them, Christine? You'll be able to ask them because I took a fucking decision."

And he slammed down the phone.

His nostrils flared. His eyes were wide and stayed open for a long time without blinking. He didn't move. And when he did blink, and then move, he

reached for the bottle of Jim Beam.

But a knock at the door stopped his hand.

And then a voice outside his flat said, "Police. Open up, Mr. Lawton."

CHAPTER 18.
HAVE FAITH.

NATHAN Holt, gazing out across the Thames, said into the phone, "I'm very concerned that we'll be shut for weeks. We're going to lose money, a lot of money – and I won't be able to pay the salaries."

"Nathan, Nathan," said the voice on the end of the phone, "it'll be fine."

"George, I'm not comfortable with any of this. They arrested Jake Lawton an hour ago. I had some reporter on the phone asking me for a comment."

"Please don't concern yourself," said George Fuad.

"Guilt's chewing me up, George. He's a good guy, Jake; he didn't do anything wrong."

"I know it's a shame, but this business in Iraq, you know. We had no idea when you hired him that he'd murdered a civilian out there. And how many more? Come on, Nathan. We don't want anything to do with that illegal war, do we? And we can't have murderers on our staff."

"It seems – it's wrong, that's all."

"I know it's a rotten thing to have to do. I know it's taking advantage, maybe, of these tragic deaths – but it's an opportunity for us to get rid of Lawton."

"He's a fall guy, isn't he," said Holt. "A Lee Harvey Oswald. Something else is going on here."

Fuad said, "What's going on here is a disaster for Religion. Twenty-eight customers died of a probable drugs overdose. How did those drugs get into the club? Do you want to take responsibility, Nathan? Ultimately, of course, you should. We should, too, Charles and I. But we have to have a sacrifice, a scapegoat. And Jake Lawton, war criminal, killer of innocent men, will do."

A silence fell. Nathan's mind reeled. He sweated, despite the wind that sliced in through the open window of his fourth-floor flat.

"Is everything all right, now, Nathan?"

It wasn't, but he nodded. "Yes, George, of course. I'm just, you know, apprehensive, that's all. I feel bad – "

"Of course you do, of course. You're a good man, Nathan. A fantastic manager. You've run a great club for us. And in the meantime, you'll be taken care of. All right?"

"If you say."

"I do say, Nathan."

They said goodnight, and Nathan put the phone down. He went to the kitchen, poured a glass of water. He drank the water and then had another and then another.

He went into the living room, walked over to the window to shut it. Night made London grey. The Thames shimmered. Sightseers strolled along the South Bank. They were wrapped against the chill.

Holt thought about what George Fuad told him:

You'll be taken care of.

He hoped that didn't mean he was going to lose his job at Religion when the club re-opened.

You'll be taken care of.

It sounded ominous, that was all.

The Fuads, sixties hippies who got rich selling cars in Thatcher's free-for-all Britain, bought the club in 1995. They took a few years to salvage it, forging Religion out of dust and rubble.

"That's how most religions are created," George Fuad said at the time.

They'd hired Holt to run the club and retreated to sunnier climes. The brothers had homes in Monte Carlo, London, and the Caribbean. They'd only visited the club two or three times in the past five years.

But that was fine by Holt. He could do it his way, and his way had been established during more than ten years of running nights and clubs in London and the south-east.

He was good at what he did, and the diversity of Religion's output drew a lot of attention. *Time Out* loved the club, *thelondonpaper* hailed Monday's The Weekend's Coming night a hit, and specialist publications loved Wednesday's goth night.

And the club's slogan, Get Religion, pissed off the Christians.

No better way to get publicity than to commit blasphemy.

Holt was born to run clubs. And now that Religion was closed, and he was staring out of his window on a Thursday night, he felt lost.

He tried to ring the Fuads again. He wanted to know if they were hassling the cops to let them re-open Religion. Shutting the club for a week would be all right. But two, even three, weeks, and it would be a nightmare.

The Fuads weren't answering.

He tossed the phone of the sofa, and puffed air out of his cheeks.

Jesus, he would've died of boredom if he didn't have this job. What would he do with himself every Friday and Saturday? Every Tuesday, every Wednesday, and every Thursday? He'd got Mondays down to a tee: his night on the town; and Sundays meant a drive down to Kent where his mum lived.

But what about nights like this?

The buzzer went. A spark of excitement ignited in Holt, and he strode over to the intercom.

"Yeah, hi?"

"Hi, good evening, Mr. Holt," said the voice, male and with a hint of an accent. "Mr. Fuad, Mr. George Fuad, has sent me to you."

Holt furrowed his brow.

Sent me to you?

That's a funny way to put it, he thought.

He wasn't about to buzz the guy up. Holt put safety first. He said, "Could you tell me what it's about, specifically?"

"Specifically?" said the voice, like he was trying the word out.

"Yes. Why has Mr. Fuad sent you?"

The man said, "To give you an offer of work while Religion is closed for business."

"A job?"

"Yes." The man sounded impatient. "A job for you. In – in Barbados, where they live."

Holt said, "I've just put the phone down on Mr. Fuad – he didn't mention anything about – "

"I know he called you, he just called me. And he said he'd look after you. Did he say that?"

Holt looked towards the ceiling.

What had George said?

And in the meantime we will look after you.

Holt buzzed the stranger in.

Two minutes later came a knock on the door.

Holt opened the door. He saw the scar on the man's face and then the knife in the man's hand.

CHAPTER 19.
THE PLAN, PART TWO.

"LAWTON'S been arrested," said Lithgow. "About bloody time that fucking war criminal got his dues. And you know what? It's me who's burying him."

Hammond rolled the joint. "He asked me about pills earlier today. Said his dealer had gone AWOL."

Lithgow said, "Lawton asked you for pills?"

"Yeah. Wanted to know where you got Skarlet."

Lithgow's nerves tightened. "Did you tell him?"

Hammond stopped rolling and glared at Lithgow. "What d'you take me for, you prat?"

"Okay," said Lithgow, "what did you tell him?"

"Hardly anything."

"Hardly anything?"

"Yeah, hardly anything," said Hammond and went back to rolling the joint, and then said, "But I did ring this journo who bought me a steak. And she wrote a story and it went on her rag's website. About Lawton asking for drugs the night after all those people died. It only took an hour to get from the horse's mouth to the stable – they're quick, these journalists."

"Oh, fucking glorious," said Lithgow. "I like that, I do," and he laughed.

They were in Lithgow's flat in Fulham, feet up on the coffee table, empty cans on the floor, and the odour of an Indian takeaway drenching the air.

Lithgow's laughter drifted away, and he chewed his lip. Hammond eyed him and said, "What're you thinking, Fraize?"

"I'm thinking," said Lithgow, "if Lawton wants the drugs so badly we should give him some – which is Part Two of my plan to crucify that bastard for trying to nail me."

"You're joking."

Lithgow stood up, grabbed the jewelled box off the shelf. He sat down, opened the box on the coffee table and said, "I got these."

Hammond said, "Jeez – fucking 'K'. 'K' for killer, man."

Hammond lit the rolley. He sucked the drug into his lungs.

Lithgow watched his mate's eyes roll up in his head. He screwed up his face, thinking. He didn't know what to do. Should he take these to Lawton's flat, get him nailed for possession, or keep this batch – just in case?

"Just in case," he said, not realizing he was talking.

"In case what?" said Hammond, slurring already.

"In case," said Lithgow, taking the spliff, "it turns out that these pills had nothing to do with those people dying. In case I'd be throwing away gold."

Lithgow smoked the joint. The drug washed into him and his legs went weak.

CHAPTER 20.
NIGHT RETREAT.

VEHICLES dashed out of the darkness and scattered the troops.

Wilson, sweat pouring down his back and from his hair, panted as the dust filled his throat.

His gaze flitted about. Officers on horseback zigzagged, racing back and forth as if they were lost. Troops on foot sprinted for cover. Dust rose in clouds, causing chaos and panic.

Shouts and screams filled the night. The squeal of brakes put Wilson's teeth on edge as vehicles jerked and bumped along the dirt track they called a road in this forsaken country.

Tribesmen broke from the night and Wilson said, "Bloody hell, bloody hell," as they hacked at foot soldiers and transport animals.

Creatures bayed and men shrieked.

Gunfire crackled and hoofs thundered.

Wilson's head snapped from side to side. He gripped his rifle, his hands sweating, the sweat pouring down the gun's varnished stock.

He froze, his nerves tightened.

A tribesman, fury burning in his eyes, his mouth wide in a screech of rage, charged at Wilson. The hostile whipped his knife about his head, moonlight splintering off the blade.

Wilson raised his gun, but the weapon slipped out of his wet hands. He cursed, and his innards felt as if they would melt. He squatted to pick up the gun. The Arab screeched and bore down on him.

A gunshot deafened Wilson. The Arab toppled off his horse and crashed to the ground, sending up a belch of dust. The hostile arched his back, blood spouting from a wound in his chest. A horseman charged from the darkness. Wilson stared at the rider, the horseman's Webley pistol held out, smoke pluming from the barrel.

"What the fuck do you think you're doing, Wilson?" said Lieutenant Jordan, stopping his horse, jabbing his pistol at the young soldier. "Get a bloody move on, man. Remember what I told you. You need to be getting back to Hillah with me – and if I don't make it – "

Jordan flinched, and gawped with shock. He opened his mouth and a gasp hissed from his throat. He grimaced and pressed his hand to his ribs.

"The bastards," he said, "the damn, heathen bastards," and he pulled his hand away. Blood drizzled from his palm and a dark wet patch spread over his jacket. "They've bloody shot me, Wilson, the bloody Arabs have shot me – come – come on, man – grab that – that mount."

Jordan wheeled his horse around and galloped away. Wilson clambered on the Arab's horse. He dug his heels into the animal's flank and it shot off after Jordan.

Horsemen sped from the darkness and hacked at the troops. Jordan fired randomly with his Webley. Wilson, clenching the rifle under his armpit, did the same, targeting hostiles as they attacked the retreating troops.

He caught up with Jordan. The road twisted and turned through scrub. All around them, it seemed, there was fighting. The air smelled of cordite.

After only a couple of minutes, Jordan's horse slowed, and the lieutenant sagged in the saddle.

Wilson pulled up his horse and dismounted. He ran to the lieutenant and caught him as he toppled from the saddle. Jordan grunted. Blood soaked Wilson's hands. He eased the officer from the horse and laid him on the ground.

Jordan licked his lips, the tip of his tongue flickering over his lips. His face blanched and his eyes dulled. He opened his mouth and croaked.

"Sir," said Wilson, "sir, don't die, sir." Wilson shuddered, the fear flushing through him. "You can't leave me here, sir. I don't – I don't know what to do."

Jordan gripped his wrist, and his nails dug into Wilson's skin. Wilson cringed. The lieutenant, his voice a whisper, said, "Get – Hillah – take – take – them – destroy – d-destroy – "

Jordan stiffened and arched his back. He opened his mouth and blood trickled down his chin. He let out a gasp and his body wilted.

Wilson stared at the lieutenant's dead eyes and felt lost and hopeless. He whimpered and rocked back and forth.

Shouts jerked him out of his depression. Hoofs hammered the earth, making the ground shake. He turned. A cloud of dust rose around the tribesmen as they charged towards him. A half-dozen, knives brandished and hate screwing up their faces, raced down the road.

Cold fear filled Wilson's chest. He leapt to his feet and dashed to Jordan's horse. He jammed his foot in the stirrup. The horse wheeled and neighed. Its head jerked back and forth. Wilson hopped around.

The hostiles closed.

"Jesus in heaven," he said, his voice shaking.

The horse spun, Wilson's foot caught in the stirrup.

The noise of the insurgents' approach deafened him. Their shouts shrilled in his ears. They would hack him to death in a minute; they would cut him into pieces and leave his remains to be carrion in this hell.

He screamed. The horse wheeled. He hopped, he sprang, he swung his leg over the saddle. He yelled.

The hostiles circled him.

They bayed for his blood.

Their knives chopped at the night.

CHAPTER 21.
DAZED AND CONFUSED.

HAMMOND wasn't sure when, or how, he'd agreed to this. But he was here, now. He still felt woozy after smoking three joints at Lithgow's. But typically, the dope had filled him with confidence. Which is probably why Lithgow was able to persuade him to get on the tube at Fulham Broadway.

An hour or so later, they got off a bus at the Three Hammers pub, where they got a drink. The booze mingled with the dope and made Hammond's head even mushier.

Then they walked over to Holland Park. And the fresh air-alcohol-cannabis compost grabbed Hammond's brain and shook it like a baby shaking a rattle.

They stood in the shadow of an oak tree.

Hammond said, "Nice night, nice spot," and gazed down the street.

Four-storey Georgian houses lined the flagstoned street. Shrubbery festooned the frontages. Flash cars parked along the pavement. Music wafted from an open window, classical stuff that Hammond didn't mind at all, the mood he was in.

But then he said, "Fraize, what are we doing here? And where is here? I've never, ever in my life been to Holland Park. Thought it was a myth, you know. Like Atlantis."

"We're here, man, to nick drugs to plant in Lawton's house."

"Nick drugs where?"

"Oh, man, Stevie, you're so fucked up. The guy who gave me the Skarlet, man. I followed him – "

"You fucking followed him?"

"Sure I did. I didn't know him, did I. You can't just trust people."

"I told him to come see you. He came from me, man."

Lithgow said, "Did you know him? Did you fucking trust him?"

"Dunno. He came up to me in the pub. You know."

"Yeah, well, that's why I'm fucking brighter than you, you fucking lamp," said Lithgow. "Know who you're dealing with, man, know who you're dealing with. I always know who I'm dealing with. Check 'em out. Upper hand, Stevie, upper hand."

"So you followed him here?"

"Fucking followed him here, the big, pony-tailed twat."

"You always do that?" said Hammond.

"I always, absolutely no fucking question about it, do that," said Lithgow. "If I go down, they go down, too, man. I'm a squealer."

Hammond furrowed his brow. He looked around again and said, "Ah, fuck it, Fraser, man, fuck it. We're not meant to be in a place like this."

"What're you moaning about?"

"My brain's fucked, man. I'm stoned. We should be indoors. I'm freaking out, that's what I'm saying."

"Steve, Steve – it'll be okay, man, be okay – it's easy, easy. Down the road here, okay, then there's a basement floor, you know, down some steps. Window was open last time, might be open this time."

Hammond shook his head. He didn't like this because he didn't understand it. He'd never broken into anywhere in his life. He started to say something, but Lithgow was off down the road, lurking under the overhanging branches that draped from the oak trees.

Hammond tottered after him, feeling sick and confused, wanting to be at home, listening to something dark and obscure and difficult on a high volume that would mush up his brain even more.

CHAPTER 22.
NADIA'S GIFT.

DR. HADDAD panted, his old brow wet with sweat and his old cheeks red with heat.

Nadia Radu got up off her knees and wiped her mouth. She went over to the mirror and checked her make-up and hair. She buttoned up her blouse and turned to face the old man. He sat on the bed, zipping himself up. He fumbled at his flies.

He said, "I never asked you for this, Nadia."

"No, you didn't."

"But you do these things – "

She said, "Do you want me to stop?"

He looked at her, his eyes wide, and said, "No, heavens, no. I may be very old, but I'm not senile, yet. It's only – I never understood – "

"You saved us, Dr. Haddad. Saved us from hell. And it's all I knew how to do. I pleased men, and I saw that I could get things."

"You only had to ask me. I would've given you anything – without this."

"I understand that," she said. "Still – we are – you know that we are eternally grateful – for all these things."

"Does it make you sick –? I mean – with an old man?"

She smiled and said, "No, only with a cruel man." She went to him and said, "Time we went downstairs. We'll wait in the living room, see if they report anything on the news." She helped him up and into his wheelchair. "You say," she said, kicking the brakes of the chair, "that it'll be tonight."

"I'm sure of it," he said. "Twenty-four hours. No more than forty-eight."

She wheeled him out of the bedroom.

At the top of the stairs, she eased him into the stair lift. His hand touched her breast and his fingers closed around it. She smiled to herself and let him feel her.

"Ready?" she said when he was sitting in the stair lift.

"Ready," he said.

She reached for the switch.

Glass shattered somewhere downstairs.

Nadia froze.

"What was that?" said Dr. Haddad.

"I don't know," she said, her voice grated by fear.

"Is Ion back yet?"

She bit her lip and listened, and then said, "No. He's not back."

"Nadia, you should go and see. If someone's broken into the cellar – "

CHAPTER 23.
THEY WILL RISE...

JERRY Landers sipped his Coke and looked at his watch. Half-ten, that was all. He'd only been on shift for thirty minutes and it felt like a week.

But the policewoman would be back soon with teas and biscuits from the machine, and he could talk to her again. Jerry liked to talk to her. She had a pretty face and a nice figure, and he never got that close to nice ladies.

Too shy.

Get out more, mum said.

He thought about the policewoman, Ruby Richards, and how perhaps he could ask her to come for breakfast. They could find a cafe at 5.00 a.m. when they both finished their shifts and ponder the night's boredom over a fry-up.

He turned towards the door with the porthole window. Strip-lights glowed in the room behind the door. The bodies lay in the room. Twenty-eight of them, cut open earlier today by pathologists at three London hospitals. And after they stitched all the skin back together, they brought the bodies here.

The unit lurked down a side street in Battersea. They housed bodies here if there was something odd about the way they died. The pathologists must've decided that this bunch were really odd because they were all ferried here that afternoon.

And Jerry got called at 6.00 p.m., Charlie the boss saying, "We need you at B13 by ten tonight, son. Don't mention it – usual drill."

He'd never been to B13, but he'd heard about the unit. Everyone at the security firm he worked for had to sign the Official Secrets Act if they worked at B13.

"Cloak and dagger stuff," said Charlie the boss. "Nudge nudge, say nothing, keep stum."

Jerry stared at the door and the light shimmered behind it. He tried not to think about the bodies, but they were stuck in his head.

He shivered and wished he didn't have to do this, but what else could Mrs. Landers's only son do? He turned away from the door and picked up the copy of 2000AD, and started reading.

"You're good for nothing, Landers," Mr. Curtis, the headmaster, had said at school.

And being *told* he was good for nothing made him *believe* he was good for nothing.

"You may as well sign on and forget about the rest of your life," Mr. Curtis told Jerry.

Ten years later and Mr. Curtis might well say, I told you so. A security guard on five quid an hour hardly suggested a transformation in Jerry's life.

A muffled thud came from the morgue.

Jerry tensed and sat up straight in the chair. He put the comic book down and narrowed his eyes. Craning his neck, he stared towards the door. The light flickered in the porthole window. He listened and heard the light inside the morgue hum. It sounded like a swarm of flies – Jerry shuddered at the thought – hovering over the dead bodies.

Something clattered inside the morgue.

Jerry gasped. A chill slid down his spine.

He looked towards the door that led out of the anteroom and into the corridor, down which PC Richards had gone to get tea and biscuits.

Where was she? She should be back by now.

He got up, the chair scraping over the linoleum floor. He breathed hard, and the smell of disinfectant got up his nostrils. The odour made him dizzy for a moment, and he steadied himself on the edge of the desk.

Another clatter from inside the morgue.

Like someone – something – tripping.

He clawed at his chest, finding it hard to breath. His heart thumped. He moved towards the door. The hum of the strip-light grew louder. Shadows danced in the dimly lit circle of glass.

He heard a moan – was it a moan?

Jerry's throat felt dry. He tried to swallow, but he didn't have any spit. He looked over his shoulder, hoping PC Richards would come with tea and biscuits, hoping she'd go in first.

No, he thought; *I'm the bloke – I should lead the way. I'll go see what's going on, then report back to her. She'll like me for that, for taking the initiative.*

You don't have any initiative, Landers.

Mr. Curtis's voice booming in his head again.

He crept towards the door. There was someone in there – he was convinced.

Too much noise for the place to be – just filled with dead people.

How could anyone have got in? Was he in the toilet at the time? Where would PC Richards have been?

Kids, maybe. Or these scary goths. These people who said they were vampires. He'd read about them in *The Sun*. The papers had gone crazy over this story. Writing all kinds of things – and they were true, no doubt. His colleagues said, *Don't believe what you read in the papers, Jerry*, but then Jerry thought, *Why would they write them if they weren't true?*

And Jerry knew there were a lot of strange things in the world. You only had to spend a couple of hours on the internet to realize that.

He was at the door. He sniffed, and a stale odour wafted from inside the morgue. He moved his face closer to the portal window. The strip-lights shimmered and hummed.

His nose was pressed against the glass. He peered into the semi-darkness. He could just make out the bodies, lying in rows on the trolleys. He could –

A dark shape whipped across the window inside the morgue.

Jerry gasped, and he felt as if someone were jabbing at his heart with a knife. He stumbled backwards, clutching his chest.

A hand fell on his shoulder, and he screamed.

CHAPTER 24.
DRUGS FACTORY.

LITHGOW said, "Be careful, you tit."

Hammond stumbled into the cellar. He kicked the broken glass off his Dr. Marten's.

"You'll wake the fucking street up," said Lithgow.

"Yeah – sorry, mate – accident – "

Hammond stared down at his feet. Glass glittered the flagstone floor. Stepping through the open window, he'd put his boot through the pane. He felt dizzy, that's all. Couldn't get his bearings even when clambering through an open window.

Lithgow had led him down the stone steps to the basement window. As he climbed down the steps, Hammond had glanced up at the street above him and felt like he was sinking. It was weird.

The sash window was open a few inches, and Lithgow yanked the top half down, and then he climbed through into the basement.

Hammond followed but he stabbed his boot through the pane, and the window shattered.

Lithgow had flinched and called him a tit.

Inside the basement, Hammond gazed around and tried to make his eyes see in the dark. He couldn't make anything out, but he could smell disinfectant and aftershave.

Lithgow scurried off, and Hammond heard him mutter to himself about a light switch, *Where's the fucking light switch?*

He must've found it.

The glare blinded Hammond.

He shut his eyes and staggered backwards. He opened his eyes. Bruises blotched his vision, and he flapped a hand in front of his face. He could hear clattering, Lithgow cursing. He shook his head, his eyes getting accustomed to the light.

"Fucking hell," said Hammond.

"Yeah," said Lithgow, "fucking hell indeed."

Chemical drums lined the far wall, their labels painted over with black paint. A cardboard box filled with emptied blister packs of Sudafed tablets was tucked into the corner.

There were flasks, beakers, and rubber tubing on the wooden table at the centre of the room. Lined on a shelf were milk bottles filled with colourful fluids. Three very old looking jars stood on another shelf.

Lithgow opened a cupboard and drew out a roll of tin foil, placing it on the table, and a box of bicarbonate.

"They got a proper little drugs factory going on here," said Lithgow. He looked around the room and went over to the shelf where the three old jars were kept. He brought them down, one by one, and stood them on the table next to each other.

"What're those?" said Hammond.

"Well, how the fuck should I know? I'm not the fucking Antiques Roadshow, am I. They just look odd, that's all. Incongruous, you know?"

Hammond studied the jars. They were clay pots. A picture had been painted on each on. The image showed a golden-haired man. The same guy was featured on each jar. The guy brandished a weapon that looked like two elephant tusks linked by a piece of wood over his head. There were objects, black and oozing, pinned to both tusks. The looked like hearts to Hammond, but he wasn't sure. Piles of bodies with holes in their chests lay around the golden-haired man. Black stuff drizzled from the wounds. *They might* be *hearts,* thought Hammond.

Lithgow unplugged the stopper from the first jar, peered inside and said, "Dust, full of fucking dust." He opened the second jar, took a look and said, "Dust in that fucker, too." He looked at Hammond and said, "Things don't look good, mate."

"You never know," said Hammond.

Lithgow pulled the stopper from the third jar and looked inside, and his mouth opened. "You fucking well *don't* know – you're right," he said, and tilted the jar over towards Hammond so he could see.

And Hammond said, "Pills," and his eyes were wide.

The door crashed open. Hammond stared at the woman standing in the doorway. She had dark hair and purple eyes that blazed. She was gorgeous, and her beauty froze him for a moment.

And then Lithgow's voice snapped him out of it, Lithgow saying, "Run," and grabbing one of the pots.

Lithgow legged it past Hammond, and Hammond looked back at the woman.

Her face went pale and she screamed, "No, no," and darted into the room, bringing a gun up from her side.

Hammond opened his mouth.

The woman fired the gun.

A massive force whacked Hammond in the shoulder, throwing him backwards. He fell against the wall. He looked down at his shoulder. Blood pulsed from a hole in his coat.

CHAPTER 25.
FOREIGN BODIES.

MURRAY, sitting in the dark in the kitchen, said, "Are you telling me that their insides were shrivelled up, and there was no blood in their bodies?"

Her contact in the pathology department said, "Not a drop. I've – we've never seen anything like it. The organs looked – old, decayed. Apart from the heart. The heart in each body had swollen, turned black, and it glistened like some – some huge, monstrous slug."

Murray raised her shoulders and shivered. She glanced over her shoulder and out of the window into the darkness. She pulled her dressing gown around her and said, trying to keep her voice low, "Do you have a name for this condition?"

Her contact said, "I don't, Christine. We've no idea. The only label I can give you, now, is blood loss."

"But you said there's no trauma wound," said Murray.

"No, no wounds to the body. Externally, at least."

"So their blood just dried up, is that what you're saying?" said Murray.

Her contact, whispering, said, "I've never seen a hundred per cent blood loss before. Forty per cent will kill a victim, but a hundred – not in bodies this recently dead."

Murray put a hand to her brow. After a few seconds she said, "You say there were marks on some of the bodies. Could that be the cause of blood loss?"

"There were incisions on a few of the bodies, yes," said her contact, "but certainly not significant enough to cause any blood loss."

Silence filled the line.

And then her contact said, "I'm led to believe that some of the victims might have practiced, um, vampirism. They drank blood. This might explain the scarring and cuts on some of the bodies. We're only talking half-a-dozen, here. You can dismiss this, Christine. It has no bearing on the deaths."

Murray said, "How do you explain the shrivelled organs, the swollen hearts?"

Her contact breathed and then said, "We don't. We can't." And then after a few moments of silence, her contact said, "But there's some unusual activity in the bodies."

Murray sat up. Her chair scraped the tiled floor. She grimaced and looked up at the ceiling. She didn't want to wake the boys and Richard. She'd already had another row with Richard when she got home. And David cried when she went up to his room, the boy saying, "Are you and daddy splitting up?"

She'd said, *No, no, darling,* and hugged him, but Murray didn't really know if that was true, and not knowing scared her.

Murray rang her contact before leaving the office, and her contact said to ring after ten and before eleven. So she'd sneaked down to the kitchen fifteen minutes ago to make the call.

Murray said, "What do you mean by that, by 'unusual'?"

Her contact said, "We found foreign DNA in the bodies."

Murray said, "Foreign?" and thought, *does she mean Albanian or Afghan and might they be illegal immigrants or, better still, foreign criminals?*

But then her contact said, "I mean, not human."

Murray's mouth opened and closed, but no words came out.

Her contact said, "Are you all right, Christine?"

"Yes," said Murray. "Not human. So animal, then?"

"No. Not animal, either. Certainly not any animal that we know of."

Murray said nothing.

Then her contact said, "There was also elements of methylenedioxy amphetamine, from which ecstasy is derived."

"The pills," said Murray. "So the pills killed them?"

"We can't say that," said her contact, "but if we can ascertain that the pills did this to their bodies, then we will be able to say that. But not now."

"What do you think?"

"Christine, I don't know what to think. I've never seen anything like it."

"I'll say in my story that the pills are believed to have been ecstasy – would that be all right?"

"That would be all right, yes," said her contact, "but I wouldn't say they killed those people."

"Okay, but I'll strongly suggest it. What else is in ecstasy tablets?"

Her contact said, "All kinds of stuff. Street drugs can contain all kinds of shit, even curry powder. What we need is a pill. We could break it down, then, see if it compares to samples we took from the bodies."

"About this unknown element?" said Murray.

"Yes," said her contact.

"Can I suggest at all what it might come from?"

Her contact said nothing.

Murray said, "Anything at all?"

"It's – no, no, you can't – it's nothing that's ever existed before," said her contact, "and if it has existed, we've never come across it."

CHAPTER 26.
FEEDING TIME.

HUNGER clawing at her belly – that's what Jenna felt before she was aware of being awake.

She came to, hauled out of whatever blackness she'd been in by a pain in her chest, as if something moved in there, and she gasped. Her gaze darted around the room, and she kept blinking because her vision was coated in red. She could see in the dark. And she could smell too, smell something that caused her to salivate.

She sat up on the trolley and looked around.

Where am I? she thought, watching others come awake. Moans filled the room. Hunger pangs pulling them out of sleep, or unconsciousness.

Jenna's head filled with her memories, and all she could see was – food.

A man she knew as her father, a woman she knew as her mother, a man she knew as – Jake.

And they were all food.

She'd seen Jake recently. Where had she seen him? What had been her relationship with him? She knew her flesh tingled when she thought of him – but was that because he fulfilled her craving for food, or fulfilled another craving?

She shook her head. She ran her tongue over her teeth. They were sharp, and strangely, she knew what they were for.

They were for feeding.

She became more aware of her surroundings, and the other figures in the room. They hoarded towards the door, and she felt drawn to them, swept up in the feeling that she was one with them.

And she sensed what they were thinking: they were thinking "food".

It was the only driving force.

Food to survive.

There was a place to go, as well. A nest.

She had a sense of where it was, and this pack of hers was headed there as well. Safety in numbers, protection of the group. She pressed at the rear of the group. They were huddled near the door. The ones at the front craned their necks, sniffing and salivating. Jenna knew what they smelled – she knew it in her head, as if she were sharing their nostrils.

They smelled blood, and it was blood she craved, and when she smelled it she would recognize it.

She licked her lips and thought about drinking its warmth and tasting its thickness, and it drove her wild.

She bared her teeth and hissed and waited for her brothers and sisters to tear open the door so they could feed on whatever lay on the other side.

★ ★ ★ ★

Jerry spun on his heels, yelling and flailing with his arms.

He hit something, there was a squeal, and a tray-full of tea and biscuits clattered to the floor. Tea spilled and biscuits crumbled, and PC Ruby Richards said, "What the hell are you doing, Jerry?"

Jerry came to and he saw Richards stand in a puddle of tea, her hands on her hips.

He said, "I-I thought I heard something move – inside," and he gestured towards the morgue door with his thumb.

Richards made a face. "I hope they're not waking up." She shook her head and said, "I'll have a look."

"Be careful," said Jerry.

She strode past him and said, "What's the worst that can happen?" and then added: "You stay here," which made Jerry feel pathetic.

Richards pressed her ear to the door and furrowed her brow. Jerry saw shadows flutter behind the portal window. The shadows could only mean that something was in there, something alive. The light wouldn't do that on its own, would it?

"PC Richards – there's – "

She stared at him and put her finger to her lips. She slipped her baton out of her belt. She'd heard something, obviously. Jerry stiffened and scratched at his chest, his skin tingling with goosepimples.

PC Richards grabbed the handle and started to open the door. Her baton was ready. Jerry swallowed. He couldn't make spit. His bladder felt heavy. He wanted to run, but what would she think of him?

PC Richards pushed open the door.

Jerry pissed himself. He stood frozen.

PC Richards faced them in the doorway.

Pale faces, evil sneers, and sharp teeth.

She turned towards Jerry, her face stretched in terror.

She screamed, her piercing voice saying, "Jerry! Phone 99 – " and she made to run towards him.

But they snatched her and pulled her into them and she shrieked, and they surrounded her and fell on her until the only thing of her Jerry could see was a twitching foot.

He called her name and felt the wetness in his pants and the fear in his chest. And all he could do as the things from the morgue burst through the door and hurtled towards him was to fall to his knees and cover his face and scream.

They ploughed into him and their teeth sank into his skin.

CHAPTER 27.
"K".

LITHGOW ran and he kept running, his eyes wide open, his chest getting tighter and tighter and his legs getting heavier and heavier.

And after he didn't know how long, he collapsed into an alley. He fell against wheelie bins, knocking them aside. He wheezed, his head spinning, and he threw up on a pile of black sacks that smelled rotten.

Still panting, he raised his head and looked out through the mouth of the alley into the road. He saw cars parked on the other side of the road, and an iron fence and trees. A park lay beyond the trees, but he didn't know which park. He didn't know where he was, but he hoped he was far away from that house and the woman who had shot Hammond.

He sat in the shadows of the alley for ten minutes, trying to catch his breath. He could hear his heart drum, and his throat burned like he'd drunk acid. He kept panting and he was thinking, *I've got to get fit or they'll catch me one day.*

He stood and grimaced as pain shot through his thighs. They felt like the muscles and the bones had been taken out of them, and they almost gave way under his weight. But he steadied himself against the wall.

A bus shot past the mouth of the alley. Seeing it gave him a spurt of energy, and he hobbled out of the passageway and saw a bus stop and the bus pulling away. He shuffled over to the shelter and checked where he was.

Lithgow huddled in the corner of the stop. His watch said it was 11.15 p.m. A bus came and Lithgow hopped on, making his way upstairs. He plonked himself in the back seat. He was headed for New Cross. With Lawton arrested, and probably in custody overnight, he could break into his flat and plant the pills.

Two break-ins in one night — I'm becoming a burglar, he thought.

He took the jar out of the inside pocket of his Crombie overcoat.

He rested the jar on his lap and he pulled the stopper out and looked inside at the pills. Hundreds of them, he thought. He could've tried to pin all this on Lawton by using a few tabs from the batch he already had in his flat.

"But, no," he said out loud, "you're far too greedy for that, Fraize."

He put the stopper back in the jar and held up the container to study it. He turned it this way and that, looking at the picture of the Greek hero-type and the dead bodies around him.

Fraser narrowed his eyes and curled his lip. He wondered if the jar would be worth anything. But he couldn't take it to an antique shop and say, *I found this, how much is it worth?*

The householders might have reported it stolen — and then he shook his head, thinking, *Not unless they want the cops to find Hammond, dead or alive but probably shot.*

"Need to think, need to think," he said to himself.

He looked at the jar again. He tipped it upside down to look at the base, and the pills rattled.

A letter "K" was scratched into the base.

CHAPTER 28.
SCAPEGOAT.

LAWTON leaned his head against the window of the N171 from the Elephant and Castle to Catford Bus Garage and watched London after dark sweep by. Traffic still busied the roads and the pavements buzzed with club-goers leaving, or looking for, a drinking hole.

Birch had let him go an hour previously. He warned Lawton that he had a right to hold him without charge for twenty-four hours if he wanted to. But he was being nice, he said.

The detective peppered Lawton with questions. He asked about Jenna, and how Lawton felt about Jenna and Lithgow. He asked about rumours that Lawton was involved with drugs. And he asked about that bullshit in Basra that was none of Birch's business.

And Lawton said he knew what was happening because it happened before, two years before.

Birch said, "What happened before, Mr. Lawton?"

Lawton shut his eyes. The memory flashed, and in Lawton's head, his commanding officer, Major Hugh Brewer, was saying, "Someone's got to go, Jake, and it's cursed bad luck that it's got to be you. I know what happened, we all know what happened, but – " He shrugged.

"I'm a scapegoat," Lawton had said, glaring out of the window of Brewer's office in the Old State Building in Basra City, where the regiment was based.

Brewer said, "It's a disgrace. This happened more than a year ago, for fuck's sake. But the press has got hold of this video. Some red-top splashed it all over their front page and some cow reporter posted it on her website – and now they're all baying for blood." The Major shook his head and said, "The war's fucked up. The politicians and the press are looking for someone to blame. They're too cowardly to accept responsibility themselves – you know what fucking politicians are like. And journalists and editors won't say sorry over their dead bodies. They've been after us ever since the bloody Americans and bloody Abu Ghraib."

Lawton said, "Don't they understand that this is war?"

"No, they don't. Their world is black and white," said Brewer. "Their world is, Take the car or take the train? Their world is, Do I have chips or jacket potato? Their world is, Have a fling with the secretary or not have a fling with the secretary? They don't live in the grey like we do; they don't live in blood and death. They don't know what war is."

"So I have to pay the price. With my career."

"You were pictured killing a civilian – an unarmed civilian." Brewer rifled through a mess of papers on his desk, found a half-smoked cigarette and lit it.

"He was neither, sir." Lawton sniffed in the tobacco and felt an itch in his lungs.

Brewer said, "I understand that, your mates understand that – but the papers won't have it, the anti-war brigade – and they're growing – won't have it. The government wants blood, and they're not willing to put their own heads on the block."

"I'm fucking outraged, sir, excuse my fucking language."

"I'm fucking outraged too, Sergeant Lawton – language excused."

Lawton shook with anger, the red mist falling. He had no problem putting his life on the line, but he expected support from the politicians who sent him here, by the press who said, Yes, go get Saddam and his weapons. But when things start to go shitty, they all turn their backs.

Brewer said, "They've fucked up royally in Iraq, I tell you. The Brits are the only ones making any headway, but we're up against image-conscious politicians and reader-hungry editors." He tried to get something out of his fag end, but he failed and stumped it out on the desk. He said, "This was a great war, Jake, but it's been a crap peace."

* * * *

Ten minutes after leaving Brewer's office, Lawton had rolled a fag outside in the mid-day heat. He looked up at the clear blue sky. He thought, *It's just like Tenerife, if you look up and ignore the tanks and weapons, the sunburned, bare-chested troops, the RPGs and mortars whizzing overhead, the explosions rattling the compound.*

Yeah, he thought – *just like fucking Tenerife.*

Lawton's gaze skimmed the compound's high walls and fixed on the sangar. They were pillbox shelters where troops on guard duty got shot at, got mortared, got RPGd.

"You know that one up there, sarge," said a voice, "that sangar's got more hits than anything else in Iraq. Taken everything, and it's still standing."

Lawton looked at the man and said, "That's why we call this place the Alamo, Rabbit."

Rabbit said, "I been taking pot-shots at insurgents this morning, sarge. Think I got a couple."

"Two less bastards to help us fuck this war up," said Lawton.

Rabbit nodded and ran a hand over his ginger razor-cut. His forehead shone with sweat, and blotches of red covered his white torso.

Lawton, fag dangling from between his lips, rolled another one and handed it to Rabbit, Rabbit taking it and lighting it with a Zippo.

Lawton said, "You need to put something on that sunburn, Rabbit. You'll be on the sick list again with it tomorrow. Medics'll be up your arse."

"Can't be bothered. Girls do sunscreen, sarge."

"And men burn, yeah?"

Rabbit shrugged. "My dad'd kill me if he thought I was putting that soft southern stuff on my skin."

"Sun'll kill you before your dad does."

They smoked in silence. The skeleton of a Land Rover trundled past, pushed by a trio of soldiers.

"That got IEDed this morning," said Rabbit, jutting his chin towards the Land Rover.

"We lose any of the lads?" said Lawton.

"They're okay, thank fuck."

"Thank fuck," said Lawton.

"Sarge?"

"Yeah."

Rabbit looked him in the eye and said, "What's going on? The lads want to know."

Lawton smiled. He plucked a piece of tobacco off his tongue. "Sent you, did they?"

"Yeah, sent me, sarge."

Lawton sighed. "You can go back and tell them they'll be getting a new Section leader."

"Fuck that. What the fuck have they done?" Rabbit's voice went high-pitched. "Demoted you? You back with the lads, now?"

"No, Rabbit, they're sending me home, that's what they're doing," said Lawton, and he tasted the bitterness rising into his mouth as he said the words.

"Home? What? R-and-R?" said Rabbit.

"No," said Lawton, "not 'rest and recuperation', more 'fuck off and die'."

"You are fucking larking," said Rabbit, the tendons in his neck cording, his eyes burning with anger.

Lawton said nothing. He smoked and looked up at the sky again trying to clear his mind of the Alamo, the war, Basra, and Iraq.

Rabbit said, "The lads won't like it."

"They'll have to like it," said Lawton.

"They'll mutiny."

Lawton scowled at Rabbit. "They'll do nothing of the fucking sort, Rabbit. And you tell them that from me."

Rabbit bowed his head and stubbed his boot in the dust. He kicked up sand.

"There's nothing to be done," said Lawton. "The bastards don't give a shit about us, Rabbit. You keep your head down, get through this, and do what we always do – fight for your mates. No one fights for us, Rabbit. Just our mates."

Rabbit's mouth quivered. He blinked and tears streamed down his cheek, eroding a rivulet through the dust coating his skin. He spat, wiped his face with a tattooed forearm, and said, "Fuckers."

"They are, Rabbit, they're all fuckers."

Lawton dropped his fag in the dust and stepped on it. He nodded at Rabbit, saying he'd see them all before he left. He slapped Rabbit's shoulder and started to walk away. But Rabbit's voice, calling his name, halted him.

Lawton turned to face Rabbit.

Rabbit stood to attention. He saluted and said, "It's been a fucking honour, sarge, a fucking honour."

Lawton bit his lip and then he said, "Me too, Rabbit."

"And, sarge," said Rabbit, his voice breaking up, "I want you remember that wherever you are, if you're in any kind of shit – " Rabbit faltered.

Lawton nodded and waited for Rabbit to find the words again.

Rabbit jabbed a thumb against his own chest and said, " – this Rabbit – this Rabbit runs with you."

And Lawton felt tears well in his eyes. He wheeled away and strode towards the barracks.

The whistle of an RPG made him duck. He turned back towards Rabbit. Shouts filled the compound. Troops sprinted for cover. The RPG tailed smoke as it swept over the wall. Rabbit stumbled away, seeing it come.

Lawton, shouting "Rabbit, Rabbit," raced back towards the soldier. The RPG ploughed into the toilets, yards away from Rabbit.

Lawton sprang off his feet, diving towards Rabbit as the RPG exploded, throwing debris and dust and flames across the compound.

★ ★ ★ ★

Lawton had left Basra a week later. The papers at home bayed for blood. The rags slapped scandal all over their front pages. Soldiers accused of atrocities and Lawton's supposed crime were among the "catalogue of shame".

But a few weeks later those same papers, with a paragraph buried on Page 30, said some of their stories weren't true.

The bus drew into New Cross, and Lawton let the memory slide away.

His heart felt heavy, and he wanted to sit on his sofa and drink himself unconscious. Rage simmered in him against the people who'd fucked up his life. He could still be in the Army, now, if officials had stood up to politicians, if politicians had stood up to the press.

Report after report proved that British soldiers didn't mistreat or murder Iraqi prisoners or Iraqi civilians. But rumour proved more interesting than fact, and the accusations still flew.

By the time he got off the bus, the time was 1.50 a.m. He walked with his collar turned up and his head down. Kids vandalized a car, smashing its windows with bricks and denting the doors with fence posts. They swore and shouted and laughed. Lawton stared ahead and picked up his pace. If he had to fight louts, he would, and he'd relished it sometimes. But tonight, he wanted to go home and drink. He strode past shops that were boarded up and past buildings that were smeared in graffiti.

This is what I came back to, he thought. *Should've stayed in Iraq. At least the Iraqis were trying to build a better country; here we're just trying to break it down.*

He turned down his street. The sodium glare of the street lamp showed him the figure crouched at the front door of his building. Lawton hastened. He recognized the would-be burglar.

The thief looked up, and his face paled in terror.

Lawton grabbed him by the collar and said, "Come visiting, Fraser?"

CHAPTER 29.
WAKING THE DEAD.

MURRAY dreamed that a phone was ringing, and in her dream she thought that if she ignored it, the ringing would stop.

But it didn't stop.

And then someone was nudging her, jabbing an elbow into her ribs. And a voice whispered her name:

"Chrissie! Chrissie! Wake up, Chrissie, that's probably for you – they're always for you."

And she came awake to Richard telling her to answer the ringing phone.

"Get it or it'll wake the boys," he said.

Murray rolled out of bed. She made her way out of the bedroom, the phone's ring shaking her out of her sleep. She went downstairs to the hall. Murray felt bewildered, unsure of the time. The LCD display on the phone read 3.12 a.m. and Murray gasped. She picked up the phone and said, "Hello," in a harsh whisper.

A coin dropped and a voice she recognized said, "Christine, it's me," and she swore at her police contact, asking what the hell they were doing ringing at this bloody time.

"Not to make small talk, obviously," said the contact.

"All right, I'm sorry. It's just – just that I'm having a bad time, that's all."

"Aren't we all," said the contact.

"Are you at work?" said Murray.

"No, just left. I'm in a phonebox near Victoria. I'm amazed that these things still work. I thought they were only decorative, these days."

"What's happened?"

The contact said, "Your soldier, Jake Lawton, he got brought in earlier tonight – "

"For what?"

"Helping with enquiries, that kind of thing."

"Was he helpful?" said Murray.

"He's a charmer, apparently."

"This I know. What happened?"

"We had to release him," said the contact. "He wasn't under arrest. Just hassling him. I think Birch sees him as a potential suspect."

"So do I," said Murray. "Is that it? Is that why you're ringing me at three o'clock in the morning?"

"No," said the contact, "something else has happened. Something really, really awful."

"Yes?" said Murray.

The contact said, "Have you ever heard of B13?"

* * * *

Lithgow, sitting on Lawton's sofa with his hands on his knees, said, "There were three of them, but I only grabbed this one. The other two were full of dust."

Lawton, kneeling at the coffee table, held the vase up and studied it as though he knew something about this stuff. He didn't, but the artefact was beautiful to him. He put it on the table and took off the lid. He scooped out a handful of pills and stared at them in his palm. Red tablets with "K" emblazoned on them. Like the "K" on the base of the jar.

"What does this letter mean?" he said, more to himself than to Lithgow. And then, looking at Lithgow, he said, "They put these letters on the pills. What do they mean?"

Lithgow shrugged. "They usually don't mean anything. They put all kinds of stuff on pills. Doesn't mean anything. The guy called them 'Skarlet', that's all. 'With a *k*.'" He shrugged again.

Shouts drifted in from the street. Lithgow glanced over his shoulder towards the window. He said, "Gets a bit noisy here, doesn't it."

"Why'd you come here, Fraser?"

"I told you, to bring you these. Wanted you to – "

"I don't believe you. You're lying through your skinny backside. Why'd you come here?"

"I think – I think Hammond, you know – the DJ – I-I think he got killed."

Lithgow told him what had happened, how they broke into the house.

Lawton said, "Why, you dickhead? Why did you break in there?"

Lithgow rolled his hands into fists. He looked down at his lap. His face turned red, and Lawton thought he would cry. "I was – " said Lithgow, "I was – was trying – oh, fuck it, Lawton, I was trying to fuck you up, man. You were giving me a hard time."

"A hard time?"

"You were hassling me, man. On my back."

"I'm trying to find out how Jenna died, you prick."

"Fucking hell, Lawton, I'm scared shitless. Those were my pills."

"They *were* your pills. You little shite."

"Yes, they were. I just got 'em off this guy in a pub. I followed him home, I knew where he lived."

"Fraser, I should chuck you out the window to those yobs in the road."

Screams filtered up from the street. *Yobs gathering for a fight*, thought Lawton. *Stoned and smashed and full of bravado – thought they were soldiers, these idiot kids. They'd piss themselves on a real frontline.*

The anger swept through Lawton's veins. "And you came round here to dump these pills on my doorstep, yes? – Yes?"

Lithgow shut his eyes and nodded. "I didn't mean to, man. I was stoned, you know. Mad, and all. Just wanted you to leave me be. And I knew the cops had talked to you."

"You fucker. I'm going to beat the bones out of you," he said, grabbing Lithgow by the collar.

Lithgow cowered and threw his hands over his head to protect himself.

Lawton stared at the shivering, whimpering thing and said, "You're not worth it, Lithgow – not worth the energy."

Lawton got up and looked at the TV. A reporter stood in front of Religion. Lawton grabbed the remote off the table and turned up the volume.

The reporter said, " – and this latest development has confounded detectives from Scotland Yard's Homicide and Serious Crime Command, and further angered the families of the dead."

They switched back to the studio, the presenter saying, "Thank you, Nita Hassan in Soho, and for those who've just joined us" – *that's me*, thought Lawton; the presenter looked grim – "a disturbing development in this story" – the presenter breathed in, stared down at his notes, and Lawton thought, *tell me, you smarmy git* – "with the bodies of the twenty-eight people who died at Religion having disappeared – "

"What the – " It was Lithgow at Lawton's shoulder.

" – from a Central London morgue, and the bodies of two people found dead at the scene. It was like they got up and walked out, a police source told our correspondent, Nita Hassan, who you've just seen there in our report."

Lawton killed the volume.

He said, "Did he just say what I thought he said?"

"I really hope he didn't," said Lithgow. "'Cause I can't see it going well if he did."

Lawton said, "Did he just that the bodies had – disappeared?"

"Yes," said Lithgow, "yes, he did. He said, Like they got up and walked out."

PART TWO.
THE PLAGUE SPREADS.

CHAPTER 30.
IMMORTAL.

ALEXANDER waited in the darkness, and the demons stalked him.

The gloom hid them, but he knew they were there. He smelled them, the stench of decay saturating his nostrils. They hissed and growled in the shadows, and whispered threats:

"We'll drink your blood – We'll drain you dry – We'll make you undead – You'll be our servant – You'll be immortal – "

And Alexander said, "I'm already immortal. I'm more god than you'll ever be. I've conquered the world. What have you conquered?"

"Death," said a voice from the darkness, "we have conquered death."

"And you suffer because of it. You're cursed to hunger for blood, night after night after night."

Laughter echoed around the throne room. Alexander wheeled around. His hand tightened on the weapon's handle. His troops had plundered the artefact from Darius's treasury. Babylon's seers had told Alexander it was the only thing that could kill the demons that ruled the city.

"And tonight," said a voice behind him, "it'll be your blood that quenches our thirst."

Alexander's heartbeat quickened. His nerves tightened like the strings of a bow. But he steeled himself, not willing to show fear.

"Now," he said.

And the torches flared, casting a glow over the throne room. Alexander scanned his surroundings.

His muscles flexed, and his throat became dry. The vampires crawled towards him through the piles of cushions, across the stacks of carpet.

Alexander's men lined the walls. They lit the torches that were fixed to the pillars. Others skulked in from behind the throne, positioning themselves near the blood-red drapes that swept down over the windows from the golden ceiling.

The vampires snarled.

"Do you fear us, now, great king?" said a deep, guttural voice. Alexander looked towards the speaker.

A colossal beast, scarlet-skinned and serpent-fanged, towered above the other vampires.

Alexander held his breath. He fixed on the vampire god. And then his gaze drifted behind the monster. In the shadows lurked two other giants, larger than the one confronting Alexander. It seemed they were waiting to see how strong an enemy he'd be. Alexander could smell the creatures. They reeked of death.

The herd corralled Alexander, closing in on him.

The giant, his head rutted by gouges, said, "Your men can do nothing to save you. They'll suffer your fate. They'll be drained of life and live forever at our heel."

Alexander raised the spear above his head.

The creature laughed and said, "You think that stick will save you, those ancient horns torn from the great hunter's head? Only a god can wield that weapon. Are you a god, Alexander?"

Alexander tightened his jaw. He glared at the creature. These hideous things had ignited terror in Alexander's army since he and his troops marched into Babylon months before. He had defeated Darius and paraded into the golden city, and its people had welcomed him. But a shadow loomed over the country.

"Undead creatures that feed on blood stalk the kingdom," said Philotas, one of his officers. "This is what Darius's slaves tell us. Darius paid homage to these demons, bringing them sacrifice in return for power."

And Alexander, sprawled on the throne that had cupped the arse of a hundred Babylonian kings, narrowed his eyes and scratched his chin.

"I pay homage to no one except Zeus – and soon, he'll pay homage to me. If these things exists, then they can be killed."

Alexander, brandishing the weapon, spat at the creature.

And the creature's face flared. Rage burned in its blood-red eyes. The beast hissed, spraying Alexander with a burning liquid. The fluid singed his skin, but he gritted his teeth, refusing to show pain.

Roars filled the throne room. The vampires sprang.

"The light," said Alexander, his voice rising over the cacophony.

And his men tore down the drapes.

Shafts of sunlight speared into the throne room. The vampires staggered away from the rays. But they only stumbled into other beams of heat.

The scarlet-skinned monster howled with fury. It lunged at Alexander.

The vampires fried, and the throne room filled with the stink of burning flesh. Alexander's soldiers swooped on the terrified creatures. The Macedonians drove their swords and spears into the vampires' hearts.

The undead's cries swept across Babylon. The smoke from their burning bodies belched out of the palace and rose into the dawn.

Alexander ducked an attack by the red beast, and as the creature swept overhead he thrust the spear upwards. A shriek burst from the vampire's throat as the tusk pierced its chest. Its body disintegrated, raining ash over Alexander. The tattered remains of its scarlet skin fluttered to the floor.

The two monsters in the shadows recoiled.

Alexander bared his teeth, and they stood white against his ash-grey face, his blue eyes glistening like crystals in dust.

And he showed the immortals his power.

"I am Alexander," he said, fury bubbling in his voice, "and I fear nothing."

He launched himself at the creatures and they flung themselves at him and they clashed as the sun splintered off the spear's ivory points.

CHAPTER 31.
KEEP YOUR ENEMIES CLOSE.

MURRAY said, "You really know how to treat a girl."

Lawton said nothing. He stared straight ahead, watching the cars stream into the NCP multi-storey. They were on the third tier, sitting in Murray's Ford. He'd e-mailed her at 7.00 a.m. He found the e-mail on her website. You could still play that video of him in Basra on her site. He didn't play it because it was on a loop in his head. He e-mailed Murray saying, "I've got something you'll want," and said where to meet him if she were interested. She was, because she was here, and now she said, "You've got a confession to make, Jake?"

And looking at her with narrow eyes and a frown, he said, "Yes, I've never seen you look better."

"All right," she said, "what's this about?"

He turned away again, looking straight ahead, into the shadows of the car park. He said, "Thirty people were killed last night in Central London, attacked in the streets."

"Yes," she said, and fear lined her voice. Lawton glimpsed from the corner of his eye that her hands were gripping the steering wheel and her knuckles had gone white.

He said, "Who will you be blaming for that?"

"Why are we here, Mr. Lawton? I've got a personal alarm, you know. Linked directly to the office and to the local police station – "

"What do you think I am?" he said, glaring at her, and then added: "Don't answer that, I know what you think I am. But I'm not going to hurt you. I just want to know. You seem intent on blaming me for these deaths, just like you blamed me for Basra, and I want to know."

"Not brought me here to whine, have you?" she said.

He ignored her and said, "How do you think those people died last night?"

Murray said she didn't know.

And then he said, "Do you think it had anything to do with disappearing bodies?"

She looked at him and her eyes were wide, and she said, "I don't know. Do – do you?"

"Have you heard anything about that? Anything more than what the news says?"

She was quite for a moment and then she said, "The bodies were being housed at this special unit in Battersea. A security guard and a police officer were found dead at the scene. The door to the morgue was open, trolleys were overturned – a mess, really. I heard it was – was like – "

Murray faltered and shook her head, and Lawton finished what she'd started to say:

"Like they got up and walked out," he said.

They looked at each other, and Lawton saw in her eyes that she'd considered that – considered the dead getting up.

"Mind if I smoke?" said Lawton, and took out his tobacco and papers.

She said, "I do."

He put the tobacco and papers away and put his hand over his face.

Murray said, "I've got a contact in the pathology department of a – a leading London hospital."

"A leading London hospital?"

"Yes," she said, and Lawton listened as she told him what her contact had told her about the bodies.

"Shrivelled?" he said.

"That's what my contact said. And the heart black, engorged, and wet."

"Okay," he said, and thought for a moment.

"What are you thinking?" she said.

He looked at her and scowled. "Do you still think I'm involved?"

Murray looked into her lap and her cheeks reddened.

He said, "All right. That's a start," and he fished out the plastic bag from his jacket pocket and tossed it into Murray's lap.

Her mouth dropped open. She looked at the bag for half a minute, and then picked it up and held it at eye level. She shook it, and the dozen pills it contained jumped about.

She said, "What are they?"

He said, "You know what they are. Your pathology friend might be able to use them. Find a cure or something."

She looked him in the eye. "Where did you get them?"

He looked away. "Does that matter?"

"Do you think I'm a fool? Are you involved in this?"

"I don't think you're a fool, Christine. I think you're wrong on a number of things, but I don't think you're a fool."

"Why did you bring them to me?" she said.

"If I took them to the cops, they wouldn't believe me, and they'd probably arrest me. They already fancy me for all this, so if I walk in with a bunch of pills, they'll take it as a confession, I guess." He rolled down the window and he leaned his elbow out of the car. "But you," he said, turning to face her, "you're looking beyond me. You're a reporter and reporters don't care about right and wrong, reporters only care about the story. And that" – he pointed at the bag of pills – "is a story."

"All right," she said, eyeing him. "What do you get out of it?"

"I get to know what killed Jenna McCall and all those others. You know people, Christine; I don't know so many – not useful ones, anyway. And I'm just using an old trick."

"An old trick?" she said.

"Yeah. It's called keep your friends close" – and he stared at her – "but your enemies closer. Let me know, Christine, or I'll let the cops know you've got those pills – and they'd want to know why you didn't tell them."

He got out of the car, shut the door, and walked toward the shadows.

★ ★ ★ ★

Murray watched him leave. He melted into the shadows, and then Murray shut her eyes for a moment, blowing a breath out of her cheeks.

Then, she looked at the pills in the plastic bag that Lawton had given her. She held them up, gave them a shake. She saw the "K" inscribed on them. She put the pills on the dashboard and took a Moleskine notebook from her breast pocket. She wrote, "K on tabs – what does K mean?" in the notebook, then returned it to her pocket.

She got her phone and called home.

David answered and something in her melted.

She said, "Hello, love, how are you?"

"I'm all right," said her ten-year-old.

"Are you sure? You sound glum."

"I'm all right – d'you want dad?"

"No, no, darling, I'd – I'd like to talk to you," she said, glancing at the dashboard clock. "Are you all right, David, shouldn't you be at school?"

"There's no school."

"No school? Why isn't there school?" she said, trying not to sound too suspicious.

"One of the teachers died."

Murray's chest grew cold. "Died?" she said, and last night's murders sprang into her mind. "Is – Is dad there, baby?"

"Okay, so you *don't* want to talk to me, now."

She said no, that's wasn't true. But David was gone and his voice came to her from a distance, calling for his dad and saying, "Phone for you."

Murray's eyes dampened and she let out a sob.

And Richard came to the phone saying, "Hello," like he was saying hello to a stranger.

"Did David not tell you it was me?" she said.

"No. He might not have recognized you. I thought you were going to take them to school this morning?"

"David said there's no school."

"There is for Michael," he said, "so you could've taken him."

"He goes on his own, on the bus."

"Oh, you know that do you? I'm fucking impressed."

"Don't curse like that in the house, not when the boys are around. Why isn't David at school? He said one of the teachers died."

"Yes," he said. "Died last night, said the headmaster. He made an announcement at the gates."

Murray thought, *Why wasn't I told? Why wasn't I there? It's my story.*

And Richard said, "Paul Gless, he was twenty-eight. Killed by a gang, they said. Thirty people died, according to the news. Is this anything to do with this story you're doing?"

"I think it is, which is why I'm here, Richard. It's why I'm home late and why I leave early. It's a big story, and I'm getting paid big – "

"I'm not sure if it's worth the money if the boys don't see their mother, or perhaps their mother doesn't want to see them."

Anger flashed white in her head and she said, "Don't you dare, don't you – how could you say – " but she trailed off, her body shaking with rage.

Richard said nothing.

Murray's rage cooled and she said, "I'm paying the mortgage, Richard. It's what we agreed. You could stay at home, write your book – I'd go and work. Well," she said, brushing a tear from her cheek, "I am working. So how's your book coming?"

She heard a breath hiss out of him.

And then he said, "You have no understanding of what it takes to write a hundred-thousand words. You've no concept of the psychological hurdles that need vaulting to achieve such a feat. You and your thousand-word rants that get re-written by – what do you call them? – the grey old men of the subs' bench. You have no idea."

"Oh, Richard," she said, "you do talk bollocks. Just get up to the study and be a writer."

"Perhaps I could do that if you come home and be a mother."

She opened her mouth to say something, but he'd put the phone down.

CHAPTER 32.
SASSIE.

THE man in the tweed jacket studied the jar and said, "And where did you come across this, um, piece?"

Lawton, casting his eyes around the antiques that cluttered up the shop, said, "I got it on eBay."

The man nodded and hummed. He stroked a penny-sized red badge on his lapel. A mobile phone poked out from the jacket's breast pocket.

Lawton found the antique shop in Covent Garden. Furniture piled high around the edges of the store. Bric-a-brac stacked on top of bric-a-brac. The place smelled musty. Gloom enveloped the shop and dust layered everything.

The man in the tweed jacket said, "You say, eBay."

"Yes, eBay. What is it, do you know?"

"It's an internet auction site, isn't it," he said, a belted out a laugh.

Lawton didn't laugh, he just stared at the man in the tweed jacket.

The man said, "Bad joke, I assume."

Lawton stayed quiet.

The man hissed through his teeth. He pushed his half-moon glasses up his nose and squinted, holding up the jar to read the underside.

"This letter, this 'K', seems recent."

"So the pot's old, then."

"I'd say quite old, yes. Do you need a value on it?"

Lawton tensed. "I want to know what it is," he said, "where it's from."

The man shook his head. "Clay, I'd say – it's – perhaps – Persian."

"Persian?"

"Or Egyptian, even," said the man in the tweed jacket.

"And how old?"

The man hummed, still scrutinizing the jar. "Could be six or seven hundred years old, I'd say." He looked at Lawton. "So do you want to sell it?"

"How much is it worth?"

The man tilted his head to the side and said, "It's worth what people are willing to pay, sir."

"And you'd say that was – what?"

"I'll give you, um, two hundred for it."

Lawton guessed the man in the tweed jacket could double or treble that by selling it in his shop. He could make even more at auction. But Lawton wasn't planning to sell. He thought this pot might give him a clue to what was happening, to what killed Jenna and why her body had gone missing.

Lawton said, "I don't think I'll – "

"Three hundred," said the man.

"No, no deal." He took the jar back from the shop-owner. "But thanks for your time, yeah?" Lawton turned to leave.

"Sir."

Lawton stopped and looked at the man.

The man in the tweed jacket said, "Sir, I'm not an expert in this kind of pottery."

You don't say, thought Jake.

"I'm a buyer, you know – that's why I tried to buy it. Please don't take offence. I wouldn't want to – offend you."

"I'm not offended," said Lawton.

"But, if I may, I could point you in the direction of someone who could offer genuine support with regards to this artefact."

★ ★ ★ ★

Dr. Melissa Rae said, "My uncle sent you?"

"Yes, he told me you were the expert," said Lawton.

"Well," she said, "I caught the bug at his shop."

I'm not surprised, thought Lawton, remembering the dust and grime in the antique shop.

The man in the tweed jacket, Dr. Rae's uncle, had directed Lawton to King's College London's School of Humanities. Lawton had been told he'd find Dr. Rae in the classical archaeology department based at the Strand Campus, a few minutes walk from Covent Garden.

Dr. Rae was a blonde in a grey hoodie, jeans, and a pair of green Converse. She'd said, "Call me Sassie," and he'd said, "Call me Jake."

The pot sat on her desk. She'd cleared away files and books to make room for it. They stared at it, as if they were waiting for something to happen – for the hero painted on it to come to life, perhaps.

"So you know where it's from?" he said.

"Incredible, really. It's Babylonian, I think."

"How do you know?"

She tilted the jar towards Lawton and ran her finger around the lip of the vessel, saying, "See here? This lettering?"

Lawton squinted. He saw tiny black shapes encircling the inside of the jar and said, "I didn't notice – "

"The language is Akkadian, which was the language of the Middle East and North Africa in the Bronze and Iron Age – up until about 100 A.D., when it became extinct."

"What does it say?"

She cocked her head to look at the script. Her hair fell over her ears, and she hooked it back. She squinted, trying to see the minute lettering. She said, "It's cuneiform, which is the writing system they used in that part of the world three-thousand, four-thousand years ago."

"So you don't know what it says?" he said.

She looked up at him, and her eyes grew cold. "No, I don't."

Lawton saw her irritation and said, "I'm sorry – it's been a rough few days, and I'm – I'm really grateful."

She nodded. "That's all right. It's an incredible piece. Can I ask where you –?"

"EBay," said Lawton, not flinching from her gaze.

"EBay – that's what my uncle said you said."

He moved the conversation along by asking, "Who's the guy with the spear?"

Sassie held up the jar and creased her brow as she studied the image on the vessel. She deliberated for a few moments, and then put the vase down on her desk.

She got went to a bookshelf and reached up for a book. A band of flesh showed between her top and her jeans. The skin was golden and smooth. Lawton felt something fizz in his belly, and he looked away. She got the book down and flicked through it, then laid it open on the desk, facing Lawton.

Sassie leaned forward, and she smelled of apples. He felt calm with her, and he'd not felt calm with anyone in years. He felt like he could sleep. It was as if she smoothed away the furrows in his life. A desire rose up in him; a desire to be in her company and smell her odour and see her skin.

"Are you all right, Jake?"

He snapped back to reality. "Yes, sorry, tired."

"Oh, would you want to do this another time?"

"No, no, I'm fine and really grateful."

"Oh, that's okay. I'm glad you brought it over. Here, look" – she indicated the book – "here's an image of Alexander the Great."

Lawton noticed the blonde hair, the boyish face, and the large nose, and the picture in the book looked like the image on the jar. But he said, "Don't they all look the same, these ancient pictures?"

"It's not an exact science," she said, "but we can deduce through educated guesswork that the image is Alexander's. Alexander the Great conquered the Persians and made Babylon his capital. That was more than two-thousand, five-hundred years ago."

Lawton said, "Babylon – you said they were Babylonian –"

Sassie said, "Its ruins lie on the banks of the Euphrates – "

A jolt of excitement shot through his veins. "Iraq?"

"Uh, yes – modern day Iraq," she said, staring at him. "The town of Hillah stands there today."

Lawton knew Hillah. And he'd heard of Babylon, too. It came back to him, now. The U.S. forces were based there. They were given a hard time for building a helipad on some ruins – Babylonian ruins, Lawton remembered.

And as if she'd read his mind, Sassie said, "The Americans have caused havoc there since their invasion. Damaged the archaeological record. Bloody morons."

She looked gloomy, her eyes fixed on the pot as if it were the only record left of the ancient civilization.

"I was there," said Lawton.

She snapped her gaze up to his face.

"In Iraq," he said. "Basra."

"I thought you might be a soldier."

"Why's that?"

"You look" – she stared at him for a few seconds with her dark blue eyes, and her pupils flared – "soldiery." And then she blinked, took her eyes away, and said, "You're not a soldier any more, then?"

He grew red and he felt the heat in his cheeks. "Not any more. Long story. I'll tell you another time.

"Oh," she said, "there's going to be another time, then?"

"If you can help me with this, I'm sure there will be."

"Can I keep it?" she said.

"No," said Lawton.

"Well, how am I supposed to –?"

"If you keep it, I'll have no excuse to come back."

He smiled at her, forcing the gesture into his eyes. They'd not had a smile in them for a while, and they struggled to find the warmth required. But when she smiled back, Lawton knew he'd pulled it off, and he felt something cruel in him soften.

She said, "I'll take a few pictures," and he then watched while she snapped images with a digital camera.

After he'd wrapped the pot up in the cloth and tucked it back in his rucksack, he thanked her.

"Thank *you*, Jake. It's incredible. A real find. And I'll let you know. This guy I know in the department, he's an expert on this period and might be able to decipher the symbols. And he's also into Babylonian mythology. I'm sure he'll be able to help us."

And as he walked along the river towards Embankment station, one word played in Lawton's mind:

"Us."

CHAPTER 33.
REMOVALS.

ION said, "Shall I kill him now?"

Nadia, looking down at Hammond, said, "No, we can use him."

"Use him how?" said Ion. Hammond lay curled up in the chest. He was naked and his body peppered with wounds. The smell of decay came off his body, the bullet wound in his shoulder starting to fester. After Nadia shot him, she'd beaten him. Then Ion came home. He stripped Hammond naked and beat him again, then burned him with cigarettes. Hammond vomited and pissed himself, and begged for mercy until he passed out. Ion, staring down at the pathetic creature, said, "I can't see any use for him other than food for the worms."

"Or food for a god," said Nadia.

Ion looked at her and lust crawled in his belly. The grey light streaming through the window shimmered off her dark hair. Madness glinted in her purple eyes, and her pale skin glowed moon-white.

And she said, "He can be the first feed, can't he."

Ion said, "Yes," and he tensed at the thought.

She looked at Ion and said, "Is everything packed."

"Everything we need. The van's waiting outside. Dr. Haddad's already over there. I set up his lab for him before dawn."

Nadia gazed around the bedroom. "Shame to leave so much of it."

The wardrobe and the bed remained, emptied of clothes and stripped of sheets. "Had we more time" – she looked down at Hammond again – "we could've taken everything with us."

Hammond and Lithgow's break-in had hurried their departure. The burglars were unlikely to have told anyone they were coming here, but Nadia didn't want to take the chance.

Ion said, "We can buy more beds, more cupboards and chairs."

She glanced at her brother and touched his arm, saying, "You're right. They're nothing. And we were planning to move – it's just we brought our plans forward, that's all."

Ion looked her in the eye, and his heartbeat accelerated. Her perfume filled his nostrils and the odour fired a longing in his belly. She licked her lips and sweat shone on her brow. He could feel the heat stream from her body. He yanked her against him, and her body lay flat against his. Her mouth opened and her eyes narrowed, and she whimpered. She shifted against him, making her breasts move against his stomach, and the feel of her sent pulses of desire throbbing through his body. He peeled back his lips and grabbed her hair, and she gasped and dug her nails into his arms.

Her phone rang.

"Ignore it," he said.

"I must – " said Nadia, pulling away.

He held her. The phone rang. He said, "Ignore it, Nadia."

"Ion, I must – " and she wrenched free of his arms. She went to the bed where her handbag lay, and sat on the bed. She took the trilling phone out of her bag, touched the choker around her throat, and answered the call.

"Ah, good morning," she said, a hitch in her voice.

Ion watched her, eyes fixed on her fingers as they stroked the band of material strapped to her neck.

"You have," she said into the phone. "That's very clever of you – it's a compliment, you should accept it" – she crossed her legs, and Ion heard the zip of nylon at her thighs – "perhaps I'll show you how grateful I *really* am one of these days" – she cocked her head and gazed at Ion, and Ion burned with jealousy – "after all this is done – yes, yes, that's right – I don't think you need to do anything, it doesn't matter anymore – no, it doesn't, we have the remains, so that's all that matters – all right, thank you – yes, we'll be in touch – yes, *I'll* be in touch, too – good-bye."

She tucked the phone back in her handbag and looked up at Ion, her lips wet and open.

"Who was that?" said Ion, trying to keep his voice neutral.

"One of our friends," she said.

"Which one? A man? All the men want to fuck you."

"Yes, they do. Some of the women, too."

Ion, his face burning, said, "What did he want? You?"

"Yes, he wanted me, Ion."

"And you said you'd show him how grateful you were – after this was done. That's what you said."

"It doesn't matter what I said." She stood and swung the bag over her shoulder, the action making her breasts quiver under her thin dress.

Ion's belly tightened. He said, "What did he say?"

"Someone brought the pot in."

Ion said, "Was it Lithgow?"

"They don't know."

"Shall I go and get it?"

"No," she said, "it's not important. It's old clay. What was inside was of more importance, and we have what was inside. Shut that chest and bring it down. We should go."

Ion locked Hammond in the chest.

"The vampires will feed again tonight," said Nadia. "And they'll bring in a harvest. We can begin the process – this one here, first. Then, Kea will rise. And from Kea we'll awaken Kakash. And from Kakash's blood, Kasdeja. And the trinity will have their Babylon again."

She swept out of the room.

Ion listened to her footsteps hurry down the stairs.

An ache for her spread through his loins.

He'd have to take it out on someone.

CHAPTER 34.
EXPERT ANALYSIS.

SASSIE, the phone tucked between her shoulder and her ear, said, "And what do you think?"

Ed Crane, his voice slithering down the line, said, "I think we should chat about them over dinner."

Sassie switched ears. She ignored Crane's suggestion. She opened the Jpegs of the jar on her laptop and viewed them while talking to him. She'd e-mailed them over to Crane for his opinion.

"I know it's Babylonian, I recognized the cuneiform," she said, "but I'm not sure what the images depict."

Crane said, "It's really *hard* to say from these pictures. I'm busy all day. Might I slip round to your dainty little apartment this evening, take a closer look at this vessel of yours?"

Sassie said, "I can see the images quite clearly on my computer screen. If you can't help me, Ed, I'll – "

"No, no, no. Of course I can help. I just wanted to be *more* of a help, that's all. You know that jars such as this one sometimes symbolized a womb, don't you."

"A womb?" she said. "Are you being helpful or lewd?"

He laughed. "Well, a bit of both, I hope," he said, and then: "Tell me, Sassie, who's the blurred chap in the background of these images? Did he bring the jar in to you?"

Sassie felt her cheeks redden as she stared at the distorted image of Jake Lawton. She said, "Yes, he did."

"He looks young and sturdy. Is he sturdy, Sassie?"

Sassie said, "He was nothing," and felt a knot of guilt twist in her belly. She brought a hand to her forehead. Her heart raced. She took a few breaths, trying to steady herself.

Crane said, "He left it there? I'm assuming he'll be back for it. Opportunity for him to see you again, Sassie. Lucky fellow, I say."

She said nothing, didn't say that Jake had taken the piece with him. After a pause Crane said, "Still there?"

Sassie said, "Are you going to flirt? Because if you are, I'll ring back when you're not in flirt mode."

"I'm always in flirt mode, Sassie. I am a flirt. And I'm sure you wouldn't have me any other way."

"I don't think I'd have you in any way at all, Ed."

He laughed again. "Well done, Sassie. Sharp as a stick. I like a woman with spunk in them, preferably – "

"All right, Ed, that's enough."

He sighed and said, "You are such a spoilsport, Sassie. All right, I'll do my very best to behave, but you'll have to forgive me if I regress – flirting is my natural state, you know."

"Okay, I'll forgive you. Now, about this jar."

"This jar," he said, "fascinating."

"The image, the warrior."

"Alexander the Great, perhaps?"

Sassie said, "That's what I thought."

"Thought right, Doctor Rae," he said.

"But the bodies."

"Bodies," said Crane, his voice distant as if he were thinking of something else. But then, his tone lightened and he said, "Yes, bodies, of course. Well, um – "

He trailed off, and Sassie waited for a few seconds.

Then she said, "Ed, are you there?"

"Yes," he said, "I was thinking, just trying to recall – you look at this image, you see the sharp teeth? The fangs? The chest wounds? What appears to be, I'd say, a heart pinned to both ends of this double-tusked weapon our hero's wielding?"

"Yes, yes I do."

"Might be a vampire thing going on here."

"A vampire thing? Like a Dracula vampire thing?"

"Dracula," he said. "Why is it always Dracula?"

"I don't know, it always is. Is there any other vampire thing?"

Crane said, "The Babylonians, they had some blood-drinking cults, you see. Lilith, the first wife of Adam in mythology, who drank the blood of babies. But many cultures have blood-drinking legends. Greek and Roman mythology had the *empusae*, the *lamiae*, and the *striges*. The word *strigoï* has been used to describe vampires in Romania since the Seventh Century. I could go on. Over dinner perhaps?"

She ignored him and said, "What about the cuneiform, do you have any idea what that might say?"

Crane sighed. "I really will need to take a closer look to make any sense of that. It's unreadable here, Sassie. What do you say? Dinner at my place?"

"I've got the cuneiform copied out here. I could just courier it over to your room," said Sassie.

"I'm five minutes down the corridor, Sassie. Why don't you courier yourself along with it? Ideally I'd like to see the pot. Get my hands on it, you know?"

Sassie knew she'd have to be in the same room as him. She felt cold, and her shoulders sagged.

"All right," she said, "I'll sort something later today, or tomorrow. But, in the meantime, what does the 'K' indicate on the base?" She looked at the image of the underside of the vase on her laptop.

Silence on the line, and she heard him breath. Sassie stared at the image of the "K".

Then Ed said, "I don't know," and then he hummed.

Sassie said, "What is it? What are you thinking?"

He paused. And then he said, "I-I don't know, Sassie, I truly don't," and she heard a tremble in his voice. He didn't know, and perhaps that scared him, she thought. Crane's arrogance was legend. He thought he knew it all. So when he came across something he couldn't explain, a question he failed to answer, it scared him.

It gave Sassie a shot of adrenalin, and she said, "Don't worry, I'm sure I'll find out. But you have been helpful, Ed, and I'm really grateful."

He said, "How grateful?" the playfulness back in his voice.

"I'm grateful, Ed," she said, "that's all."

"Dinner 'grateful'?" said Crane.

"Not at the moment."

"Oh, coffee 'grateful', then?"

"Perhaps. When I can get the jar over to you."

"Oh dear, 'perhaps'. That's not very hopeful is it?"

"It's the best I can do, Ed."

"Ah well, I'll just have to settle for sex 'grateful'. How's that?"

"It's just a thank you 'grateful', I'm afraid."

He chuckled, and his laugh trailed off. Sassie was about to say good-bye when Crane went, "By the way, where did your sturdy chap find this treasure?"

Sassie said nothing. She stared at the screen and thought of Jake Lawton and his steel-grey eyes and his scar-flecked face.

CHAPTER 35.
THREE'S COMPANY.

LITHGOW said, "Why didn't you tell the fucking cops where the house was, Lawton?"

Lawton said, "I want to go and have a look. See if Jenna's body's there. See if it's anything to do with this stuff."

"It is, I'm telling you. That woman shot Hammond. I'm fucked if I'm going back there. Tell the cops, let them sort it out."

"I might do after I've been over there, after you've shown me the way."

Lawton had no intention of telling the cops. He was keeping well out of their way. They were sniffing around a little too much, looking to nail him for this shit. He'd been out all day, wandering, not going home in case Birch and his troops were waiting for him.

Lithgow said, "No, no, no, no. No way. Tell you what, Lawton – I'll tell you where it is, draw you a fucking map – yeah, that's what I'll do, man, draw you a fucking map. I'll even top-up your Oyster card, pay for your journey. How's that? How's that? But there's no way – no fucking way I'm coming. Oh, oh, even better: I'll tell the cops myself."

"And then," said Lawton, "they'll know you distributed the drugs, that you're the heart of this mystery. They won't leave you alone then, you know."

"I'll get my dad on to it."

"Daddy can't save you from this one."

"I'm not coming with you. Take her instead," he said, gesturing to Sassie.

Sassie looked up from her white wine. They'd been sat in Ye Olde Cheshire Cheese a quarter of a mile from Sassie's office for two hours. The old tavern, rebuilt after the Fire of London in 1666, provided booths where they could conspire. Lithgow cradled a pint of lager and Lawton glanced now and again into his Bells and water. He'd ordered it, but not touched it yet. He was trying to test himself, putting temptation right there in front of himself to see how long he could abstain.

Lawton looked at Sassie and said, "Sassie's not coming."

Sassie straightened in her seat. "I am," she said.

"It's too dangerous," said Lawton.

"Yeah, right," said Lithgow, "then it's too dangerous for me, too."

"Go home, Sassie; I'll let you know what we find."

"No way, Jake, I'm coming with you."

"There," said Lithgow, "she's coming with you. That means you don't need me. You see? She wants to go – I don't."

Sassie had called Lawton earlier and told him about vampires and blood-cults. She asked him where he got the jar, and this time he told her. He told her about how this all stemmed from the deaths at Religion. He told her about Jenna.

Sassie told him, "My blood's just run cold," and asked to meet.

He said he'd be going to the house that night to see what he could find. Sassie still wanted to meet up with him, so he said, *Where?* And she suggested the pub, which stood a few minutes away from the campus.

Ignoring Lithgow, Sassie said, "Where d'you think the bodies that disappeared from that morgue might be?"

Lawton shook his head. He dropped his eyes to the whisky. He licked his lips and imagined the liquid scalding his throat. He knew this wasn't thirst; he'd known thirst. Out in the desert he had to drink twenty litres of water a day. In Basra they put their bottle in a wet sock to keep it cool.

"Do you think the bodies might have been stolen?" she said.

Lawton looked at her. A flicker of fear flashed in her eyes.

"I don't know?" he said.

Eyes still fixed on Lawton she said, "Do you think – do you actually believe that – "

She couldn't finish, but Lawton knew where she was going. His skin goosepimpled, and he shivered. She was hinting at something impossible. But the thought gripped his insides and twisted. He couldn't believe what he was thinking.

Like they got up and walked out.

He shook his head, trying to dislodge the thought.

He stood. "I think we should go. Come on, Fraser."

"No, man, I don't — "

Lawton took his phone from his pocket, dialled, and said, "Police, please. Scotland Yard — "

"All right, all right" said Lithgow, lunging at him.

Lawton shoved Lithgow back into his seat. He took the phone from his ear and said, "I'll do it, Fraser. I'll ring them. Are you coming?"

"All right, you bastard."

"And I'm coming too," said Sassie, getting to her feet.

Lawton looked at her, ready to tell her, *No way.* But her dark blue eyes fixed on him and he saw the will in her and let it be.

CHAPTER 36.
FIRST BLOOD.

HAMMOND, naked and hanging upside down by his ankles, said, "Help me, please help me," his voice like gravel.

Pain seared through his body. His right side, from shoulder to waist, pulsed and the skin was bruised. After she'd shot him, the woman had beaten him. The agony was unbearable. He'd fainted many times and after that he'd only been vaguely aware of being beaten again. And then, in his semi-conscious state, he recollected a man coming, beating him even more, and burning him with fags.

He remembered begging the woman to get a doctor for his gunshot wound but she'd spat on the injury and said, "Let it fester."

He could feel the wound starting to rot; already, the odour of decay belched from the injury.

Hammond felt sick, and he'd already vomited. The sick pooled at the bottom of the pit over which he was hanging.

He called for help again, and his voice echoed off the walls. He scanned his surroundings.

Being upside down, he found it difficult to make sense of where he was. And the more he focused, the sicker he felt. But he could see that he'd been left in a cave that was as large as the aircraft hangars he'd worked in at Broughton in North Wales, where they designed parts for the Airbus super-jet.

He wished he were still there now, messing about with the lads. But he gave it all up three years ago, deciding to go pro as a DJ.

And look where it fucking got me, he thought.

Damp smeared the walls of the cavern and moss coated much of the rock. The ceiling was panelled wood, and it seemed to undulate now and again – another sensation that didn't help Hammond's nausea.

He looked down at the ground. An area the size of half a football pitch had been panelled with varnished wood as well, and around this skirted the original rock. A few yards away from where Hammond hung, a cage stood.

Hammond looked down into the pit. The grave had been hollowed out of the earth. It was at least eight feet deep. The sides were slick with slime, and the bottom sprouted weeds. The earth in the grave looked pale and bloodless.

Hammond heard a rumble, and he struggled. The manacles clasping his ankles cut into his flesh. The chain linking the manacles to the horizontal post that spanned the pit rattled.

Hammond said, "Who's there? What going on?"

He saw a wheelchair and the legs of the woman pushing it. He twisted round and saw an old man sitting in the chair. He looked ancient. He wore a trilby, a red feather or something pinned to the brim. A bowl, one you'd have pudding in, sat on his lap. The woman behind him was the bitch who'd shot him and Hammond said, "You shot me, you fucking shot me! Please, please it hurts. You've got to get a doctor."

"You broke into our home," said the woman.

"It wasn't my fault. It was Lithgow. He made me do it."

The woman said, "Forced you, did he, Mr. Hammond. Threatened you. Couldn't say no, could you?"

"No, that's right, please," he said, but he was swaying too much and he felt dizzy and he swung away from the woman and the old man.

He froze. A girl, late teens, crouched on the wooden platform, looking up at him. She wore goth make-up, and her skin was death-pale. Dark bags hung under her eyes. Hammond stared into those eyes and fear chilled his spine. They were green, but in the green there was a trace of red; like someone had injected dye into her iris. He shook the chill way and said, "Hey, hey can you help me? Please, please I'm really in pain. I-I'm Steve Hammond, Captain Red, that's it, Captain Red. You know me, yeah. You come to Religion? To the goth night, there?"

A grin started to stretch across the girl's face.

Hammond smiled back. He sensed hope, salvation.

"Yeah," he said, "you know me, that's great. Hey, can you help?"

Her mouth widened into a smile and her lips peeled back, and her teeth showed. Hammond yelled and struggled against his chains. Piss swelled his bladder. His insides churned, and terror crawled up into his throat.

She hissed at him, and spit sprayed from her mouth.

She sprang at him and he screeched, not knowing what she was, his brain reeling to find a description.

"Fucking vampire," he said, screaming till his throat burned, "fucking vampire."

And she came for him and he pissed himself, his urine running down over his belly and chest and neck, into his face.

A figure shot into Hammond's eye line, grabbed the girl by the hair, and tossed her aside.

"Find your own food," the man said to the girl.

She hissed at him and scuttled away.

The man looked at Hammond, and Hammond saw his scarred face and recognized him. He was the guy who came to ask Hammond if he knew any dealers who'd be interested in a free sample; he was the guy who said, "What about this Lithgow? Can we trust him?" And then he realized he was also the guy who'd beaten and burned him when he was half alive earlier on.

He was the guy.

Hammond realized how deep the shit he was in actually was.

He said, "It's you, it's fucking you, oh fuck. I didn't see you, honest, I didn't see you. I won't say a thing, please. I won't, I won't. Please don't hurt me, please don't hurt me again."

The scarred man laughed. He made his way to the other side of the trench, where the woman and the cripple still waited. Hammond swung around with him. The scarred man stood near the edge of the pit. He stared at Hammond for a moment, and then glanced over his shoulder at the woman.

Hammond said, "I'm sorry I broke into your house, man, but it was Lithgow, you know. I can tell you where he lives and everything, but I really, really need a doctor. I'm going to die, man."

"Yes you are," said the scarred man.

Hammond stiffened. His throat moved, but no words came out.

The woman wheeled the cripple forward. The cripple opened the bowl on his lap. He held it out over the pit, and spilled out the contents. Ash rained down from the bowl and sprinkled the bottom of the grave. The old man tossed the bowl into the trench. The woman rolled him away from the edge.

"W-what's going on?" said Hammond. "W-what was that stuff? Tell me. Oh, God. Please don't hurt me, please let me go. I don't want to die – "

"Too late," said the scarred man, and he whipped his hand across Hammond's face.

The hand moved quickly, but Hammond caught a flash of steel.

Coldness enveloped his body. He tried to breathe, but his throat felt wet and clogged.

A hissing sound like air leaving a tyre filled his head, and his eyes began to blur.

He felt so weak, so light-headed.

He dropped his head and looked above him, down into the pit below him.

And the blood from his open throat gushed over his face, hot and coppery to the smell, and it spilled into the trench and splashed over the ashes, and the ashes bubbled and hissed.

CHAPTER 37.
GUARD DOGS.

NIGHT crawled over London and the light started to slip away. Lithgow said, "It looks empty – let's leave," and he turned to go.

Lawton grabbed his collar and dragged him back. He said, "Safer for us to have a nose around, then."

"This is where you got the jar?" said Sassie.

"This is where Fraser, here, *stole* the jar," said Lawton.

"I didn't steal it."

"You broke in and you stole it, Fraser," said Lawton.

Lawton looked up and down the street. Darkness and silence. He gazed up at the house. There were four floors. The windows were dark. The place felt empty to Lawton; it felt dead.

"Okay," he said to Lithgow, "show us how you got in."

Lithgow moaned and led them down the steps. The sash window stood open.

"That's convenient," said Sassie, a shudder in her voice.

Lawton gave her a look. She shouldn't have come. He said, "You'll be all right. Stay close to me."

She shuffled up to him, pressing against his arm.

They got in easily, and Lithgow found the light switch from before. The basement was empty. Dust covered the concrete floor. The paint peeled off the walls.

Lithgow said, "They've cleared out. There was a drugs factory in here."

He told them what he and Hammond had found in the basement.

Lawton sniffed and screwed up his face. "What's that smell?" he said, more to himself than a question to the others.

Sassie sniffed. "Can't smell anything; nothing but 'old'."

"The jars were over here," said Lithgow, indicating the shelf, "three of them lined up."

Lawton ignored him. They'd moved out, obviously. "Your break-in stirred them up a bit, Fraser. They didn't hang around."

"Maybe they were moving anyway," said Lithgow.

"They had something to hide. You say the drugs were produced in here."

Lithgow said yes.

Lawton said, "So you were in here, having a nose – what happened then?"

"I had the jar, ready to go, then the woman, she came through that door and shot Stevie."

"Which is when you ran," said Lawton.

"Too fucking right."

"You're a good man to have around in a crisis," said Lawton.

Sassie said, "Are you two married? You bicker like an old couple."

Lithgow said, "Lawton turned me down. Said I wasn't pretty enough."

Sassie laughed. The door burst open.

Lawton said, "Look out," and lunged towards her.

A pale man with bleached hair wrapped an arm around her throat and pulled her towards the door.

Sassie reached for Lawton as he sprang forward, but the pale man dragged her away from him.

Her face blanched and her eyes gaped.

Lawton clawed at the air, trying to reach her but not managing to, and saying, "No, Sassie, no – "

And the pale man opened his jaws and showed his fangs and moved his mouth towards Sassie's white throat.

★ ★ ★ ★

"And here," said Ion Friniuc, leading the way, "is where the good stuff happens," and he laughed, continuing down the wooden stairs that led into the cavern.

The Professor stopped halfway down the stairs and his gaze skimmed over the underground hideaway. Above him, strip-lights hummed like they were living things that hung from the panelled ceiling.

He looked down, and saw what he knew to be vampires staring up at him. A cluster of a dozen or so glared and sniffed the air. His legs weakened, and he wanted to turn around and go back upstairs to Nina.

"They can smell your blood, Professor," said Ion.

He touched his emblem.

He swallowed, wetting his dry throat.

"Does it work?" he said, holding up his symbol.

"Yes," said Ion, "of course," and he flicked at his ponytail, which was held in place by what seemed to be a strip of red leather. "How do you think we survive? Come down, Professor, for fuck's sake."

The guided tour had started out promisingly, an audience with Nadia Radu in her office, before he was shown into Dr. Haddad's lab. The old man was still making pills. The Professor stared at the chemist while Mrs. Radu explained how they moved here to the new base.

She'd said, "Those idiots forced our hand when they broke in. We had to get out of the Holland Park property. No doubt the police will be nosing around at some stage."

The Professor, still staring at Haddad, had said, "Funny to think that I'm in some way related to this old fellow," and then looking at Mrs. Radu, he added. "Delicious to think I'm in some way related to you, Nadia."

Ion's voice pulled him out of the memory:

"Professor, come down, I said."

And the Professor scurried down the wooden stairs, eyes fixed on the vampires the whole time. They moved towards him, and his belly crawled. He rushed up to Ion's side, and Ion barked at the vampires. They balked and shuffled away.

Ion laughed. The Professor looked at him. He was a towering man. Muscles bulged under his black T-shirt. The scar etched on his face made him look even more fearsome. His sister had given him that. Cut him when he was a child.

"Why?" the Professor had asked him once, rubbing his hands together, sweat on the palms, and Ion had answered, "Because she loved me."

The Professor thought, *I wouldn't like to know what she does to the people she hates.*

"A good place, Professor," said Ion.

"Yes, it's – it's remarkable, Ion."

Ion said, "I have to let them out, now. It's feeding time. The city's crawling with them already."

The Professor said, "I've seen the news."

"It doesn't matter. The more the merrier, eh?"

Ion left him and walked across the panelled platform that covered much of the floor area. The vampires followed him, and the Professor gasped when he saw more of the creatures appear from the shadows and join the troop of undead tailing Ion.

He's the Pied Piper of Vampires, thought the Professor.

Ion stooped and turned to look at the Professor, and the vampires did the same. For a moment, he thought Ion would order them to attack, and he took a step backwards.

And then Ion said, "Will you try to sleep with my sister again, Professor?"

The Professor swallowed and took another backward step. He said, "I've never – I have nothing but respect for Mrs. Radu, I've never – "

"Don't lie," said Ion. "Everyone tries to sleep with Nadia. Nadia's Nadia. She's irresistible." He smiled and said, "Even to me."

Ion turned away and walked towards the far wall, the vampires following like dogs after a pack leader.

A steel ladder clambered up the far wall. Ion climbed it, and at the top he unbolted what appeared to be the underside of a manhole cover. He climbed down, calling a vampire to him. He pointed up the ladder and said, "Go get food," and slapped the creature on the back of its head. The vampire darted up the ladder. The Professor gasped at the creature's agility. It barely seemed to touch the rungs. Another followed, then another. Vampires swept up the ladder and disappeared into the manhole.

"Where does that lead?" said the Professor.

"To some sewer, then a tunnel, then out near the Thames," said Ion.

"Will they be followed when they come back?"

Ion glared up at him and said, "Would you follow them?"

No, he wouldn't. Not unless he had his emblem. And even then, he'd follow far behind. He said, "Will they all come back?"

"Maybe. Not all of them are here, anyway. They're scattered all over the city, by now. A few are still at the house in Holland Park. We left them there," he said, "as guard dogs."

★ ★ ★ ★

Sassie screamed. The pale man tried to bite her. She jammed her hand under his chin and forced his mouth away from her throat.

Lithgow screamed and cowered away.

The pale man, his head forced back, hauled Sassie out of the basement.

Lawton regained his balance, but the pale man was almost through the door. Another figure crashed into the basement, barging into the pale man and Sassie. The pale man lost his grip, and she slipped away from him, running into Lawton.

The other figure, a man with orange hair, snarled and showed sharp teeth, and he charged into the basement.

He went straight for Lithgow.

The pale man found his footing and came for Lawton. Lawton, holding Sassie, stared into the pale man's eyes. They were tinged with red, as if blood had leaked into their colour. He only looked into the eyes for a couple of seconds, but it was enough time for him to see something he could only describe as evil.

Then he punched the pale man in the face.

The pale man reeled away, and his legs buckled under him.

Lithgow shrieked.

Orange Hair stumbled towards him. Orange Hair said, "Remember me, you cunt? You sold me that pill for a tenner, and look at me now."

Lawton shoved Sassie aside. The pale man tried to get up, and Lawton kicked him in the face, but he just shook his head and staggered to his feet.

Lawton glanced across at Lithgow. Lithgow flailed against his attacker. Orange Hair laughed and baited Lithgow. He pounced and bit Lithgow in the arm. Lithgow squealed and flapped.

Sassie's attacker lunged again.

Lawton swung an elbow and it cracked against the pale man's chin, and he lurched against the wall.

Lawton looked at Sassie. "Go help Fraser."

Lithgow screamed.

The pale man, not a drop of blood on his punched, kicked, and elbowed face, came forward again, baring his teeth.

Lawton kicked him under the chin. The pale man's head snapped back, but he shook the blow off and came forward again.

"You can't beat me down, tough guy," said the pale man. He snarled, showing fangs.

He lunged at Lawton and Lawton put his guard up, throwing punches and elbows at the pale man's head. It was like hitting a punch bag — the thing kept coming back. Lawton grabbed the pale man's collar and threw three rapid punches into his opponent's nose. The nose flattened against the pale man's face, but no blood came out — just some black fluid, oozing down over the pale man's mouth.

And then he opened his mouth and hissed at Lawton.

Lawton glanced over at Lithgow. Orange Hair had his teeth buried in Lithgow's arm. Lithgow screamed and thrashed about.

Lawton, holding off the snarling pale man, said, "What the fuck *are* they?"

Sassie said "You know what they are, you know," and she grabbed a splinter of wood the length of a cricket bat. It looked like the remains of a table leg. She drove the sharp end into the middle of Orange Hair's back. He screamed and wheeled around, letting go of Lithgow. He tottered towards Sassie, but only made a few steps.

Orange Hair turned black, like he'd been singed. He shrieked and burst into flames, and then exploded into dust, which created a cloud around Lithgow and Sassie.

Lawton's attacker clawed at him and Lawton looked him in the eye and said, "So now I know how to kill you."

Lawton shoved the pale man away.

Lithgow screamed that he'd been bitten.

Sassie said, "Stab it in the heart."

Lawton fended off another attack. He was tiring. His arms felt as if they'd been drained of strength; he'd thrown that many punches.

Lithgow howled, saying he was going to die.

Sassie scoured the basement. She found another slat of wood, the leg of a chair splintered off.

She said, "Jake," and tossed it to Lawton, and he caught it just as the pale man came again. Lawton batted him across the temple with the chair leg. His skin broke, and black fluid seeped from the wound. But the blow didn't hinder him: he growled at Lawton and came again.

Lawton drove the stake up into the pale man's solar plexus, lifting him off his feet. The pale man, staked on the chair leg, started to twitch. His mouth opened and closed, and he started frothing. He croaked, and then his skin scorched and he came apart, his flesh and everything in it falling into dust.

Lawton stepped back, looked at the pale man's remains: motes hanging in the air, peppered around the floor.

"Jesus Christ," he said.

Lithgow again cried that he was dying. Sassie, trying to comfort Lithgow, said, "We need to get out of here."

Lawton said, "What have I just seen?"

★ ★ ★ ★

Jenna slipped into the basement and watched Jake's legs slide through the window.

She sniffed the air, smelling the thick, warm blood flowing through his veins. She heard the sound of his running feet, and they faded and faded until there was only silence.

And then his odour was gone, leaving nothing but the stale smell of this basement and the dusty remains of her companions.

She'd seen them destroyed, and it terrified her.

She'd come down after them when they all smelled blood in the basement. But when the guys went in, she stopped at the door because she recognized Jake's voice.

She drew away, lurking in the shadow of the stairs that led down to the basement. She listened to the struggle, taking a peek around the door now and again.

And she peeked just at the moment Jake drove that piece of wood through Heiko's heart.

Heiko could've run away when she saw Jake arm himself, but he'd been obsessed with food. Jenna knew this because it obsessed her, too. The hunger gnawing at her the entire time, and only one thing would sate it.

Blood.

She was so hungry she'd almost barged into the basement. She could smell the boiling blood in Jake's veins, in Fraser's veins, in that blonde thing's veins. She could hear the throb-throb-throb of their pulses, and it drove her mad.

But she somehow held back.

She'd watched Jake, and although he was only food now, something had burned deep inside her when she saw him.

She didn't know lust anymore, or love – only hunger; but the feeling wasn't quite that.

It was gone, now, whatever it was. In its place, hunger came again.

Blood, she thought, *I must get blood.*

Without blood in her belly it felt like a thousand insects were crawling just beneath her skin.

It could drive you mad, this hunger.

She scanned the basement and saw everything in the red hue her new eyes allowed. She looked up at the window and to the night outside, and she saw the darkness and all that moved in it as shades of red.

Jenna hissed, craving food. They'd been told to be guard dogs, here. There were half a dozen of them, the other three taking care of the upper two floors. But since her troop was dead, what was the point in staying?

She'd go out and nourish herself.

She thought about her family, who were now only blood.

She thought about her friends, named them all in her head, but felt nothing but the urge to feed from them.

She thought of Jake and the blood in him, and she ached for his liquid.

Jenna growled and sprang for the window.

CHAPTER 38.
HISTORY AND MYTH.

LITHGOW sobbed and shivered, saying, "I'm going to die, I'm going to die."

Sassie, rolling up Lithgow's sleeve, said, "Let me have a look, Fraser," and he settled down.

They'd got a cab back to Lithgow's flat in Fulham. The cabbie got worried when Lithgow started to cry, saying he'd turn into "one of them", he'd "die and walk the streets at midnight". But Sassie calmed him down by saying he'd be all right, and Lawton calmed him down by telling him to shut his gob.

Lawton poured Famous Grouse into glasses. He'd got the bottle out of Lithgow's drinks cabinet.

Lawton jabbed a tumbler-full into Lithgow's hand. "Drink that, let Sassie have a look," he said.

Sassie studied Lithgow's arm while Lithgow gurgled down the liquor.

"You're all right," she said, "it didn't even break the skin."

"There you go," said Lawton, "thick-skinned after all, Lithgow."

Lithgow relaxed a little, whisky spilling down his chin. "I thought I was going to die. Thought I–I'd turn into – they were vampires, weren't they, they were fucking vampires."

Sassie and Lawton looked at each other, like concerned parents sharing eye contact after a terrible revelation from their child.

Lawton said, "I've never seen anyone die like that – turn to dust."

"Well, we all turn to dust," said Sassie, her cheeks red, knowing it was bullshit.

And Lawton said what she'd expected him to say: "Not two seconds after being stabbed in the heart, we don't."

"Oh, my God," said Lithgow, "oh, my God."

Sassie said, "Do you think those pills made them like that?"

Lithgow said, "Oh, my God," again and again, pouring himself another drink.

Lawton said, "We've got to find those people who were in that house. We've got to find out who owned it. If they're anything to do with this. Any idea where they went, Fraser?"

Lithgow shook his head.

Lawton said, "My respect for you has gone up from zero to half-a-per-cent after discovering you kept Famous Grouse in your drinks cabinet. Try a bit harder to remember, and it might go up another notch."

Lithgow screwed up his face and shook his head again.

"Did you know them, Fraser?" said Sassie.

"No, I didn't," he said.

Lawton said to Sassie, "What d'you think they were, those things? D'you think they were – you know, what Fraser said?"

Sassie said, "Ed told me the Babylonians had blood-cults. Maybe there are people worshipping Babylonian blood-cults in London. It is a multi-cultural city, and we do have freedom of religion in Britain."

Lawton said, "And there's Druids carrying out human sacrifice in Wimbledon, and the Home Counties has Satan worship on Sunday afternoons."

"You're not far from the truth," said Sassie.

Lithgow whimpered. Sassie sat on the settee and swigged at her drink, and she winced. She handed it to Lithgow, who slurped it down.

Lawton said, "Whatever they are, at least we know how to kill them."

"We still don't know what that cuneiform on the lip of the jar said. That might hold a clue," said Sassie. "And I'm not sure why there's an image of Alexander on the vase. Have you got a computer, Fraser?"

Five minutes later, Sassie and Lawton sat next to each other at the table, Googling "Alexander the great legends myths vampires vases" on Lithgow's Macbook.

They got millions of hits and Sassie said, "You've really got to be careful with the internet. Everything you read has got to go through a bullshit filter."

Sassie scrolled through the links. Lawton leaned in and he smelled her. His arm rested against her arm, and she made no attempt to move away.

"Okay," she said, "let's have a look at this," and she opened a link that took them to a blue-coloured page with Courier type, which Lawton had to squint to read.

Sassie's eyes skimmed the page, and as she read she hummed. Lawton tried to follow the words. But he'd never been much of a reader. And the number of words crammed on the screen made his eyes blur and his focus wane.

Sassie said, "According to this one, Alexander the Great entered Babylon victorious after defeating the Persian king, Darius."

"And that's history or myth?" said Lawton.

"That's history, that's truth – it happened in 331BC at the Battle of Gaugamela," she said.

Lawton looked over at Lithgow. He was sitting on the couch, nursing his uninjured arm. He had a tumbler of Famous Grouse in his hand, and Lawton could smell the whisky. An itch for the drink played in chest. He could imagine the fiery liquid burning his throat and washing that itch away.

But then Sassie said, "And when Alexander led his armies into Babylon, it says here," and Lawton returned his attention to her as she continued: "He issued an order that none of his troops should enter the homes of the Babylonians."

"Do you think that's true?" said Lawton.

"I don't know. Says it's a local account. I don't know."

"All right," said Lawton, "but why issue that ruling?"

Sassie, her finger tracing the lines, said, "Doesn't say. Okay, let's go back to Google, here. And" – she typed in "ruling homes Babylonians" after the list of words in her initial search, and then hit the GOOGLE SEARCH button – "we'll see what comes up."

What came up was another mile-long list of hits.

Lawton blew air out of his cheeks.

Sassie trawled through the list, then opened one link.

A black screen popped up, blotched by yellow and orange lettering declaring it to be the website of THE ALEXANDER MYTHS. The colours were so violent that Lawton flinched.

Sassie, reading the yellow-on-black writing, said, "Says that Alexander had heard that demons ruled Babylon, and they dwelled in all the homes. He made the ruling to protect his troops, and then set about finding the demons."

"And did he find them?" said Lawton.

She shook her head. "Doesn't say."

They trawled through a dozen websites, each offering strange and impossible details about Alexander the Great.

Lithgow snored on the couch, and Lawton envied him.

Then Sassie said, "Look at this," and Lawton turned to the screen, which was now yellow with red and blue text. Sassie said, "Here, look, it says that Alexander fought three demons and destroyed them. He – look, Jesus – he kept their remains in jars stolen from Darius's treasure chest and – bloody hell, Jake – and had images of himself as a conquering hero defeating the monstrous army painted on them."

★ ★ ★ ★

"I'll take you back," said Lawton.

Heat rippled through Sassie's belly, and her skin goosepimpled. Without thinking she said, "Okay," and stood.

"Hey," said Lithgow, leaping to his feet, "hey, you're not leaving me here, are you? What if those things come back? What if they've got a taste for me?"

"Don't worry, Fraser," said Lawton, pulling on his coat, "it'd be a first for anyone to have a taste for you."

"Jenna did, you bastard."

Lawton tensed. Colour rushed into his face. Sassie saw anger flash in his eyes. He glared at Lithgow, who sagged back into the settee.

Lawton said, "I'll be here at 8.00 a.m., Fraser, so you be ready."

"Wh-why?"

Lawton said, "We're going to see Christine Murray, going to tell her about what we've found today."

"No way, Lawton."

"The only way, Fraser."

CHAPTER 39.
BLOODY REPORTER.

METROPOLITAN POLICE HQ, SCOTLAND YARD – 10 A.M.,
FEBRUARY 9

MURRAY said, "Can you tell me if my story" – she held up a copy
of the paper – "published this morning is true, Dr. Frome?"

The pathologist, a red-haired woman with pink-framed glasses,
opened and closed her mouth, but no words came out. Her cheeks
flushed, and she looked across to Commander Peter Deere and
Superintendent Phil Birch.

Birch had gone purple, and he glowered at Murray.

Deere wore a frown, and sweat gathered in the furrows on his brow.
He didn't like Saturday morning press conferences, Murray knew that.
He wanted to be on the golf course on Saturday morning.

Deere said, "This is a leaked document, and we don't comment
on leaked documents. The results of the port-mortem examinations
have not been made public. Inquests have opened on the twenty-eight
victims of the Religion tragedy. The actual, official post-mortem results
will be made public by the coroner, during the inquest."

Journalists shot questions at Deere, Birch, and the pathologist.
A press officer tried to bat the queries away, but they kept coming.
Cameras flashed and microphones were thrust forward.

Murray smiled and sat back in her chair. She laid the paper in her lap and read the front page headline:

BODIES DRAINED OF BLOOD

And then a sub-deck read:

Nightclub dead's organs "had shrivelled".

The press officer got control of the reporters and said, "One at a time, one at a time, please."

Murray's arm shot up.

The press officer said, "You've had your question, Christine."

But a guy from *The Sun* with his hand up glanced across at Murray and said, "No, let her ask a question. Go ahead, Chris," and the others said, "Go ahead, your show, Christine."

Silence fell and Murray said, "And could you confirm if my sources were correct when they indicated that the bodies had been drained of blood?"

Deere leaned into the microphone on the table in front of him and feedback squealed. He flinched, gathered himself, and said, "We don't comment on leaked reports."

"I understand," said Murray, "that there were no trauma wounds on the bodies – can you give us an idea how the blood could have been drained?"

Murray stared at the pathologist. The tag sitting on the table in front of the pink-spectacled woman said her name was Dr. Pauline Frome. Dr. Frome stared right back at Murray, her face fixed in a frown.

Deere said, "We're still looking into that, Christine, now – "

Murray said, "How's the investigation going, Superintendent Birch? You seem to be adding to the body count every night. Thirty on Thursday, forty-seven last night – more than a hundred people dead in three nights. Do you have any idea what's causing this?"

Birch's eyes burned with fury. He said, "We are continuing our investigations," in a robotic voice.

A *Mirror* reporter said, "Do you believe it's anything to do with drugs?"

"Certainly," said Birch, "drugs were involved in the first deaths at Religion. We've yet to ascertain if drugs were involved in the latter tragedies."

The *Sun* reporter who gave way to Murray said, "Have you looked at the possible link to terrorism?"

"We don't know," said Birch, "of a possible link to terrorism."

"Yes, but have you *looked* at a possible link to terrorism?" said *The Sun* man.

Birch craned out his neck and said, "No, we haven't."

Deere said, "There's no evidence to suggest that this is linked to terrorism, ladies and gentlemen."

"Well," said a BBC London reporter, "what is it linked to, Commander Deere? What do you say to Londoners who think you've lost control of the streets, who are too scared to go out after dark?"

Deere said, "We say that we've *not* lost control of the streets and we *do* advise Londoners to take special care if they're outside after dark. But we must remember, these terrible events have been mostly contained in the central areas of the capital. This is not a London-wide incident at the moment."

Murray shot her hand up again and before anyone gave her the go-ahead, said, "Some of these people who died at Religion, they described themselves as vampires" – Deere and Frome squirmed – "and I understand, as my report states, that a few of them had incisions on their bodies. Do you link these incidents to vampirism?"

A hush spread through the room.

And after a few seconds Deere said, "No."

"No?" said Murray as the other journalists started to shout questions again.

"How do you explain the blood loss, then?" said another reporter.

Deere's wide, fearful eyes flitted around the room. His mouth opened and closed, but no words came out. Birch hunkered down next to him, his cheeks purple with rage. Dr. Frome stood up and said something to the press officer before striding out of the press conference.

Murray, shouting over the cacophony, said, "Has the drug 'K' got anything to do with this? Have you tested the drug, yet?"

Birch fixed her with a glare, and Murray felt the hatred shoot from his narrow eyes.

CHAPTER 40.
THIS CHARMING MAN

SASSIE, arms folded, watched as Ed Crane studied the jar.

Lawton had brought it in that morning, reluctantly handing it over before heading out to meet the journalist, Christine Murray.

Sassie yawned. She wanted to be home, in bed. But instead she'd had to drag herself over to the college, the only place she'd meet Crane – there was no way she'd let him come over to her flat, and she needed his expert eye; so it was college or nowhere.

Crane, eyes on the jar, said, "Late night?" He raised an eyebrow and glanced at Sassie, and she felt her cheeks redden. He said, "You're blushing, sweet Sassie. You know" – he turned to face her – "you are the sauciest saucepot in the School of Humanities, and I can't understand why we've not gone beyond that delicious kiss we shared at that lovely riverside pub so recently."

Shame flared on Sassie's face. She said, "Four years ago, Ed – I-I was a student – I-I was drunk, and you took – I was – that's enough – "

He laughed, gazed at the jar again. "It was only a kiss, Sassie. Tongues, that's all."

"Ed, please – "

"Why so embarrassed? We're both adults."

She gritted her teeth. Her legs felt drained of strength. She slumped into the chair behind her desk and wished Crane hadn't come here. She glared at him, and felt hate rise in her breast.

Crane laughed again and ran a hand through his dark hair. Sunlight splintered off his ruby ring. He put the jar down on Sassie's desk and took the chair opposite her. He draped an ankle across his knee and laid his hands on his inner thighs.

Sassie steeled herself and let the anger and the shame seep out of her. She said, "Are you able to help me, Ed? Do you know what the cuneiform says?"

He leaned forward and took hold of the clay pot once more, rolling it around in his hands. He looked at it and said, "Doesn't mean anything."

"Nothing?"

"All it says" – he twisted the pot around, reading the cuneiform on the lip – "is that this is the property of the Kings of Babylon – or some such nonsense." Crane shrugged and placed the pot back on the desk. He scratched his chin and said, "Do you know where this friend of yours got it?"

"No," said Sassie, "I don't."

"I mean, it might be stolen, don't you think?"

"It might be, but that's not my business, is it – not mine, not yours."

"You don't think?" said Crane. "You don't think we have a responsibility to return it to the rightful owner?"

"Only if you know who the rightful owner is, Ed."

He chuckled. "I see – of course." He narrowed his eyes. "Was there – anything in the pot, do you know?"

"When?" she said.

"When your – um – friend found it?"

"I don't know if he did find it. I think he bought it on eBay."

"He – eBay –? " said Crane, blowing air out of his cheeks.

"Ask him yourself, Ed. He'll be here in a while to pick it up," she said, and then: "What about vampires? You said that Babylonians had vampire cults."

Crane shrugged. "Ancient peoples had all kinds of cults."

She took a breath and said, "You know these deaths – "

"Yes, I know. It's all over the news. *Standard's* full of it every day."

"Well, what do you make of it all?" she said.

"Now there's a non-sequitur: from vampire cults to deaths in London."

She felt the colour fill her cheeks. "The bodies have disappeared, Ed."

"Gangs, drug lords, I don't know," said Crane, and he brushed his shoulder as if he were wiping away dust. "I'm surprised at you, Sassie. I think you need to have dinner with me so I can put you back on the straight and narrow. You need to get out more."

Sassie shut her eyes. She tried again, saying, "Do you still think the depiction on the jar is Alexander the Great?"

Crane said, "Looks like the image we have of him. But then he could be one of many Greek heroes."

"And these things, these bodies with their hearts gouged out? You still think they could be depictions of vampires?"

"Could be a depiction of demons, could be anything; could be humans – Alexander's countless enemies," said Crane. He looked at her and shrugged. "I'm not being helpful, am I, Sassie."

"Of course you are, Ed, of course – I'm grateful – "

"Are you? How grateful?"

"Don't start that again."

"Well," he said, "I didn't actually get the coffee you promised me."

She ignored him. "Do you imagine," she said, the image of a vampire turning into dust after she drove a stake through its body vivid in her mind, "that these deaths, these massacres, could have anything to do with – vampires?"

Crane tutted and pulled a face. "Sassie, don't be ridiculous."

CHAPTER 41.
CHEMICAL REACTION.

MURRAY said, "You did *what?*"

Lawton told her again what had happened at the house in Holland Park the previous night, and again she gawped at him at shook her head.

They were huddled around a table at the far end of a Cafe Nero in Kensington High Street. The smell of coffee had brought Lawton to life. He was on his second cup of black Americano. Lithgow sipped at a green tea. Murray gulped from a bottle of orange juice.

Leaning across the table towards Lawton and keeping her voice down, she said, "So these – things – they just burst into dust when you – " and she made a stabbing motion with her hand.

Lawton nodded. "I think we'd be right to say that something unusual's happening."

"The authorities are denying everything," said Murray.

Lawton took a slug of coffee. He said, "Do you think they know anything?"

"They always know something," she said.

Lawton flicked through a copy of *The Daily Express* that lay on the table. Every paper ran with the story. They had it either on the front page, or as a spread on the inside. Lawton pointed to a story headlined:

Sales of crucifixes rocket over "vampire" attacks.

"Yes," said Murray, "and church attendances have boomed, too. People going to all the denominations asking for holy water. And the churches are saying, 'You don't need relics, you need Christ.' And then the Catholic Church, say, 'Here's some holy water, and come to Confession, come to pray, God will save you.' Some of the crazier churches are preaching the end of the world. There's a loopy bunch saying that it's all aborted babies coming back to avenge their murders."

Lawton said nothing. He stared into his coffee, brow creased.

Murray said, "Are you sure about last night? What happened in that house?"

He glared at her. "What're you saying?"

"Well," she said, "you admit to not sleeping, and liking the odd drink. And him" – she gestured to Lithgow – "he's a drug dealer and – "

"Him," said Lithgow, "has got a name."

"All right," she said, "Fraser. But you're talking about murder, here. You – you murdered those guys."

Lawton stared at her for a moment and then he said, "You can't murder dead things."

"Yeah," said Lithgow, "those guys weren't alive – and I know for a fact that they weren't alive."

Lawton said, "Tell her, Fraser."

Lithgow said, "Those two guys, they died at Religion. I-I fucking sold them the pills, okay. And I saw them collapse, froth at the mouth, die. One of them was called Tim Jackson, the one with orange hair. The other guy, I think he was called Heiko, that's what they'd called him at Religion that night – Heiko."

Murray bent down and fished in her bag. She brought out a Moleskine notebook and flicked through the pages. She looked at a page and bit the nail of her right forefinger. She said, "Timothy Allen Jackson."

"Is - is Jenna on that list?" said Lawton.

Murray nodded her head. "Jenna McCall, yes."

Lawton's chest tightened. He shrugged the feeling away, and said to Lithgow, "Are you sure about him, Fraser?"

"'Course I'm sure. I never forget a customer."

"So you're admitting," said Murray, "that you sold him drugs. You admit that you distributed those pills."

"Hang on – " said Lithgow.

Lawton said, "Forget that, Christine. You can't keep chasing the wrong people. You chased me for years – blaming me for something I'd never done."

She said, "You shot – "

Lawton held up a hand and scowled at her. "No one cares anymore. You didn't get your story."

"I got the footage."

"You got the footage. Good for you. And I've never thanked you for posting it on the internet," said Lawton. "But look at me here – I'm willing to forget your attempts to destroy me, I'm willing to do the bygones bit." He leaned in and spoke in a hiss: "There's something weird going on in London that's got nothing to do with me, that's got nothing to do with Fraser – "

Murray said, "He distributed the pills, he's just admitted it."

"Doesn't matter," said Lawton. "Whoever wanted these pills distributed would've got them out there without Fraser's help. He was the one stupid enough to be taken in by it."

"Hey," said Lithgow, "if you're going to insult me, I'd appreciate if you did it behind my back. You know I got bitten last night. I'm a fucking martyr, I am."

Lawton ignored him and said, "You know what the word is for these things, Christine – you know what's running around after dark killing people. We've got to find a way to kill them."

"Why?" she said. "Why us?"

Lawton sat back in the chair and folded his arms. "Because it's something worth fighting for. I'm not going down without having tried to do something."

"I can't do that, I can't fight," she said. "I can only write about these things. That's all I can do."

"What do you do when there's no one left to read what you write, Christine?"

"Yeah," said Lithgow, "because what we saw last night, they can't read is my guess. And if they could, they don't give a shit about your stories."

"So," said Lawton, glancing at Lithgow, "you're with me then?"

Lithgow frowned. "Well, no, I mean – my suggestion is that we run away."

"That's great," said Lawton.

"But what we saw last night was weird, man. It was too much for me, too much. Those bodies, Tim, Heiko, the others too, they're wandering around London, man. And they're biting people and making more people like them. They're hungry, and they're feeding on us."

Murray furrowed her brow. "Hungry?"

"They're vampires, Christine," said Lithgow, "blood-sucking, undead vampires."

★ ★ ★ ★

The red-haired woman said, "We had deaths last night."

"Yes," said Nadia Radu, "we had deaths. We'll have deaths, now."

"Deaths make me nervous, that's all."

Nadia smiled. "We can't have this without death."

"Of course, but seeing as I – well, it doesn't matter."

Nadia frowned at her and said, "No, it doesn't."

The red-haired woman grimaced and brought her handkerchief to her nose. "The smell in here is terrible." They were in a fourth-floor room: a foxhole, no window, plaster peeling off the walls, the ceiling rotting away.

"Chemicals," said Nadia. "Dr. Haddad's magic."

The women looked at the old man. He stood at the table pouring liquid into beakers. He then pinched some dust from a plate between his fingers and thumb and sprinkled it into the liquid.

"Some of Kea's remains. We combine it with the other materials needed to produce the tablets," said Nadia. "Kea's DNA, being vampiric, requires blood. When ingested, it will devour the blood from the host body, killing it. The DNA will then meld with the host's DNA and create a vampire."

"And then, those vampires will – kill and feed, making more vampires," said the red-haired woman.

"Until London is ours."

"And," said the red-haired woman, "where does that leave us, Mrs. Radu?"

Nadia looked the woman in the eye. She said, "It will leave us in power. We will be the Nebuchadnezzars, the Dariuses, of the 21st Century. It'll be like the golden age of Babylon. A king or queen on the throne – you, perhaps – and the trinity watching over us all. We'll harvest food for them. Slaves will build us a city of gold, a London the world will envy and fear. We'll flush out her sewers, her slums, feed the dregs to the vampire legions."

"Which will then make more vampires," said the red-haired women.

"No. Some victims will be slaughtered. A land of vampires would be pointless. They can't run things. They've not got that human capacity for logic, for reason – they only feed. They'll be an unconquerable army, though. They'll provide us with all the weaponry we need to defend ourselves, to defeat other cities – other nations. It'll be like Babylon again."

"Tell me about the resurrection," said the red-haired woman.

Nadia said, "We poured some blood over Kea's remains, starting the process of bringing the great demon to life again, feeding the ashes with the nourishment they need. His body will take a while to rebuild itself, to feed off the blood. We're creating life from dust. We're making a god."

The red-haired woman nodded.

Nadia said, "The vampires will feed and kill again tonight, and they'll be stronger. They can start bringing living victims back, with which we can feed our god. Kea will soon rise. And Kakash will follow, then Kasdeja, and the three will be one again and we'll have our Babylon."

The red-haired woman blew her nose. The reek of chemicals was getting to her. But Nadia thought, *She can stay here and watch Dr. Haddad for a while. He's owed that, this little miracle man.*

The red-haired woman said, "We've got a bit of trouble, though. I understand there's this soldier – "

Nadia nodded. The soldier. The scapegoat. He was meant to take the fall for the drugs, but he was more trouble than they'd thought. She said, "We'd been led to believe he was a washed-up drunk. But it doesn't matter. It doesn't matter what anyone does; it doesn't matter who our enemies are. They can't stop us. The plague will spread, our enemies will die. They all die in the end."

CHAPTER 42.
DEATH BED.

PTOLEMY leaned over Alexander's face and said, "Do you want to tell me where the vessels are, My Lord, and the weapon?"

Alexander, sweat coating his skin and his lips chapped and bloody, grabbed Ptolemy's arm. Alexander's mouth opened and closed as he tried to speak. Ptolemy smelled the rot emanating from the king's body. The general grimaced at the stink of decay. He straightened and stood up, looking down at Alexander lying on the bed. The incense burning around the bed filled Ptolemy's nostrils, and he breathed deeply so the smell could flush his senses clean of the reek of decomposition.

He looked around the king's bedchamber. The room was gloomy because light made Alexander sick. He'd been like this for twelve days. They'd attended the banquet organized by Alexander's friend, Medius of Larissa. They got drunk, and Alexander took a girl he'd met at the banquet to his chambers. Ptolemy, as one of Alexander's seven *somatophylakes* – his personal bodyguard – followed.

And he watched the drunken Alexander strip naked, and the girl strip naked. They slipped into the bath together. The girl licked the king's face. And then she bit his throat. Alexander stiffened, but she held him fast. She drank from his veins for a while, then stood in the bath. Blood oozed from her lips. Ptolemy, gazing at her nakedness, felt a flush of excitement fill his loins. He had the urge to drag her from the bath and ravage her himself.

But he'd die.

Alexander's whore was a vampire.

And she'd been sent to avenge the murder of her gods years before.

Ptolemy shut his eyes and shame reddened his cheeks. Eleven years older than Alexander, he'd been the young king's friend since childhood. They'd been tutored together by Aristotle. They'd fought together in Alexander's victories. They drank together and they pillaged together.

And now, Ptolemy had done something he would never have thought possible.

He had betrayed the man who was closer to him than a brother.

"Power," said Ptolemy's wife, Artakama, the Persian princess he'd married at Susa the previous year, "that's what you'll have. More power than you'll know. You can build an empire far greater than Alexander's, an empire remembered for eternity − if you help avenge their deaths."

Ptolemy had seen Alexander kill the trinity of demons, and he'd joined in the butchery himself. He and the other *somatophylakes*, and a group of a dozen warriors, laid into the other creatures as the sun's rays charred them.

Ptolemy collected the trinity's ashes into the clay pots that had Nebuchadnezzar's words scrawled around their edges. He commissioned artists to paint Alexander's victory on the vessels. The trinity's human servants were exiled or executed. Babylon, it seemed, had been purged.

But then, Artakama came into Ptolemy's life.

And love's the strongest poison of all.

"Help us," she said, "help the descendents of Nebuchadnezzar avenge the death of their gods."

Had the vampire girl, who had watched Ptolemy as she dressed, drained Alexander of blood, he would've died and risen again as an immortal.

"But he is already immortal," said Ptolemy as he and Artakama conspired, "so you can't kill an immortal."

"The vampire can drink some of his blood," said Artakama. "There will be poison in his veins. More powerful than any poison man can find. This will kill him in days."

Days, thought Ptolemy now, standing above his king; *it's taken almost two weeks.*

But Alexander, *Shahanshah*, king of kings, was no ordinary man.

Ptolemy kneeled next to his friend and asked again: "Tell me where the vessels are, My Lord. The vessels and the spear, and I will take them to safety. The demons can't be allowed to return. Their henchmen are in the city, already. They are the ones who poisoned you, My Lord. For the sake of your legacy, you must tell me where they are."

Ptolemy hadn't thought for years about the clay pots and the two-tusked spear Alexander wielded that day.

But now he needed them.

Artakama and her people needed them.

"We'll find a way to resurrect our gods," she'd said, "and they will make us powerful, Ptolemy. They will make you a king."

Ptolemy bent his head towards Alexander. The young king's breath rasped. Blood oozed from the bite mark on his throat and sweat drizzled down his face. His chest rose and fell as his lungs fought for air.

A noise came from Alexander's throat, something that sounded like: "Stateira."

Ptolemy frowned and leaned closer, saying, "Stateira, My Lord? Did you say your wife's name? Stat – "

"Stateira," said Alexander, more clearly this time.

"She has them?"

Alexander nodded, and then said, "Look – look after – her, b-brother – take her – her and my – sons – and the – vessels – into your house – and – " He coughed, sprayed spit into Ptolemy's face.

Ptolemy winced, and then wiped the saliva from his face as Alexander's fit passed.

Alexander grabbed his arm and said, "Listen – l-listen, brother – destroy – destroy it – destroy the ashes – destroy them – " His throat clogged, and he arched his back.

Ptolemy stood and turned towards the door, saying, "Slave. Slave, *Shahanshah* is in pain. Find the doctor. Go, slave, or I'll have you cut open."

Ptolemy heard footsteps running off on the other side of the door. He looked down at his friend. Alexander's face had turned yellow. A string of spit slavered from his mouth.

Ptolemy said, "Forgive me, friend, forgive me."

CHAPTER 43.
TERRIFYING TRUTHS.

LITHGOW strode alongside Lawton, breathing hard, sweating, trying to keep up. He said, "What do you think she'll do, now?"

"I don't know, mate. Let's hope she believes me," said Lawton.

"Believes you? This is about you, isn't it?"

Lawton glanced at him and frowned. "Yes," he said, "it's about me."

"What about me, man? I've been bitten."

"You didn't get bitten, Fraser, that thing's teeth didn't break through your fucking jacket."

"I could turn into one of them."

"Might make you shut up," said Lawton.

"And even if I don't, I could still get poisoned."

"You won't get poisoned. Didn't you hear what I said? It didn't break the skin, you crybaby."

Lithgow said, "This is about all that bollocks in Iraq. About you shooting that towel head – "

"He didn't have a towel on his head," said Lawton.

"But it's about that business, that's what this is about. You getting friendly with Christine Murray. You want some sort of fucking redemption."

"I don't want redemption," said Lawton, picking up his pace.

They were headed for the tube station to catch a Circle line train that would take them to Embankment. Police carrying guns milled around the station entrance, and Lawton halted. Lithgow bumped into him and said, "You do, you want redemption – you're looking to – to – to redeem yourself, man. You're looking for atonement."

Lawton turned on him and snarled, saying, "I'm not fucking looking for fucking atonement or redemption or forgiveness or anything. I'm looking for something to fight for, Lithgow. Something I can stand up for and defend."

Crowds veered around them, glancing at Lawton as they moved down the street.

Lawton said, "They took that away from me. She, that Christine bloody Murray woman, took that away from me. The M.O-fucking-D took that away from me. The politicians, the papers – they took it away."

Lithgow leaned back as Lawton raged into his face. And then Lithgow said, "I know what you are."

"What?" said Lawton, getting out of Lithgow's face.

"You're like a ronin, aren't you, man."

"A what?"

"A ronin. A samurai who's been shamed, who hasn't got a master. The Army was your master, Jake, and now you've had to leave your master. You're a drifter and you're looking for someone to serve."

Lawton stared at him for a few moments. Then he spun away, and strode down the road.

★ ★ ★ ★

Murray watched Lawton and Lithgow leave the coffee shop. She thought about what they said:

Vampires.

They didn't exist, of course, but perhaps the myth had some truth in it. The legends of blood-sucking creatures had to have a source, and that source could be true.

A disease, maybe, she thought. She felt a jolt of excitement. That's what it was: an ancient plague that had somehow been unleashed in modern day London. An affliction that gave the sufferers the appearance of being dead for a few hours, and then when they regained consciousness, they went around attacking people – and drinking their blood.

Vampires.

Her phone rang and she flinched. She answered it. The voice said, "I can't be on the phone for too long."

Murray said, "All right, just tell me," and her skin flushed with anticipation.

"The pills," said Murray's contact in the pathology department of a London hospital involved in the case, "contained elements of methylenedioxy amphetamine, from which ecstasy is derived."

"They were ecstasy?" said Murray.

"For all intents and purposes, they were ecstasy tablets. However – "

Murray gritted her teeth and thought, *Get on with it.*

Her contact got on with it: " – the pills also included that unusual DNA sample we found in the bodies."

Murray shuddered. She said, "What does that mean?"

"It means that the pills were ecstasy pills, but, like all street drugs, they included other substances – including warfarin, by the way, which thins the blood."

"And this unknown element that you found in the original bodies?" said Murray.

"Yes. This, um, 'unknown' element found in the victims came from the pills – it seems."

"Do you know what it is?"

"Like I told you before, Christine – we don't. It's just – just the weirdest thing. And I think – I don't know this for sure, so don't even quote me off the record – but I heard some guys talking – and I think, I think they said – "

Her contact faltered. Murray squeezed the bottle of orange juice. The drink spurted from the bottle and splashed on the table. Murray said, "What? What?"

"Sorry," said her contact, "people walking about."

"What did you hear?"

"I heard them say the element, the unknown one, that it appeared to be very, very old. I mean, *really* old. I mean ancient. That's what they said."

CHAPTER 44.
LOCKING HORNS.

KING'S COLLEGE LONDON, STRAND CAMPUS — 1.16 P.M.,
FEBRUARY 9

LAWTON put his phone away. "That was Christine Murray," he
said. He felt cold. His throat was dry, so he coughed and swallowed. It
didn't do much good, but he tried to speak.

First he told them about the bodies, that they had no blood in them
and that the organs were shrivelled. "Like the life had been sucked
out of them," he said. "But the hearts, they're engorged, blackened,
coated in slime." And then he told them about Murray's phone call,
Murray ringing to tell him that the pills called "Skarlet" contained
some unknown substance that was "ancient".

And then he said what he, Sassie, and Lithgow had experienced at
the house in Holland Park the previous evening.

Ed Crane leaned against the window, arms folded. He wore a sneer
and kept winking at Sassie.

They were in Crane's office, overlooking the river. His office was
larger than Sassie's cluttered corner. Box files stood in neat rows on
shelves. Ancient looking books lined the walls. The clay pot depicting
Alexander and the vampires sat on the windowsill.

He sat down at his desk, putting his hands behind his head.

He said, "Surely there must be a logical explanation to what's going on. What do the police think?"

Lawton said, "I'm not sure they think anything. They're as confused as everyone else. They like to manage an investigation, keep it on a leash. But this one's tugging and pulling away from them."

Crane said, "Might it be possible that someone who's obsessed by all these myths, this vampire nonsense, could be perpetrating these crimes?"

Sassie shrugged. "How do you drain the blood out of twenty-eight bodies without leaving a mess or a mark?"

Lawton said, "The people who died last night, and on Thursday night, they had" – he furrowed his brow; a chill flushed his veins – "had bite marks on their necks. The kind you see – "

He faltered.

"See where, Mr. Lawton?" said Crane. "In the movies?" He chuckled.

Sassie said, "Ed, when I drove that stake into that thing at the house, it turned to dust. Right in front of my eyes. That's not normal."

"No, not normal at all," said Crane. "But I don't think it's normal, Sassie, to drive stakes through living people."

"They weren't living," said Lithgow. "They were dead. They died at Religion. I saw them die. And – and Hammond, my mate Steve Hammond, he got killed in that house. Murdered by a woman with a gun."

"Quite a story," said Crane. "We keep peeling back the layers. Women with guns, stakes through the heart   "

"Is there anything in the Babylonian myths about the dead coming back to life?" said Sassie.

Crane shrugged, steepled his fingers. "I'm assuming you're talking about vampires here."

Sassie and Lawton glanced at each other.

Crane chuckled. "It's ridiculous, really. Sassie, we're academics. We deal in facts. Myths, legends, superstitions, they're for" – he threw a hand in Lawton's direction – "the plebs. People whose reading and writing is limited to *The Sun* and – and an Army recruitment form."

Lawton glared at him, arching an eyebrow. He wasn't taking the bait. This was more important than Crane's childish game, and his reasons for playing it. Lawton guessed it had something to do with impressing Sassie.

Sassie said, "Okay, Ed, you don't have to be a wanker about this."

"A wanker?" he said. "I'm not the one claiming to have killed vampires."

"I'm not saying that," said Lawton. "I'm only telling you what I've seen and what I know. I thought maybe someone clever like you could help us find the answer. But if you prefer playing 'my-dad's-bigger-than-your-dad' games, then fuck you, mate."

"Now," said Crane, "there's no need to get aggressive, is there," and he had a smirk on his face that Lawton wanted to rip off.

Sassie said, "Can we stop this."

Lithgow, gnawing at his nails, said, "Does this mean that all of those people who died at Religion are going to be – " He trailed off, creased his brow and looked at everyone in the office in turn. And then he said, "Have those dead people come back to life?"

"Good grief," said Crane, "what silliness. And what do you plan to do, all of you? Hunt them down like you're little Van Helsings and drive stakes through their hearts?" He laughed, a patronizing guffaw intended, Lawton was sure, to make anyone in his presence feel inferior. Then Crane frowned and glared at Sassie. "Do you know this man, Sassie? This" – and he looked Lawton up and down – "Jake Lawton character?"

"Ed – " said Sassie, but she wasn't allowed to finish.

Crane cocked his head, looked at Lawton through narrowed eyes. "Why did you leave the Army, Mr. Lawton? Not as if you got sick of the killing, was it? Care to tell us?"

Lawton felt rage pulse through his head. He looked Crane in the eye and Crane paled, turning away. The academic looked at Sassie again, eyes wide now. He said, "He killed a man, Sassie, this soldier of yours."

"Breaking news, Crane, fucking breaking news" said Lawton, his fists clenched. He twitched, fighting the urge to launch himself at Crane.

"Oh, hasn't he told you, Sassie?" said Crane, and Sassie looked from Crane to Lawton, her cheeks red and her eyes wide. Crane said, "He doesn't think much of you, does he. Mind you, it was all over the papers a couple of years ago. And on the internet, too. You can see it. I'll e-mail you the link." He made a face, like he'd smelled something bad. "It's nasty."

Sassie stared at Crane, her face flushed. "It doesn't matter who he is or what he's done. I don't need to know his secrets; he doesn't need to know mine. All we're doing is trying to – trying to save people."

Crane winked at Lawton and said, "She's a good kisser."

Lawton lunged at him, and Crane's face blanched, his mouth gaping. He threw himself off the chair and scrambled across the office, saying, "Don't touch me! I'll sue, I'll bloody sue."

Sassie, reaching for Lawton, said, "No, Jake, don't," and Lawton felt the rage leach out of him when she held his arm.

Crane, ashen faced, cowered in the corner.

Lawton grabbed the vase from the windowsill and stormed out of the office.

Crane, shouting after him, said, "That's an artefact. It should be in a museum."

Sassie glowered at Crane, and Lithgow, looking down at the academic, told him, "You shouldn't make him angry, you know. He's a bastard, is Jake Lawton."

Crane said, "I know – I've seen the footage."

CHAPTER 45.
A BITTER TASTE.

LAWTON swigged his Scotch and thought about what had happened in Crane's office.

Sassie eyed him with fear after they left Crane's office. He thought of the academic and anger flashed in his head. Had Sassie's voice not doused his rage, he would've gone for the man. He wanted to rip the fuckwit's head off. He *would've* ripped the fuckwit's head off.

"I *will* rip the fuckwit's head off," he said, staring at the cracks in the plaster above the door to his flat.

He thought about the video.

That fucking thing was on the internet, downloaded by fanatics in Iraq and anti-war campaigners in Britain, and every nutcase in-between.

"And all thanks to you, Christine," he said, holding up his glass in a toast.

He slugged down the Scotch, poured another. He felt fuzzy, now, the drink mushing up his brain. But that's how he liked to feel. That was the only way he could get any sleep, even if it were only a couple of hours.

The papers had been full of shit when the footage got out. All of them slagging off the war, slagging off the politicians, slagging off the troops, slagging off Lawton.

The phone rang. He picked up, and it was Murray.

"I was just talking about you," he said.

"To who?"

"To myself."

"Sign of madness," she said.

"So they say."

"I'm sorry to break-up your evening of self-abuse and depression, but I've found some stuff out about the house."

Lawton sat up. "In Holland Park."

She said, "Yes, in Holland Park. It's owned by a Dr. Afdal Haddad. British. He's in his nineties, now. A chemist by training. Cardiff University. He ran a private practice for years. Homeopathy. Firm called F&H Wellbeing. He's a wealthy individual. Had a couple of staff there, assistants. A" – she paused; Lawton heard papers being shuffled – "Nadia Radu and Ion Friniuc. Again, British citizens."

"Where d'you find this stuff out?"

"Where do I find anything out?"

"I don't know," said Lawton. "Where?"

"I've got contacts. This one came from a copper. But it's not difficult. Information's available if you know where to look. You can find out anything if you want to."

Lawton said, "Anything else?"

"Nadia Radu was married to a Viorel Radu," said Murray, "a minor diplomat in the Romanian embassy during the Ceaucescu regime in the Eighties. He was much older than her. He's dead now. Died in a car crash in 1999. As to the Holland Park property, neighbours said they didn't really see much of Haddad or the other two. They were well-to-do, though. Had posh dinner parties, lots of well heeled sorts coming and going."

"Funded by drugs," said Lawton.

"Might be. A chemist. Guns."

"Guns?"

"Yes," said Murray. "Lithgow's pal, Steve Hammond getting shot. And no one knows anything. Police have got nothing on it."

"Lithgow didn't want to report it. Thought he'd get into trouble for breaking into the house."

"There's more trouble than breaking and entering facing that one, I tell you   facing us all. Another mystery to consider, as well."

"Too many mysteries. My head hurts."

Murray ignored him and said, "Have you heard anything from Nathan Holt?"

"Since he lied about me to the police, you mean? No, I haven't."

"Well, he's gone."

"Gone where?"

"I don't know or I'd find him. He's not answering his phone, he's not at his flat, his mum's in Canterbury and she's frantic. Police haven't logged him as a missing person yet, but it won't be long."

"He might've left the country, gone into hiding."

"He's the sensible one," said Murray.

"What about the Fuads? What does your reporter's nose sniff on them?"

"Nothing. They're notoriously publicity-shy. They've never given interviews, never made public statements, never had their pictures taken. They announce everything through their PR firm. And even the PR firm's out of reach at the moment."

There was silence between them for a moment, and then Lawton asked: "Any idea what's going on?"

"Yes, I've got an idea. The papers have got ideas. People have got ideas about what's going on. But no one's willing to do more than speculate at the moment."

"So what's your idea?" he said.

"You're drunk – you give me yours, first."

"I think," he said, "that Lithgow was on the mark this morning."

That word in his head:

Vampires.

"Do you?" she said.

"I do. Do you?"

"I might do."

There was nothing left to say. They agreed to get in touch the following day. He said goodnight and she said, *Stop drinking.* He put down the phone and finished his Scotch. He went for a refill, but he'd drained the bottle.

He got up, went over to the kitchenette. He found another bottle, Tesco own brand, and took it back into the living area. He sat on the sofa, picked up the TV remote and considered watching a film. He thought about it, and then tossed the remote aside. He couldn't concentrate on a movie, on music, on anything. This business crowded his mind. The dead at Religion. The disappearing bodies. Holt gone, now. Hammond getting killed. More dead people.

But there was one bright spot on all of this.

Sassie perked him up from the start. He'd not felt such a surge of affection towards anyone in a long time. Not even Jenna, who'd been in and out of his life since they were teenagers.

He thought about Sassie. He remembered her eyes today after Crane's bollocks about the footage. She'd looked terrified, and cowered from him.

Shouts wafted in from the street and broke his train of thought. Louts heading off to find trouble, he guessed. Yobs reeling around after an afternoon on booze and cannabis. Saturdays were always the worst.

A flash of anger burst in Lawton's head. He almost leaped to his feet and stomped downstairs to the street to confront them, but he stopped himself. It was stupid. One-on-one, he might have been able to deal with them, but if he faced a dozen or more, he'd be in trouble. He had no physical fear of any man but he would always avoid confrontation, always turn the other cheek unless things got hairy. As an ex-soldier he got a lot of shit. People just didn't like him – from the middle class snobs at their dinner parties berating the war and the "violent" troops, to the scum on the street who'd read too much tabloid shit and wanted to show their mates how hard they were.

Screams sliced the darkness. Lawton sat up and listened. Curses filled the air. The sound of running. Horns blaring.

Bit wild out there tonight, he thought.

And then he remembered the dead from last night, and the night before. And he thought, *Are they walking about, those carcasses?*

He furrowed his brow, got to his feet. He started to cross to the window. His doorbell went and he flinched.

Kids mucking about?

It buzzed again. He pressed the intercom, said, "Yeah?"

A voice he thought he'd heard the last of said, "Hi, Jake, will you let me in?" and the chill it brought in it wake flooded his veins.

His throat felt dry. His mind reeled.

The voice said, "Will you let me in?"

He pressed the red button and waited. He heard footsteps coming up the stairs. There was a rap on the door. For a moment he didn't think any of it was real: the voice asking to be let in, the knock on the door, him reaching out for the handle.

He opened the door.

Jenna stood there, grinning at him.

PART THREE.
BATTLEGROUND.

CHAPTER 46.
THEY WILL FEED ...

BARRY Corbett peered through the bus's window as the vehicle crossed Blackfriars Bridge, heading south. There was some problem up ahead, and the bus slowed. Horns blared, and he could hear pedestrians and drivers shouting and arguing. The bus came to a halt.

People dashed through the gridlocked traffic. He heard screams. Some of the other passengers craned their necks to see, saying, "What's going on?" and "D'you see anything?" and other languages as well. There were a lot of languages in London, these days, and you could hear most of them on the bus.

A woman sitting next to him had been jabbering away into her mobile phone, and Barry couldn't understand any of what she was saying. Except "Blackfriars Bridge, Blackfriars Bridge," sprayed here and there during her rant. He wanted to say, *There's no need to shout;* but that never made a difference. She'd have just glared at him, and carried on shouting – English or not.

He didn't know where the woman was from till he saw a badge on her shirt: a green globe on a yellow background. *Brazil*, he thought. He was good with flags. He'd learned them as a kid through his interest in football.

And there was no flag more famous in football than the flag of brilliant Brazil.

He'd seen them win the 1970 World Cup final in Mexico City, thrashing Italy 4-1 in the final.

Samba soccer, he thought.

He'd flown over with some mates to watch England defend the trophy they'd won at Wembley four years previously.

"We start saving now," said Colin Makerewicz, son of a Polish dad who'd fled his war-torn country twenty-five years before. And Colin, on a crest of an English wave as his adopted country beat West Germany in the '66 final, said, *Let's go to Mexico in four years time.*

Four of them – Colin, Barry, Arthur Crossley, and Terry Hayes – saved money like Gordon Banks saved shots and headed off to Mexico on a trip of a lifetime.

England flopped, losing 3-2 to the bloody Germans in the quarterfinals after being 2-0 ahead.

But Brazil, with Pele, Jairzinho, and captain Carlos Alberto, made up for it and the four pals had a great time. Sun, soccer, and sex.

That felt so long ago. All the lads were gone. Colin and Arthur dead, and Terry jailed for murdering two kids in the early Eighties. Strange how they'd been friends and not known he was a pervert. Now in his seventies, his wife long dead, too, Barry did nothing much but travel from his home in south London to the city centre or Stamford Bridge. Today had been a washout: a dull 0-0 at home to Hull City. There'd been a minute silence before kick-off for these people who'd died over the past few days.

The Brazilian woman next to him asked what was going on outside. The London Eye flickered in the distance. For a moment, Barry's gaze was drawn to it. But he drew his eyes away and looked at what was happening on the bridge.

Fights broke out.

Groups of wild looking people attacked passers-by, held them down and bit into their throats.

Barry pressed his face to the window. The London air filled with noise. The bus driver got out of his cab and leaned out of the door.

A snarling man threw himself at the bus window through which Barry stared. Barry flinched and jerked away. The man bared his teeth. He had – fangs. Sharp canines like a dog. He had brownish-red eyes.

The Brazilian woman next to Barry screamed.

The bus driver screeched. Two women dressed like punks dragged the driver off the bus and into the street, and they fell on him. Barry stood up, saw the driver kicking and struggling. But the punks held him down and they tore at his throat with their teeth.

Barry's heart raced and a sweat broke on his nape. The other passengers started to panic. They shouted, explaining what was happening outside, as if Barry or anyone else needed to be told – they could see it all themselves.

A car skidded and crashed into the bus. The passengers screamed. Barry got thrown into the aisle. The Brazilian woman fell on top of him. Passengers screamed as the bus tilted on its wheels. The vehicle clanged and creaked.

The Brazilian woman got up, and she reached out to help Barry. He took her hand and she smiled as she tugged him to his feet.

Something black and lightning quick ploughed into her and whipped her away.Barry's gaze darted after the woman. A black-clad figure with bleached hair gnawed at her neck, and blood splashed on her yellow shirt as she struggled.

Shrieks pierced the air. Passengers tried to rush off the bus. They opened the emergency door at the back and spilled out of the vehicle. They hit the Tarmac, piling up on top of each other. Some got up and trampled on the ones who'd got out first. Passengers clogged the bus's aisle. They barged and pushed, trying to make it to the emergency exit. Fanged things swept on to the bus.

Barry thought, *You haven't swiped your Oyster card*.

And that bizarre thought made him scream.

He scrabbled to his feet. The Brazilian woman stopped shrieking. The bleached-haired man who'd killed her glared at Barry, and Barry's legs sagged.

Blood streaked Bleached-hair's pale face. The dark liquid frothed in his mouth. But Barry could see the yellowing fangs.

Bleached-hair's eyes were red-hued and cruel, and they seemed deep set in his bony face. His eyelids were smeared with black make-up.

He crawled towards Barry, hissing as he came. Barry staggered backwards. A passenger booted Bleached-hair in the chest, and he jerked.

But the kick didn't disable him.

He snarled at his attacker, and leapt at him. Bleached-hair sank his fangs into the man's neck and thrashed his head from side to side, and the man screamed and blood sprayed from his shredded throat.

Barry felt cold, and he couldn't move.

But when Bleached-hair, his face dripping blood, turned on him again, Barry found the will to get the hell out of there.

Screams filled the air around him. He didn't know what was happening. He leapt to his feet and dived through the emergency door.

His bones rattled as he hit the road, and for a moment he thought he'd lie there and wait for one of those creatures to finish him off.

But he got on all fours. His gaze darted about the bridge.

Pale-skinned creatures baring their fangs attacked people. Assaults broke out all around him. Screams deafened him.

What the hell's going on? he thought. It's those monsters the papers said were roaming the streets. His next-door neighbour had told him, *Barry, buy a crucifix*; but he'd laughed.

Not laughing now, Barry, he thought.

He scuttled towards the side of the bridge and got to his feet. He had his back to the river and he stared at the carnage on the bridge.

Something grabbed his collar from behind. He went cold. He looked over his shoulder. A moon-white face leered up at him. The woman tugged at Barry's coat. She clung to the bridge, the Thames shimmering beneath her. She showed her teeth and hissed.

Barry felt himself teeter.

He said, "No, no," as she yanked at his coat.

He was going over. A scream filled his throat.

He lost his balance and slipped over the edge of the bridge. The hissing woman chewed into his throat and his bladder emptied. He toppled over, and the woman plunged with him.

And as they fell, entwined, she sucked the blood from his throat.

Barry's insides melted as he plummeted and then the water hit him, cold and hard, and the icy river pulled him and his attacker down and dragged them deep into its guts.

The river gushed into Barry's throat and filled his lungs, and the woman sucked at the streaming vein in his throat.

He thrashed and screamed as Thames water filled him and the blood left him.

★ ★ ★ ★

Aaliyah said, "So you slept with her, yeah? You got drunk and you slept with her."

J.T. shrugged and said, "It was nothing, man. Just some bitch, that's all. You're my woman, girl, you're my – "

She slapped him across the face. He staggered away down the platform. Passengers waiting for the Northern Line looked away. Aaliyah went after him, threw a kick. Her dress flitted up, showing off her smooth, brown thighs and a guy on the other side of the platform wolf-whistled and then said, "Come over here, bitch, and I'll give you pleasure if you're man's giving you pain."

Fury boiled in her and she wheeled round, glaring at the man. She spat out a volley of curses and abuse. He gave her the finger, called her a whore, and strutted off down the platform.

"You fucking bitch," said J.T., swaggering towards her. His cheek was red where she'd hit him.

"We're done, J.T.," she said, "over and done."

"We're not over till I say we's over."

Aaliyah felt a little twist in her guts, her anger sapping as fear took hold. J.T. had laid hands on her before, and it wasn't a good thing. She'd not been able to go to work for days, till the bruising faded. She backed away from him, saying, "You're on CCTV, J.T.; don't go hitting me."

"I don't give a shit, bitch. You never fucking beat on me, yeah? You never beat on me. You never put a hand on me 'less it's to worship my dick, yeah?"

Aaliyah's gaze darted around the other passengers. Leicester Square tube station was busy, but no one seemed to want to help her. She backed up, towards the end of the platform. A rush of cold wind brushed her legs from the tunnel.

Bastards, she thought; *cowards* – everyone turning their backs, walking the other way like they all did apart from the Samaritan in the Bible story Mum used to tell her when she was little.

Always help other people, Aaliyah, Mum would say. But Aaliyah grew up and found that helping people didn't get her the things she wanted. She found that helping herself seemed to work better, and that got her J.T. and all the other guys before J.T., with their bling and their labels and their cars.

"Get away from me, J.T," she said.

"I ain't getting away from you, ever, bitch," and he was closing in on her and she moved back towards the tunnel.

"You having trouble, chicken?"

She looked across the platform. Three black guys stood there. They wore suits, but they looked bedraggled. Their faces were ashen and their eyes were dark red.

J.T. looked across the platform at them and said, "Fuck you, blowjob, you stay the fuck out of it, nigger."

The black guy glared at J.T. and J.T halted. The black guy said, "Why are you using the American vulgarity with me, son? Are you American?"

"No, I fucking ain't. Keep the fuck out of my business with my woman."

"Your woman doesn't seem very happy."

Aaliyah saw that J.T. was jittery. She turned to the guys and said, "Leave it, okay, I'm all right."

"You don't look all right to me, honey," said the man.

J.T. said, "Don't you fucking 'honey' my woman, you fuck," and he pulled out his gun and screams swept through the tube station and passengers cowered and hit the floor.

But the three guys over on the other side just stood and stared at J.T.

Aaliyah said, "J.T., put the gun away, babe. Put it away, please." She glanced up at the CCTV camera. It fixed on J.T.

He started firing.

Aaliyah threw her hands over her ears.

The three guys leaped across the line.

Aaliyah held her breath as they hung in the air.

The train blared its horn. It whipped out of the tunnel. The trio jumped over it. The brakes screeched.

J.T.'s gun barked. The bullets whacked into the flying men, but there was no blood, no damage.

Aaliyah squatted and screamed.

The train shrieked to a halt.

Two of the guys plunged down on J.T. and he thrashed about, cursing, punching. But they held him down and clawed at his throat with their hands.

The other man, the one who'd spoken to them and called her "honey", loomed over Aaliyah.

She looked up at him. His eyes were brown with a red shade to them, like rust. She stared at them, not able to look away.

Screams filled the platform. Passengers rushed off the train and up the stairs. Underground staff hared down to the platform to see what was going on.

J.T. yelped and kicked as the men put their mouths over the wounds in his throat.

The suited man leered at Aaliyah. He had fangs. His tongue flicked over his lips. "Now then, honey," he said, and moved towards her.

Aaliyah screamed.

CHAPTER 47.
INSTINCT.

"YOU'RE dead," said Lawton.

"Sort of," said Jenna.

He watched her glide into the flat, the door shutting behind her. He felt dizzy and confused. He wasn't sure if this was a dream. It must be, he thought; must be dreaming. And he said, "Are you real?"

She faced him, grabbed his wrist and put his hand on her breast.

"How's that for real?" she said.

Her breast was firm and warm under her white shirt. The shirt was stained brown, streaks of dried blood whipping across the frilly neckline. Passion stirred in Lawton's belly. He looked at her eyes. Blood seemed to have seeped into their natural colour. His insides twisted: Jenna's eyes were like the eyes of the things they'd killed at the house.

Red eyes, he thought.

Skarlet's poison.

He yanked his hand away.

"What's happened to you?" he said. "All of you who died that night?"

"We're part of a brave new world, Jake."

She turned and moved into the flat. She brushed her hand over the table in the living room.

"Still not used to Mr. Sheen, then," she said.

She threw herself on the couch and leered at him.

"Don't you find me alluring, Jake?" she said.

He did, but he didn't know why. She should sicken him. Her deathliness, the hint of decay when she swished past him.

But he found her far more desirable than he'd ever done before. His heart raced and sweat broke on his goosepimpled skin. There was something – he shook his head – vile about her that drew him in; something abominable and delicious.

It twisted his mind.

He said, "Have you been on drugs?"

"No, just the drugs that" – she hesitated – "killed me. The pill Fraser gave me in the hope that I'd do him again."

Jealousy flared in Lawton's chest. He stayed standing. He kept alert. He didn't trust her.

He said, "Killed you? So you're dead."

She shrugged. "Ish, I guess. But do I look dead to you, baby?"

She did – pale and drawn.

"I killed things like you at the house," he said.

"Don't worry," said Jenna. "There's plenty more where they came from. And after tonight there'll be more still."

"What do you mean?"

"I mean were breeding, Jake. We're making more like us. It's weird. I know who you are, who my parents are, I still know who I am. But I feel nothing – no love, no hate, no" – she shook her head – "no emotion at all. I feel nothing. Only instinct."

"Instinct. What instinct?"

She grinned at him and licked her lips. "To feed. Nothing else. You don't need anything else. It's better than sex ever was, even with you."

She stood up, almost floating off the couch.

Lawton stepped back and braced himself.

She sashayed towards him. "Although you were pretty good, if I remember."

He took another step back.

She came to him and looked up at him and laid a hand on his arm. Her skin felt clammy. He could smell a hint of roses through the odour of decay coming off her.

She squeezed his bicep. "You're so muscley, so hunky," she said.

He said, "What do you want?"

She looked him in the eye and he knew she wasn't a living thing then.

She said, "I want to feed."

"I got some ready meals in the fridge."

She hissed, showing her fangs. He'd seen fangs like this before.

Lawton said, "Nice teeth."

"All the better to bite you with." She sniffed deeply. "I can smell your blood, Jake. I can smell it pulsing through your veins. I can hear it throb through you. Do you know what blood smells like in the vein?"

Lawton steeled himself. "I've no idea."

"Like heaven."

"That's not a very practical description since we've not really experienced heaven."

"Big thoughts there for a soldier boy," said Jenna. "Spending too much time with that clever little blonde."

He shoved her away. She hissed at him.

"I saw you," she said, "saw you at the house, killing Tim and Heiko, I saw you and could've killed you."

"Get out, Jenna."

The anger left her face. She looked sad and his heart softened. "Don't send me out there, Jake."

"I thought you liked it. Go feed," he said.

But Jenna said, "I don't want to. I want to stay with you." She moved to him again. "I want you to feed me. I want you and me to live forever, Jake."

CHAPTER 48.
DOMESTIC.

"AND you come home late, stinking of testosterone and fags and – and filth," said Richard, waving the beer bottle around like a baton.

"While you stink of beer and self-loathing," she said. "Where are the boys?"

"Where do you think they are, Chrissie? At" – he squinted at his watch – "ten-thirty at night. Huh? Ten and twelve year olds. I tell you, it's a fucking – "

"Don't curse – "

" – surprise that they're in bed."

Murray threw off her coat and sat on the sofa. He was slumped in the armchair, a six-pack of Stella Artois already down to a two-pack.

She said, "What are you talking about?"

"You have no idea about your own kids, do you." Richard's face was red and puffy, and the skin glistened with sweat.

"What are you talking about, Richard?"

"These lads, these boys that I have to care for on my own, these boys are going off the rails."

"Off the rails?"

"Michael, in particular, is disruptive at school."

"I didn't know – "

He sat up. "Of course you didn't know, you stupid cow, you're never here."

Murray winced.

She said, "W-what kind of disruption?"

"Bullying – "

A chill leached through her. "Bullying?"

"Abusive towards his teachers. His work in decline."

"What about David?"

"Learns by example. Worships his older brother. Out with him till all hours – "

"Richard, why do you let them stay out?"

"Why do I let them?"

Murray said, "You're drinking. You're drunk, that's why. You get drunk and let them run riot."

He said, "I'm here, on my own, looking after two adolescent boys. While you're – "

She let a silence fall between them. Richard slumped back in the chair. Spit oozed from between his lips.

She said, "This is what we agreed. That I'm making the better money, so you would look after the boys at home. This is what we agreed."

Richard said, "I gave up my career for yours."

"This is what we agreed. You agreed. You said, 'I'll do some work at home, write my novel.' Those were your words, Richard."

He shrugged drunkenly, almost falling from the chair. "It's not working, I'm not happy. I want to renegotiate."

"Renegotiate? Don't use long words when you're pissed."

"I didn't think you'd be away for so long – these hours you're working, Chrissie – "

"I'm working to bring home a good wage, Richard. I work these long hours because I get paid for my time. I get paid for the stories I find. And with what's going on in London today, do you expect me to sit back and let other reporters get all the good angles?"

He didn't respond, just stared at the television that was silently showing Michael Caine in Zulu.

She said, "I thought you were going to support me. This is what we'd agreed. You support me for five years, see where I can get to."

"You put ambition over your kids' well-being – "

She leaped to her feet, anger searing her breast. "How dare you, how dare you!"

He flinched, but Murray went on:

"We sat at the kitchen table two years ago," she said, "and discussed this. I asked you and asked you, Are you sure? Are you certain this will work? And you said that it was okay. 'You go ahead,' you said. 'I'll write my novel when they're at school,' you said. How dare you, Richard."

He stared at the television. Wave after wave of Zulu attacked Roarke's Drift.

"Are you listening to me, or sulking again?" she said.

"I don't want to talk about it, now."

"Good, neither do I," and she stomped out of the living room. She went into the kitchen, sat at the table and started to cry.

Her phone rang and she reached into her trouser pocket. The words PRIVATE NUMBER flashed on the screen.

She furrowed her brow and answered.

The male voice said, "Sorry to call so late, Christine, it's Phil Birch."

She pulled herself together and said, "Mr. Birch, what a delight."

"I'm sure," he said. There was a lot of noise in the background.

"What's all that shouting?" she said.

"Have you seen the news?"

Hot, sour liquid came up from her stomach; she retched. She looked at the radio perched on the fridge and though about switching it on. She told Birch she hadn't seen the news.

"Well," he said, "London's gone to hell, that's what's happened. And — I'm not happy about this — but Commander Deere thought, perhaps, a reporter, embedded as it were, with the police, might help our communication with the outside world."

"Embedded?" she said. "That's very — war-like."

"It's a pretty war-like situation, Christine." He sniffed. "I want to make it clear I'm not happy about it."

"You said."

"But I've little choice."

"Good."

"So if you're not doing anything, I can send a car to pick you up within the hour."

She said, "I can make my own way."

Birch said, "I'm telling you that's not a good idea. You're chances of making it are slim."

CHAPTER 49.
ALL HELL.

LITHGOW barged through the crowd. His heart raced and adrenalin flushed his system. Screams and shouts filled the nightclub.

Management had just switched on the lights, and the clubbers were surging towards the exits. Doormen tried to hold back the tide.

Trapped in a sea of bodies, he looked over his shoulder.

One of the vampires hurled itself from the balcony and crash-landed into a cluster of bodies. The clubbers screamed and scattered. The creature pounced on a fallen girl and sank its teeth into her neck. She screeched and thrashed. A man – her boyfriend, perhaps – started pummelling the creature around the head, but it wouldn't budge.

Like a fucking pit bull, thought Lithgow. He'd seen those dogs fight, once. Wouldn't let go once they got their teeth into something.

A doorman, tank-solid, tussled with another vampire. The doorman tried to keep the thing away from his neck, holding it at bay with his strong arms. But another creature leapt on he doorman's back and bit his throat. The first vampire bypassed the strong arms and buried its teeth under the doorman's chin.

Got to get out, thought Lithgow.

He'd only come here to get blinded after the crazy day he'd had. He didn't want to think about what he'd seen last night in Holland Park, what he'd learned today.

But fifteen minutes ago, before he'd even downed a couple of pints, it all kicked off. A scuffle broke out at the door. Bouncers were strewn around the entrance as six vampires invaded the club. They'd started attacking clubbers right from the off – no subtlety about these creatures: *they want blood*, thought Lithgow, and they were getting blood.

Fights broke out. Lads tried to batter the vampires away, not realizing what they were, what little chance they had of surviving.

Lithgow felt hot and sweaty, pressed in this surge of bodies. Screams filled the club.

How the fuck had this happened?

It was all his fault; his greed.

He started to sob, his rage growing.

He pushed against the bodies in front of him, forcing his thin frame through the gaps in the crowd.

There were shrieks behind him. The crowd pressed forward.

The vampires must be herding us forward, picking off the ones at the back, he thought.

Lithgow looked again, craning his neck to see over the wave of bodies washing towards the exit.

Some lads had gathered into groups and were attacking the creatures. A gang had one surrounded, and they were giving it a kicking. It rolled around and hissed as the boots smacked into its body.

The vampire got on all fours, his muscles corded. He jumped, clearing the circle of attackers. They watched it shoot out of their midst like a rocket. It landed a few yards away, and they charged at it again. But this time it was ready and it threw itself at the group, knocking the lads over. The youths were dazed. The vampire attacked one of them, tearing out his throat. Blood fountained from the wound. It attacked another youth, butchering him, blood spouting from the shredded throat. Another vampire joined in the attack, pouncing on a fallen youth, holding him down and – instead of tearing out the lad's throat – sunk its teeth into his neck, sucking the blood from him.

They're killing some and feeding off others, thought Lithgow. He wondered how you became a vampire. Did you have to have your blood sucked out, or would those who were just killed, murdered, change too.

He didn't know.

Maybe that woman Lawton had been talking to knew something.

Lawton, he thought; *the bastard*.

The man he hated most, the only one he could trust. The only one who'd believe him. He had to get to him.

Ten minutes later, Lithgow finally succeeded to tumbling out of the club. Fresh air flooded his lungs and made him dizzy. He got himself together. Horns blared and screams saturated the air. Traffic gridlocked Charterhouse Street. Sirens wailed, and helicopters swooped above the streets.

Lithgow thought, *It's like the end of the world.*

CHAPTER 50.
BEGGING FOR BLOOD.

JENNA said, "If I don't have blood, I'll die. I'll die in three days, Jake. I'll wither away, turn to dust. I have to have it, Jake."

He said, "What d'you want me to do about it?"

She tilted her head. "You always helped me out, Jake. Always looked after me."

"That was before you died and got up again."

"It's still me, though," she said.

"It's not, is it. You've said it's not. You said you feel nothing." He looked into her bloodied eyes, and they chilled his bones. What was he doing talking to this creature that used to be Jenna McCall?

She squinted and said, "I still remember, you know."

"You're lying."

She moved towards him.

"Stay where you are," he said. "I know how to kill you."

She opened her mouth in a gasp and he saw her fangs. She said, "Jake, that's a terrible thing to say."

Lawton stared at her. What should he do? Kill her, making it one less of these things, or let her go and hope he'd never come across her again?

He thought about the future.

What would happen with these creatures roaming the streets?

He hoped the authorities had a grasp on things, but knowing the authorities like he did, they probably didn't.

Beaureucrats, red tape, "computer-says-no" – that's what it was like.

"I want you to leave," he said.

"I'm starving," she said, clawing at her belly, "You can't imagine what it feels like. It's like cold turkey but a million times worse."

"I wouldn't know. Just deal with it. It'll pass."

Jenna frowned and said, "Yeah, when I wither away, a dried up old hag."

He thought about that and guessed it would be better that she did die.

"Okay, then," she said, shrugging, "I'll go get blood elsewhere. I wouldn't kill you, you see. Just take enough. And it wouldn't do you any harm, as long as I didn't take it all. I mean, a forty per cent blood loss will probably kill someone, but I'd only take about half that – just a little to keep me going. You'd only suffer tachycardia. Rapid heartbeat. Your blood pressure'd be normal, and you'd be right as rain in a couple of days."

Lawton raised an eyebrow and said, "Your two years at medical school came in handy then. Bet your dad'd be proud. That he'd not wasted all that money on your education."

She hissed. "Fuck him and my family. I'll fucking kill them next. But won't bother with their blood. Rip their fucking throats out."

Lawton steeled himself, ready for an attack. But Jenna appeared to relax. The lines around her eyes and on her brow disappeared and her skin smoothed out again.

"Fine," she said, "I'll leave. I'll find myself an innocent victim, drink all their blood, make another one like me." She shrugged. "That's all I can do if you're not willing to help me, Jake."

His throat dried out. "Why don't you take a little, let them live? Like you were going to do with me?"

Jenna said, "Can't do that. Only do that for you. Something in me still beats for you, honey." She reached out and brushed his arm. Her touch sent a shiver through him. She said, "And that's my offer – you live, but they, well, they become undead." She looked at him, her tongue flickering over her lips, back and forth. "So what are you going to do, Jake? Let me take my fill, or send me out there to make more of me."

CHAPTER 51.
EMBEDDED.

PHIL Birch, shouting over the helicopter's rotor blades, said, "The city's going wild. There's death everywhere."

Leicester Square had been cordoned off. Yellow police tape bordered the area from Charing Cross Road to Whitcomb Street. Police cars and emergency vehicles sat at each end of the roadblock, their sirens flashing blue. Paramedics attended to the injured and the dead. Units of armed police patrolled the area. Helicopters, like the one deafening Murray right now, wheeled over London, casting their spotlights over the streets.

She scribbled in her notebook and thought of Lithgow's description of the killers: Vampires. Vampires? No – never. That's nonsense; superstitious nonsense.

"People are getting their throats ripped out, they're being drained of blood," said Birch, his voice matter-of-fact. "And I've got something else I'm supposed to show you." He sighed, didn't show much enthusiasm. Deere had foisted her on to Birch, and the detective made an effort not to hide his irritation.

"Since you seem to know what's happening before we do," Birch had told her with a sneer when she arrived, "your friend Commander Deere thought you might as well be centre stage. You pissed him off at that press conference this morning, I'm telling you. Pissed him off so much he wants you in his pocket. I'd have locked you in a cell till this was over if it was me."

He led her to a white van. They got in the back. Three techies stared at banks of screens. Wires dangled everywhere, like vines in some electronic forest.

One of the techies rolled two chairs over, and Murray and Birch sat.

"What are we looking at?" she said.

Birch said, "Michelle, run the Northern Line tape."

The techie reached over and flicked a switch, pointing Murray to a blank screen that flickered to life. A CCTV image showed a Tube platform.

"This is from a couple of hours ago," said Birch.

It showed a black guy firing his gun across the platform. A girl, tall and attractive in a wisp of a dress, shouted silently at him. A train burst out of the tunnel. Three figures appeared from the top of the screen. Murray gasped.

"Yeah," said Birch, "they leaped across the platform, over the bloody train, would you believe it."

Two of the men attacked the gunman, pinning him to the floor.

"They rip out his throat here," said Birch.

"Thanks for the commentary, Detective Superintendent Birch," said Murray.

Birch muttered. On the CCTV footage, the third man cornered the girl. He closed in on her and she cowered. The other two seemed to be nuzzling the gunman's neck. The man pounced on the girl, swept her over his shoulders, and bounded into the tunnel. The other two raised their heads. The faces were covered in blood. They dived off the platform and into the tunnel. The gunman's body twitched on the platform. Blood spouted from his ravaged throat. Someone rushed up to him, kneeling next to him, and waved for help.

The techie switched off the tape and Murray asked what on earth she'd seen.

"Those three attackers were" said Birch, checking his clipboard, "Adam N'Tenga, Daniel Fisherman, and Horace Whatling. Brokers in the City."

"Have you caught them?"

"No, we haven't."

"How did you manage to I.D. them so quickly?"

"We had them already, Christine."

She scowled at him. "What d'you mean?"

"They were three of the victims killed the night after the Religion incident – with the blood drained from their bodies."

CHAPTER 52.
DEATH'S KISS.

LAWTON shoved her away, and she hissed. Blood stained her lips. He put his hand to his throat, and the wound smarted.

"You taste good, Jake," she said. She licked her lips, washing the thick fluid into her mouth. She swallowed, half-closing her eyes.

Nausea swept over him, and the room floated in front of his eyes. He reached out his hand and steadied himself against the wall.

"Get out," he said.

"You saved a life tonight."

"Get out before I kill you, Jenna."

"I don't think you can," she said.

"Don't tempt me."

She glided past him and he smelled blood on her breath. He closed his eyes and what they had done played out in his mind:

She'd walked up to him and sank her fangs into his throat. He'd flinched at the pain, but she held him. Her breasts pressed against him. She stroked his body. He could hear the pulse of his blood. It throbbed in his head as it streamed out of his vein and coursed into Jenna's mouth.

Jenna opened the door. She said, "I'll see you again."

"No you won't."

"You will, Jake. Every time you give me blood, you'll be saving a life, you'll be keeping another human from joining us. You save one life, you save many, yeah?"

She shut the door, and he listened to her race down stairs and out of the front door.

He straightened, but his legs trembled. He staggered through to the kitchen, and threw up in the sink. He poured himself some water and drank.

His phone rang. It was in the living room and he listened to it, thinking he wouldn't be able to get to it without tripping. It stopped ringing, and he tottered back to the living room. He slumped onto the couch.

I should've killed her, he thought; *turned her into dust like we did those things at the house.*

The phone rang again. He picked it up and said, "What?"

"Jake, Jake, It's me, Fraser."

"What the fuck do you want?"

"Let me in, man, I'm downstairs. It's a fucking nightmare out here. It's like hell."

★ ★ ★ ★

Lithgow said, "You let her drink your blood?"

"Yes, Fraser, I did."

"You're mad," said Lithgow, hands on his head, pacing the flat, "you'll turn into – her, one of them."

"I don't know, I don't think so. I think you need all your blood drained for that."

"Oh, right, so you're a fucking expert on vampires, now, are you?"

"I'd say I was pretty up to date, wouldn't you?"

Lawton drank sweetened tea, trying to get his energy back up. Lithgow told him what had happened in the club and what he'd seen in the streets. But Lawton felt too weak to do anything. He wanted to sleep, that's all; sleep and wake up to a world that had righted itself.

Let others sort this one out, he thought.

Lithgow said, "You look really pale, man. Really sick. If you're a vampire by tomorrow morning, I'm – I'm – "

"You're what, Fraser?"

"I'm running away."

"Yes, I'm sure you will."

Lithgow plonked himself down in the armchair. "This is mad, man. What's going to happen? How are they going to kill them all? Every time they bite someone they – "

"Drink their blood."

"Yeah, whatever – but when they bite someone, that someone then becomes a vampire – just like the films, man. Oh, crazy, crazy."

"And who's to blame for all this?" said Lawton, scowling at Lithgow.

Lithgow looked at him and frowned.

"Who's to blame?" said Lawton.

"Not me."

"Yes, you."

"I didn't make those pills," said Lithgow.

"You handed them out. Made money doing it." Lawton coughed, and his head went spinning.

Lithgow said, "You told Murray I wasn't to blame."

Lawton sighed. "Yeah, well, that was me being soft in the head."

Lithgow leaned forward. "What are we going to do, man?"

"What I'm going to do is sleep" – he got up, and his legs buckled – "and get my strength back. What you do, Fraser, is up to you."

"I can't go back out there, don't send me back out there."

Lawton's shoulders sagged. "I won't do that. Kip here. Sofa's all right. Tomorrow will be better."

CHAPTER 53.
COUNTING THE COST.

MURRAY tolled up the night's carnage: Fifty-seven people dead, eighty injured, and at least twelve unaccounted for, according to the BBC website. She had the Sunday papers spread out on the kitchen table, but they'd yet to catch up with "Savage Saturday", as MailOnline, the *Daily Mail's* website, described it – newspaper deadlines were an archaic burden in the world of 24-hour news.

She sipped her coffee and stared at the laptop's screen. She scrolled down, reading the story. There were quotes from witnesses describing terrifying attacks all over London. She read about "carnage on Blackfriars Bridge" as "vampires" attacked a bus. She clicked on a link to a story about London's religious leaders calling for prayer. She read quotes from Jacqueline Burrows insisting that the police and the government were in control on the situation.

"Mum?" said the voice.

She looked up. "David. You-you startled me."

"Sorry," he said, standing in the kitchen door in his Arsenal pyjamas.

"Hello," she said, and felt herself flush, not able to find any other words.

He nodded, stayed in the door.

"Come in, let me make you breakfast," said Murray. She stood, going to the cupboard to get cereal.

He shuffled into the kitchen and said, "I-I don't have breakfast."

Murray said, "You don't have breakfast?"

"No, Mum, I don't."

"Why, David?"

"Because. Because I don't."

She sat down opposite him, shut the laptop. She said, "Doesn't Dad make you breakfast on school days?"

"He used to, but I don't eat breakfast. I'm not hungry in the morning."

"You're up very early today. Why's that?"

He played with his hands and said, "Couldn't sleep."

Murray touched his hair. "Are you all right?"

"Don't know?"

"Tell me, David."

He looked at her and his eyes were wet, and Murray felt a jolt of grief in her breast. She bit her lip, fighting the urge to weep.

David said, "It's just crap, isn't it."

"Crap? What do you mean by that?"

"Our teacher died – Mr. Gless – "

"That's terrible," she said, "I'm so sorry."

"And everyone else, they're dying too."

"There have been a lot of deaths, but it'll soon get back to normal."

He said, "Kids at school say it's, like, the end of the world. They say it's – it's vampires."

Murray shuddered and said, "No – No, David, don't – don't listen," and she held his hands. They were small and cold, and she squeezed them and closed her eyes.

"B-but everyone's saying it, Mum. The papers, too. And you work for the papers," he said.

"Papers, they only ask questions, David. They ask questions, that's all."

"And the internet, too – all my Facebook – "

"Facebook?" she said. "You're on Facebook?"

He frowned. "Yeah. All my mates are on Facebook."

Murray felt herself grow cold. She said, "You're – you're too young, David, you should be eighteen."

212

"I'm not a kid, I'm not too young," he said, yanking his hands away from hers. "Michael's on there – "

"Michael's too young – does your dad know?"

David shrugged. "I don't know."

"You shouldn't be on those pages, not yet."

"Everyone else is," he said.

"Well, I'm telling you – "

"Why are you telling me anything?" he said, standing up. "You're never here, I never see you for anything," and he stormed out of the kitchen, Murray calling after him and feeling him being torn from her breast.

★ ★ ★ ★

Lawton's phone rang. He crawled out of bed and rifled through the clothes he'd cast off last night before he collapsed. His throat was dry and he felt weak. He found the phone in a shirt pocket and answered it.

"Hi, Jake, it's Sassie," she said.

"Hi, Sassie, you okay?"

"Yeah, yeah, I'm okay. You?"

"First class," he said.

Silence fell. And then he broke it:

"Sassie, what Crane said yesterday, that needs explaining."

"All right. Although you don't need to explain. I mean, you're not answerable to me or anything."

Lawton noticed he was naked, and slapped a cushion over his crotch – it didn't feel right talking to her with his balls out.

Sassie said, "Did you hear what happened last night?"

He said he hadn't, and she told him. "How many died?" said Lawton.

"TV says many dozens."

"Many dozens."

"U-huh. And the say people are missing. Some kids and women, a few old people, too."

The bedroom door burst open and Lithgow stormed in. He flapped a piece of A4 at Lawton. Lawton scowled and waved him away.

"But this is important," said Lithgow.

"Okay – could you hang on, Sassie?"

She said she could and Lawton took the sheet from Lithgow. It was a printout of a BBC News page, a Manchester news item. It was dated six months ago.

"Sassie," said Lawton, "Fraser's just handed me a printout – "

"I did it last night, switched on your computer," said Lithgow, hopping from one foot to the other like an excited schoolboy.

Lawton nodded at him, then continued speaking to Sassie:

"It says that three antique vases were stolen from a flat in Manchester six months ago."

She said, "Really?"

"Yeah, and there's a picture of one of them. It's our vase."

"Really?"

"I found it," said Lithgow. "I dug that out."

Lawton mouthed "yes" at him, then went back to his conversation with Sassie, saying, "What are you doing today?"

She hummed. "Usually I go for Sunday lunch, you know; drink at lunchtime; stroll by the river; lazy days. How does that sound?"

★ ★ ★ ★

"You're not as useless as you look, Fraser," said Lawton.

"I know. Amazing, isn't it, man. I just saw the vase last night. In your cupboard."

Lawton scowled at him, and Lithgow went red.

Lithgow said, "It's okay, man, I was trying to find some mugs. You don't have many mugs."

"Just these two," said Lawton, holding his own up and gesturing at the one Lithgow had.

"Yeah, but no green tea."

Lawton shook his head and sipped his coffee. "Not in this house."

"So, anyway, I saw the vase. Then I switched on your computer, and Googled stuff. Came up with that." He pointed at the A4 sheet like it was treasure he'd discovered. "So did I do all right?"

"Good dog, Fraser. I'm impressed. But you do have a lot of making up to do."

Lithgow frowned. "What d'you mean, man?"

"Those pills, mate. This is why we're in this mess."

Lithgow's face stretched in sadness and his shoulders sagged. Lawton, for the first time, felt sorry for him. He told Lithgow not to worry:

"You didn't kill them, did you. You just made them into vampires."

"You think that's what they are?" said Lithgow.

Lawton thought about it. He thought about Jenna feeding on his blood. He hadn't told Sassie.

Lithgow said, "Hey, I'm glad you're not one, anyway."

"Told you," he said, rubbing his neck.

"Looks like a love bite. With two little pinpricks inside it. Does it hurt?"

"Stings a bit. And I feel weak. Any idea how long it takes for blood to return to its normal levels?"

Lithgow shrugged. "Hey, can I come to Mancs with you? I can do the accent: All right, all right" – he strutted about like a Gallagher brother, imitating them – "I'm 'ard me, I'm 'ard. Come on, then, come on, la'."

Lithgow stared at Lithgow's pantomime and thought about going north. He'd rather spend the time with Sassie, explain to her about Basra. But he had to let Lithgow join the party – he'd done well, finding this stuff.

Lawton said, "As long as you sit in the back and don't make any noise."

CHAPTER 54.
CHICKEN COOP.

SCREAMS echoed around the cavern.

Nadia Radu strutted down the stairs. She sneered at the women and teenagers in the cage.

They whined and cried and shrieked, they rocked back and forth and rattled the bars.

Ion jabbed a cattle prod into the cage. Sparks flew. The one that got singed screeched and stumbled away.

Nadia stood next to Ion and smelled the sweat and the pee wafting from the cage. She cringed and fanned her hand in front of her nose.

A dozen victims were rammed into the cage, dragged here the previous night by vampires out hunting. Their wrists were handcuffed, and when they shivered and rocked, their chains jangled. The miserable figures were blood-stained and sweat-stained, and dust coated their skins and their clothes were torn.

"Would you moan and beg if you were in their position, Ion?" she said.

"No, I'd be trying to think of a way to get out," he said.

"Not pleading like this pathetic lot?"

"They're kids, Nadia – kids and girls," he said.

She glanced at Ion, and her eyes slid up and down his body. Her blood quickened, and the skin at her throat flushed. She stroked her choker, the material leathery. Ion leered at her. She'd taken him into her bed last night, and like always he proved to be her best lover.

She said, "Not feeling sympathy for them, are you?"

"Me? Sympathy? You know that I don't have the capacity for such weak-minded rubbish, Nadia."

She turned to face the prisoners, studying them. They cowered and cried. A crust of teenagers who a few hours earlier had swaggered through the streets now wept for their mothers. A young woman who looked like she was the bitch in her yard yelped in terror. A hen dressed in a veil with an L-plate stuck on her chest sobered up in rapid time.

"You're pathetic," Nadia said to them.

"Please let us go," said the young woman. Her skin was dark and she was beautiful. The woman wore an orange mini-dress. Sweat poured down her face. Dirt streaked her arms. A heel had snapped off one of her silver shoes.

"And what happens if we don't?" said Nadia.

"Please," she said, and then some of the others joined in saying, "Please, please, please," too.

And then the hen said, "What are you going to do to us? Is this all a joke? Did Karin put you up to this? Fucking bridesmaid, I'll fucking kill her. I'm not fucking amused. I'm getting married next Saturday, and my fiancé's got contacts. So if you don't let me go, you'll be in trouble."

"What kind of trouble?"

The hen stuttered and then said, "Just major fucking trouble."

Nadia glanced at Ion, and nodded. Ion stepped forward and jabbed the cattle prod through the bars. Inside the cage, they recoiled and shrieked. He yanked open the door and stepped in, flashing the prod around to keep then at bay. He grabbed the hen by the hair. Her veil crumpled in his hand. She screeched as Ion dragged her out of the cage. As he stepped out of the door, the orange-dress woman and a youth rushed forward. Nadia slammed the door on them.

She pressed her face to the cage and she was nose to nose with Orange-dress, and Nadia saw the will in the woman's eyes.

"Watch," Nadia told Orange-dress.

She turned and strode over to the pit. A crossbar hung over the trench. Ion hauled the hen towards the hole in the ground. She kicked and screamed, and tried to bite him. The manacles around her wrists and ankles made it difficult, but she was fighting for her life. Ion punched her on the jaw, and she sagged in his arms. He laid her on the wooden floor. He belted a leather strap around the hen's ankles. A hook dangled from the leather strap. The hen moaned and started

217

coming to. Ion hoisted her on his shoulder. Her skirt rode up her thighs and Nadia curled her lips at the hen's puckered backside. Ion carried her to the pit and hooked her on the crossbar. She hung upside down, her veil fluttering above her head.

The hen came to and screamed and struggled. Ion picked up a pole and latched it into the belt around the hen's ankles. He slid her across the crossbar so that she hung over the middle of the pit.

The others in the cage moaned and cried. Nadia glanced over her shoulder at them. A half-dozen vampires had circled the cage. The vampires mocked the prisoners. The vampires spat at them, and they clawed at the hands trying to rattle the bars.

Nadia turned her attention to the screeching hen.

Ion stared over at the cage and said, "All of you, watch this – watch your destiny," and his voice echoed through the cavern.

He whipped a knife out of the scabbard fastened to his belt.

He sliced the blade across the hen's throat.

Blood spouted from the wound. The prisoners saw and their screams intensified.

The hen twitched. The blood spewed from her open throat, and splashed down into the dust that coated the pit's floor. Her flowing veil turned scarlet.

The dust sizzled and cooked and sparks flecked from it, and in the sparks Nadia saw life.

★ ★ ★ ★

Aaliyah gawped at the hen, who was swinging like a pig. The blood poured down into the pit.

Aaliyah sobbed, and her insides wrenched. She felt sick and wanted to puke. She was going to die here, in this fucking cave. She'd be sliced open like a pig. Who were these maniacs? Were these things spitting at her from outside the cage really vampires? She'd read stuff on the internet, and J.T. had warned her about them after those goths died in Soho. She thought about J.T. and what happened to him at the station. Was he a vampire, now? He got his throat ripped out, his blood spouting all over the place. Was he going to turn and come looking for her?

Adrenalin flushed her veins. And staring at the butchered bride-to-be, she thought, *If I'm going to die, I'm going to die like a fucking warrior queen, not like some clucking hen.*

The bride-to-be was called Teresa, and she was getting married next weekend – well, not now she wasn't. Aaliyah had asked her name and then said, "We'll be all right, girl," when the hen cried about having to get back to Leeds tomorrow morning to pick up her dress. But it wasn't all right, because seconds later the hen got her throat sliced by that dark-haired bitch.

Aaliyah's gaze skimmed around their surroundings. The cavern was the size of a cathedral. Damp darkened the walls and moss grew out of the rock. The place smelled of decay and methane. Strip-lights illuminated the cave. A ladder crawled up one wall and led up to a manhole cover in the ceiling. Behind Aaliyah, stone stairs led up to a metal door.

The others brought in with her cried and screamed. They tried to struggle, but these weird things that killed J.T. and brought her here kept lunging and baring their fangs.

"They're fucking vampires," said a kid in a baseball cap. There was a bunch of kids, all in hoodies and caps, and they were crybabies, every fucking one.

Aaliyah said to them, "If we don't put up a fight, we're all going to die like that girl, okay. You want to die like her? Or you want to die with guts?"

A hoodie said, "No way. If we do what they tell us, they gonna let us go, innit?"

Aaliyah said, "Yeah? You fucking think so, crybaby? You think they going to say, Hey, you all behaved really cool. Go home and don't say nothing about what you seen, yeah?"

The hoodie cried. The lad in the baseball hat sobbed, too.

Aaliyah said, "You're pathetic. You think you're tough, but you're pathetic."

A middle-aged woman in a grey business suit said, "We should pray."

"Yeah? I been praying all my life and no one's listening, lady," said Aaliyah.

"Jesus will listen," said the woman.

"He ain't listened to you all your life. Why's he going to listen now?"

"Because we are in torment."

"We're in shit, not in torment."

The dark-haired man with the scar and the ponytail strode over. He frowned at them. Aaliyah looked past him. Teresa's body had

219

been lowered, and two vampires – that's what they were, no denying – dragged off her carcass. Aaliyah felt sadness for the bride-who'd-never-be and her waiting groom.

But then she thought, *Fuck them, now – it's all about me.*

She steeled herself. She guessed the dark-haired man would grab her next. Terror clutched at her heart, and her bladder felt loose. She wanted to cry and scream.

But there was no way she'd die without a fight.

The others wailed and begged as Scarface approached. He saw Aaliyah stare at him, and he leered at her. She wondered if he was a vampire, too. She couldn't see any fangs in that mouth.

He was sexy, though, and although she'd never dated white guys, she'd fuck him to get out of here.

Her nerves tightened and her muscles tensed. He swung the cage door open and gritted his teeth. He reached out, and grabbed for Aaliyah's hair. But she sprang forward and bit into his hand. She sank her teeth into the soft bit just between the thumb and the forefinger, and the guy yelled.

The dark-haired woman and the vampires raced over.

Aaliyah bit harder, knowing she didn't have much time.

Scarface, spitting and shouting, punched her, and stars exploded in front of her eyes. But her jaw clamped tighter on his hand. She tasted blood, warm and coppery. He hit her again, and pain flared in her head. The vampires grabbed her hair, hissing at her. They pulled her off. Blood spouted from the man's hand. The vampires lapped their tongues at it as it spat from the wound. They threw Aaliyah aside, not interested, going instead for the blood pulsing from the man's injury. He kicked one of them away. He yanked the rag that held his hair in a ponytail and waved it at the vampires. They recoiled. "Get away from me, you dirty cunts," he said, panic making his voice high-pitched.

The dark-haired woman who'd killed Theresa said, "Away, away," and harried the vampires, her fingers around her collar. They scurried off, hissing.

"The bitch bit me," said Scarface.

Aaliyah's vision cleared. The vampires, half-a-dozen of them, lurked a few yards away. They licked their lips. They slavered like dogs waiting for a bone.

The woman said to the man, "Go get that seen to. We don't want your blood all over the place, they'll get a taste for it – go."

He ran off, saying over his shoulder, "That whore, she's going to die slowly and painfully, tell her that."

The woman leaned over Aaliyah and Aaliyah said, "You want some, bitch?"

The woman laughed. "You're feisty."

Aaliyah said, "Yeah? You're fucked," and kicked out.

But the woman dodged the heel. "Hold her down," she said, and the vampires bounded forward.

The creatures pinned her legs and torso down. Aaliyah fought back, but they were too strong for her. They stank of rotting food, and it almost made her throw up.

"Go ahead, fucking kill me, then," she said. "Kill me, you bitch." Tears streamed down her face. She knew she was going to die, and although she wanted to go like an Amazon, here she was weeping like a baby.

"Ion wants to kill you slowly, and when he means slowly, he means *slowly*," said the woman, "he means days of pain like you've never known."

Aaliyah sobbed. "Let him. Bring him on, the fucking gay boy."

The woman smiled. "No, you're far too much fun to be meat and carcass. I have a better idea for you, tigress. Throw her in."

And the vampires hauled her off, her face scratched and bruised, her knees tearing. Her heart raced and blood thundered through her. And she heard the others scream and wail and beg like cowards, and cursed them for being so weak.

CHAPTER 55.
CONFESSIONS.

THEY listened to the news as they headed up the M25 and the news said terror stalked the streets of London.

"They don't half exaggerate," said Lithgow from the back of Sassie's Mini.

The headlines told of death and carnage. Witnesses expressed fear, officials called for calm, analysts spouted bullshit.

Lawton switched off the radio. "I know what it's like; I saw it," he said.

It had been difficult getting out of London. Traffic crawled, and armed police carried out checks on vehicles leaving the city.

But Lawton felt good being out of London, felt as if a weight had been lifted from his shoulders. He glanced across at Sassie, her eyes fixed on the road. He said, "I want to tell you what happened in Basra."

"You don't have to. I've already seen," she said.

Lawton glanced in the rear view mirror and saw Lithgow sleeping.

"I don't want you believing what you hear from people like Crane, from the press."

"Okay," she said.

"I didn't murder an innocent man, Sassie. I didn't kill an unarmed civilian."

"Okay," she said again.

And then Lawton told her.

★ ★ ★ ★

Basra, Iraq – November 2004

TWO men stumbled out of the knackered VW. They had backpacks strapped to their bodies. They made their way through the crowd, towards the Shia mosque. Dust rose up as they strode across the road. Panic spread through the crowd. Kids started to point. Traders started shutting down their stalls.

Lawton ordered the Scimitar to stop. The vehicle jerked to a halt. He leaped out of the tank, Rabbit and Billy Tell backing him up. He told them what he'd seen and they saw what he saw. They moved quickly, the crowd parting, the crowd pointing and shouting towards the backpackers racing towards the mosque.

Lawton licked his lips. His throat felt like sandpaper. He could hear his pulse throbbing in his ears.

Shouts filled the street. People spilled out of buildings. The backpackers screamed as they headed for the mosque. Worshippers scattered.

Lawton shouted at the backpackers.

One of them stopped, turned to face Lawton, Rabbit, and Billy Tell. The backpacker was young, late teens, sweat pouring down the creased skin of his face. He bared his teeth and raced towards the soldiers. The crowd screamed and spread. Lawton said, "Shoot him, Rabbit."

Rabbit fired. The onlookers cowered. Blood sprayed from the backpacker's head. His body flew backwards and hit the ground. Dust coughed up around his body. He was almost sitting up, the backpack preventing him from lying prone.

Lawton, chasing down the other backpacker, told Rabbit and Billy Tell to disengage to get bomb disposal here – now.

The mosque doors swung shut as the other suicide bomber reached them. He turned to face the street. The worshippers ran about, shouting prayers, calling on their god. Lawton, twenty yards away from the backpacker, shouldered his SA80 and said, "Hands in the air, down on your knees," and then he said, *Down, down*, in Arabic.

But the suicide bomber looked up to heaven. He said, "*Allah akbar*" – God is great – and held his arms up to the sky. And then he reached into his pocket.

Lawton told him, *No* – first in English, then in Arabic.

The bomber took out a mobile phone. He held it up. He stared at Lawton and grinned. He said, "Come, English animal, come die and watch me go to Paradise as you go to Hell. Come die."

Lawton stalked him. His throat was dry. The heat was stifling under his body armour. But the armour wouldn't protect him if the bomber triggered his device. The bomb would blow the doors off the mosque, kill Lawton and anyone else hanging around when they should've fucked off.

Lawton, hands sweating on the rifle, kept moving towards the backpacker. The bomber started to pray. He held up the mobile phone. He was waiting for Lawton and Rabbit and Billy Tell to come close enough. The other two Scimitars in the convoy had unloaded, now, and there would be more troops down here any minute.

The bomber was going to take as many infidels with him as he could.

He stopped praying and opened his eyes. He whipped out a pistol from under his flak jacket and shot an old man cowering at a wall. The old man slumped. Screams filled the air. Someone tried to drag the old man's body away.

He's drawing me in, thought Lawton.

Lawton would take him alive if he could.

But these guys weren't scared of dying and weren't soft about killing.

The man aimed at Lawton. Lawton fired. The man screeched and his gun hand exploded – blood and bone. The weapon hit the ground. He still held the mobile phone in his other hand. He went stumbling down an alley and Lawton started after him.

From behind someone said, "Be careful, sarge, cover's coming."

Lawton followed the bomber, and the bomber stumbled, his rucksack heavy on his back. He fell on his backside. Blood pulsed from where his hand should've been. He scuttled backwards, kicking up dust.

A group of children came up the alley. Lawton waved them back, but they kept coming. They pointed at Lawton, knew they'd get sweets, football stickers. The bomber heard them, looked over his shoulder.

He looked back at Lawton and laughed.

The bomber said, "They will go with you, English animal. The apostates."

He raised the mobile phone. He started chanting his prayers.

Lawton said, *No, no, no, put it down, put the fucking thing down.*

The kids raced up the alley, kicking up dust.

The man's thumb hovered over the CALL button. He prayed, a babble flooding out of his mouth. The kids kept coming. The dust blinded Lawton.

The bomber screamed, went to press the CALL button.

Lawton shot him through the head.

CHAPTER 56.
BATTLE LINES.

THEY stopped to fuel up. Lithgow snored in the back seat. Sassie filled the car while Lawton went into the store to pay and stock up on food. He came back with crisps and pasties and chocolate and water.

She fired up the Mini and guided it out of the service area, joining the M1.

Lawton waited for her to say something, but she didn't so he said, "Do you understand why I did it?"

She said, "I don't – agree with the war."

"That's not the point," he said. "Do you understand why I did what I did?"

"I – he – he was fighting for what he thought was right."

"He was going to walk into a mosque and kill innocent people, and then he was going to kill a bunch of kids."

Her face went red and she said, "What? Like the Americans don't do that? And our army? Like they haven't killed innocent people in this war?"

Lawton bristled. He said, "You can't see the difference?"

"Killing's killing."

"Okay," he said, "we blow up a weapons dump that Saddam – that nice man who murdered thousands of his own citizens – built next to a school. The school gets blown up, and ten children die. We didn't target the children, Sassie. And it's not a good thing they died."

"No, it's not."

"That man I killed was going to walk into a mosque and, on purpose, kill innocent people – on purpose, Sassie – " He sighed. The rage faded. There was no way he could win.

If you'd not been in a war, you'd never understand – Lawton knew that. The Major was right when he said that most people don't live in the grey place where soldiers do, that place where right and wrong, good and bad, sometimes doesn't exist.

Lawton was angry with Sassie for being so simplistic. He was angry that she still accused him of killing.

Then she said, "I don't blame you."

"Thank you."

"You're just a tool."

He didn't respond. He let his temper pale. He knew that he'd always be alone in this. Only those who'd been in the same place would understand. Guys like Rabbit, like Billy Tell.

Staring out the window he said, "Sometimes we have to fight, you know. Sometimes we have to go to war."

"I just think fighting's wrong."

He said, "You didn't think that the other night when you drove that piece of wood through that thing's heart."

She said nothing. Lithgow snorted in the back seat. The M1 whipped by.

★ ★ ★ ★

Two hours later at the Norton Canes Service Area on the M6: Lawton drank coffee at Costa; Sassie browsed the magazines at WH Smith; Lithgow sat with his feet up on the table next to Lawton, crunching his way through a packet of boiled sweets.

Lawton got up and walked out of the cafeteria, over to WH Smith. He stood behind Sassie. She was flicking through a copy of Marie Claire. He said, "I've got something to tell you."

Without turning, she said, "Oh yes. How many more people have you killed, then?"

"I've killed plenty, but I'm not apologizing."

She spun round, fire in her eyes. They held each other's gaze for a moment. And then he said, "Jenna came round."

She creased her brow. Lawton realized how strange this matter-of-fact statement sounded: he'd just said that his dead ex-girlfriend dropped by his flat.

Sassie shook her head and her mouth opened and closed. Lawton rubbed his neck and looked away.

He said, "She was – wasn't alive, Sassie. She wasn't her. She was – something else. Like those things in the house."

He told her what Jenna had said about not feeling anything, only hunger, only animal instincts.

He said, "And she said she needed blood. They survive by drinking blood."

Sassie reached up and touched his throat. She tugged down the collar of his shirt. Her skin paled and her eyes widened and in a voice gravelled by fear she said, "No, no."

CHAPTER 57.
OLD SOLDIER.

THE block of flats loomed over the estate. The old man lived on the second floor. Lawton smelled urine as they climbed the stairs. Graffiti plastered the walls. Shouts echoed along the walkways.

"This is lovely," said Sassie, grimacing as she scanned her surroundings.

"Yeah, a country fit for heroes," said Lawton.

She said, "A man his age should not be living in a place like this."

Tom Wilson's granddaughter, Margaret Wilks, let them in. They'd phoned ahead, Lawton saying he was a former King's Regiment man. Tom Wilson's Manchesters had become the King's Regiment in the 1950s.

Margaret Wilks had been reluctant to let them see her grandfather. But Lawton heard the old man shout, *Who's there, Meggie?* and when she explained, the old man said, *A Kingsman, eh.*

"He's very frail. He's almost a hundred-and-six, you know," said Mrs. Wilks, a blonde in her mid-fifties. She led them through the hallway into the living room. The flat was neat and tidy. A television was on but turned down, and the old man sat with headphones on, watching the set. He watched *Saving Private Ryan*, the opening scene depicting the Normandy landings. Lawton knew those twenty-four minutes on screen were about as realistic as film could get in representing what war was like.

Tom Wilson was thin and small, his skin covered in liver spots and wrinkles. But his eyes were wide and sharp, staring at the screen.

Mrs. Wilks went over to him saying, "Granddad," but the old man was fixed on the film.

She lifted the headphones off the old man's head and Lawton heard the gunfire and the shouts spilling out of the television. He felt a pressure in his chest. Those sounds weren't special effects to him. He'd heard them for real, seen their consequences.

Tom Wilson had as well.

The old man's eyes narrowed and they scanned his three visitors and then they settled on Lawton. "You're the Kingsman," said Wilson.

Lawton felt a rush of pride. He went to Wilson and took the veteran's hand, introducing himself as Former Staff Sergeant Jake Lawton, King's Regiment, "proud to meet you, sir".

Wilson gestured for them to sit. Lawton took the armchair next to the old soldier, Lithgow and Sassie huddling on the two-seater settee. Wilson asked his granddaughter for tea, and she went through to the kitchen.

"I read about you," said Wilson, eyes on the film. "I got my great-grand-daughter to look you up on this internet thing – like a library the size of the world. All manner of rubbish in there."

"And did she find me?"

"Yes, she found you." Wilson turned to look at Lawton. "And I don't believe a word of it, son. I know what war's like. Not like those poncey journalists."

"Thank you, sir."

Wilson flapped a hand. "Ah, don't call me, sir. I made sergeant like you did. The name's Tom and I'll call you Jake. Is that right?"

Jake smiled. "Yes, that's right. And those are my friends, Dr. Melissa Rae and Fraser Lithgow."

"I know why you're here. I've seen the news from London, read the papers." He glanced over at a copy of *The Sun* with the headline "HELL" plastered across the front page. "How did you find me?"

Lawton explained about the report of a break-in at the flats. He said they had one of the vases.

Wilson sat up straight and his eyes widened. "You have one?"

Lawton said Lithgow had come across it, and that it was one of three.

The old man clutched his chest. "Margaret, bring my pills."

"Are you all right, Tom?" said Lawton.

"Yes, fine," said Wilson.

Mrs. Wilks came through with a tray containing mugs of tea, a plate of Digestives, and Wilson's pills.

"Are you all right, granddad?" she said, throwing a glance at Lawton.

He swallowed a pill and said he was fine. Mrs. Wilks nodded and distributed the tea and biscuits. Then she went out into the kitchen and switched on the radio. Music wafted into the living room.

Wilson said, "She doesn't like to hear my war stories. Upsets her."

Lawton nodded.

"Well," said the old man, "best I tell you my story, then you can tell me yours."

Lawton said okay and Wilson took a deep breath.

He said, "We were based in Hillah. Were you in Hillah, lad?"

Lawton shook his head. "Americans and Poles in Hillah. I spent all my time in Basra."

"You know that the ruins of Babylon are near Hillah, don't you?" said Wilson.

Lawton looked at Sassie. "Yes, we do."

"And do you know about Nebuchadnezzar? How he built Babylon?"

Sassie came forward, and kneeled next to Lawton's armchair. She put a hand on Lawton's hand. He skin was warm and soft. She told the old man she knew about Nebuchadnezzar. She said, "Nebuchadnezzar's father, Nabopolassar, defeated the Assyrians and Babylon became independent again."

"Clever girl, isn't she?" said Wilson, grinning at Lawton.

Sassie's nails dug into Lawton's hand, and he felt her bristle.

Wilson said, "Nebuchadnezzar, when he became king, ordered the city rebuilt. He built the Ishtar Gate, he built the Hanging Gardens – he made Babylon a golden city again."

The old man faltered, coughing. Lawton stiffened. Wilson held up a hand, indicating that he was fine. He grabbed the remote and switched off the television.

He went on: "But you see, lad," addressing Lawton, "Nebuchadnezzar had help. Story goes that his dad had allies when he defeated the Assyrians. Demonic allies. Nabopolassar unearthed three demons, destroyed, so the legend goes, by Abraham." He shook his head and frowned. "Says nothing about it in the Bible, though. At any rate, Nabopolassar raised up the demons and in return they helped him defeat the Assyrians. And after Nabopolassar's death, the demons helped Nebuchadnezzar rebuild Babylon."

"And these demons were . . . " said Sassie.

"Were vampires, love," said Wilson. "Vampires. Bloodsuckers. Parasites. They were given slaves and criminals to feed on, transforming these victims into a vampire army that helped Nabopolassar, and then Nebuchadnezzar." Wilson shrugged. "So the legend goes."

"And what about the vases?" said Sassie. "They depict – well, we think it's Alexander the Great. And those bodies, they're his enemies."

Wilson said, "This is one legend: when Alexander conquered Babylon, he defeated these monsters, destroyed most of the vampire army, as well. Nebuchadnezzar's descendents, the vampires' human allies, fled."

"And the vases?" Sassie said again, her nails digging into Lawton's flesh.

"Those vases were stolen from me," said Wilson, "but they should never have been stolen. I should have destroyed them, and destroyed what was in them. Just like it said on the lip – that old cuneiform."

"The cuneiform means nothing, Mr. Wilson," said Sassie. "It's praise for heroes, that's all."

Wilson's eyes filled with fire and he said, "Who told you that? That's a lie. Those words are a warning. A warning that if ever Alexander, master of the world, dies, the vessels and their contents should be destroyed. Only Alexander, it says, can prevent the return of the dark magic that raised those monsters. And if any magician gets that power again, the world will be destroyed, the demon trinity will reign over Babylon – or wherever they happen to be; London, maybe."

Sassie's hand tightened on Lawton's.

"What was in them, those old pots?" said Lithgow.

Mr. Wilson looked over at him. "You found them did you?"

"Um, well – yes," said Lithgow. "There were pills in the one I – um – found, and dust – dust in the other two."

"Not dust," said the old man. "Ashes. And I should've got rid of them like my lieutenant said. I should've destroyed them." He sagged, as if the air had been pushed out of him.

"Where did you find them?" said Sassie.

"Find them? Oh, we didn't find them. We stole them. And they were stolen from me, and then" – he nodded at Lithgow – "your friend here stole one of them."

Lithgow said, "I didn't − " but Lawton raised a hand to silence him.

"Where did you steal them, Mr. Wilson?" said Sassie.

"We stole them in Hillah in 1920."

CHAPTER 58.
FINDING THE TREASURE.

HILLAH, MESOPOTAMIA – 11.32 P.M., JULY 23, 1920.

"QUIETLY, now," said Lieutenant Guy Jordan, "let's not make too much of a song and dance of this, Wilson."

They sneaked in through a window. The house was decked in silks and carpets. A smell of incense drifted through the room. It made Private Tom Wilson feel giddy. They'd walked from the garrison and crossed the Euphrates by the bridge made of fifteen boats. Hillah stood on both banks of the river. Date gardens surrounded the town on each shore. The river was about a hundred yards across, and the only way over it was the bridge.

"Keep your eyes open, lad," said Jordan. "We can't trust these bloody Arabs."

Wilson swallowed, but he had no spit. His legs felt drained of strength. He shouldn't be here – he should be back home. *Christ, I'm only seventeen*, he thought. He lied when people asked him: told them he was eighteen. But he felt an idiot for joining up two years ago. Fifteen years old. A kid; a stupid, head-full-of-dreams kid. He'd seen enough mud and blood in the trenches of France to last a lifetime. He'd only lied about his age so he could be with his brother, Bill. And then Bill got killed, and Tom, in a daze of mourning, found himself in Mesopotamia, fighting Arabs.

When they were skulking through the narrow streets under moonlight, Wilson recalled notes issued in May 1919 by the 17ᵗʰ Indian Division on how to fight Arabs:

"Do not get rattled by his unexpected appearance."

Easier said than done, thought Wilson, trying to make some spit to wet his mouth and throat, his gaze skimming the gloom inside the house.

Wilson and Jordan were armed, so any attacks would be seen off. But killing locals wasn't a good idea. They were trying to get on with the population, to win hearts and minds. Killing insurgents was one thing; murdering innocents was asking for trouble – military and diplomatic. If they did get caught here in this house, he'd let Jordan explain their nighttime jaunt through Hillah.

Guy Jordan had arrived in Mesopotamia in March, along with Brigadier-General Aylmer Haldane, who was to lead the Mesopotamian Expeditionary Force.

He'd latched on to Wilson when he saw the youngster reading a copy of *Dracula* by Bram Stoker. Wilson liked those scary stories; he'd always loved ghostly tales as a kid. The copy was tattered by now, but he still dipped into it, enjoying its creepiness.

"You're interested in vampires, Private?" Jordan had asked.

Wilson said he liked scary stories, that was all.

Jordan asked if he'd heard of Babylon. "It's three miles to the south of Hillah," said the lieutenant. "Did you know that, Wilson?"

Wilson shook his head, not understanding why he was being asked.

Jordan had said, "If you like scary stories, son, I've got a scary story for you."

And Jordan told him.

A week later, here they were, breaking into this house in Hillah.

Jordan said, "Careful, now, Wilson."

Wilson gripped his Lee Enfield 0.303 rifle. His eyes were wide, but they weren't getting used to the darkness.

"Sir, do you know what you're looking for?"

"Of course I bloody know," said Jordan.

Jordan crept through the house, and Wilson followed. Wilson looked down, careful not to stand on anything that looked like a body. The Arabs slept on the floor, so it was easy to step on them. Mounds of bodies seemed to fill this room.

"Lord in heaven, here they are," said Jordan, his whisper startling Wilson.

Wilson went up to him. The lieutenant had opened a chest. A musty smell breezed from it, and Wilson wrinkled his nose. Jordan lifted a sack from the chest, laid it on the floor. Wilson could barely see, moonlight the only illumination. He squinted, watching Jordan unwrap the sack. Dust belched from the material. Wilson gasped when he saw what was inside. Three clay pots with a similar painting on each.

And a pair of horns or tusks joined by a shaft.

"The two-horned spear," said Jordan, holding up the weapon by the ends, "made from the bones of a great hunter, the father of demons."

The shaft had been wound in a material that looked like leather.

Jordan gripped the handle and said, "Skin."

Wilson felt dizzy.

Jordan said, "The skin of that same hunter, Wilson," and he grabbed one of the pots, saying, "Look – the same as this image. Didn't I tell you? Alexander the Great."

Wilson saw that the man painted on the vessel held a replica of the weapon that lay on the cloth.

"We must take them," said Jordan, "even if it costs us our lives, one of us must get them back to England."

"Put them back, you dogs," said a voice in Arabic from behind Wilson.

He and Jordan turned. Three figures stood in the dark. A lamp flickered, momentarily revealing their opponents. Jordan laughed. Three boys, two of them were teenagers, perhaps thirteen or fourteen, and the other couldn't have been older than five.

Wilson, using the smattering of Arabic he'd picked up, told the boys to get back and let them leave.

"You'll not leave. We'll die before you leave with those," said the tallest boy.

"Tell him we'll shoot them, Wilson," said Jordan, gathering the artefacts in the cloth. "Tell them we're British soldiers and if they prevent us from carrying out our duties, we'll arrest their parents tomorrow and have them tried and executed."

Wilson didn't say that. He asked the boys if they were brothers and where their parents were.

"Our family is gone. We're all that's left," said the tallest boy.

Wilson translated.

Jordan, after packing up the treasure, stood and pointed his Webley pistol. He had it aimed at the eldest boy. "This is what's left, then?" he said. "All that remains of their human serfs – three children." And he started laughing. He cocked his pistol.

Wilson said, "No, sir, we can't shoot them."

"Why ever not?"

"They're children."

"They are the servants of hell, Wilson."

"We can't."

"I can," said Jordan.

He fired. The boy dived to the side. The middle boy raced forward, a knife in his hand. Wilson raised his rifle and batted the boy aside.

The eldest lad got up, rushed forward. Jordan didn't miss this time. The bullet struck the boy in the chest. The lad stumbled backwards. A dark stain spread across the youth's shirt.

The youngest boy screeched. He sprang forward. He struck Wilson in the arm, and Wilson felt a pain shoot up into his shoulder. Wilson shoved the child aside and glanced down at his arm. A knife jutted out of his flesh. The blade stuck out the other side. He gritted his teeth and moaned, feeling sick.

The middle boy said to the youngest one, "Run, run and commit your life to looking for these dogs," before Jordan put the pistol to his head and fired. The boy's head burst in a halo of blood and brain.

Wilson, dropping to his knees, saw the youngest boy race out of the house.

Lamps flared in nearby houses. Shouts came from outside in Arabic, voices flashing with rage.

Wilson thought, *We're going to die.*

But then he heard English voices shouting, "Put down your weapons. British Army. Put down your weapons."

And Wilson, the pain pulsing through his arm, fainted.

CHAPTER 59.
LOST BOYS.

TOM Wilson rolled up his sleeve. "Little bastard stabbed me," he said, pointing to a scar on his old, brown skin. "Went right through."

"Did they catch him, the boy?" said Lawton.

"No, they didn't. Got lost in the crowd. Disappeared, the scamp."

"You didn't tell your superiors?"

Wilson shook his head. "We were in enough trouble. We were up for punishment, but the next day we were ordered to relieve the town of Kifl."

"What happened to Jordan?" said Lithgow.

"Died that next day, July 24th. On our way to Kifl, we'd stopped off at a canal, the Rustumiyah. About fifteen mile from Hillah. Couple of thousand Arabs attacked us. We were ordered back to Hillah. It was chaos. Arabs picking us off. We lost two hundred men, Jordan among them. I was lucky to get back to Hillah in one piece. A dark time for the Manchesters, lad."

Lawton said, "Were you sent home?"

"No. I were out there for a few more months, had to keep the artefacts hidden in my kit. Then I got injured, got sent back to India."

Sassie said, "Tell us about the robbery, Mr. Wilson."

He shrugged. "I'd gone out. Very lucky."

"Yes, you were. It would've been terrible for you," said Sassie.

"No, love," said Wilson, "for them. Lucky for them. I'd've got my old Webley pistol out, shot the bastard between the eyes." He pantomimed a gun with his finger, and aimed it at Lithgow, who curled his lip. "Don't worry, son – can barely see you from here. I'd probably miss – "

"Oh, good," said Lithgow.

" – and hit you in the balls."

Sassie glanced at Lawton and rolled her eyes. She said, "The burglary, Mr. Wilson."

"Yes. I was down the Legion. I go every Wednesday. Play dominos, have a stout. Meggie comes to get me, brings me home. That night we got back to find the place ransacked."

"They'd taken the pots," said Lawton.

"Aye, lad. The pots." He shook his head and frowned. "I should've destroyed them. Like Jordan said. His last words to me, *Get them home safe, Wilson, and bury them deep – bury them deep.*"

"Why didn't you?" said Sassie.

He shrugged. "We sometime don't do the right thing, do we. I don't know. Life got in the way. Came home, first time in years. Put them in the attic at my Ma's place, forgot about them. Thought nothing. Then I got wed, they followed me around. Ended up here twenty years ago when my wife died. Then the lassie, my great great granddaughter, she put them on the internet thing – this eBay, she called it. I'd forgotten. They'd slipped my mind – slipped to the *back* of my mind, let's say. Then she goes, 'Gramps, I've put some of your old stuff on eBay; Mum said I could,' and I says, 'That's fine, love,' and, well, here we are."

"That's how they found them," said Lawton.

"Oh, aye – that's how they found them?" He looked at Lawton. "You know who 'they' is? They're the descendents of Nebuchadnezzar. Those vases contain the ashes of the demon trinity."

Lawton clicked his fingers at Lithgow. Lithgow jerked, opened up his rucksack. He took out the Tesco bag, handed it to Lawton.

Lawton unwrapped the plastic bag, showed Wilson the vase.

Lawton said, "Brought it back."

Wilson sneered. "Anything in it?"

"Nothing."

"Means they've got the ashes out. Means they're trying to resurrect their demons," said the old man. He glanced over his shoulder, and called towards the kitchen: "Another cup of tea in here, Meggie – and bring the bottle, love."

★ ★ ★ ★

Murray said, "Where are the boys?"

"Out, Chrissie," said Richard, "out doing what boys do."

Murray felt a chill seep through her insides.

"Richard," she said, "it's almost five o'clock, they should be inside. It'll be dark soon."

He chuckled and drank from the can of Stella. He'd not turned to acknowledge his wife, just continued to stare at the Sky Sports channel.

He said, "You don't buy into this 'don't be out after dark' nonsense, do you?"

"Richard, I do buy into it. Dozens are dead. There are people missing. There are *children* missing."

His eyes stayed on the TV. A blonde girl talked about football. Murray grabbed the remote and switched off the television.

Richard Murray glared at his wife. "Don't do that," he said.

She saw fury in his eyes; she'd never seen fury there before – only boredom.

He reached for the remote and she yanked her hand away. "Not until you tell me where my children are."

"*Our* children," he said, "*our* children whom I look after. I don't know where they are. I spend all day wondering where they are and in return all they do is wonder where you are, Chrissie. So where" – he flicked beer at her – "the fuck" – and he did it again, flipping the can till it shot booze in her face – "are you?"

"Richard – you idiot." She wiped her face. Beer filled her eyes and ran down her cheeks. "You're drunk, you fool. Drunk. And you've let our kids go out there at a time like this."

"Times like what?"

"Don't you know what's happening?"

"Yeah," he said, sneering, "vampires," and he pantomimed ghosts, making hooting noises.

Murray slapped him. He stopped fooling and his mouth dropped open. The colour leached from his cheeks. He cupped his jaw in his hand. She stared at him, and her breast grew cold and tight.

"You bitch," he said. "You hit me."

She thought about apologizing, but swept her regret aside. She said, "Where are the boys?"

"You bitch," he said, staring at the floor.

"Tell me, Richard, tell me where they are or – or I'll have you arrested for abandoning them."

He stabbed a look at her. "Me abandon them?"

Her blood quickened. "Where the fuck are they!" she said.

He froze. Probably because he'd never heard her swear like that before. She thought she'd faint, and urged him again to tell her where Michael and David could be.

"The park," he said, "they always congregate at the park – kids, teenagers."

She said nothing. She turned and stormed out of the house.

CHAPTER 60.
ANCIENT WEAPON.

TOM Wilson held out his glass and Lawton poured whiskey into it. Lawton smelled the liquor's sharpness. He could imagine its taste.

The old man, nodding to indicate his glass was full enough, said, "Time for drinking's arrived, lad. Nothing else we can do, now. Drink and pray, if the black magic Alexander warned about has been rediscovered."

"So these demons," said Lawton.

"Yes: Kea, Kakash, and Kasdeja – incubus, vampires. Not quite dead but not alive, either. Feed on blood. Hunt at night."

"Kea," said Lithgow, "Kea and Kakash and – and the other one. 'K' on the pills, man, that's what the 'K' stands for on the base of the pot."

Sassie and Lawton glanced at each other. Lawton felt a pressure in his belly. He didn't want to believe this kind of stuff, but what he'd seen made it real.

Wilson said, "They're rebuilding Babylon. Right here in England, in London."

He took another gulp of the whiskey. He put the glass down, pointed a bony finger at it and Lawton poured a drop of booze into the tumbler.

"More than that, son, if you want me to tell you the story. Helps the memory you see," he said, tapping his temple. Lawton filled the glass to half and Wilson nodded, then continued:

"When Nebuchadnezzar became king, he was protected by these

monsters. Nothing could defeat an undead army. Immortal creatures. Nebuchadnezzar provided victims, the trinity provided protection. Babylon grew, became a magnificent city. Powerful, magical, legendary – but maintained by corruption, by rot and decay."

"You brought them to Britain," said Sassie. "In those pots."

Wilson groaned and shook his head. "I know. I know I did, and I curse myself every day and wish I were dead, I really do. But I could't die before someone knew. But who'd believe me? Who'd believe an old soak like me?"

"They might do, now," said Lawton.

"They might," said Wilson. "But who can I trust?"

"Us," said Lawton. "You can trust us."

Wilson sighed. "The weapon we stole, the two-horned spear that can kill these monsters. That's what Alexander used. Every king since Nebuchadnezzar made the same contract with the trinity, you see. Even Darius, who Alexander defeated. These human serfs, they'd hidden this weapon. Darius kept it safe, and all the Babylonian kings before him, right back to Nebuchadnezzar. They kept it away from trinity and they helped those kings rule Babylon. There's a legend says that Abraham made it from the horns of Nimrod the hunter, first king of Babylon and father of vampires. Killed the three demons with it, like I said."

Wilson coughed, took another sip of whiskey.

"But Alexander didn't wipe them out," said Lawton.

"No. And they got their revenge. He died after being bitten by a vampire. Didn't turn him, just poisoned him."

Lithgow gasped. Sassie's grip on Lawton's hand tightened.

Lawton felt a wire slice at his insides. He rubbed his neck. He'd started to feel better in the last few hours, but what if there was poison in his blood? What if some plague lay dormant in him? His mind drifted. He would kill himself before he'd become what Jenna was.

Wilson said, "After Alexander's death, Nebuchadnezzar's descendents – led by Ptolemy, who became Pharaoh of Egypt – fled with this weapon and they also stole the ashes of the vampire trinity, which Alexander had stored in the pots."

Lawton stared at the clay vessel that stood on the coffee table.

"So,' said Sassie, "you're saying – let me get this straight – you're saying that the descendents of Nebuchadnezzar, servant of these demons, are still around in the Twenty-first Century and they stole these – these old pots from your flat."

"That's it, love," said Wilson. "Story goes that a few vampires escaped Alexander's slaughter. A few of Nebuchadnezzar's descendents did. Many went to Egypt with Ptolemy, helped him become Pharaoh. Some, they say, came to Europe – Eastern Europe, Romania, the Balkans – places where vampire legends are rife." The old man shrugged, drank some whiskey. He said, "But I've no idea how the spear and the pots got back to Hillah. My guess is that the descendents thought they could raise the demons, get their help to kick us Brits out." He shook his head and sighed. "Jordan wanted the ashes destroyed, and he was right. He knew that they could never be allowed to survive. He knew they could be used as a lethal weapon if anyone, ever, got down to resurrecting them: imagine a vampire army."

"I'd rather not," said Sassie.

Wilson finished his drink. "But," he said, "the burglars didn't take everything, you see," and he struggled out of his chair. Lawton helped him. "You wait there." He trudged into the kitchen. They heard him chattering to his granddaughter.

Lithgow, pale and wide-eyed, said, "Do you believe all this?"

Lawton said, "I don't know what to believe. What do you think those things we killed in the house were?" He rubbed his neck.

Sassie said, "Are you worried about Alexander dying after being bitten?"

"Do you think I need to be?"

"I don't know."

Then Lithgow said, "It's mad, that's what it is, mad." He came over and checked the whiskey bottle, but Lawton told him to leave it alone. He stomped back to the sofa. Then Lithgow stared towards the kitchen, his jaw dropping. Lawton followed his gaze, turning to see Wilson totter into the living room holding a double-ended spear with points that looked like bulls' horns.

★ ★ ★ ★

"The boy who stabbed me," said Wilson as Lawton held the weapon and studied it, "is still alive, I'm sure of that. He could only be in his nineties," he said as if it were young.

The weapon rested on Lawton's palms. Two horns or tusks, each two feet long, joined by a shaft that was wrapped in… flesh. Lawton's fingers closed around the grip at the centre.

Was this really bone and skin? he thought. What was it Wilson had said?: the bone and skin of Nimrod.

Wilson said, "Nimrod was supposed to have built Babylon. He dug up the dirt of the pit and built the city. I guess those monsters came from the pit, I don't know – ha! – that's just me adding to the myth."

Lawton felt awe. He'd never thought about history like this before. But something so ancient, something that had been in the hands of men thousands of years ago, moved him. He could sense their strength in the weapon, hear their battle cries, see Alexander wield it as he faced Kea, Kakash, and Kasdeja in Nebuchadnezzar's palace almost two thousand five hundred years ago.

Could he wield it now?

"The trinity can only be killed if you stab them in the heart with this," said Wilson. "The heart, that's the only living thing in their bodies. Black and bloated by evil. Sunlight will weaken them; their skins are thin, you see. The others, your common-to-garden vampire, sunlight, ultraviolet light, will do for them. Their flesh is like paper; burn them up, it will. As does any penetration of their black, bloated hearts. But not the trinity. Only this spear will destroy those bastards."

"We've killed a couple," said Sassie.

The old man perked up. "Have you?"

She told him about it and he bounced in his chair. "I wish I'd seen one. All I did was fight off bairns." He shook his head and lowered his gaze. "And now I know I should have destroyed those old clay pots. Thrown out the dust, cast it into water or something – the canal when I got home from the wars. Look what I've done."

He shuddered. Sassie put a hand on his arm. She said, "You're not to blame, Mr. Wilson. You stopped them. They could've released plague back then."

"Well," said Wilson, "I don't think they had the science back then. Today, they know more things, don't they. And these pills you mention. Someone clever made those. I don't think those Haddad boys – "

"Haddad?" said Lithgow.

"That's right," said Wilson, "the boys were three brothers, called Haddad – "

"Haddad," said Lawton.

Wilson said, "Name's obviously familiar to you."

They told Wilson about the house in Holland Park and its owner. And the old man said, "Afdal Haddad. That's got to be him, then, got to be. Bloody hell. Bloody hell, that's bloody terrible. He's still alive. He's the magician Alexander was worried about. He's making them come alive. He's resurrecting the trinity."

Lawton stared at the weapon. He said, "Then we'll just have to kill them again, won't we. And this time we won't fuck up."

CHAPTER 61.
A MOTHER'S TERROR.

THE park lay empty and dusk fell.

She called out the boys' names, but no one called back; there wasn't a sound.

Where are my children? she thought; *where are my boys?*

She tried again. "Michael, David. You've got to come home. School tomorrow."

Nothing. Murray shivered, tears in her eyes.

She phoned Richard and said, "They're not here. Anywhere else they could be?"

He sounded concerned for the first time, and her hate for him cooled.

He said he didn't know, perhaps the school, perhaps around the shops.

"They always *say* they go to the park," he said.

Murray almost said that it wasn't just her, then, who had no idea about their children. But she didn't. She felt an appeasement was coming between her and Richard, and didn't want to threaten that possibility.

"All right, I'll have a look," she said, and hung up.

She rang the newsdesk at the *Mail* and asked if there were any news. Lindsey, the forward planner, said things were quite. "But things don't seem to kick off until after sundown," she added. "Maybe it really is vampires after all." And she chuckled.

Murray told Lindsey to let her know if anything happened, that she was looking for her sons.

Darkness had crawled further over the city while Murray had made her calls. She looked at her watch: almost 6.00 p.m. – it would be pitch black soon. She shivered, and dread tightened her chest. She looked around. Suburbia stood silent. She thought at least there'd be teenagers hanging around. But there was no one.

A bus rumbled past. A few cars whipped by. She waited outside the park for a while, looking back over the expanse. The woods lay dark at the far end of the park. Murray felt a finger of fear crawl up her spine. She sensed something in those trees watching her, but she knew it was paranoia chewing at her reason.

Come on, she thought; *get a move on.*

She headed towards the shops.

CHAPTER 62.
KIDS WILL BE KIDS.

DAVID Murray watched his brother drink from another can of beer. They were blue-and-white stripe Tesco ones. David looked at his mobile phone, thought about phoning dad. David didn't like this; didn't like being out after dark and didn't like seeing his brother drink. But then dad was drunk, too, when they left the house. He felt tears well in his eyes and wondered if Mum would mind if he called her. She was always busy, always writing her stories for the paper. She'd written about Mr. Gless dying; she'd written about all the terrible, scary things that were happening. David pressed the PHONEBOOK key, deciding to ring him Mum. He filed through the names, came to MUM in the phonebook.

But then the girl, Sophie, she said, "Does David want one?" her head cocked to one side. He looked back at her, his finger hovering over the CALL key.

Michael said, "No way, he's only ten."

David moved his finger away from the key. *Only ten.* Yeah, and if he phoned his Mum, that would prove that he *was* only ten; only a kid. And he didn't *want* to be only a kid. He wanted to be like Michael.

"You was drinking when you was ten," said C.J., popping open another can.

"Yeah," said Michael, staring at his younger brother, "but I was more mature."

"Man, leave your little brother be," said C.J., taking a swig of the beer and making a face.

C.J. was thirteen, the eldest there. He mixed with older boys, and his brother was a rapper. Not a famous rapper – "he will be soon, yeah," C.J. would say – but a guy who hung round a local studio, smoking weed and making tunes.

Michael, Sophie, and C.J. sat in the porch, David leaned on the gate. He tried to look cool but he didn't know how. He'd look cool if they gave him a can of beer and if Sophie gave him one of her cigarettes.

"Yeah," said Sophie, "he's all right, ain't you, David?"

His cheeks were hot and a sweat broke out on his back. "Yeah, I'm okay," he said. "Can I have a can, then?"

"No, you can't," said Michael, drinking from his can and puckering his mouth.

Why's he making that face? wondered David. *Does the beer taste bad?* If it tasted bad, why did they drink it? Because they were all making the same face.

So he asked and they laughed at him, Michael calling him a stupid kid.

C.J. got up, reached into his hoodie pocket and brought out a can of spray paint.

"What're you doing?" said Michael.

"Leaving my sign, innit."

"What? On the school door?"

"Yeah, why the fuck not?"

David glanced up at the CCTV camera pointing down at the porch. Another camera spied on them from inside the reception area behind the sliding glass doors. The school was really old. Made of stone and looking like a Victorian prison David had seen in a book. Bits of it were modern, though: the glass doors, the double-glazed windows, the CCTV and security systems, and all the inside was new, too. It wasn't a bad school, but he was looking forward to leaving in September and going to the comprehensive with Michael. Maybe they'd let him have beer and cigarettes then.

C.J. shook the can of spray paint and it rattled. Then he painted the word "Sidewalk" – his street name – on the glass doors in blue. Sophie giggled.

Michael stepped back to admire C.J.'s handiwork, spilling beer from the can. Booze and the fumes from the paint got up David's nose.

Then C.J. stepped back to have a better look at what he'd done.

"Cool, yeah?" he said.

"Cool," said Sophie.

"Yeah," said Michael.

David said, "We should go home, Mike, it's half-six almost. Mum'll be home and – "

Eyes still on C.J.'s artwork, Michael said, "Who gives a shit? She doesn't, does she?"

"She's a reporter, man," said C.J., "you better watch it. Some of the guys, they don't like me hanging with you, man."

"Why?" said Michael.

"'Cause your mum's a reporter, man. They make things up, scare people. They're making all kinds of stuff up, now, man. About, you know, vampires and stuff. Just shit, man, innit."

David's anger rose again.

Sophie said, "Yeah, my step-dad, he says it's the end of the world. Devils and angels preparing to fight for our souls."

"My mum's trying to help," said David, and they all turned to look at him. He couldn't see their faces clearly in the gloom, but he could tell C.J. was smiling.

"See? That's why you ain't cool, little boy," said C.J. "That's 'cause you're a mummy's boy."

And Sophie laughed, and Michael laughed, too.

David's insides tightened and his head started spinning. He balled his fists and gritted his teeth. His fury erupted, and he hurtled towards C.J., fists flying.

C.J.'s mouth dropped open, and he froze in the headlights of David's rage.

David caught C.J. with a punch to the side of the head, and C.J. dropped his spray paint and his beer, the beer leaking on the schoolyard.

C.J. threw his arms over his head, stumbled backwards, David raining fists, cursing him for insulting his mum, saying, "Don't laugh at my mum, you bastard!"

C.J., recovering from the initial assault, rallied. He was bigger and stronger than David. He straightened, grabbed the smaller boy's arms and kneed him in the belly. The air rushed out of David. Pain burned a hole through his stomach. He doubled up and crumpled to the floor.

"Little shit," said C.J., and kicked David in the backside. The pain made him scream. He curled up into a ball. Tears filled his eyes. C.J. said, "I'm gonna cut you, you little queer," and David saw a flash of steel.

"No," said Sophie, and tried to bat C.J.'s knife hand away.

"Yeah," said Michael, "yeah, C.J., it's cool. P-please don't hurt him, yeah? He's only a kid – stupid kid, that's all."

David could hear the terror in his brother's voice, but he didn't want Michael begging on his behalf. He didn't want Michael joining in with C.J. in insulting his mum.

His mum worked hard and she was hardly ever there, but she was their mum.

"You okay, David?" said Sophie, kneeling next to him.

David's tummy hurt. But he nodded he was all right and struggled to sit up. Sophie put a hand on his shoulder. C.J. glared at him, brandishing his knife. David wanted to throw up. Michael stood to the side, hands held out as if trying to calm the situation. He was saying, "He's just a stupid kid, C.J. He's a bit mental, that's all. Sorry, man."

C.J. waved the knife. "I don't give a shit. I'm going to cut him." And he strode forward. Michael screamed, "No, please," then moved out of the way. Sophie put her arms up. C.J., eyes blazing, tramped towards David, blade held out.

The hoodie bounded off the roof of the school and landed behind C.J., and before C.J. could do anything the hoodie grabbed him and bit him in the throat. C.J. dropped his knife. He made a screaming shape with his mouth. He started to twitch in the hoodie's grip. The front of C.J.'s jeans turned dark and the air filled with the stink of piss.

Sophie screamed. David sensed her being whipped away from him. He turned and saw a pink-haired woman holding Sophie's limp body in her arms. Pink Hair grinned at David and he saw her fangs.

Pink Hair said, "The boys, too."

And David sensed someone standing above him. He turned away from Pink Hair and Sophie, and looked up. He wanted to pee.

Mr. Gless, his dead teacher, stared down at him.

Mr. Gless's clothes were stained, and he smelled like a wheelie bin that hadn't been emptied in ages. The teacher's skin was chalky and his eyes were reddish. He smiled at David, and David cried when he saw his teacher's teeth.

Michael screamed, but David didn't take any notice. He was too fixed on Mr. Gless, standing above him.

Mr. Gless said, "Hello there, David Murray."

The hoodie dropped C.J.'s body on the yard and the boy's carcass twitched, like it was doing a breakdance. The hoodie had blood all over his chin and he said, "Come on, let's get going."

Mr. Gless said, "Detention for you, Murray," and scooped David up in his arms, David, screaming, dropping his mobile phone, yelling for his mother.

CHAPTER 63.
HEADING HOME.

"FEEL like a hero again, do you?" said Sassie. "A soldier? With your new weapon?"

Lawton stared ahead. The M1 stretched out before them, traffic-thick. "No, I don't feel like a hero, I've never felt like a hero. I've only ever felt that there's a job to do."

"This is so cool," said Lithgow. He sat in the back with the spear on his lap.

"Wrap it up, Fraser," said Lawton. "We don't want the law stopping us and finding that."

"What did you make of the old man?" said Sassie. "You got on like a house on fire, you two. Old soldiers, eh."

"What is it you've got against soldiers, Sassie?"

Her eyes stayed on the road. Lawton saw her knuckles turn white as she tightened her grip on the steering wheel. They'd left Manchester an hour ago, and Sassie floored it. They'd been quiet during the drive while they digested the information.

Sassie said, "I went on the march against the war. You know?"

"Yes, I know."

"There were so many of us," she said. "Everyone speaking out against the war. We were convinced that the government would listen – listen to the people. I mean, it's supposed to be a democracy. But they didn't listen. They went to war."

Lawton said, "That's not my fault, is it. That's not a soldier's fault. We just do our jobs, Sassie. It's what we sign up to do."

"Killing."

"You think it's all killing? Do you think that's all I did in Basra? You go ask the Marsh Arabs if they're better off now we made the Euphrates flow over their land again and what that did for their economy. Saddam built dams, diverting the water from their marshlands. He tried to wipe them out, Sassie. He killed twenty per cent of their people. You go ask them if all I did was kill."

A silence fell. But after a few moments Lithgow said, "That's war, though, isn't it. There's always been wars and we can't help that."

"I didn't know you cared," said Sassie.

"Yeah, well, it's all very well being against war," said Lithgow, "but what if we'd listened to those people who were against war in the 1939? I wouldn't be partying every week, would I? You wouldn't be allowed to moan, Sassie."

"Moaning, am I?" she said, but the conviction had left her voice.

Lawton glanced at Lithgow in the rear-view mirror and saw the glint in his eyes.

Lithgow said, "I think they went to fight the war for the wrong reason, I do. Just politicians talking shite. But I don't think it's bad that Saddam Hussein's gone. I used to be in Amnesty when I was at school. Did you ever hear what Saddam did over there?" He screwed up his face. "What he did was – was fucking dreadful, man, fucking off the scale."

"What George Bush did was off the scale, too," said Sassie.

"You're joking. He was just a jerk, that's all. Americans could slag him off without disappearing and getting their daughters raped. And loads of Americans did slag him off. They fucking hated him and said so. He was a dickhead, but you can't compare, Sassie. You got your moral bearings mixed up, man."

"Don't call me 'man', Fraser," she said.

"I'm not, man, Sassie, I'm just saying."

Her face was red, and tears leaked from her eyes.

"The world's a fucked up place," said Lawton. "It's got too many injuries, by now."

Sassie blew air out of her cheeks. She switched on the radio. A news headline said that more people were dying in London.

CHAPTER 64.
BACK TO SCHOOL.

SITTING in the car, Murray rang the newsdesk, and Anil, one of the news editors, picked up. Murray said, "I can't find my children. Is there anything happening?" her voice trembling.

"A few attacks reported already. Are you able to, um, file?"

Murray felt a cold sweat break at the back of her neck. She fanned her face with her notebook. Bile rose up into her throat.

"My kids are missing, Anil. I can't do anything," she said.

"I'm sure your boys'll be fine," he said. "There are attacks, but most people out of a night are perfectly safe. Odds are against anything happening to them. Bet they'll be home when you get there."

She thanked him and put the phone down.

Murray didn't share his confidence. Terror clawed at her chest. She wouldn't be happy until David and Michael were in the car with her.

She U-turned and headed down the road towards the school. A lorry cut her up as she came to a junction. She slammed her horn, and he slammed his.

She parked outside the school. The wrought iron gates lay open. She got out, walked up to the school building. The word "Sidewalk" had been spray painted on the glass doors. It was fresh, she smelled the paint. And she smelled beer, too.

Shadows lurked around the yard. She said, "David? Michael? Is there anyone here?" Her voice echoed around the schoolyard. She studied the building, and it chilled her: so gray and ominous. Do we teach our children in such places? And then she felt shame rise in her chest: *I hadn't noticed what my son's school looked like,* she thought.

Murray stepped forward towards the main doors. A night-light cast a weak glow over the steps that led up to the door. She pressed her face to the glass, looked inside. She turned, went down the steps. She saw the can of spray paint, and cans of beer. Booze pooled on the yard.

Her heart felt heavy, and she wanted to cry. She started to walk towards the car, and kicked something. It skittered across the yard, clattering against the open gate. Murray went after it, crouched. A mobile phone. She picked it up. She looked at the screen. The screen said MUM.

CHAPTER 65.
CHAOS ON THE STREETS
OF LONDON.

THEY hit traffic and roadblocks in London.

Lawton tuned the radio, found a traffic info station. The announcer said that police were limiting traffic into Central London. Soho, Leicester Square, and Shaftesbury Avenue were affected. Buses and the Tube had also been hit, said the announcer.

The DJ came back on and said, "So are there vampires stalking the streets of –?"

Lawton turned off the radio.

Sassie, crawling along the A400 Kentish Town Road, said, "How are we supposed to get home?"

"We can go to mine," said Lawton. "It's not much, but it's home."

"Yeah, it's lovely," said Lithgow.

"Okay, which way?"

Lawton said, "Turn into Highgate Road."

They drove on. Traffic thickened the closer they got to the guts of London. Cabbies raced through the gridlock. Bus passengers waved fists and shouted as their journeys were slowed.

Sassie said, "So how come a London boy gets to join the King's Regiment? Isn't it for northerners?"

"My dad lived in Birkenhead. He worked at the Tranmere Oil Terminal. I'd not seen him in years. I was raised by foster families in

London after my mum died when I was two. He'd fucked off a year earlier. I found out where he lived when I was fifteen. Went up there at sixteen. It didn't go to plan, the meeting. He wasn't interested. I hung around the North West for a few months, doing odd jobs. Slept on the streets. I was kipping outside this newsagent's one evening, saw a poster for the King's Regiment. I joined up the following day."

Sassie said, "I thought you were an orphan. That's what the papers said."

He said, "You read that rubbish in the end, then. Well, that was a lie, too. My dad's still alive, but I guess I'm dead to him. Had a new family by the time I found him. He was a Scouser down in the big smoke in the Seventies, doing some building work. My mum was a barmaid at a New Cross pub. He was a bit of a wag, you know. He moved in, they had me, he moved out. They spent a year together. My mum died of a drugs' overdose, social workers found me."

Sassie said, "I'm really sorry."

"Why?"

"For all that. No wonder you joined the forces."

"You think useless cases like me join the forces, then?"

"No, I mean – you didn't have – many choices."

"I had choices," he said. "Everyone has choices. I could've knuckled down at school, got my O-Levels. I chose not to. I could've got a job, an apprenticeship or something. Chose not to. I could've gone with my mates, caused mischief. I chose not to. We've all got choices."

She said, "Did seeing your father – I mean his reaction to you – make you join up?"

"It did. I had no real family down in London. I was seeing Jenna, knew her mum and dad. But I was a kid, you know. Typical teenaged boy. Not ready to settle down. I knew I'd end up on the streets. I was sixteen, and didn't want to go back in with a foster family. You know, sixteen and he thinks he's a big man."

"And when you got – when you left the army. You came back."

"Back to New Cross," said Lawton. "Old stomping ground. Get drunk, feel sorry for myself, feel anger towards the people who fucked my life up."

"You're angry?" she said.

"Fucking furious," said Lawton. "I had a good life. I had order and discipline. I was doing well. A staff sergeant with prospects. It was my life. Imagine if they told you, Sassie, that you'd have to leave your university tomorrow and you'd never work in another one all your life. You could never study, do your research ever again. That's how it felt, I guess." He shook his head. "Politicians took over. Press wanted blood. I got sacrificed."

"You should stop drinking," she said.

"Yeah."

"I think that a part of you enjoys all this chaos."

"Gives me something to do. Gives me a war to fight." He turned and stared at her. "Gives me someone to fight for."

She glanced at him, and then cast her eyes back over the road. She said, "Are you fighting for Jenna?"

"Her. Everyone. You."

"Me?"

"Jenna's gone. She's – whatever she is. But you're with me. You're alive and breathing. But then you don't like war."

She said, "No. But sometimes you have to fight them."

Lithgow snored in the back of the car.

Sassie said, "What about Jenna?"

"What about her?"

"Will you – do you still like her?"

"No, not like I did. And it was only 'like', really. We were kids. We just got together, you know. Like kids do."

"She's not human anymore."

"No, she's not."

"Not the Jenna you knew. They're none of them the people they were."

"No, they're not. I know that." He rubbed his neck. "Jenna's not alive anymore – but I still think I'm going to have to kill her."

CHAPTER 66.
STEAMING ON SUNDAY.

JED, aged fifteen, with hate in his eyes and a Stanley Knife in his pocket, scanned the commuters travelling south on the Bakerloo Line.

He and Marty had got on at Kensal Green. They were hunting – hunting some dipshit they could rob for cash, mobile, or an MP3 player. They were going to steam through a train, nicking anything they could.

Loads of kids being loud filled the carriage. Posh cunts from Harrow who joined the Bakerloo Line off the Metropolitan Line. They were headed for Oxford Circus, Jed guessed. Sunday night out on the town. Finish off the weekend. Headed for the clubs and bars with shiny lights and stupid cocktails; not the clubs and bars he tried to get into – dark and grimy and drug-infested.

The train rumbled through Queens Park, heading towards Kilburn Park.

Jed got the rage and said, "What the fuck you looking at, cunt?" to a tall, gangly ginger nut.

The ginge flinched, and his freckles showed on his scared, white face.

A girl, slutty in a short red dress, stabbed a look at Jed and said, "Leave him alone."

The ginge touched her arm, mouth going, "No, no, no," and Jed strode over. Another guy, spiky blonde hair, stocky, stepped in front of ginge and the girl, the girl – mouthy bitch – still going, "Fuck off, pondlife," to Jed.

The blonde guy held out his hands, saying, "Cool down, mate – " but Jed smacked him – a right hook across the jaw. The guy went down. Girls screamed. The mouthy bitch stopped talking and gawped as the blonde lad hit the floor. Ginge looked terrified, and Jed thought he could smell piss.

Marty grabbed his arm, said, "Come on, mate, leave it – leave it, Jed."

Girls attended to the wounded gay boy and Jed spat at them, calling the blonde, "Fucking queer."

He stomped back to the other end of the carriage. Commuters hid behind newspapers, magazines, anything, to keep away from him. Marty said, "What're you doing, nutjob?"

"He fucking stared at me, that carrot-head," said Jed.

"Yeah? Well do him after. We're robbing someone, and you just got us tagged."

Jed glanced over at the group he'd attacked. They were on their phones.

"They're calling the pigs," said Marty, "so we get off at Warwick Avenue."

The train screeched and rattled as it hurtled through the tunnel. Jed watched the wankers phone the cops. His heart raced, and a cold sweat broke out on his back. He could feel anger rise in him again, and he clenched his fists.

Marty, jabbing a finger at the group, said, "We know you," and he swaggered down the train to square off – he was just trying to scare them, Jed knew that. Other passengers cowered. Marty said, "We can find you, right?"

"Leave us alone, you scum," said the mouthy bitch in the red.

Marty backed up, still squaring his shoulders, still jutting out his chin.

Jed held the rail to steady himself. His head spun with fury and fear. He'd fucked up. Marty'd be pissed off if they couldn't rob someone and get away with it.

They got off at Warwick Avenue. The raced up the stairs, out into the night air. Jed breathed hard, and felt dizzy. But it was good to have fresh air. The tube felt stifling. He lit a fag and spluttered, still not used to it after a year of trying to smoke.

"You cunt," said Marty, shoving him.

Jed staggered away, almost dropping his fag.

Marty said, "They got you on CCTV doing that. Well, you can take the fall, wanker. You ain't taking me down with you, right?"

"He was fucking looking at me, Marty."

"Yeah? Well I'm looking at you, now."

"What was I supposed to do? He pissed me off. He looked at me," said Jed.

Marty strutted off, swearing under his breath. He gobbed on the pavement. A white van was parked on double yellows. Jed narrowed his eyes, thinking, *That wanker in the van looks dodgy parked there.*

Marty neared the van. The rear doors burst open. Three goths leaped out. Jed's heart punched his ribs. The strength drained out of him. The goths grabbed Marty. They dragged him into the van. He gawped at Jed, his eyes wide and scared. The back door shut and the van sped off.

"Think you're tough, sunshine?" said a voice behind him.

He wheeled round, dropping the cigarette. A dark-haired girl in a frilly white shirt glared at him from the tube entrance. She could've been pretty. But her skin was pale – like it had too much powder on it. Dark rings cradled her eyes and the eyes themselves – fuck, they were red almost; red and blue, like a bruise. She smelled weird, like something dead. Like that dead dog Marty and him burned down by the river a few weeks ago. They'd poured lighter fluid on the carcass, threw a match on it. The putrid dog sizzled and swelled, and the belly burst open and entrails spooled out, charring and fizzing in the flames.

Oh, the fucking stink . . .

The girl opened her mouth and showed her fangs. Jed's insides went cold. He legged it down the tree-lined street. His chest tightened as he gasped for air. He dared a glance over his shoulder.

He screamed.

The girl flew after him.

Yeah, he thought, *that's right:*

She's fucking flying.

She took mighty leaps, covering loads of ground. She sprang off the sides of buildings back onto the pavement, then lunged forward again, gaining on him. She laughed and called out, saying, "Come on, little boy, let me bite you."

Onlookers legged it. They screamed and shouted, watching this woman – *woman? More like an animal. Bounding like that* – hunt him down.

A car skidded and crashed into a lamppost. Horns blared as the traffic behind tried to avoid a pile-up.

"Oh, my God, look at that," Jed heard people say.

He started to cry, panic like a tight belt around his belly. He'd stay on the main road. He'd be all right with all the people watching.

Then he thought:

Hey, she's just a fucking girl.

Seeing Marty kidnapped had panicked him. They were goths, like this girl flying after him. Perhaps they were circus people, or something. Had they robbed a goth lately? They were always robbing someone, and Jed rarely remembered.

He stopped running, out of breath. He turned to face his pursuer and took out his blade.

His legs buckled when he saw her spring off a window ledge two floors up, and land on the pavement ten feet in front of him.

Crouching, she licked her lips. "Big tough man, are you?" she said.

"W-what the fuck d'you want, bitch?"

"You, sweetie. I want you. I want your fucking fluid."

A thrill fizzed through his belly. She looked dirty. Like she could do some pretty nasty things. She wasn't that much to look at, now, but she might have been hot once. Goths looked weird, anyway. He'd seen tributes on YouTube yesterday, a bunch of them died at this Soho nightclub from a drugs overdose. And then he remembered seeing those headline boards for the *Evening Standard*. And rumours on Facebook. Yeah: Vampires; it was all about vampires.

Jed, shaking and shitting himself, fronted up to the girl and said, "Yeah? What're you going to do?" and jabbed his knife towards her.

She stood up. "I'm going to suck you."

Jed felt his nerves tighten. "Oh, yeah? And I'm going to cut you, bitch."

She hissed and strutted towards him. He wanted to back up, but he didn't. Stood his ground like a soldier. His palms sweated, the knife greasy in his grasp. He'd slice her open if he had to. Or smack her, deck her with a punch. Smacking a bitch was nothing. His dad always smacked his mum and his sister, telling Jed, *You've got to do it to keep 'em in line.*

She didn't stop coming. He smelled her. He wanted to throw up, bile filling his throat. Shouts filled the air. Two men were fighting where the car had crashed into the lamppost.

Jed stepped back. The girl glided towards him.

"Hey," he said, raising blade, "you leave me – "

And she sprang forward.

Jed yelled.

She ploughed into him, and he got thrown off his feet. Her nails dug into his shoulders. Her feet jammed into his hipbones. He crashed to the pavement, her on top of him. She hissed and showed her fangs and Jed smelled her breath and he almost passed out. He wet himself and screamed, tried to push her away, sliced at her shoulder with his knife, shredding her shirt, her skin – but there was no blood. She nuzzled his throat and growled in his ear. Her teeth punctured his skin. It stung, and he shrieked. He thrashed about, trying to shove her away. But she held him tight.

He heard voices saying, "What are they doing?" and, "Are they screwing on the pavement?" and then another voice saying, "She's a vampire, one of those vampires."

Jed kicked out weakly as the blood pulsed out of his body and the girl made sucking noises at his throat. He felt scared, but he still, weirdly, had a hard-on. And it would be the last thing of him to die.

CHAPTER 67.
A GOD FORMING.

NADIA Radu's god took shape. *Tonight and tomorrow night's batch should do it,* she thought.

She stared down into the pit. The stench of decay washed up from the trench. The ashes Dr. Haddad had spilled into the grave days ago were thickening. The blood poured over them last night had mixed into a mud-like substance, coppery in colour. A body shape lay in the mixture, as if it were trying to push itself up from beneath the sludge. It was long, some six and a half feet in length. The head was thrown back and the mouth seemed open. There were cavities where the eyes would be, but there was no form to the face yet. The torso was a block of blood-coloured soil, but at its centre the shape split, forming what would be the creature's legs.

Screams filled the cavern. Ion and the vampires bringing more victims. He'd have parked the van in the backstreet, then dragged out the terrified youngsters. They were all young, or female. Children and women were easier to handle, that was all. Nothing to do with that Hollywood nonsense of a vampire needing virgin blood, she thought, smiling to herself.

The street nearby had been blocked off, so very few suspicious eyes would spot what Ion was up to. And those who did see were unlikely to say anything. They weren't the sorts to contact the authorities around here. Streets away, of course, it was different. Lights turned to darkness quickly in London. Turn a corner and you were in hell without realizing it.

She looked up from the shape in the pit to the stone steps leading down into the cavern. Half a dozen teens were being shoved down the stairs by vampires. The kids cried. One or two, a lad with a baseball cap, tried to fight back, but he was soon weeping with the rest of them.

She thought, *The city gives up its young for sacrifice. That's how it's always been.*

"Only six tonight, Ion?" she said.

"It's chaos out there. Roadblocks everywhere. It's difficult to drive around without being stopped. We're causing panic, Nadia."

"Good. They should be terrified. But if they think this is hell, they don't know what's coming in a few days' time."

She stared into the pit.

The shape seemed to move, a breath coursing through it – life pulsing through it. But it didn't, of course. Only her imagination. She smiled and felt a thrill rinse through her.

CHAPTER 68.
TOUCHING HISTORY.

THE two-tusked spear lay on Lawton's kitchen table.

"And what do we do now that we've got this thing?" said Sassie. She ran her fingers up and down the length. She was touching a relic once brandished by Alexander the Great.

Sassie grasped the grip. It felt too thick to be skin. Human skin, at least. It didn't bother Sassie that this was supposedly human bone and human flesh – she was an archaeologist; this was an artefact. She tried to pick the spear up, but it was heavy. Lawton appeared at her shoulder. He put his hand around hers on the grip. She looked up at him and fire swept through her veins.

He said, "We go to war, Sassie."

"Against whom?"

"Against whatever's spreading this plague. And if it's those demons Tom Wilson spoke of, then we go to war against them."

"Did you believe him?" said Sassie.

"I believed what he said. I don't know if it was true, though."

Lithgow sat on the couch, watching TV. He spooned cold beans into his mouth straight from the can. Through a mouthful of Heinz he said, "There's more killings. And some kids have disappeared tonight, they're saying."

Lawton looked at Sassie, and she felt the weight of his eyes. He smelled of man, and she liked that. It had been a long time since she'd smelled a man like this. You didn't get many of them in academia.

Ed thought he was a real man. Ed who'd lied about what the cuneiform on the vessel said. Ed who might not know what it meant, but didn't want to look ignorant in front of her because he was so arrogant.

But Ed wasn't like this. He'd not seen blood and war and carnage. Her principles warned her away from a man like Jake Lawton. But her body said he was what she wanted.

Maybe this is history, too? she thought. Women always went for the warrior, the male who could protect her, who could – Sassie's gaze slid down Lawton's chest, over his belly, then shot back up to his face – give her sons.

Something trilled inside her, and she gasped. She drew away from him, went to the sink and poured herself a glass of water.

Lawton asked if she was all right and she nodded, saying yes she was fine, and she drank the water.

Shouts carried from the street outside. Sassie froze, her eyes wide.

Lawton said, "Don't worry. Usually just yobs."

She'd noticed that when they drove down the street. Boarded up shops lined the pavement. Graffiti marred the walls. Holes gouged the road. She'd parked up and asked Lawton if her car was safe, and he'd said he couldn't say if it was.

Outside the flat, a window smashed. Sassie imagined some lout hurling a breezeblock through her windscreen.

"I got attacked out here," said Lithgow, "by vampires."

Lawton looked at him. "No you didn't. I don't think they're this far south. I think they're contained around Central London, where they" – he paused – "died. Or where they lived."

"Jenna came here," said Lithgow.

Lawton rubbed the wound on his neck. Sassie said, "Let me have a look at that," and she came to him. He tilted his head to the side so she could look. "Can you sit," she said, so he sat at the kitchen table. She leaned over him and smelled him. She studied his injury. A bruise the size of a fist stained the right side of his throat a few inches below his ear. Two teeth marks had punctured the skin at the centre of the bruise. "She bit into your carotid artery," said Sassie. "Do you have iodine, anything?"

"In the bathroom, Fraser," said Lawton, "go get some iodine."

Lithgow tutted and went through to the bathroom. Sassie heard him rummage around in there. She looked into Lawton's eyes and he looked up into hers. Her hands slid up his neck and into his hair. It was thick and warm. Her insides ground.

"You're just not my type," she said, her face going to his.

She pressed her mouth to his mouth, and her skin burned from thighs to throat. He pulled her down to him, and she sat on his lap and gasped into their kiss when she felt his hardness against her bottom. She moved against the erection and the heat in her grew more intense until it felt like her insides were liquid fire. Her tongue found his tongue and her fingers laced through his hair and his odour saturated her nostrils.

"Found it," said Lithgow from the bathroom.

A cold sweat broke on her body. She pulled away and got off Lawton's lap, striding to the sink. She grabbed the empty glass and pretended to drink. Her heart raced.

Behind her Lithgow said, "Get it yourself next time, trooper," and she heard the bottle being slammed down on the table. "You look a bit red in the face, Jakey boy," said Lithgow, "better let your nurse take a look at you."

Sassie blushed.

A phone rang and Lawton answered it.

★ ★ ★ ★

Murray told them her boys were missing and she cried.

It was 10.00 p.m. They'd met her at The Gallery, a pub not far from her Pimlico home. They'd driven here through streets crawling with predators, manned by roadblocks. Usually a five-mile, fifteen–twenty minute drive from New Cross, it took them almost an hour.

Sassie put her arms around Murray's shoulders and said, "I'm sure they'll be fine, Christine."

Murray went into her pocket, took out a mobile phone and put it on the table.

"That's David's phone," she said, and told them how she came to find it. And then she said, "I can't get a hold of Michael on his phone, either. I don't know what to do. I feel so useless. The police, they let me inside, you know. Gave me access to the whole investigation. But what good has that done me? I'm a useless mother, and my children, my children are gone."

She put her head in her hands and cried, her body trembling. Sassie tried to comfort her, but it wasn't helping.

"It's okay," said Lawton, "we'll find them."

Sassie frowned at him, as if saying, *Don't give her false hope.* But it was the only hope he could offer. He looked at Sassie, now, and remembered her taste and her touch. Gazing at her, everything else slid away to leave only her and him. Nothing existed except the two of them.

And then Murray said, "Where do we start? What can we do?"

Lawton came back to the present and said, "We start by looking for trouble."

Lithgow said, "What?"

Lawton said, "If we're in an area where they're known to attack, we can track them, follow them. They've obviously legged it from that Holland Park place. Well, perhaps if we get one of them, they can lead us there."

"It's dangerous," said Murray. "More dangerous than we let on. They're attacking people out in the open. They don't seem to care about anything. I've seen CCTV footage. It's scary."

"Good," said Lawton, "scary makes you sharp."

"Doesn't make me sharp," said Lithgow. "Makes me want to shit my pants."

Lawton looked at him. "You don't have to come. Stay here." He glanced at Sassie. "You too. Get back to the flat and get safe." He wanted to touch her face, but he didn't.

She stared at him and said, "I'm coming with you."

"You're not, Sassie."

"Stop me," she said.

CHAPTER 69.
MY BROTHER'S KEEPER.

DAVID Murray clutched his brother's arm. He wanted to pee, but some of the others had already done that, and it smelled sour in here. David could feel Michael shaking and whimpering. He didn't want his older brother to be scared – he wanted his older brother to be brave and to protect him.

But they were only kids.

The thought forced a sob out of him.

Only kids.

What could they do against this terrible thing that was happening?

They'd been herded out of the back of the van. They'd had to travel here with those sharp-fanged, red-eyed monsters hissing at them and forcing them to cower and huddle together. Mr. Gless had been one of them. They said Mr. Gless was dead yesterday, but he didn't look dead to David – he didn't look alive either. Mr. Gless was a vampire. All these things were vampires.

The children had cried and screamed all the way here. Sophie wept and shrieked for her mum, and David wished his mum were here, too.

The van had parked in a dark alley. It had reversed down the dead end, so the kids couldn't make a run for it. One or two tried, but the vampires pounced them on.

The driver, a tall man with a scar on his mean face and a bandage around his hand, hurried them through a door marked FIRE EXIT. They herded the children down a dimmed corridor, and down some steel stairs. Their feet clanked on the metal, their cries echoed off the walls. The place smelled of chemicals and it made David queasy.

"Wait," the scarred man said, and barged through the shivering children. He slid open the scissor door of a wire-caged elevator. The scarred man and the vampires shoved the youngsters into the elevator, which then groaned and moved downwards. It came to a halt against a rusting, iron door. The scarred man slid the bolt aside and opened the door. A breeze rushed through the door, filling the elevator, and carried with it a smell like dead meat. David recoiled. The others cringed too, and put their hands over their noses.

The vampires and the scarred man forced them through the iron door, down the stone steps, and into a cavern – and that's when they really started to panic.

They were shoved into a cage that barely had room for the ten of them.

The cavern was the size of David's school hall, big enough for more than a thousand kids. There was a panelled floor, and at its centre a hole in the ground. Above the pit, there was a bar – *like the crossbar of a goal*, David thought.

The bad smell came from the pit. It was like that dead fox David and Michael found in the park a few months ago. Maggots had crawled all over it. The guts had swelled and burst out of the fox's belly. Flies buzzed around the carcass. David threw up and Michael had called him gay.

But that's what this place smelled like. Putrid and horrible. And David really wanted to puke again. Then someone else did. He heard the retching sound. And then more cries and screams.

The scarred man stood in front of the cage and grinned at them. "Screaming brats," he said. "Who'll be first, then? First is best, because second and third and fourth – they all know what's coming."

Sophie's face stretched with fear and she rattled the cage. "Please let us go, please," she said.

A woman appeared from behind the cage. She was beautiful and dark-haired and she stood next to the scarred man. She gazed at the youngsters in the cage and said, "Five tonight, five tomorrow."

"Why not all today?" said the scarred man.

"Dr. Haddad says to do this slowly."

"He's almost alive, Nadia, let's finish it tonight."

She put a hand on the scarred man's shoulder. "He knows best, Ion. He's brought us this far." She moved away from the man called Ion, and said, "Start it, now."

The man called Ion opened the cage door and everyone in the cage moved back, huddling against each other. David smelled sweat and pee, and his ears rang with cries. He said, "Michael, what's happening? I want to go home."

Michael clutched his brother's hand and said, "It'll be all right. We'll be all right," but his voice was shaking and his body trembled.

The Ion man reached inside the cage. His grabbed Sophie by the arm and Sophie screeched, trying to hold on to Michael. But the Ion man was strong and dragged her out of the cage before slamming the door shut again.

Michael gasped and stiffened next to David. Sophie shrieked and kicked. The Ion man heaved her over to the pit. She tugged against him, but she was just a girl and he was a man.

Three vampires, including Mr. Gless and the hoodie who'd killed C.J., put their faces between the bars of the cage and bared their teeth. David's legs went soft, and he thought he'd faint. They had fangs like snakes, and the front teeth were stained a reddish-brown colour that David knew was blood.

The Ion man handcuffed Sophie's hands behind her back. She screamed and thrashed about, saying, "Don't hurt me, please, let me go – Mum, Mum, please," in a high-pitched voice.

David wanted to put his hands over his ears, but he thought it was right he should listen. He should be able to tell people what happened to Sophie and why these people – this Ion, that woman – should pay for her death.

The Ion man fastened a leather strap around Sophie's ankles. A hook was clipped to the strap. The Ion man hoisted Sophie on his shoulder. She yelled at him to stop and to please put her down. He eased the hook over the bar that crossed over the pit. The muscles in his arms flexed as he held Sophie's weight for a second – and then he let her hang by her ankles from the bar. The Ion man stepped back.

Sophie looked down into the pit underneath her and her screams came in short, rapid stabs. David trembled and whined, Sophie's terror infecting him, and the others, like a plague.

"What's happening, what are they doing?" said Michael, tears in his voice.

But David didn't want him to ask that. David wanted him to answer those questions. Michael was his big brother, and he should know why this was happening, why they were going to die like this – die like –

And he saw how.

The Ion man took out a knife. He stood at the edge of the pit with his back to the cage, staying in front of Sophie, so David and the others couldn't see her.

But when the knife slashed from right to left, and left to right, and Sophie stopped crying, David knew what had happened, and he peed himself.

The Ion man moved aside. Sophie twitched. Blood poured over her face from the gash in her throat, and rained into the pit.

David shrieked.

CHAPTER 70.
DADDY'S BOY.

LITHGOW knew he'd fucked up. After Lawton, Murray, and Sassie left the pub, he found a corner table and cradled his pint. He phoned his dad and his dad said, "What have you done, now?"

Lithgow said he'd done nothing but just wanted to talk.

A silence filled the line and then Lithgow said, "Dad, have you been following what's going on?"

His dad said, "Of course. Do you think I live in a cave? Why? Do you know something about it?"

"No, no, I don't," said Lithgow, loosening his collar. He took a gulp of Guinness. "But I know people who know people, kind of thing."

"Oh, do you, now."

"And I kind of know how it all started," said Lithgow.

His dad took a few deep breaths and then said, "You know how it started? Does that mean you know who's responsible?"

"No," said Lithgow. "I don't know that."

"All right, Fraser. Well, how about you explain to me how it started."

And Lithgow told him about the pills called Skarlet killing people in Religion. And about those dead people disappearing and then coming back to life, and the word "vampire" being mentioned.

"So, Dad, do you reckon that whoever, kind of, distributed those Skarlet pills at Religion — handed them out without knowing what would happen — do you think they'd be done for murder — seeing as the victims died, then got up again?"

His dad paused before answering, and then said, "Are you on drugs, Fraser?"

"No, Dad, no."

His dad sniffed. "This talk of vampires is nonsense. And I won't even deal with that. Whoever distributed those drugs could be accused of manslaughter. But if the victims are, um, alive, as you say, then supplying would be the worst of it." He paused. "Get out of London for a while, Fraser. I mean, if you're involved – "

"I-I'm not, I – "

"Well," said his dad, "get out anyway, perhaps – for the moment, at least. Until – until things have, um, settled down. Then – then you can come home – come back, I mean. I could try to help you but – but I'm not sure at this time – "

"Dad, you're waffling."

"Well, I'm a barrister, son, that's what I do."

"Yeah, right. So you say, get out of London."

"That's what I say, Fraser."

"Yeah, thanks, Dad."

"Fraser?"

"Yes?"

"Listen to me – just this once."

They said goodbye. Fraser hung up. Ten minutes later, he'd finished his pint and raced towards Pimlico tube station. His father had always given him good advice, and Fraser had mostly ignored it.

Weaving through crowds, he thought he'd continue that tradition.

CHAPTER 71.
A VAMPIRE IN
EMBANKMENT STATION.

BARRY Corbett crawled out of the Thames. Slime hung off his clothes. He stank of the river. Hunger gnawed at his belly.

He'd woken up in the cold, dark water. A thump in his chest had brought him out sleep, as if an electric generator had been turned on in his heart. Panic gripped him, and he thrashed about. He thought he'd be out of breath, that he'd drown, and started to claw his way up to the surface.

But he gulped water into his lungs and nothing happened – just a chill seeping through him and a bad taste crawling around his mouth. He wasn't drowning. He swam to the surface. The hunger in his belly grew and he knew, without knowing how, what would get rid of his craving:

Blood.

Barry, scrambling up the bank, remembered how he got there. The bus stuck in traffic, getting hit by that car. People screaming and shouting. The woman dragging him over the edge of the bridge. Her teeth sinking into his throat as they plunged into the Thames. The strength draining out of him. The darkness swallowing him. Death making him limp, making him debris.

The river took him west, under Waterloo Bridge. His body got tangled up in the wreckage of the riverbed. He stayed there for a day, a carcass. But then the poison from the woman's bite made him live again, and he came out of his death stronger than he'd ever been. And if he could feed, he'd feel stronger still. Out of the river, his nostrils filled with the odour of blood, thick and metallic. He slavered and flicked his tongue over his teeth. He felt fangs in his mouth and knew what they were for.

He clambered up through Embankment underground station. Commuters avoided him. They cringed when they saw him, when they smelled him. Water drizzled off his body and he trailed it behind him. Slime draped over his shoulders and down his arms. Saliva tendriled from his mouth, vines of it hanging down his chest. He could hear heartbeats pump in his head, the blood coursing through all these people around him. The smell drove him crazy.

Feed, his mind said, *feed*.

His throat clicked.

His mouth snapped open and closed.

His insides were on fire.

Barry snarled.

A London Underground official in his blue blazer came up to him and said, "You've got to get out of here, mate. I'm going to have to call the police."

Barry hissed in the official's face, and the man flinched. Barry shoved him, and he stumbled, fell on the concourse. The official, pissed off at being on his arse, said, "Hey, you bastard, you're – "

Barry pounced, leaping through the air, ploughing into the official. The guy screamed, tried to fight. Barry sank his teeth into the man's throat and blood filled Barry's mouth and it was the most wonderful thing he'd ever tasted.

★ ★ ★ ★

Lawton, Murray, and Sassie got off at Charing Cross. They'd left Sassie's car at Pimlico, no chance of getting through the congestion that was building in the streets.

Stepping out of the station, they heard the commotion down Villiers Street, where Embankment tube station stood. Crowds spilled from the station entrance. Travellers strolling down towards Embankment turned round when they saw the panicked faces of those darting out of the station.

Lawton said, "They're in there, there's one of them in there."

He strode into the crowd swarming up the street.

Sassie called his name and Murray told him to wait. But Lawton muscled his way through the throng. He glanced over his shoulder and said, "You two stay there and keep an eye out."

Sassie looked at him with fire in her eyes. A yearning for her put a knot in his guts. The crowd swept past her. He turned away and moved towards the station entrance. The screams and shouts faded up Villiers Street. Sirens filled the night. Lawton heard voices saying, "Police! Police!" and boots trampled the road behind him.

Lawton stepped into the station.

The silence chilled him. Shadows fluttered in the gloom. Two figures lay, one on top of the other, on the concourse. Lawton skulked towards them. He heard the sucking sound that sent a rush of fear into his guts. The same noise he'd heard when Jenna drank his blood.

"Hey," said Lawton, drawing the two-horned spear from the leather scabbard strapped to his back. The silver-haired vampire, his head adorned with weeds and slime, looked up. The Underground official lay dead. The vampire hissed at Lawton, blood frothing in its mouth. The creature stood. Water dripped off its coat. The smell of rot came from the monster, and Lawton creased his face.

Lawton heard the footsteps behind him and a voice said, "Step away, mate, we'll handle this."

Lawton glanced over his shoulder. Three armed police in protective vests. They aimed Benelli M3 shotguns at Lawton, at the vampire. Lawton said, "Those won't work."

"They work on elephants," said the goateed cop in the middle.

Lawton stepped to the side saying, "Okay, mate, but that's" – he turned back to the vampire – "not an elephant."

Speaking to the vampire, the goateed cop said, "Armed police, sir, move away from the body or we'll shoot."

The vampire stepped towards them.

"Back, sir, back," said Goatee.

The vampire moved forward.

"Sir, I'm warning – "

The vampire flew.

Lawton flinched as the shotguns cracked. The blast tossed the vampire aside like it had been yanked on a rope. The creature hit the floor, skidded along the concourse, smoke coming of its body where the pellets hit. The cops raced after him.

Lawton said, "Be careful."

Goatee turned and said, "It's okay, we know what we're fucking – " and the vampire sprang to his feet. The creature bit into Goatee's throat. The two other officers fired. The pellets peppered vampire and policeman, tearing chunks off the cop's body. The vampire snapped its head from side to side. The officer twitched. His throat came away in a hunk of meat. Blood spouted from the wound. The vampire shoved his kill aside. The red blood on its face contrasted with the white of its skin.

The other cops fired again, backing away. The vampire staggered back, came forward again.

Lawton thought, *Fuck this,* and he rushed forward.

One of the cops ran out of ammo. The vampire pounced. It sank its teeth into the cop's face, and the cop screamed. His colleague yelled and started battering the vampire with his shotgun.

Lawton shoved the third copper aside. He grabbed the vampire by his collar. The material was wet. The cop having his face bitten off screamed. Lawton hauled the vampire off the officer, and tossed the creature aside. The cop cradled what remained of his face. Blood pumped from between his fingers.

The vampire stood. It flew at Lawton. Lawton braced himself.

The vampire bared its teeth, bloody with bits of flesh pressed between them. The stench of river and death filled Lawton's nostrils. He lunged and drove the tusk into the vampire's chest. The vampire's face showed shock. It tried to claw at Lawton's face and started to squeal. Lawton shoved the point deeper into the creature's heart. He felt bone crack and flesh pop.

The vampire slid up the spear until he was face to face with Lawton and Lawton smelled the fucking awfulness of the thing's breath. The odour made him want to puke, but he steeled himself, tightening his abs. The vampire's jaws snapped inches from Lawton's face. Then it shrieked and a gout of black blood shot from its open mouth, splashing over Lawton's face.

Lawton groaned.

The smell of burning filled the air. The vampire's skin charred and cracked. The creature convulsed on the stake. It clawed at Lawton's shoulders. Smoke belched from its body and its eyes started to blacken.

Arteries of fire laced the vampire's flesh, now. Flames ignited all over its body. Fire spat from its nostrils and its ears. The heat singed Lawton's skin. The reek of burning flesh was overwhelming. The vampire shrieked. Fire engulfed it, and Lawton felt the heat. The vampire's body erupted into ashes and the ashes rained on the concourse and over Lawton, and Lawton stood, his skin and clothes grey with the vampire's dust, gripping the spear of Abraham.

CHAPTER 72.
BLOOD CRAZY.

LITHGOW, racing for the tube, saw the bus stop and sprinted for it. He leaped on to the bus, just as the door shut behind him. He went to swipe his Oyster card, and the driver said, "No need for that, man, we're going back to the depot – it's crazy, man, streets are wild."

Lithgow, finding a seat, glanced out of the window.

Vampires lunged out of the shadows, pinning their victims to the pavement to suck their blood. Vampires hurled themselves at buses and cabs and cars, clawing at the windows. Vampires got trapped under the wheels and mangled. Twisted, gnarled vampires crawled around on the road, leaving behind them a trail of slime. Their damaged bodies didn't stop them – their hunger drove them on. Even dismembered vampires lashed out at passers-by. One creature, torn in half from the waist down, reddish-black slush pulsing from its torso, tripped a girl and mounted her. The half-vampire tore at her throat and drank her blood.

Lithgow, sitting now, pressed his face against the window and watched open-mouthed as hell rose up. Even in his wildest trips, his craziest drug binges, he couldn't have imagined such things.

Screams filled the night. Someone grabbed his shoulder and he turned, fear burning his skin. But it was just a girl, early twenties, her face stretched in terror.

"What's going on?" she said.

"I don't know," he said.

"M–my friends have been killed b–by those things. I saw them being attacked and I–I jumped on this bus."

"Yeah," said Lithgow, his eyes wide with fear. The bus crawled along. The driver honked his horn. Over-turned vehicles, blood–drained bodies, and hunger–crazed vampires cluttered the road.

Vampires clattered against the bus, some latching on to the vehicle, trying to tear through metal and smash through glass to get at the food inside.

"Are they – are they vampires?" said the girl.

Lithgow looked her in the eye. Her eyes were green and tearful. Lithgow said, "Yes, I think they are, and I think I made them."

He didn't know why he told her that, but she felt safe. It felt like she would take his confession, and nod, and comfort him and say it's all right.

But the girl gawped. She stood and stepped into the aisle and pointed at Lithgow, saying, "He made them, he made these monsters. He made them."

Lithgow's blood ran cold.

Commuters turned their attention from the carnage and looked towards the girl, who was going:

"It's him. He started it. He says he made the vampires, he made the monsters."

Two youths stormed up to the back of the bus and one of them, a skinhead, said, "What're you saying?"

The girl said, "He told me he made them, he created them – he's to blame."

The skinhead glared at Lithgow. Lithgow tried to say, *No*, but his throat was dry, and he shook his head.

Another voice said, "It's him, him at the back," and passengers flooded down from the top deck to hear the commotion.

"You made them?" said the skinhead.

"You fucking bastard," said the other youth, an Asian in an Adidas baseball hat, "my girlfriend got killed last night." And he surged forward, and the skinhead surged with him, and they bumped each other. And from behind them, the girl kept saying, "It's him, it's him," and the other passengers shoved their way up the bus towards Lithgow.

He felt the strength drain out of him. Sweat coated his body. He panted, and the blood went from his face. He grabbed the emergency-door handle and yanked and yanked and yanked, and his throat clogged, and the door wouldn't open and he could hear the passengers shout and the girl scream, "It's him, it's him."

The baseball hat and the skinhead elbowed each other to get at him, and they reached for him. Lithgow yelped, feeling their hands on his shoulders, and he wrenched the handle and shouldered the door and the door opened and air and noise rushed into the bus and Lithgow dived out of the emergency door. Hands clawed at his legs and voices called him a bastard and a murderer and told him to get back here.

He hit the road, hands first. Pain shot up his arms, jarring his shoulders. Headlights swept over him and horns blared.

He covered his head, ready for the hit.

Tyres screeched. The car skidded, smoke hissing from the wheels. It stopped a yard from Lithgow. The driver popped his head out of his window and started to curse Lithgow. A vampire shot out from between the parked cars. The vampire wrenched the man's head, stretched his neck out, sank its teeth into the man's throat.

The car blocked traffic. Horns honked and drivers screamed. Headlights flared on full-beam. Helicopters swooped overhead, throwing down their spotlights. A megaphoned voice said, "Stay in your vehicles, stay in your vehicles."

Lithgow jumped to his feet. The vampire pulled the driver out of the car and dragged him into the shadows to finish its meal.

Lithgow's gaze flitted around. Passengers spilled out of the bus and pointed at him, one saying, "It's him, he's made them, get him," another saying, "There's the bastard, there he is," and they started towards him.

Lithgow clambered over the bonnet of the car that had almost hit him. He scooted round to the driver's side. He opened the door, leaped in. The engine still running, he jammed the car into gear and floored the accelerator.

The car jolted and stalled.

He cursed – and then something caught his eye. He looked right, out of the open driver's side window.

"Fuck," said Lithgow.

The vampire shot from the shadows.

Lithgow started to roll up the window.

The vampire bared its teeth, hurtling forwards.

Lithgow rolled like mad, whimpering.

The buss passengers, coming for him, clambered over cars. Vampires attacked them, sweeping some away into the shadows.

The vampire dived for the window.

Lithgow screamed, rolled like crazy, the window shutting as the vampire's hand shot through the gap.

Lithgow yelled out, jammed the vampire's wrist in the window. Bone snapped. The vampire snarled, clawed at the glass with its other hand.

Lithgow fired the engine, slammed the accelerator. The car shot forward. He dragged the vampire along, weaving through traffic.

He looked in the rear-view mirror. The baseball hat and the skinhead pointed after him and he knew they were saying, *It's him, it's him.*

The vampire Lithgow was dragging along bumped off cars. Its fingers opened and closed in the car. It snarled at Lithgow, and Lithgow tried not to look the thing in the eye because every time he did, he wanted to piss himself.

He drove straight, pinballing vampires and pedestrians out of the way.

Helicopters hovered over Central London. Their spotlights threw a great shower of light over the city. Lithgow sped towards the glow.

He came to Parliament Square, the vampire still attached to the car. Lithgow looked around. Camera crews filmed the chaos on the green outside Parliament. Vampires attacked reporters, attacked tourists, attacked buses and cabs.

Lithgow's eyes skimmed over Big Ben.

And something cold crawled up his spine.

He slowed the car and said, "Jesus Christ," in a whisper, and stared up at the clock. A figure stood in one of the faces, more than three hundred feet above Parliament Square. It hung on to one of the clock's hands, watching the chaos below.

The figure, Lithgow guessed, wasn't human.

CHAPTER 73.
SILVER SCREEN.

THE EMPIRE CINEMA, LEICESTER SQUARE — 11.30 P.M., FEBRUARY 10

CRAIG Truman, nineteen and desperate to make his move, stroked Lisa's thigh. Lisa slapped his hand away. Craig, assistant manager at Lyte's Electricals near Waterloo, tutted and folded his arms. He stared up at the screen. Sylvester Stallone rampaged through the jungle.

Funny she'd wanted to see *John Rambo,* he thought. Craig didn't think it was a girl's film. But Lisa said she liked Stallone. A pang of jealousy twisted in Craig's gut.

Maybe if I was muscled beyond nature, she wouldn't play so hard to get, he thought. He got off with her last weekend at Bar 242 on the South Bank. He got her number, said he'd call, obviously didn't. He left it a week, played hard to get, then rang saying, "Hey, babe, it's me," and she went, "Who's me?" and Craig said, "I had my tongue down your throat at Bar 242 on Saturday, babes, and no lady ever forgets my tongue."

She turned out to be a tough nut, but he finally persuaded her to come on a date, asked her what movies she liked, what kind of food.

"I want to see the new *Rambo,*" she'd said, "and I fucking love Chinese."

"All right," said Craig, "let's do Sunday, babe."

Craig, shit hot on technical stuff, had sat next to her in the cinema and gave her the gist on THX, saying, "It's a high-fidelity sound system, innit, which is just a mark of quality, yeah. Stands for Tomlinson Holman's eXperiment, okay, and he, like, invented it for George Lucas."

But Lisa goes, "Whatever," and hogs the popcorn and, now, just slapped his hand away.

Lisa stared at the screen. He'd already tried to put his arm around her, but she shrugged that off. He'd tried to nuzzle her throat – she jerked away. And now she wouldn't let him stroke that smooth, caramel-coloured leg.

Bitch, he thought; *ice-cold bitch*.

He slumped in the seat. He was getting nowhere. He looked around. The cinema was packed, more than thirteen hundred customers. The sound of war thundered from the speakers. Rambo ran riot, his enemies dying by the dozen. The cinema screen split open and a figure leaped out.

Cold fear flushed Craig's veins. He thought for a second that a character from the film had sprung out into real life.

Rambo flapped around on the ragged remains of the screen.

The audience started screaming. The figure that tore through the screen dived into the front rows. Fists flew, curses filled the auditorium. Rambo fired on a torn screen. Explosions deafened Craig. He stood up, grabbed Lisa's arm. She said, "What's going on?"

The audience panicked. More figures spilled out of the tattered screen. They dived off the stage and into the audience. The audience started to stampede. Shouts and screams filled the cinema. The film kept rolling. The sound was spot-on. *THX for you*, thought Craig, and then, pulling Lisa out of her seat, he said, "Come on, we got to get out of here."

The lights came on. The invaders sweeping out of the screen raced up the aisles. Fights broke out as people tried to flee the cinema.

Craig yanked Lisa's arm, and got her out into the aisle. He shouldered into the traffic, barging someone out of the way. Craig pulled Lisa into the wave of people rushing for the exit. She screamed. She slipped from his grip. He turned with his mouth open, ready to call her name, but the air was knocked out of his lungs as the crowd thudded into him, carrying him off his feet.

"Craig, Craig" – Lisa shrieking his name – "Craig, Craig."

He pushed against the tide of bodies. Someone threw a punch at him saying, "Get the fuck out of the way."

A pale man, shaven headed, flew through the air and bombed into the crowd. The impact scattered bodies. Craig got dominoed by the stumbling crowd and he fell on bodies and bodies fell on him.

He tried to get up. A foot rammed into his chest. It blew the air out of him. Feet trampled him. He threw his arms over his head, but the feet pounded at him. He kicked out, tripping some of the stampeders, and they fell on top of him. He struggled to breathe. Panic filled his heart. He clawed and punched and kicked. And through the chaos of bodies he saw Lisa. The shaven-headed guy straddled her, his face nuzzling her throat.

Rage flashed in Craig's chest.

He said, "Lisa," but his voice died in the swarm sweeping over him. A man fell across his chest. A woman tripped over the man. Someone else piled on top of her. Craig screamed and struggled. The bodies heaped on top of him.

"I can't breathe, I can't breathe," he said, but his screams died in the panic. A body rolled across his face. He scrabbled at the body. Feet trampled his legs. Someone stood on his balls and it lit a fire in his groin. An arm pressed down across his throat. A leg blocked his mouth. His lungs became tighter and tighter. The pressure in his head grew and grew.

He called for Lisa again, but only in his head because he had no breath for words. And he kept calling her till the life was crushed out of his body.

CHAPTER 74.
HOW DO WE STOP THIS?

A POLICE van drove them up Charing Cross Road towards Leicester Square. Murray had shown the cops a letter from some senior officer giving her access to the investigation. The cops were reluctant at first, but Murray persuaded them she and her companions would be safer with the police.

And then one of the armed officers who had seen Lawton kill the vampire at Embankment said, "Let them come with us, this guy" – jabbing a thumb at Lawton – "seems to know what he's doing."

They'd eyed the spear, but Lawton guessed that the cops were happy for people to arm themselves at a time like this.

Crowds choked the streets. They looked scared and confused. The van crawled along Irving Street. A radio crackled and the copper took the call. A cacophony of voices crashed through the airwaves.

"What's that?" said Murray.

"Riot at the Empire cinema, up ahead," said the Inspector, a man called Suleiman.

Lawton slid open the van's door. He leaped out into the sea of bodies. He turned, saw Sassie trying to follow him. He said, "Stay in the van, Sassie, stay in the fucking van."

The colour washed out of her face. The rage in his voice had stopped her dead. But then Murray put a hand on Sassie's shoulder and said, "He's right. Stay here."

He backed away, looking into Sassie's dark blue eyes and saw the yearning in them, and he showed her the yearning in his. But the fear growing in him made it difficult. And he said, "I'll see you again," then turned and barged through the crowd.

People poured out of the Empire. A figure flew out of the exit, ten feet above the panic.

Vampire, thought Lawton.

The creature plunged into the throng. The crowd rippled out – like someone had thrown a rock into a lake. Screams grew louder. The vampire grabbed a woman from behind, tearing into her throat with its hands, lapping at the blood. Her friends swatted the creature, but it held on.

Blood crazy, thought Lawton as he sprinted over, wielding the spear.

"Out of the way," he said, and the friends moved aside.

Lawton drove one end of the spear into the vampire's ear, through its head, and out of the other ear. The creature shrieked. Lawton shook the spear and the vampire flapped like a rag doll. Lawton pulled the spear free. The hole in the vampire's head was the size of a tennis ball. Black fluid pulsed from the wound. The vampire staggered about like he was pissed. Lawton glanced at the woman. Blood bubbled out of her throat. Her friends were comforting her.

Lawton turned on the vampire. The vampire, unsteady on its feet, snarled at him, called him a "Bastard." It stumbled towards Lawton, the creature wailing like a distressed dog. Lawton thrust the spear into the vampire's heart and the thing burned and burst into a cloud of ashes.

"Jesus Christ," said someone, "it's just blown up."

"Vampires," said another voice, "vampires."

Voices babbled around him. Two more vampires sprang out of the cinema.

"Over here," said Lawton, trying to grab the vampire's attention.

The vampire turned, caught his eye, and came for him with its teeth bared.

Lawton jabbed with the spear, but the vampire evaded the attack. The creature clawed Lawton's cheek and he felt the blood hot on his face. He stumbled away.

A voice said, "Look out."

Lawton wheeled around. A female vampire raced towards him. Lawton swiped at the creature with the spear. The weapon's point gashed a wound across the vampire's face. Black blood oozed from the wound.

The vampire who'd torn Lawton's cheek sprang forward again. Lawton kicked out, caught it in the midriff and sent it staggering away.

Lawton's strength drained out of him. Blood seeped from his face, and the bite on his throat throbbed. His vision blurred and the screams and shouts around him faded in and out.

The crowd formed a circle around him. It was like they were watching a street fight.

"They're coming again," someone said and Lawton thought, *Yeah, thanks — why don't you fucking help me?*

The female vampire pounced. Lawton plunged the spear up through its solar plexus. The creature screeched and thrashed and clawed, and the crowd, as one, made a gasping sound.

The male vampire bounded for him, now. Lawton saw the attack coming, but he had the female vampire pierced on his spear. Then, she withered and erupted, dusting the concrete and Lawton with her remains. But it was too late. The male was nearly on him. Lawton braced himself. The creature's scarlet-stained eyes held his. Its jaw widened and Lawton saw the fangs.

The car swept in from the right, crowd screaming and scattering as it skidded into Leicester Square.

The vehicle slammed into the vampire. The creature wheeled through the air and crashed into a Starbucks window.

Lithgow, in the driver's seat, said, "Looked like you could do with a hand."

"Yeah," said Lawton, "I had some issues, you're right. But you took your time."

"Picked up a passenger," said Lithgow, gesturing at the vampire attached to the car. "Get rid of it, can you?"

Lawton went round to the driver's side. The vampire trapped by its arm in the window snarled and clawed at the car. Lawton drove the spear through the middle of its back. The creature stiffened and wailed, then dissolved into dust.

"Better finish the other one off," said Lithgow.

The creature crawled through the shattered Starbucks window. Shards of glass jutted from its face. Lawton kicked it in the head. The vampire slumped, rolled on its back. Lawton skewered it through the heart, and it scorched and softened and went to dust.

Crowds stampeded through Leicester Square. They screamed above the noise of helicopters and sirens. Another pair of vampires burst out of the cinema. And other creatures bounded into the Square from other directions.

"Get away," said Lawton, waving his arms at the crowd, "just get out of the area."

Flashing blue lights blinded Lawton. Emergency vehicles raced into Leicester Square.

Vampires chased the fleeing crowd.

Police marksmen shouted warnings:

"Down! Get down! We'll fire! Armed police!"

Like that's going to make a difference, thought Lawton.

And it didn't.

The coppers fired. The vampires danced as the bullets ripped into them. Then they turned on the cops, clawing and tearing and biting.

Fuck, thought Lawton. His body was weak, but he found strength somewhere. Dragging the tip of the spear along the Tarmac, he strode towards a pair of vampires tussling with a marksman.

Lawton raised the weapon, ready to strike.

And he thought, *How the hell do we stop this?*

CHAPTER 75.
JENNA'S GONE.

MARK McCALL stared at the photo on the front of *thelondonpaper*. The hairs on the back of his neck prickled and the blood drained out of his face. He moaned, put his head in his hands.

The grainy CCTV image showed his dead daughter straddling a youth in a Maida Vale street. Jenna's face was turned to the camera. Her complexion was pale. She scowled at the camera. Dark fluid oozed from her mouth. The same black liquid poured from the youth's throat and pooled on the pavement.

Sitting in a cafe not far from the Metropolitan Police's headquarters, he stared out of the window. Last night's debris littered the streets. He'd got here at 7.00 a.m. as usual, ready to wait outside Scotland Yard for news of his daughter's death. He travelled in on the No. 53 bus from New Gate Rail Station, then picked up the No. 11 from Parliament Square to Victoria. A fifteen-minute walk down Victoria Street got him to Scotland Yard. The journey usually took just over an hour – today it had taken two. Police had cordoned off streets. The City crawled with armed units. Forensic officers scuttled around in their white overalls.

Picking up the *London Lite* and *thelondonpaper*, the capital's freesheets, McCall went to the cafe for tea and toast. He only ate because his wife told him to. His appetite had waned since Jenna's death. But Sarah said,

"You have to eat something, keep you going, so promise me that you'll have some toast, at least."

So he did, for Sarah.

He'd also bought *The Sun* and the *Daily Mail*, and their front pages howled at the indignity and uselessness of the authorities in handling the crisis.

The *Mail* accused sub-cultures of distributing drugs that gave the impression of death. And the paper attacked the "weird, unnatural" desire in some humans to drink blood.

"All this talk of vampires is misleading," said the Leader column. "These are not vampires in the fictional sense – that is a nonsense. These are sick, perverse individuals produced by a sick, perverse society."

The Sun's front page blasted the words:

WELCOME TO HELL

in red capital letters, and then a sub-deck below saying:

LONDON MORE DEADLY THAN BAGHDAD

He turned again to *thelondonpaper*. He studied the image again. There was no mistaking; it was Jenna – or what was left of Jenna.

Her face seemed cold, and he'd never seen her look with such fury before. The caption under the picture said, "A 'vampire'" – they'd put the word in quotes, to pretend it wasn't real, maybe – "attacks a youth outside Warwick Avenue tube station in Maida Vale last night."

McCall bit his finger to hold back the tears. His child was an animal. His Jenna was gone. His blood boiled. This was Lawton, all Lawton.

"Bad news," McCall had told his wife when Jenna first brought Lawton home when she was a schoolgirl. He was sixteen, she was fourteen, fifteen. Then he went and joined up, broke Jenna's heart, and that made it even worse. The Army, for Christ's sake. "Soldiers, nothing but trouble," McCall had said.

"Give him a chance," Sarah told him, "he seems nice enough – and he treats Jenna well."

"We'll see. I tell you, if he lays a finger on her – "

"What, Mark? What will you do?" His wife glared at him and he'd felt the shame rise up in him. He'd balled his hands into fists. But then he'd counted back from ten and turned his back on her like they'd told him to do at the counselling sessions. And then she'd put a hand on his shoulder and told him it would be all right.

Well, fifteen years on it wasn't all right.

It was worse – worse that they'd lost Jenna, firstly, to some weird sub-culture, then lost her to some bizarre drug, and then found out she attacked people in the street.

And things weren't good at home, either.

The old anger flared up in McCall. The old anger that made him raise his hand and made Sarah cower.

"Anything else, mate?" said the cafe owner.

McCall asked for another tea. He studied the picture of Jenna again. He'd lost her, now – he knew that. And because he'd lost her, someone had to pay. And that was Lawton. McCall clenched his teeth and balled his fists. If the fury erupted again after all these years, it would erupt in Lawton's face.

McCall got up, threw a tenner on the table.

The owner put the tea down on the table and said, "Your tea, mate," as McCall stomped out of the cafe.

CHAPTER 76.
DISCOVERIES.

LAWTON said, "Let's go over it again."

Murray, scanning the paperwork spread out on her kitchen table, bit her lip. She plucked a sheet from the carpet of papers. She furrowed her brow and began by going through everything they knew about the house in Holland Park and Dr. Afdal Haddad. "And now we know he was originally from Iraq," she said.

"Which links him to the vessels," said Sassie.

Sassie had napped for a while on an armchair in the corner of the kitchen, and now she sipped black coffee to keep fatigue at bay. Lithgow was grabbing some kip on Murray's sofa. Richard Murray provided the coffee and tea and toast, and Murray smiled at him. They shared the loss of their boys. Richard had cried when they'd got back that morning, realizing he'd been stupid the night before. Sassie went on, her eyes filled with fire. Murray looked at her, wishing she could have some of the younger woman's enthusiasm. But it was rage and fear that drove Murray now. She glanced at Lawton. He looked pale. Gauze covered the wound on his cheek. The bruise at his throat was livid. How many other injuries did he have? Murray knew he'd been shot five times during his Army career – "That man's got five bullet holes in his body for you," a major ranted at Murray when she was writing her story about the incident in Basra. She wondered how long he could go on.

Sassie said, "Everything Tom Wilson said makes sense. We've got to find their lair. Like Alexander found their lair. He trapped them all there, in Nebuchadnezzar's palace. And then he" – she looked at Lawton – "faced the trinity and killed them with this." She placed her hand on the spear, which lay on the table in its scabbard. "That's what we've got to do."

"So you're saying there's a Nebuchadnezzar's palace here in London?" said Murray.

"I don't know," said Sassie. "I'm just trying to think what we can do." She paused. And then said, "Could they be going back there? Planning a return to Babylon, rebuild the city?"

"Saddam tried that," said Lawton. "He started to rebuild Babylon. Then the U.S. Army mowed it all down."

Sassie said, "Could they still be at the house in Holland Park?"

Murray shook her head. "Police trawled that place with a fine tooth comb. There's nothing left."

"And the house isn't on the market?" said Lawton.

"No – still owned by Haddad."

Richard went through to the living room. Murray watched him go. She remembered why she loved him. And then grief ached in her heart. Why had it taken the loss of her children to make these feelings return, to make them come together again? She bit her lip to stem the tears.

"Was Haddad and the Radu woman that lived with him in a relationship?" said Lawton.

"Don't know," said Murray.

Sassie said, "Why are they bringing vampirism to London?"

"Afdal Haddad" – they all turned as Richard came into the kitchen holding a laptop; he read from the screen, which cast a glow on his face – "came to the UK in 1921 as a six-year old. An Anglo-Arab family who came over here in 1900 took him in. This family sponsored Haddad, paid for his schooling. In 1946 this family had twins. In the late 1980s the brothers set up a homeopathic clinic in Holland Park with Haddad called – "

"F&H Wellbeing," said Murray, her nerves fraying.

"That's right," said Richard. "These twins, they made a lot of money in the Eighties selling cars."

"F&H," said Murray. "Fuad and Haddad."

Her husband nodded. "George and Alfred Fuad."

Nausea washed through Murray.

Lawton said, "Religion."

Murray looked at him and said, "You can find out anything if you want to," her voice thin and fragile.

CHAPTER 77.
BRICK WALL.

DETECTIVE Superintendent Phil Birch said, "You're not running this investigation, Christine, I am."

Murray leaned across Birch's desk. "My sons are missing."

He frowned and scratched the back of his neck. "I realize that. There are many people missing. And we're doing our best – "

"Best is not good enough," she said, slamming the desk. The heat rose up in her, and she was trembling. She said, "If my boys are dead, I'm coming after you."

"Don't threaten me. I'm serious: do not threaten me."

"Then why don't you go there, go to Religion?"

He said, "We've been to Religion. Our initial inquiries were centred on Religion. There's nothing there, is that clear?"

"No, that's not clear."

"I'm afraid it's about as clear as it's going to get."

"Have you been in contact with the Fuads? Have you found them?"

Birch looked at his clipboard, which lay on the desk in front of him. He fumbled with the red ribbon laced to the clipping mechanism. He raised his gaze to her again and said, "We've – we've been in touch, yes, and we're satisfied with the answers they provided."

"They're involved, Mr. Birch, and – "

He jabbed a finger at her saying, "I'm warning you, Christine, don't get on your high horse with this one."

She sat back, the fire leaving her cheeks. She said, "What do you mean?"

"I mean don't get yourself a crusade. Didn't work out with the soldier, did it. I hear you're good mates, now. Hear he's been a bit of a" – Birch sneered – "hero over the past couple of evenings. So my officers say."

"Jake Lawton's courageous. It doesn't mean he didn't do what he was suspected of doing. Even bad men can be brave."

Birch paused for a moment. And then he said, "It might be best for all of you – Lawton, yourself, all of you – to keep out of trouble over the next few days."

Murray cocked her head. "Is that a threat?"

He laughed. "Heavens, no. Advice, that's all. It might get – well – fraught out there."

"I think we can cope with fraught, Mr. Birch. Jake Lawton can cope with fraught, I think."

He bared his teeth. "I'm telling you, don't interfere with our investigations."

"Then get a search warrant for Religion."

"We don't need," he said, his cheeks red, "a fucking search warrant for Religion."

"Does Commander Deere know about this? Maybe I'll go see Commander Deere."

"Maybe you should. Your pal Peter Deere. Dear little Peter the pen-pusher."

Murray tensed. Her mouth opened, but she said nothing.

Birch continued:

"He knows his place, Christine, so he won't help you anymore. He got you in with our investigation, didn't he, but you won't get anything else out of him. He's not for this world much longer."

"What does that mean?" she said, her throat dry.

"I mean exactly that – he's not for this world, the world of the Metropolitan Police. He's retiring at the end of the year, so he's keeping his nose clean. Maybe you should consider retiring, too. You could both get a little cottage in the country. I hear things aren't too healthy in the Murray household, so a love-nest with sweet Peter might be just the thing."

The strength leached out of Murray. She tried to speak, saying, "How – how – " but that's about all she managed.

Birch slammed his fist on the desk and Murray flinched. He said, "It's over, Christine. We're in charge. My advice is as before: keep out of trouble, don't get involved. This is a nasty, nasty situation."

"My – my children – it's – it's Religion."

"It's not. It's not Religion. Religion is out of bounds. I'll have anyone caught snooping around there arrested. Do you understand?"

She gathered herself, regaining her strength and her bite. She said, "No, I don't understand," and stood up.

"That's a shame," said Birch, "a great shame."

"I'll go higher."

He smirked. "You go higher, Christine," he said. "You go as high as you like."

CHAPTER 78.
VISITORS.

LAWTON arrived at his flat at 10.50 a.m. He felt thirsty, hungry, and weak. He made a coffee, rolled a fag.

He sat at the kitchen table and put the scabbard containing the spear in front of him on the Formica. He planned to grab an hour's rest and then head back into the city to meet up with the others.

Before they'd left Murray's house, Lawton shared a moment with Sassie. They held each other and kissed. She'd asked if they'd ever get through this, and he said they would. But he didn't know if this was true or not.

She'd gone home to sleep, Lithgow had remained on the sofa in the Murray's living room, and Murray had gone to Scotland Yard.

He'd got a call from Murray just as he was getting off the bus at New Cross Underground Station, phoning to say how her meeting with Birch had gone. She was crying, and Lawton couldn't understand what she was saying. Then she stopped crying, made more sense, and said Birch wouldn't help them.

"He warned us off," Murray had said to Lawton. "Told us to keep away from Religion, keep our noses clean."

"Not much chance of that, is there," he'd said, and promised her again that they'd find David and Michael.

She said she didn't know what to do. "Birch won't go for a warrant."

Lawton thought for a moment, and then he'd said, "Ask Fraser. His old man's a barrister. He might help."

He turned on the radio. Trouble filled the news. London in turmoil. Central areas cordoned off. Limited travel. More deaths, more disappearances. CCTV images showing Saturday night's victims walking around.

The dead becoming alive.

Or something like *alive*, he thought, remembering Jenna's touch, cold and clammy. Decay wafting off her. Her eyes tinted red. And no human – living or dead – had fangs like hers.

He rubbed his neck. He still felt weak, as if he'd been drained of strength. He'd blindly ignored his condition last night and fought on adrenalin. He was used to that. They'd often had to do that in combat. Forget your thirst, your hunger, your pain, your fear, and just focus on the task.

He drank the coffee, smoked his roll-up.

He drew the spear out of the scabbard.

He'd not known much about Alexander the Great until the past couple of days, although his first platoon sergeant, a guy called Jim Quinn, had mentioned him.

Quinn had said, "Alexander the Great led armies at sixteen. What do sixteen-year-olds do these days? Hang about street corners, mug old ladies, and nick cars."

But Lawton, like the rest of the lads, chuckled, thinking Quinn was a bit of a swot. Now, he regretted not listening to the platoon sergeant.

He remembered himself at sixteen. Leading armies? Not likely. Hanging around street corners, more like. He never mugged old ladies or nicked cars, though.

He sardonically toasted himself with the coffee mug for not going down those paths, at least.

Lawton poured the coffee down the sink, rinsed the cup. He heard the building's front door open and footsteps – two sets – clumping up the stairs. The footsteps stopped outside his flat and someone knocked on the door.

Lawton frowned.

He wrapped the spear in it scabbard, tucked it under the table. He went to the door, opened it. His chest grew cold. His eyes fixed first on his neighbour, a constantly smiling Bangladeshi youth who worked in an Indian restaurant down the road.

The youth wasn't smiling, though, and he had a gun to his head.

The tall man with a scar running down his face was holding the gun and he said, "Good morning, Mr. Lawton."

The gun went off. Lawton flinched. He smelled cordite. Blood pumped from the Bangladeshi youth's temple. The youth toppled over and hit the corridor floor. The scarred man strode into the flat, gun aimed at Lawton, Lawton stumbling backwards with his hands held out, his mind reeling.

The scarred man smiled and said, "You next, Mr. Lawton."

★ ★ ★ ★

"Ed? What are you doing here?" said Sassie.

He stood at the top of the stairs outside her door and gave her a grin. "Thought I'd come to see how my favourite researcher's getting along," he said.

"Fine, thanks." She stopped at the top of the flight. Her legs felt heavy and her shoulders sagged. She wanted to get into her flat and sleep. Ed Crane was the last person she could cope with – she wasn't sharp enough, at the moment, to deal with his banter and fend off his flirting. "I'm just very tired, Ed. Can't this wait, whatever it is?"

He folded his arms and raised an eyebrow. "I always wait for you, Sassie. Waiting for an answer to my declarations of love."

She groaned and shook her head, went for the door. "Sorry, Ed, not in the mood."

He grabbed her arm and glared at her.

Her mouth went dry; she froze, her muscles feeling like lead.

His mouth turned into a smile, but it didn't make it up to his eyes. He said, "Wondered how your research into this Babylonian vase's going, that's all. I've some information. You know, thought I'd help my number one girl."

Sassie stared at him. She needed sleep. But if Ed had something useful to say, she wanted to hear it. For Jake's sake, for everyone's sake. She couldn't risk not knowing. She considered him for a moment, and then drew away, putting her key in the lock.

"Ten minutes," she said, "I'm knackered."

★ ★ ★ ★

"But first," said the scarred man, "you give me the spear."

305

Lawton, hands held out in a surrender pose, glared at the gunman.
"Now, Lawton."

Lawton stared at the scarred man. The gunman's face wavered, a
frown creasing his forehead. A vein pulsed at the stranger's temple, and
his Adam's apple bobbed.

"Lawton" – more haste in his voice – "I want the spear. I know you
have it. We know you went up to Manchester, to see the old man."

Heat flared in Lawton's cheeks: they'd been followed.

The scarred man said, "Give me the spear of Abraham, or I'll kill
you."

"And then what will you do?"

"I'll ransack your" – Scar's eyes ranged the flat, and he curled his lip
– "home and find it myself."

"I die either way, then?"

Scar shrugged.

"All right," said Lawton, "if I'm going to die, you can have what you
came for – but first, I want to know a few things."

Scar smiled, lowered his gun and held it close to his waist, still aimed
at Lawton. "All right, for amusement."

"Are you vampires?" said Lawton.

"Ha! Funny man. We're human."

"So what are these creatures running around London?"

"They *are* vampires. They need blood. Three days without it, they
die."

"How else can they die?"

Scar's eyes narrowed. He studied Lawton for a moment. Then he
said, "I'm sure old Mr. Wilson, the hero of Mesopotamia, thief and
killer of children, told you."

Lawton tensed.

Scar laughed. "We know you've been up there. We have eyes
everywhere. You can't do anything without us knowing about it,
Lawton. We're like Big Brother."

"Did you steal the jars from Wilson's flat?"

Scar's brow creased. "Steal? They were ours in the first place. Our
family. He stole them from us. Lucky we found them. His great great
granddaughter, stupid little bitch, put them on eBay. Then we guess:
if he's got the vases, he's got the spear. We bid for them, say we'd pick
them up. I get the address. I go up there. Lucky he wasn't in. I'd have
cut him into a thousand pieces."

"Then I'd have cut you into a thousand more."

Scar chuckled, threw a glance towards the kitchen area saying, "I'm bored with this now. Tell me – "

Lawton sprang forward. Scar flinched. The gun fired. The bullet zipped past Lawton's ear. Scar raised the gun to fire again. He yelled as Lawton swatted his gun-hand away with his left hand. Lawton swung his right elbow, cracked Scar above the eye. Bone snapped, skin sliced, blood spurted from the wound. Scar lurched, fell, hit the floor.

Lawton went for him. Scar kicked out. Lawton avoided the attack. He kicked, catching Scar in the thigh and Scar screamed. He bared his teeth, his cheeks reddened with anger. He fired the gun.

The bullet thumped into the ceiling, gouging through the plaster.

Lawton dived on top of Scar. He grabbed Scar's wrist. Blood ribboned down the gunman's face from the eye wound. Lawton rained fists on the man. Scar lashed out, clawing at Lawton's face. They rolled, they cursed, blood sprayed. The gun jammed between their chests. Lawton felt the barrel press into his ribs.

If Scar pulled the trigger . . .

Lawton gritted his teeth. He tried to twist the man's wrist. Swung punches at his head. Scar hammer fisted Lawton bicep, making it go dead.

The barrel angling up towards Lawton's heart ...

Lawton's muscles tightened.

The gun fired.

Lawton flinched and felt a bolt strike his chest, and pain filled his head.

Scar leered up at him.

Lawton felt a warm wetness spread over his chest.

★ ★ ★ ★

"Will he help?" Murray had asked Lithgow, and Lithgow had said, "You're not his son, so he just might."

And Murray asked the same question again: "Will he help?"

Lithgow, chewing his nails, told her, "Dad's one of those barristers who love going up against the cops, so if you say you're trying to get them to search Religion, and they're refusing, he'll probably start salivating and help you out."

Bernard Lithgow's offices were near Victoria Station. The waiting room smelled of varnish, and it made Murray dizzy after her lack of sleep. She wondered how Lawton and Sassie were getting on while she waited for Lithgow senior, and she thought about her children.

She gazed around the waiting room. Hunting scenes hung on the panelled walls. A piece of scarlet cloth, old and worn, was framed. Murray stood and went over to the framed cloth. It was a rag, stained and ancient. It lay on a white satin background in the glass case. The frame was gold.

A memory flared in Murray's mind and she tried to retrieve it, but it was lost before she grabbed it. She shook her head, her brow furrowed.

She thought, *Where have —?*

"Mr. Lithgow will see you now, Mrs. Murray," said a voice.

Murray turned. A blonde woman, mid-twenties and glossy, peered from behind a door.

"Thank you," said Murray to Lithgow's assistant.

She entered his chambers. The assistant, throwing a smile towards the QC, left and closed the door.

Lithgow senior sat behind an oak desk. The barrister, beckoning Murray, absent-mindedly brushed the desk. He was in his fifties, tall and lithe, and Murray saw Fraser in the man's face.

"Sit," he said, and Murray sat. Still he brushed at the desk. His cheeks were flushed, and his Oxford shirt open at the neck. Murray thought, *He's just been having sex with that girl.*

Lithgow senior said, "Very unusual situation, Mrs. Murray. Why do you think the courts should issue a search warrant?"

Murray explained, telling him that the owners of Religion had links with the suspected owner of the house where a vessel containing drugs was found.

"And," said the QC, taking a yellow legal pad from a drawer in his desk, "why is it, do you think, that the Metropolitan Police are unwilling to pursue this warrant?"

Murray said she didn't know, couldn't understand why. She said her sons had disappeared, that she thought they were victims of whoever was responsible for these murders, "and I think they're being held at Religion," she said.

The barrister scribbled on the legal pad with a pencil.

"Any proof?" he said.

"No proof," she said.

His eyes narrowed and he chewed the top of the pencil. He said, "Have you spoken to Detective Superintendent Phil Birch?"

She said she had, but had no luck.

Lithgow senior nodded and hummed.

"You know, Mrs. Murray," he said, "I'm not sure I can help you at all – I don't think a court, any court, would issue a warrant on just a hunch – "

She started to say something but he raised a hand.

He said, "But what I will do is put in a few calls. I know Mr. Birch. I know a minister in the Home Office. I'll guarantee you, if there is any truth to your allegations, we'll try our best to dig them out. How's that?"

"Well," she said, "it's a start. But I – I don't know how much time – "

"I understand, I understand. You're a concerned mother. I'm a concerned father, as you know. But this is all I can do."

Murray nodded, and got up.

Lithgow stood, leaned over the desk to shake her hand. He said, "Give my regards to that son of mine, if he's still around? Still around, is he?" Lithgow's eyebrow arched.

"Yes," said Murray, feeling something twist in her gut, "yes he is."

She said goodbye and turned, walking out of the office.

Behind her, Lithgow clicked an intercom and said, "Estella, would you come back in here. I seem to have lost my – my – yes, yes, that would be delightful, Estella."

The door opened. Estella the blonde bounced in. She smirked at Murray and sashayed past her, breasts moving, hips swaying, heels clicking on the varnished floor.

"Shut – shut the door, Mrs. Murray," said Lithgow.

She glanced over her shoulders. Estella perched on the edge of the desk. She watched Murray until Murray had closed the door. And after shutting it she listened outside for a moment. A groan came from inside the office. It sickened Murray, and she moved away, backing off across the waiting room. Then the red rag in the gold frame caught her eye again, and she turned to look at it.

A muffled moan came from behind the barrister's door, but it faded as Murray focused on the scarlet cloth.

And a cold, slick fear crawled up from her belly.

★ ★ ★ ★

Ed Crane said, "That's nonsense, Sassie. You're an archaeologist. You deal in facts, in truth."

"I know, Ed, but – but I can't deny what I've seen," she said. Her throat was dry. She eyed him. She wondered about the cuneiform on the lip of the clay pot. Crane said it didn't mean anything; Wilson said it was a warning. Had Crane got it wrong, or was he lying?

He folded his arms and leaned back in the armchair. "And what have you seen?" he said.

"I've told you, I've told you what I've seen. I drove a stake" – she got up from the sofa, started pacing the room – "through someone's chest who then turned to dust before my eyes. And I've seen people attacked in the street. I've seen my friend drive a stake through things that have also just – " She stopped pacing, looked at him. "That's what I've seen, Ed."

He leaned forward, put his elbows on his knees and rested his face in his hands. He said, "I'll admit that there are awful, awful things happening. But we can't revert to pseudo-science, pseudo-history, to explain these events. We research, we consider, we evaluate, we conclude – a reasonable answer will show itself if we keep our heads, Sassie."

"I wish you were right." She turned and faced the window. The streets lay quiet under a constant drizzle.

Hands fell on her shoulders.

She spun around and drew away from him, and he smiled at her, saying, "Hey, delicious, don't be jumpy."

Sassie shuddered. She said, "Ed, I need to sleep – "

"Good, where's the bedroom?"

"No, Ed, please."

He stepped towards her. "You and me, we've got to get friendly, you know."

Her temper blazed. "Ed, would you please – "

He closed the space between them, and she leaned away from him. He grabbed her arms. Sassie grappled with him.

"What are you doing?" she said.

"It's all right," he said, "it's all right, come – "

She kicked his shin and he yelped, letting go of her. Sassie stepped back, tears welling in her eyes. Fear flushed coldly through her veins. She said, "I want you to go. I want you to go – "

He slapped her across the face. She reeled away. Her skin burned, as if someone had laid a red-hot poker across her skin. She stared at him, mouth open and tears rolling down her cheeks. She tried to say something, but shock had muted her.

Ed sneered and came towards her.

Finding her voice, she said, "Ed – Ed – what are you – Ed –?"

He seized her arms and shook her like a rag doll. Her bones rattled and her neck whiplashed.

"You fucking little bitch," he said, "you'd better start appreciating me, because if you don't you'll be fucking meat, I tell you, fucking strung up like a pig and bled."

He shoved her against the table. Hot liquid washed up her throat and she retched. She wanted to shout for Jake, but she knew he wouldn't come.

She tried to say Ed's name again, but nothing came out, only a gasp.

He grabbed Sassie's hair, and the pain ripped through her scalp. He dragged her across the room, and she screamed. Ed shoved her against the wall and slammed himself against her, knocking the wind out of her. Then he mashed his mouth against her lips.

Her bladder chilled and felt heavy, and she almost puked again. She couldn't breathe, his mouth pressed against her mouth. She started to choke. Panic made her body twitch and her lungs filled with hot fluid that she couldn't throw up. She dug her nails into his shoulders, struggled against him. Her vision blurred. Her head felt as if it were swelling, filling with blood.

Sassie bit his lip until she tasted his blood in her mouth.

Ed screeched, pushed himself away and put his hand to his mouth. Blood pulsed from his split lip. He glowered at Sassie. "You little cow," he said. "Enjoy taking bites out of people, do you? Right – we'll see if you like a taste of you own medicine."

He strode towards her. Blood poured down his chin. He raised his fist. Sassie moaned and begged him not to hurt her.

He was on her and she cowered and screamed.

He punched her on the jaw.

Her head snapped back against the wall.

White light exploded in front of her eyes.

And then everything went black.

★ ★ ★ ★

He rolled away from the body and put his hand to his chest. Blood soaked his T-shirt, a dark stain seeping through to dampen his skin. He got up, stared down at his chest. He took his T-shirt off and dropped it next to the dead man. He crouched next to the body, checked for a pulse in the neck. Blood masked the man's face. His eyes stared up at the ceiling. His mouth stood agape. The gunshot had burned away the man's shirt and charred his skin. Blood bubbled from a wound near the centre of his chest.

Right through the heart, thought Lawton.

He went to the door, looked into the corridor. The Bangladeshi lay dead. The poor guy had never hurt anyone. He'd always been polite to Lawton, always smiled and said hello. Probably faced abuse since he came to this country, but still managed to be civil with everyone he met.

Even his killer, Lawton supposed.

The Bangladeshi had probably thought he was doing Scar a favour, letting him up into the flats. Then he got a gun pointed at his head, and his brains blown out.

Lawton dragged the Bangladeshi into the flat and locked the door. He laid the youth next to the scarred man. Lawton got a blanket out of the airing cupboard and draped it over the Bangladeshi's body.

He left Scar uncovered.

Lawton thought about how he should handle this. He had two dead men on his floor, one of whom he'd killed himself; in self-defence, in a struggle, but still – the police would presume him guilty before discovering he was innocent.

He thought of phoning Murray, telling her what happened. He nodded to himself, deciding that was the best option. He went to the phone, then the Crazy Frog ringtone started up.

Lawton looked at Scar.

The phone vibrated in the dead man's jacket. It looked like a rat trying to get out from under his armpit – while singing the Crazy Frog tune.

Lawton shook his head, scattering the bizarre image from his mind. He squatted and reached into Scar's pocket for the phone.

The phone's screen read, PHONE #3.

Lawton pressed the answer button and put the phone to his ear. He didn't say anything.

A voice Lawton recognized but couldn't identify said, "H–hello? Hello, Ion? Ion, is that – are you there? Have you got the spear?"

Lawton thought, *Where have I heard that voice?* He trawled his memory. Static filled the line. It sounded like the man was calling him from the top of a building in a gale. Lawton heard traffic in the background.

The man said, "Ion, can you hear me – it's a really bad line."

Lawton walked over to the kitchen, turned on the radio and found static. He brought the radio up to the phone and said, "I can't hear you."

"Bloody hell, Ion. That's a really bad line. You sound weird. Have you got the spear? I've got the girl."

Lawton's guts turned cold.

The man said, "I'm taking her over there. Shit, this line – I'm going to have to go, Ion." The man said, "fuck," and hung up.

Lawton dropped the phone and switched off the radio.

He stared into space, his chest growing cold.

I've got the girl.

What did that mean? Which girl?

The strength drained out of him. He leaned on the counter. He knew the man meant Sassie. And then he knew who the voice belonged to.

Energy pulsed through his body. He grabbed a shirt, pulled it on. He went for the door, unlocked it, threw it open and –

The man clubbed Lawton across the face.

313

CHAPTER 79.
A LIONESS PROTECTING
HER CUBS.

MURRAY strode up Old Compton Street. Armed police wandered about. She looked at her feet, hiding her face under the brim of a baseball cap.

They weren't going to stop her – not with their curfews, not with their guns, not with their plots and their conspiracies.

She weaved through pedestrians and police, keeping her head down. The drizzle made the back of her neck wet. She stopped at a street corner, glanced up.

Religion stood on the opposite corner. A slab of wood covered the entrance. A sign read, CLOSED UNTIL FURTHER NOTICE. Yellow police tape crisscrossed the wood. She walked around to the side of the club, up a narrow, single-lane street. The tall, narrow windows were dark. They stood ten feet off the ground and stretched up the building's height. Seven of them lined the side of the building like guards standing watch.

Murray walked up the side street, gazing up at the windows, trying to think how to get in.

A black Toyota 4x4 swept across the street ahead of her and shot down an alley at the rear of the club.

Murray trotted up the street. The road, lined with warehouses and garages, was quiet and she faltered for a second, thinking if it was wise for her to be here on her own.

Then she realized *why* she was here: David and Michael.

She jogged up the street and came to the corner of the building. She peered around and saw the car, about fifty yards down the passage. The alley was narrow, only slightly wider than the 4x4. The driver would only have a foot or so either side to open his doors. She made a mental note of the registration number.

A man squeezed out of the driver's side door. He was late thirties, lean and handsome. He came round to the rear of the vehicle and lifted open the back door.

A woman with a sack over her head lay in the boot. Her hands and feet were bound with tape. Murray gasped and her nerves tightened.

The driver sat on the edge of the boot and made a call on his mobile. He chewed his nails, waiting for the call to be answered. *No one at home,* thought Murray when the man put the phone back in his pocket. He hauled the blindfolded woman out of the 4x4 and hoisted her over his shoulder. He shut the door and appeared to be tapping the wall. A screech of metal put Murray's teeth on edge. Then, as if walking through the wall, the man disappeared into the building.

Murray sneaked down the alley and came to a metal door. Dents calloused its surface and rust scabbed the paintwork. On the door frame there was a security panel. That's what the man was tapping: a code on the keypad. She flipped up the security panel's cover and stared at the numbers.

No hope, she thought.

She put her hand on the door. She gave it a nudge, not expecting it to open.

It didn't.

She looked up. A CCTV camera pointed down at her.

Sadness filled her heart. Her eyes welled up. She felt fear and loss for her sons. Were they in here? She would claw through the door with her hands if she had to, if she knew they were here.

She bit her lip and lowered her head, the brim of her cap hiding any tears she shed from the watching camera.

Murray wanted to crouch against this wall in this alley and weep. She wanted the world to close in on her, the ground to swallow her. She wanted to sleep and let this pass away.

But not until David and Michael were safe.

She braced herself.

She banged on the door.

"If my children are in here – I'm calling the police. I'm a journalist. I'll have coppers and camera crews crawling all over the place unless you" – she held her NUJ card up to the camera – "open this door. You've got missing children in this building."

No answer.

She banged again, using her fist this time. Her skin chafed on the metal. But Murray didn't care. Panic grew in her. She hammered the door again, saying, "Open this door. I'll ring the Army. I'll get the SAS. You'll regret this. I'll – I'll kill you, you hear, I'll kill you if you hurt my boys."

But no one answered.

Murray was out of breath. She tried to calm down. She thought about what she could do. Ring for help, maybe. The police? But they still didn't have a warrant.

She rang Birch, and he picked up after five rings.

"Your rights have been rescinded, Christine," he said. "Go home, let us take care of things, now."

"But I saw this man, I saw him carry in a body," she said.

"It's theatre-land, Christine. It could be anything. A dummy, anything. It's not enough, all right."

She raged at him, saying he was endangering her children and that she'd have his job.

Birch was quiet for a moment, then he sniffed and said, "I don't think so," and hung up on her.

She walked away from Religion, back along Old Compton Street. She passed an electronic goods shop, TV's silently flickering behind barred windows. She looked at the screens. A woman was making a speech. The woman paused and wiped her mouth with a red handkerchief. But not really a handkerchief – too frayed; too leathery.

A memory flared.

Murray's legs buckled. Hot, sour liquid gushed up into her throat, and she put a hand over her mouth. She felt clammy and sick and doomed.

The woman on TV was Jacqueline Burrows.

CHAPTER 80.
THROWN INTO THE PIT.

CRANE tossed Sassie to the ground. Dust rose and filtered through the pores in the sack covering her face. The dust went up her nose, into her throat, and she coughed and spluttered against the tape covering her mouth.

Crane tore the sack off her head.

Lights blinded her for a few seconds. Then her eyes adjusted. She stared up at the strip-lights on the ceiling.

Crane stood above her, leaned down and sat her up. Her wrists and ankles were bound with tape.

She tried to speak, tried to tell him to let her go, but couldn't with tape over her mouth. And in her frustration, she kicked out at him.

A woman said, "She's a hot one," from behind Sassie.

Sassie twisted around to see.

A dark-haired woman strutted by and went to stand next to Crane.

"Nadia Radu," said Crane, "this is Dr. Sassie Rae, a nosy researcher who should've listened to me instead of taking a fancy to that meddlesome soldier."

"He's not a concern to us any longer," said Radu. "Ion paid him a visit."

Sassie's stomach tensed.

"I called Ion," said Crane, "asked him if he had the spear, but it was a terrible line."

The woman glanced at her watch and said, "He'll be back any minute."

"Will the others be here?"

"They'll all be here tonight."

Ed rubbed his hands together.

Sassie struggled again.

The woman smirked.

Crane said, "Shall I stick her in the cage with the others?"

"No, Professor. Put her in the pit with that other girl. Another princess for our Lord Kea. A meal for when he awakens."

Sassie screamed through the tape covering her mouth. Crane grabbed her wrists and dragged her to her feet. He sliced the tape binding her ankles so she was able to walk. She kicked at him, but he skipped out of the way.

Nadia Radu strolled off.

"Bitch," said Crane, baring his teeth. He grabbed her hair. He hooked his hand into the crook of her elbow and yanked her towards the panelled flooring at the centre of the basement. A cage nearby held five youngsters. Sassie stared at them. They were sleeping, all of them huddled together.

She wondered if Murray's children were among them.

Crane ushered her towards the trench in the wooden floor. She smelled something and it made her dizzy. She wished she didn't have to breathe through her nose.

Crane dragged her to the edge of the pit and forced her to look into it. She thought she'd faint. That's where the stink came from: the smell of blood and meat; the smell of death and decay.

A girl lay curled up in the corner of the pit. Blood covered her tattered dress and coffee-coloured skin. Her hair hung in clumps, matted with blood. Sassie saw her chest rise and fall.

Sassie's eyes skimmed the rest of the grave. It was about eight feet wide and twelve feet long, and around seven feet deep. Blood soaked the ground. And in the blood, at the centre of the trench, a human shape was forming from the gore. It was red and raw, sinew and muscle, arteries and veins, blue and red and purple. Steam rose up from the shape and it smelled like rotting food.

Sassie stared at the figure.

And it pulsed.

A scream locked in her throat.

The thing was alive.

Sassie struggled against Crane.

He laughed. "Time to meet your maker," he said.

He shoved and Sassie fell into the grave. She hit the slime knees first and her legs sank into the soft, fleshy ground. She stared at the face of the thing coming alive in the trench. The odour was stronger, now. It made her want to be sick. She shuffled from the cadaver.

Sassie started to gag. She yanked against the tape trussing her wrists. She tore at the tape over her mouth. Her feet gouged through the slime. Vomit filled her throat.

Her mind screamed: *I'm dying, I'm dying.*

She started to choke. The vile-tasting sick filling her throat and mouth. Her eyes were wide. Tears streamed down her face.

Crane smirked down at her. He waved, and walked away from the edge of the pit.

And then a shadow passed across her vision.

Sassie curled up into a ball as terror shredded her nerves.

A hand, cold and oily, pressed down over her taped-up mouth.

★ ★ ★ ★

Stars flashed in front of Lawton's eyes. He reeled away from his attacker.

The man, snarling as he charged, held the club out again – ready to swing at Lawton, ready to strike him another blow.

But the man didn't see the bodies, rage tunnelling his vision, and he tripped over them. His face stretched into an expression of shock. He stumbled towards Lawton and threw out his arms to stop himself from falling on his face.

Lawton grabbed his chance. He lunged forward and slipped inside his attacker's guard to prevent the man from hitting him, the man's blows glancing off Lawton's forearms and elbows. Lawton brought his arm down in a chopping motion, smashing it into the attacker's collarbone.

The man yelled out in pain and dropped his weapon.

Lawton grabbed the man by the collar and swung him round, tossing him against the wall. The man's head whipped back and struck the plaster. He swayed, and his eyes rolled back in his head. Lawton let him go, and the guy slumped to his knees next to Scar and the

Bangladeshi.

Lawton pointed at the bodies and said, "You do that again, McCall, and you'll end up joining these two."

McCall cradled the back of his head with one hand, and rubbed his shoulder with the other.

Lawton grabbed the baseball bat and tossed it over to the kitchen, where it clanked against the oven. He kicked the door shut, then slumped into a chair.

"Want to tell me what that was about?" said Lawton.

McCall wasn't listening. He stared at the bodies and then looked up at Lawton, saying, "You did this?"

"Only Scar-face over there. The other one's my neighbour. Scar killed him."

"Who is he, the guy with the scar?"

"I don't know," said Lawton.

"Jesus, you've got dead bodies in your flat, there's dead bodies on the streets – things are going to hell."

"What are you doing here, Mark? What the fuck was that all about, attacking me?"

McCall got up. He reached inside his jacket. Lawton bristled and was ready to fly at the man again. But McCall brought out a rolled up newspaper. He flung it at Lawton saying, "Front page."

Lawton unrolled the paper.

"Recognize her, do you?" said McCall.

Lawton stared at the CCTV image of Jenna straddling a youth.

"You did this to her," said McCall. "You were always trouble," and his voice broke and he started to cry, his body shuddering with emotion. "I was right. I knew it'd end like this. With me losing her."

McCall cried for about a minute, Lawton letting him, and then he wiped his face, saying, "No point crying, Crying won't help, will it. I'll get no sympathy from you, Lawton – not that I'm looking for any."

Lawton said, "It doesn't matter what I say – you've never liked me, and chances are you never will."

"No, that's right – I never did like you. Never liked soldiers. Soldiers are always trouble in my book. Always looking for a fight, always looking for a war."

"Maybe you're right. But I'm telling you, I never led Jenna into any of this. She had a mind of her own. If she wanted to do something, it was up to her. And the goths were harmless; they're all right. But it was nothing to do with me, whatever she did. We weren't together, Mark."

"But she always loved you, Lawton. Always spoke about you. You should've stopped her then, if you didn't like it; you had an influence."

"She wasn't mine to stop. People can do what they like."

"No they can't. If she was my wife, my girlfriend, I wouldn't have let her get involved."

"This is stupid. You're going to blame me whatever I do. If I'd saved her life a thousand times over, you'd still find something wrong with the way I did it." Lawton went to the sink, poured a glass of water. "You'd better get out of here, Mark. Forget everything. Jenna's gone, now. She won't be coming back to you."

"You bastard."

"Forget it. I'm not taking the blame anymore. She was your daughter. You're passing the buck because you couldn't control her – like you controlled Sarah."

McCall glared at him. His face reddened and Lawton noticed the man balling his fists. Lawton didn't care. He drank his water. He said, "You've got too much of a temper on you to cause me any trouble, Mark, and if you do I'll fucking hurt you. Get out and go home to your wife. Treat her well for the time you have left, for fuck's sake."

"I hate you, Lawton."

"Yeah, yeah, get a new tune, McCall. I don't give a shit. I tried my best with you, was always polite, courteous. But you were a shit with me from day one. So fuck you and your grief. Fuck you and your anger. I'm sorry Jenna's gone, but it's not my fault. I can't bring her back." He rubbed his neck. The wound she'd made still smarted. The blood she took made him weak. He went on:

"If I see her again, I'll tell her to give you a call – pay you a visit. I'm telling you, you won't like that."

McCall's eyes skimmed over the bodies.

Lawton's nerves tightened.

He knew what McCall was after.

McCall went for Scar's gun.

321

CHAPTER 81.
THE COLLABORATOR.

MURRAY strode towards Leicester Square. Police presence was heavy there since the previous night's carnage. Sweat coated her body, and her clothes stuck to her skin. She fought to stem the panic flooding her heart.

Jacqueline Burrows had the red cloth as a comfort blanket. Bernard Lithgow had a scrap of it in a glass case on his wall. And she remembered where else she'd seen it.

She flashed her letter from Deere at the two constables manning the roadblock at the end of Wardour Street, leading into Leicester Square. She hoped Birch's threat to revoke her invitation hadn't filtered down to the bobbies on the beat. The coppers took their time, creasing their brows as they read the letter, handed it back and forth between them. Murray looked around while they pondered. Crowds pressed at the barrier, craning forward to see what was going on. One of the officer's said, "All right, then," and moved the barrier aside so Murray could pass.

A white tent covered the Square. Forensics officers trawled for evidence. Uniformed and plain-clothed police milled about.

She saw him and picked up her pace.

Rage flared in her breast. She clenched her fists, ready to pile into him. David and Michael flashed into her mind.

"Birch," she said, fifteen yards away from him.

He turned, and his face turned the same colour as the ribbon flapping on his clipboard.

Turning to face her, he said, "Get yourself away from here, Christine, or I'll have you arrested – "

She reached him, flicked the ribbon and said, "I know what this is about, Birch, I know, you bastard."

He blanched, leaning back away from the force of her anger.

Murray was shaking. She said, "I'm going to Deere, to the Chief Constable, let them deal with scum like you – but not before you tell me where my sons are, you evil bastard."

Detectives and uniforms glanced over towards them.

Murray looked around and said, "Your Detective Superintendent is in on these murders. He's helping these monsters."

The cops closed in.

Birch smiled and said, "Christine, that's a ludicrous allegation."

The fury leached out of her and she realized what she'd said: it was a stupid allegation; it made her sound like a madwoman.

Uniformed officers were coming closer, some of them smiling, trying to make Murray calm down.

One copper said, "Are you all right, sir?" And Birch said, "Perfectly. She's missing her boys, that's all. She's angry. An angry mother," all the time looking Murray in the eye and smirking.

"All right, madam," said a blonde with sergeant's stripes, "let's go and have a cup of tea – "

Murray wheeled around to face the blonde. "I don't want a fucking cup of tea, you bitch, I want my boys back and this bastard – "

But before she finished, cops grabbed her.

"Be gentle," said Birch.

They dragged her away, back towards the barrier. She screamed, calling Birch a bastard, calling him evil, a murderer.

The two cops who let her through looked sheepish as they eased the barrier out of the way so the officers could shove Murray back into the crowd. She turned, faced the blonde sergeant who said, "Count yourself lucky, lady."

Murray said, "Birch is in on these killings. He's in on it and Jacqueline Burrows at the Home Office, she's in on it – "

The crowd gasped and whispered, Murray hearing things like: "Burrows?" and "Home Office, that's what she said" and "Conspiracy, I told you."

"Go home," said the blonde sergeant, "and let us do our job."

"You can't," said Murray, "because he" – pointing back to where Birch would be – "won't let you."

CHAPTER 82.
ARE YOU WITH ME OR AGAINST ME?

LAWTON pushed the gun into McCall's mouth, and McCall's eyes widened with terror.

Lawton said, "I haven't got time for this crap, McCall. Now, you either help me or you fuck off – I don't care which, but I am giving you the option. And that's really, really nice of me under the circumstances."

McCall stared up at him, his lips an "O" around the barrel of the gun.

McCall had reached the gun a second before Lawton, but Lawton kicked it out of his hand. He'd smacked McCall across the head, retrieved the gun, and then stuffed it into McCall's mouth.

And now Lawton said, "So what's it going to be? Do you want a crack at the people who actually killed Jenna, or are you going to ignore the real villains just because you hate me?" He could feel the rise and fall of McCall's chest beneath his knee. He could smell the sweat pour from the man's body.

McCall shut his eyes and nodded.

Lawton stood. "Okay," he said, "Let's go."

Ten minutes later they were on a bus from New Cross Gate to Canada Water.

Lawton held on to the handrail as the bus rumbled through streets strewn with uncollected litter. A copy of *London Lite* flapped across the road, pages spilling out of it. A poster for the We Are Londoners campaign – the "one" in "Londoners" standing out in red – peeled from a lamppost.

Lawton scanned the other passengers. He could sense their fear. Vampires had targeted buses over the past few nights. Lithgow nearly got nailed on one. But Lawton knew, as the sun streamed into the vehicle, that they had nothing to worry about, now. It was only when the sun went down that the vampires came out.

His army rucksack hung on his shoulder. The spear in its scabbard was strapped to his back. He didn't know what it might have looked like to passers-by. A guitar, maybe. He might look like a busker. Anyway, he didn't give a shit. Anyone tried to stop him, they'd not get far. The scarred man, the one referred to as Ion by the voice on the phone, his gun was tucked into the rucksack. And if Lawton had any trouble of the human variety, he'd bring out the pistol.

He thought of Sassie and hoped she was all right, and that after this was done they could get kissing again. His rage mellowed as her sitting on his lap last night, her lips on his mouth, came to his mind.

She'd been warm and soft and delicate. She was in his head, now. This was how soldiers with wives, with girlfriends felt before they went into battle: their loved ones on their minds. A mixture of fear and desperation, excitement and apprehension. Nerves tight, ready to explode into the enemy.

He thought what thousands of soldiers had thought; he thought: *Will I ever see her again?*

CHAPTER 83.
FINDING AN ALLY.

THE woman tore the tape off Sassie's mouth, and Sassie gulped in air. The reek of methane and decay filled her head, but at least her lungs were able to function.

"I'm Aaliyah," said the woman with bloodstained skin. "And we're in shit."

Aaliyah freed Sassie and then they stood over the human shape forming in the dust and blood at their feet.

"I've no idea what's happening," said Aaliyah, "but they hang kids from that rail up there, slice open their throats, and the blood fucking rains down into this pit."

"Oh God."

"I get splashed every night. It's horrible. I thought they were going to kill me, but they chucked me in here with that – " She made a face and gestured at the form growing in the blood and slime.

"It's – it's Kea," said Sassie, "they're resurrecting Kea."

"Who's Kea?"

Sassie told Aaliyah and Aaliyah shook her head. "I've seen crazy, crazy stuff over the past couple of days. My man J.T., he got killed by them. Got bitten and they drank his blood."

"They're all over London."

"So how do we get out of here?"

Sassie looked at Aaliyah, really for the first time. She was tall, and probably elegant and beautiful under the mask of dried blood and muck that soiled her skin and her tattered dress.

"Have you tried?" said Sassie.

"Have I tried? You bet I've tried." She showed Sassie her fingernails, dirty and bloody and torn. "I've tried to claw myself out of here. And they just look down at me and laugh at me and spit at me."

"Who does? How many are there?"

"There's the woman – bitch. Then a good-looking guy with a scar down here." Aaliyah ran a finger from the corner of her right eye to the edge of her mouth. "He just smirks at me. And then you got those things, those – "

"Vampires," said Sassie.

"Is that what they are?"

"I think so. I know it's mad. And this thing" – Sassie indicated the pile of flesh at their feet – "will come alive very soon. And we're its first meal."

Aaliyah sobbed. "I'm going to die in this hole? I don't wanna die here, honey."

"Neither do I," said Sassie. "But my friends, they know about these creatures, and they know about this place. They'll come." But she didn't know if she believed that. Her legs felt weak. Fear rinsed her veins. She wanted to scream and cry and beg for mercy. She wanted Jake to rescue her.

She looked at the shape in the blood-soiled earth.

It would stand about seven feet tall. Sassie imagined it rising out of the pus, looming over them. Its shadow would fall across Aaliyah and she as they huddled together and cried. It would corner them in this pit and destroy them.

The thought made Sassie quake and she wrapped her arms around her chest, trying to stem the panic surging through her.

"Getting to know each other?" said a voice.

Sassie snapped out of her nightmares and looked up. Crane stood at the edge of the trench gazing down at them.

"Ed," said Sassie, "for heaven's sake, Ed, what are you doing? Please let us out."

"Come on," said Aaliyah, "help us."

"Help you?" said Crane, furrowing his brow. "Sassie, I offered to help you. Had you been willing to be my – friend, well – you wouldn't be in this, well, hole."

"I'll be your friend, any kind of fucking friend you want, honey," said Aaliyah, "if you let us go."

"Tempting, very tempting. But there's going to be a show tonight, and you're the support act. I'm really looking forward to it, so I can't spoil it all by helping you – despite my lust for a pair of blood-stained, mud-soiled whores."

"Fuck you," said Aaliyah.

Crane laughed and walked away.

He kept on laughing, and the mocking, spiteful sound echoed around the cave.

Sassie clamped her hands over her ears to block out the noise.

But his scorn still seeped into her head.

CHAPTER 84.
CONSPIRACY THEORIES.

MCCALL, shaking his head, said, "That's madness. You're making up stupid conspiracy theories instead of doing your job."

But Murray said, "It's true. They're all involved. I know they are."

She looked at Lithgow, bit her lip, her brow rutted. She took a drink of her vodka, eyes still on Lithgow. Lawton looked at her, then at Lithgow. He tried to work out her expression.

Fear? Concern?

What was going on?

But then McCall said, "You're accusing a government minister, and a senior police officer of being involved in the murder of – of hundreds of people."

Murray spluttered.

"Yes, she is and I believe her," said Lawton. "I believe you, Christine. Now, are we going over there and forcing our way in, or are we sitting on our arses in this pub all day?"

"I'm not going anywhere with you," said McCall.

"Fine," said Lawton, "I told you to come along or fuck off. You can fuck off, then."

McCall stared into his beer. "My daughter's been taken from me – "

"And my sons from me," said Murray. "That's why I'm here. It's got nothing to do with what happened a few nights ago at that club anymore. We're up against more than drug dealers. We're up against

330

creatures we know nothing about. We're up against a conspiracy that involves a minister in the Home Office."

McCall shook his head. "I just can't – "

"Then don't," said Lithgow. "Don't bother. Do what Jake says. Just go, yeah? Look, man, I'm scared shitless. I'm not a soldier like this one" – he jutted a thumb at Lawton – "I'm just a bank clerk who's likely to lose his job any day, now. Today's just one too many sickies for their liking. But I'm with Lawton. I want to be counted. D'you know why? Because I want my life back. I want to mope about all day and party at night. I want beer and drugs and sex. I want to stroll home at night without fear of attack. I want to watch MTV and The Playboy Channel, and read NME. I want to travel on the bus with my feet up on the seats. I want the right to shout at a copper, without being dragged off somewhere and getting beaten up. I want not to be scared of politicians like Jacqueline Burrows. I want the freedom to be apathetic and bored and to lounge about. That's why I want this to stop. It's completely selfish, but that's why."

Lawton looked at Lithgow and nodded, and then he turned to face McCall, saying, "Well?"

McCall said, "I want someone to blame for Jenna."

"Yeah, and now that you're not getting to blame me, you've got to find someone else. And we're giving you someone else."

McCall nodded. Lawton, satisfied they were all on board, glanced towards the door. He shot a look at the clock above the bar. The pub was near London Bridge. Sassie should've been here by now. He'd left a message on her phone.

Murray must've read him. She said, "Try her again."

Lawton dialled and her mobile went into answerphone again. He listened to her voice and left a message telling her to call. Fear coiled in his belly.

"You go over to her flat and we'll hang on, wait here for her," said Murray.

"Are you okay with that?" said Lawton.

"We are, Jake," she said.

"What about your –?"

"You're going to save them, aren't you," said Murray. "That's what you promised me."

CHAPTER 85.
FURY.

JACQUELINE Burrows's ministerial limousine crawled along the alleyway and stopped outside Religion's rear door. Burrows didn't worry about being conspicuous. So what if someone saw the car trundle up this passageway? What would they do? What could they do after tonight?

Meadows, her chauffer, opened the door, and she squeezed out. The driver punched a code into the security panel and pushed open the door, the hinges creaking.

He said, "Are you all right, now, Mrs. Burrows?"

"Yes, thank you, Peter. You go back."

The driver reversed out of the alley. Burrows shut the door. Her skin tingled. She took a breath and walked along the dimly lit corridor. The air was stale, the whiff of decay in the atmosphere.

She followed the instructions Nadia Radu had given her earlier, and came to a door on the third floor labelled MANAGER. Without knocking – she was a government minister; she didn't need to knock – she entered.

Nadia Radu, Professor Ed Crane, and a High Court judge called John Petrou stood in the middle of the room. The window stared down at the street. A year planner hung on the wall. A bottle of champagne perched in an icebox on the desk. Petrou and Crane drank bubbly from flutes. They toasted Burrows.

"Jacqueline," said Nadia, greeting her with a kiss on both cheeks.

"Come have some champagne."

Nadia poured her a glass, and Burrows clinked glasses with Crane and Petrou.

"When will the others arrive?" said the minister.

"In dribs and drabs during the day," said Nadia. "We'll all be here by sundown. Then, the last of the blood will be spilt and Kea will rise."

"Where's Dr. Haddad?" said Burrows.

"Still in his little lab, holed away like the eccentric scientist he is," said Nadia.

Burrows saw a wrinkle of concern on Nadia's brow. "You're not drinking, Nadia?"

"Ion is missing."

Crane said, "I spoke to him a few hours ago. He'd gone to retrieve the spear from Lawton's flat. The line was terrible, though. Couldn't really make out what he was saying."

Burrows glared at him. "It *was* him you spoke to, wasn't it, Professor?"

Crane's face creased. "How d'you mean?"

Burrows said, "I mean, it was Ion you spoke to. You say the line was bad. You say he'd gone to Lawton's place. Anything could've happened. You were supposed to confirm that Ion had retrieved the weapon."

Crane's face blanched. "I – I – I did."

Nadia grabbed Crane's collar. Rage flared on her face. "You *did* make sure it was Ion, didn't you?"

"I – I – said I did."

Burrows said, "You said weren't sure, that's what you said, Professor Crane."

"That's true," said Petrou.

"I said I spoke to him," said Crane, his eyes wide.

"Phone him again," said Burrows.

"I'll do it," said Nadia. She got her phone from her bag and dialled, biting her lip as she waited for her brother to answer.

Burrows could see the fear in the woman's eyes. Nadia's knuckles turned white, such was the grip she had on the mobile. After almost a minute, she drew the phone from her ear. She glared at Crane, and Crane, his voice high pitched, said, "Don't look at me like that, I don't know where he is."

"That was your job to find out," said Burrows, sipping the champagne.

Nadia said, "If anything's happened to my brother, I'll have you crucified. Do you understand? I will have you crucified."

"Get over to Lawton's flat," Burrows told Crane, "and find out what's happening. Find Ion."

Crane said, "You're jok – "

Burrows, baring her teeth, said, "I'm not fucking joking, you decadent, useless creep. Get over there or I'll hammer the nails into your hands and feet myself."

Crane bristled. He said, "You – you can't – can't threaten – "

Nadia lashed out. Her nails gouged Crane's cheek. Blood oozed from the four stripes whipped across his skin.

Nadia said, "Go find my brother, you bastard, go find him and bring him back to me."

Crane stumbled out of the office, and they listened to his footsteps stagger down the corridor.

After a while, after giving Nadia time to calm down, Burrows said, "I understand your fury, Nadia – I share it. We can't have fuck-ups at this stage, can we? But we've so much to look forward to. I say we toast."

"What are we drinking to?" said Petrou.

Burrows glanced at Nadia. The dark-haired woman's face burned with wrath. Burrows said, "To friends reunited."

"Friends – "

"And," said Burrows, "to an age of monsters."

"An age of monsters – "

CHAPTER 86.
THE CODE.

ADRENALIN pulsed through his veins.

She wasn't here. The door lay open. A table had toppled over. The curtain pooled on the floor, torn down from the window.

Lawton dropped his rucksack. He steadied his breathing, tried to slow down his racing heart. He needed a clear head to think.

Shutting his eyes, he focused on the voice on the phone:

Bloody hell, Ion. That's a really bad line. You sound weird. Have you got the spear? I've got the girl.

That's what he'd said: *I've got the girl.*

The man meant Sassie. Who else could he mean?

Sassie and the spear went together.

Have you got the spear?

No he fucking didn't have the spear, thought Lawton; *he's fucking dead in my flat. And when I find you, you'll be dead too, Crane.*

Lawton grabbed his rucksack and raced out of Sassie's flat.

★ ★ ★ ★

Murray said, "I'm sure we'll find her, and we'll find my sons."

"Ed Crane's involved, Birch, Burrows — who else?" said Lawton. "How many know about this?" He looked at Murray and her eyes were wide, her face white. He said, "What's the matter?"

She said, "Nothing it's — it's just — "

"How are we supposed to get in?" said Lithgow.

They were loitering in Soho, a few streets away from Religion.

"Knock at the front door?" said McCall.

Murray asked Lawton if he knew the security code that opened the rear door. He said he didn't. He looked up at the windows. They were unreachable. Unless you started to scale the building, make a scene. And he doubted if they opened, anyway. From the inside, they were never on show; always covered by those red drapes.

A 4x4's rear end poked out of the alley.

"That's him, that's Crane," said Murray.

"Wait here," said Lawton. He crossed the road and trotted up the narrow street leading up to Religion. It was a dead end, so rarely had any footfall.

The 4x4 crawled backwards out of the alley. Lawton couldn't see the driver yet – which meant the driver couldn't see him, either.

The vehicle reversed out. Ed Crane cocked his head from side to side, checking his wing mirrors. There was blood on his face and he looked flustered. He saw Lawton, and his mouth dropped open.

Lawton opened the door and grabbed Crane. Crane started screaming. He slammed the accelerator. The 4x4 screeched out into the street, lurching over the pavement. Lawton jerked, got dragged along. But he held on, digging his fingers into Crane's arm.

"Let me go, let me go," said Crane, twisting the steering wheel.

The 4x4 veered, Lawton almost losing his grip and getting tossed into the road. But he leaped up onto the doorframe. He kicked Crane's foot off the accelerator. Crane punched him in the face. Lawton's vision blurred, but he held on. Threw punches – one, two, three – into Crane's temple.

The 4x4 reversed into a parked Volvo. Crane slammed backwards into his seat. Lawton lost his footing, stumbled off the vehicle.

Crane shook his head, coming to after being punched. Crane's foot pressed the accelerator, Lawton thinking, *He's going to get away, he's –*

Lithgow dived into the 4x4 through the open driver's door, landing across Crane's lap, and wrestled with the professor. He bit Crane's hand. Crane shrieked. Lithgow snatched the keys from the ignition.

"Bastards," said Crane, thrashing under Lithgow's weight, "bastards."

★ ★ ★ ★

336

Lawton, holding Crane up against a wall, said, "Where's Sassie? Where are the kids?"

Crane, bleeding from the nose and from a scratch on his cheek, said, "You – you should be dead. Ion – Ion was – was supposed to sort – "

"Like you see, Ion *didn't*," said Lawton. He rammed Crane against the wall, Crane's head snapping back and cracking against the bricks. Crane's eyes rolled back in his head and he sagged in Lawton's grasp, but Lawton gave him a shake. "You're not falling asleep on me, you shit. Where are they? Are they in here? In this fucking club?"

Crane laughed.

Murray said, "Jake – Jake, you can't don't hurt him, don't – "

Fire in his eyes, Lawton looked over his shoulder at Murray and said, "I'm going to find your sons, I'm going to find Sassie, I'm going to make him take us inside, Christine, or beat the security code out of him. If you're not up for that, then take a stroll around the corner."

Crane, his voice a croak, said, "You'll get nothing out of me."

Lawton bared his teeth and stuck his face in Crane's face. "You've seen that video of me, haven't you, Professor, you've seen me shoot that – unarmed man. Well, you should see what we did to his mates. You might have degrees in archaeology; I've got degrees in pain and suffering. I'll show you my qualifications if you don't tell us how to get into this fucking building. Give me the code, Crane. Give me the numbers."

Crane said, "The number's fuck you fuck you fuck you fuck you."

McCall, at Lawton's shoulder, said, "Is this blowjob responsible for what happened to Jenna?"

Crane smirked and gurgled.

"I think that's a yes," said Lawton.

"Jake," said Murray, "I can't let you do this."

Lawton step back, letting go of Crane. Crane slumped to the floor. Lawton, arms held out, said, "Fine, we'll let him go, Christine. How's that? Shall I do that?"

Lawton looked at her, waited. Murray's mouth gaped. She stared at the wounded Crane. She turned her back.

Lawton reached for Crane, dragging him to his feet, ramming him up against the wall again. Lawton said, "I know you've got Sassie – you rang me. 'I've got the girl,' you said. Remember the static? That was the radio in my kitchen – where I'd just killed your mate Ion." Crane grasped Lawton's wrists and tried to release the grip on his throat, but

Lawton didn't budge, saying, "You're going to get us in there, Crane. Give me the code."

"Okay," said Crane, "here's the code: you're dead, you're dead, you're dead, you're dead. Ha! You're all going to die, you know that. No-nothing you can do about it. You, Sassie, this lot, the kids, everyone – die and – and nothing you – you can do."

"We're getting into Religion, with or without your help," said Lawton.

Crane sneered, showing the blood in his mouth. He said, "You're not. You can't. Police won't help, will they? Won't listen. Bet you've tried, bet you've begged." He started laughing, blood and spit dribbling down his chin.

"I know who set up this security system, Crane," said Lawton.

"Do you? Give yourself a medal, tosser," said Crane.

"Guy called Cal Milo. Doorman here."

"So what?" said Crane.

"Is he in on this? Is he one of you?" said Lawton.

"Doorman?" said Crane. "Are you joking? Doorman? No, Lawton, we only allow people with brains, you see – brains and education. We don't let morons join us. Morons will be food for our gods and our monsters."

Lawton nodded. "Thanks, Crane."

Crane curled his lip, not understanding why he was being thanked. Lawton didn't bother telling him. But he knew, now, that Milo wasn't part of this. And he could safely ask the brickshithouse of a bouncer for the code. The worst that could happen was that Milo would smack him and tell him to fuck off.

Crane tried to struggle against Lawton, but Lawton wasn't letting go.

"Where are my children, Mr. Crane? Are they in there?" said Murray, her voice quiet and calm at Lawton's shoulder.

Crane, his voice high-pitched, said, "Your children are going to die, bitch. Die like you lot. Die like pigs. Their blood spilling down into a trench from their dead little bodies, their throats sliced open."

Murray lunged over Lawton's shoulders, clawing at Crane's face, Crane yelping as her nails raked his cheeks. Murray screamed at Crane, Lawton squaring his shoulders, making a barrier between her and Crane.

Lawton said, "Mark – Fraser, get her – get her – "

And McCall pulled Murray away, telling her to calm down, that it was okay.

Crane, his face a mess now, started laughing.

Lawton put a stop to that: he punched Crane in the mouth, knocking him out.

CHAPTER 87.
I KNOW A MAN WHO CAN.

THE lift, smelling of piss and littered with used condoms and empty beer cans, didn't work. Lawton took the stairs, three at a time. Graffiti smeared the walls. Broken glass crunched under his feet. Syringes with rusting needles were scattered around.

Lawton got to the third floor. The sun blinded him when he stepped out of the stairwell. He took a moment, then stared along the walkway. A crust of teenagers, four or five of them in hoodies and baseball caps, loitered up ahead.

Lawton strode forward, glancing down towards the car park that lay in front of the building. A couple of kids, ten or eleven, kicked a football back and forth against Crane's 4x4. Lawton had dropped the others, including Crane, off at Murray's house. A fifteen-minute drive to the grim estate not far from Waterloo station, where Cal Milo lived, had taken forty minutes because of congestion.

He thought about things during the drive. And after parking the vehicle he rang Lithgow. He told Lithgow what he was planning and what Lithgow should do if things went tits up. He told Lithgow he trusted him, and Lithgow said he didn't know if he was good enough to help. Lawton said, *Yes you are,* not sure if Lithgow was up to it or not.

The estate was formed of three four-storey flats built around a patch of grass littered with pizza boxes, empty bottles and cans, and the charred skeleton of a burned-out car. A row of shops and takeaways, some of which were boarded up, stood on the opposite side on the grass.

Lawton approached the group of teens blocking his way.

One of them, sixteen and lanky, stepped forwards, strutting. The teen said, "Where you goin', bitch?"

Lawton didn't falter. He snatched the teen by the collar and tossed him against the wall and carried on walking. He heard the boy sob behind him, but he didn't care. Some of the kid's mates shouted after Lawton, so Lawton turned and took a step towards them. They legged it, leaving the youth Lawton threw against the wall huddled there, weeping and cradling his arm.

Lawton turned away and walked on.

Many of the flats were boarded up or caged. Cracks webbed the windows. Piss stained the doors. Shouts filled the air, but Lawton ignored them.

He came to the door he was looking for and knocked.

The door opened and Lawton looked up into the face of the man and said, "Hello, Cal."

Cal Milo furrowed his brow, then raised his eyebrows in recognition. He let Lawton into the flat. A woman breast-fed a baby in a living room cluttered with toys. A toddler waddled among the toys, tripping over them, tossing them around.

Milo led Lawton into the kitchen and shut the door. Lawton smelled washing-up liquid. The sink was full of plates swimming in foam.

"Washing up," said Milo, like he had to explain himself – as if a big tough man like him was embarrassed he had to do household chores.

"Yeah, I can see," said Lawton.

They small-talked while Milo made coffee.

They sat at a Formica table and Milo fidgeted with a Star Wars figure of Darth Vadar.

"His arm came off," he said. "Ty snapped it. Ty's the two-year-old who's making a nuisance of himself in there."

"How many you got?"

"Two. Ty and the baby. Baby's three months, now. Big blow losing the gig at Religion, mate. Gave me a regular wage. Now the wife's got to do three nights a week at the chippie across the road, tide us over. And that chippie's fucking Baghdad central, mate. Not nice."

"Sorry about that, Cal."

"What about you? Fixed up any more work?"

"Nothing yet," said Lawton.

Neither man said anything. Milo tried to fix Darth Vadar's arm. Lawton drank his coffee.

Then Milo said, "You been keeping an eye on all this murder, then?"

"I have a bit, yeah."

"There's all kind of weird stuff going round. Rumours about vampires, zombies, all kinds. They say it started with those people who died at Religion. The pills they took made them monsters."

"Yeah, we think so."

"Who's 'we'?"

"A few of us. Trying to fight this."

"There – done," said Milo, standing Vadar up on the table. "Mine, you know. Had a whole set when I was a kid. Kept them spick and span. Then along comes Ty and snaps off an arm, a leg, a head – kids, eh."

"You fixed the security system at Religion."

Milo nodded. "Yeah, I did. Holt said he'd give me a good deal, so I sorted it through my brother's firm."

"What's the code for the door?"

"The code?"

"Yeah, the keypad. The code."

Milo shrugged. "Which door? Every door's got its own system. We set them up individually, like Holt asked."

Lawton told him which door and Milo rubbed his chin.

"I'd have to check, Jake," he said.

"That'd be great."

"Why d'you ask?"

"Because we need to get in. Because that's where the monsters are, Cal. Because unless we get in today, I think we're all going to die."

Milo stared at him for a moment. "Is this bullshit?"

Lawton shook his head.

Milo played with Darth Vadar again, moving the toy's arms about. And then he said, "Any chance of a rumble?"

"Big time."

"I'll get my coat."

"We're taking a detour down to Peckham."

CHAPTER 88.
BETRAYED.

MURRAY, watching the sun redden and slip towards the horizon, rested her head on Richard's shoulder while he stroked her arm. "It's going to be nice tomorrow," she said.

He said nothing.

She said, "Perhaps we'll take them over to France. Remember when we used to do that?"

She felt him shudder and she closed her eyes, fighting back the tears. He kissed her hair and went to the window to draw the blinds. He came back to her and she reached out her arms and he came into them. They held each other and then she sat on the bed. After a moment, he sat next to her and she put her head on his shoulder again, and felt his arm wrap around her.

"I'm going to ease off the work," she said. "Perhaps you and I, perhaps we could write a book together. About, I don't know, about us – about all this. When we're a family again."

"We are a family," he said.

"Yes – yes, I meant when the boys – the boys are – " but she faltered, and started to cry, and he started to cry too, and they shook against each other, their desperation coming in waves, crashing against them, making them rock, making them unstable, threatening to uproot them and toss them apart.

A mobile phone ringtone, playing the song that went, "the candy man can", made Murray jump. It came from downstairs, either

Lithgow's or McCall's. Or maybe Crane's. She wiped her face saying, "What's that? Who's is it?"

"Stupid bloody ringtone," said Richard. "Why do people need such stupid bloody ringtones?"

Murray coughed out a laugh, and she kissed her husband. She got up, went to the door. "Let's go downstairs," she said.

She opened the door.

Lithgow's voice downstairs went, "Hello?"

Murray stood at the top of the stairs, blew her nose on a handkerchief.

Lithgow saying, "Dad – "

Murray's nerves tightening, her insides melting.

Lithgow going, " – yeah, yeah, we're okay, we're at – "

Murray trying to scream, "No," but no word coming out, just a breath.

And then Lithgow saying where they were.

CHAPTER 89.
RABBIT.

LAWTON walked into the pub, and it was Wild West stuff – everyone turned to look at him.

A fruit machine pinged and croaked in the corner, the guy playing it stopping for a second to glare at Lawton. Two youths played pool. One of them eyed Lawton, his head canted to one side. He slapped the pool cue on the palm of his hand, like a teacher would slap a ruler.

Lawton smelled tobacco and dog, and then the dog – the look of a pit bull about it – barked and bounded from behind the bar. Lawton stood up straight and drew back his shoulders, towering over the dog. The pit hunkered down and barked up at him. Lawton stepped past the dog and it capered about, as if demanding Lawton's attention.

Lawton went to the bar. The landlord, sleeves rolled up to show a forearm-full of tattoos, polished a pint glass with a stained cloth.

"Shut up, Frank," he told the dog, and the dog shut up. And then, glowering at Lawton, he said, "Yeah?"

Lawton leaned on the bar and scanned the pumps. He ordered an orange juice. When the landlord plonked it on the bar in front of him, Lawton said, "Did Rabbit come home from the war?"

The landlord stared. "Why? What's he done?"

Lawton smiled. "He *did* come back, then."

"I asked you what he's done."

"Nothing. Is he here?"

"Depends who wants him."

345

"Tell him Sergeant Jake Lawton's here."

The landlord narrowed his eyes. "Copper?" he said.

"No," said Lawton, "comrade. You're his uncle?"

"Might be." The landlord backed away, still watching Lawton. He said, "Sandra, keep an eye on the bar," and a blonde filing her nails jutted her chin at the man.

Lawton drank his juice. The landlord disappeared through a door at the back of the bar, and his feet clumped up the stairs. Lawton kept his eyes fixed on the door.

Muffled voices came from behind the door. Feet raced down the stairs.

Rabbit shot out of the door, his eyes wide and his mouth gaping.

Lawton straightened and smiled at him.

Rabbit ran out from behind the bar and came up to Lawton, grabbing his hand in both of his and shaking until he almost pulled Lawton's shoulder from the socket.

And Lawton said, "Rabbit – Rabbit, calm down."

"Sarge, sarge, sarge – oh, man, oh, man – I thought you was fucked after that shit – I thought they'd put you in jail and throw away the key – "

"Thanks, Rabbit."

They sat at a corner table, Lawton with his orange juice, Rabbit with water.

Rabbit said, "You know I had a bit of trouble with the booze, so when I left the Army eighteen months ago, I quit."

"Me too," said Lawton. "How does it feel?"

"Like shit, that's how it feels. You?"

"Yeah. This stuff's not the same. Doesn't burn your throat and sear your insides – doesn't shake you up, does it."

"Might as well drink piss," said Rabbit.

Lawton said, "What've you been doing with yourself?"

"Came down to London after I got out. A year after you left, sarge. My uncle's given me a job and a place to live here. I do some bar work, a bit of kicking heads when it needs doing – that's all. You?"

Lawton told him.

Rabbit shook his head. "We fight and die for them, and they don't give a shit about us. It's like someone's got to do the dirty work, but those who do it, sweep 'em under the carpet after it's done. Country doesn't like soldiers. Don't think it ever did. You told me back in Iraq, you remember? We fight for our mates, that's all. No one else. 'Cause no one else gives a shit."

Lawton nodded. He drank. He glanced over at the bar. The landlord – Rabbit's uncle – polished glasses. He eyed Lawton and gave a nod, Lawton nodding back.

"Anyway, London's gone to fucking hell, hasn't it, sarge?"

"It has," said Lawton.

"Papers say it's worse than Iraq. But then they wouldn't say it's *better*, would they? How many copies would that sell? And what the fuck do journos know?"

A silence fell, and Lawton scanned the pub. The pool players were back to their game and the fruit machine flashed its lights trying to tempt another punter to part with a few pounds.

Lawton said, "You remember what you told me in Basra?"

Rabbit looked him in the eye. "I do remember, sarge. I told you where to find me. I'd be here, in my uncle's pub. Peckham way. Down from the north to the Big Smoke. I do remember."

Lawton said, "D'you remember what else, Rabbit?"

Rabbit stared at him and they were silent for a few seconds.

Then it was Rabbit who spoke, saying, "I said, 'This Rabbit runs with you,' that's what I said." He paused, looked Lawton in the eye. "Going to battle with you, sarge, it was like… it was like you knew you'd get out alive, you know. All the boys said so. 'He's got your back has the sarge; he'll get you out if you do what he says' – we all knew it. Called you 'The Lawman' – Jake 'The Lawman' Lawton. 'Cause you laid down the law and you stuck by it, lived by it, and if your Section did the same, they'd get out with their balls. They always did. You never lost a man. You saved my skin don't know how many times. Fuck me, even when they'd kicked you out that day, if you hadn't been there that RPG would've put this Rabbit in a hole."

Lawton lowered his gaze, blinked. Then he looked at Rabbit again and said, "So you're with me?"

"You don't even need to fucking ask. It's a fucking honour."

CHAPTER 90.
REVELATION.

LITHGOW said, "My dad? No way."

"I was in his office," said Murray. "I saw this rag on his wall, framed."

"Rag," said Lithgow, "what do you mean rag?"

"Like this," she said, going to Crane, who was sitting, McCall's hand heavy on his shoulders. Murray grabbed Crane's left hand, flashed his ring finger. The kitchen light splintered off the ruby set in gold. Crane laughed, yanked his hand away.

"That's a ring," said Lithgow. "What are you talking about?"

"Your dad had a piece of cloth, old, torn, stained, on his wall," said Murray. "Crane's got a piece set in his ring – "

Crane said, "Clever bitch, aren't you," and McCall cuffed him round the ear.

Murray continued:

" – and Jacqueline Burrows, she's got a cloth, the same cloth as your father. So has Phil Birch. Ribbons tied to that bloody clipboard of his."

Richard Murray said, "Chrissie, what are you saying?"

"I'm saying that Fraser's just given away where we are. They know we're here."

Lithgow said, "No way, no way," pulling at his hair. He looked towards Crane saying, "Is this true? My dad."

"Who's your dad, my little doomed friend?" said Crane.

Murray said, "The barrister – "

Crane said, "Oh, we have many barristers – "

Murray saying, " – Bernard Lithgow – "

Crane started to laugh, blood in his mouth, and caked around his nose. His cheeks raw from Murray's nails. McCall cuffed him round the ear again, telling him to stop laughing, answer the fucking question.

Crane spat at McCall, got slapped again, then said, "Yes, your daddy's a top man. I'm a good friend with Bernard Lithgow. So you're his offspring. The distributor. The guy who set it all up for us."

Lithgow's face went bleach white.

Murray felt anger grow in her chest. She glared at Lithgow and said, "You bastard, Fraser, you little shit. You've betrayed us, you've – "

Lithgow, backing away, said, "No way, man, no way."

McCall said, "I'll wring your neck, you skinny little shit. You went out with my daughter, too. You killed her, you murdered her."

Richard calmed McCall down, telling him to keep an eye on Crane.

Murray still burned, though, fury simmering in her veins.

And then Lithgow said, "Have you told Jake?"

"What?" said Murray. "That you've betrayed us? Been stringing us along all this time?"

"I haven't, I haven't," he was saying, his face creased.

Murray said, "I've not told him yet. I was waiting for the right time. When you weren't there. I didn't want to accuse you outright, Fraser. I wanted to talk it over with Jake."

Lithgow, his voice a squeak now, "Talk it over, then. Talk it over. I'm innocent. I've done fuck all, man. I've helped. I got us to Manchester. I helped catch that bastard," he said, pointing at Crane.

"They fell for it, Fraser," said Crane.

"Shut up, Crane," said Lithgow, "don't lie, don't wind them up – tell the truth: I didn't know anything – my – my dad – oh, fucking hell," and tears filled his eyes.

"He's a good actor," said Crane. "Had me fooled, too. They said we had an insider. Well done, Fraser, good man."

"Shut up," said Lithgow, face turning red, tears rolling down his cheeks.

Crane said, "Your dad'll be proud – "

Lithgow screeched, launching himself at Crane. Murray tried to stand in Lithgow's way, but got shoved aside. Richard lunged forward, grabbing Lithgow round the waist, Lithgow throwing punches in Crane's direction but nowhere near to hitting the man. Richard dragged him away saying, "It's okay, Fraser, it's okay," and Crane laughing.

McCall picked Crane up off the chair, swung him round, and punched him on the chin. Crane's legs buckled and he slumped to the kitchen floor, out cold.

Richard pinned Lithgow, still crying, still saying he was innocent, against the kitchen door.

Murray went over and said, "Tell me the truth, Fraser."

"I am, I am. I knew nothing. I've said all this: I got the drugs through Steve Hammond. He told me I didn't have to buy them, just distribute, make a profit. Hammond got me the contact, told me where to meet this guy. They came to him, asked for a dealer, he sent them to me. Christ."

"And now Hammond's dead," said McCall. "How bloody convenient."

"It's not for me, it's not," said Lithgow. "If he was alive, he could tell you."

Richard let go of Lithgow and Lithgow stumbled across the kitchen, steadying himself against the fridge-freezer.

"He denied being involved in drugs when I spoke to him," said Murray.

"He would, wouldn't he," said Lithgow. "And he – he was a liar, man."

McCall said, "I guess you are too, Lithgow."

"No," said Lithgow, "no, I'm not. Not on this. I want Jake, here. I want to see Jake."

"He'll be here," said Murray.

The doorbell rang.

Murray said, "Might be him," and she walked out of the kitchen, through the living room. Her heart raced. All the strength seemed to have left her, and she felt dizzy. She stopped, touched her brow. The doorbell rang again. Lawton was here, she thought; they could sort this out, now.

She opened the door, ready to say, "Thank God you're here," to Lawton, but her throat clogged and her voice didn't come out.

She stared, her body cold.

Detective Superintendent Phil Birch, with four hefty-looking men in black T-shirts behind him, said, "Good evening, Christine."

PART FOUR.
RESURRECTION.

CHAPTER 91.
ARMY OF 3.

LAWTON found that a part of Central London had been virtually blocked off – from Tottenham Court Road tube station along Oxford Street to Oxford Circus station, down Regent Street to Piccadilly Circus, west to Leicester Square tube, then up Charing Cross Road to Tottenham Court Station again.

Police crawled all over Old Compton Street, Poland Street, Shaftesbury Avenue, and Wardour Street.

But Lawton, Rabbit, and Milo got in using Milo's security firm credentials. The van sported a Milo's Security logo. The men wore blue overalls showing the same logo. The cops let them through, no problems.

Lawton tried to call Murray but couldn't get an answer. He furrowed his brow and stared at his phone. They'd been round to her house in Pimlico, but there was no one in. Then he'd called Lithgow and again, no response, the line going straight to answer machine.

Milo spotted his concern and said, "Trouble?"

Lawton said, "I've got a feeling it might be."

They parked on Frith Street, opposite a gallery. Soho Square opened up behind them. But the street was quiet and shadows fell from the tall buildings. Milo slapped a SECURITY AT WORK sign in the van's window.

Lawton then called Ray Brewer, the guy who did all the light shows at Religion, hoping Ray was all right. He got through and they spoke for five minutes. Ray told Lawton what he wanted to know, and then asked something Lawton didn't know: "When will all this be over, Jake? When can we get back to work?"

Lawton told Milo and Rabbit about the call, and he told Rabbit what he wanted him to do, saying at the end, "And then wreck the fucking thing so no bastard can switch them off."

They went into the back of the van, checked the weapons. The rear smelled of wood. They'd bought piles of foot-long ash posts from the builder's merchant in Peckham. Rabbit had been sharpening them into stakes in the back of the van. Sawdust lay thick on the floor. Lawton strapped the spear in its scabbard to his back. He clipped a torch and a knife in its case to his belt. Milo piled handfuls of stakes into a rucksack, and swung it over his shoulder. Rabbit armed himself too, stakes slipped into the hoops of a tool belt around his waist, stakes in the pockets of his boiler suit. Then he brushed sawdust from something he'd brought into the van that was wrapped in a duvet.

Milo said, "What the fuck is that?"

Rabbit said nothing, just unrolled the duvet to reveal what was wrapped up in it.

Lawton stared and said, "Jesus Christ, Rabbit. Where the fuck did you get that?"

"Off an insurgent. Holed it away. Sneaked it out when I came home."

Milo said, "What the hell is it?"

Lawton said, "How do you smuggle an RPG-7 out of Iraq into the UK?"

"With a lot of balls, sarge," said Rabbit, "that's how."

Milo said, "It's a what?"

Rabbit, stroking the weapon, said, "Rocket-propelled grenade launcher. Pop a stake into the hollow tube, here. And" – he raised the weapon to his shoulder.

"Jesus, Rabbit," said Lawton, "We get the picture."

Milo said, "You mean to shoot wooden stakes at vampires using that thing?"

"It can fire warheads, blow up tanks at a range of a hundred metres," said Rabbit. "Imagine what it can do to one of those things."

Lawton saw Milo trying to imagine.

Rabbit said, "What about your mates, sarge?"

"I don't know," said Lawton, staring down at his phone. Fear coiled in his belly. He licked his dry, chapped lips. Times like this, he could do with booze.

"Where'd you seen them last?" said Rabbit.

Milo stroked the RPG like someone stroking a dog he'd been told might bite.

Lawton told Rabbit he'd dropped them off at Murray's place and then spoken to Lithgow less than an hour later. He said Sassie had been taken, he was sure of it, and Murray's kids too. And now he thought Murray, Lithgow, and McCall had also been taken.

"Seems we've got a fight on our hands," said Milo, feeling the weight of the rocket-propelled grenade launcher.

"Odds are stacked against us," said Lawton.

And Rabbit, smacking his lips, said, "That's just the way we like it, eh, sarge?"

CHAPTER 92.
CHOOSING SIDES.

THE woman who had shot Hammond said, "Where's my brother?" Her eyes were wide and hatred sizzled in them. "Tell me where he is or I'll have you all butchered right now."

Lithgow's chest fluttered with fear. He was sweating, his head spinning. The copper named Birch and a crowd of heavies had swarmed into Murray's house and bundled them into the back of a Transit. They'd brought them here to the club. They beat Jenna's dad after he put up a fight. He'd cut one of the heavies with a bread knife before they overpowered him. Richard Murray had a swollen eye after trying to defend his wife, but Mr. Murray was no fighter.

Where the fuck was Lawton?

Where the fuck was Dad?

Was it true what Murray said? Was his dad part of this? Lithgow felt sick, wanting to throw up. He couldn't be, not his dad. He was a pain in the neck, yes, but not a killer, not like these people.

Murray said, "Where are my sons, you cow? I'll kill you."

The woman said, "I am utterly terrified. Where's my brother?"

They'd been hauled up into a room with no windows. It smelled of disinfectant. Empty shelves lined the wall. They were coated in dust, festooned in spiders' webs.

Birch and his heavies kept an eye on Lithgow, Christine and Richard Murray, and Mark McCall. The thugs, muscled and ugly, wore black T-shirts and had what looked like red leather laces tied around their wrists.

The woman who shot Hammond perched on the windowsill, dust from the sill powdering her navy trousers. Next to her, his face swollen, stood Crane, and it was Crane who spoke, saying, "The soldier killed him, Nadia. And these bastards, they helped. They're all responsible."

The woman's face turned purple and she twitched. She seemed about to throw herself forward, lashing out at any of the four of them – Murray, her husband, McCall, or Lithgow.

Then the door opened.

The woman settled back on the windowsill.

Lithgow's mouth dropped open.

He felt nauseous.

He made the shape of the word, "Dad," but no sound came from his throat.

Bernard Lithgow glared at the captives. And then his eyes settled on his son, whose mouth still formed that dad-word shape.

And then his dad went, "Speak up, Fraser, will you."

And Lithgow found his voice, saying, "Dad, what's going on? Why are you here? What's happening?"

Murray said, "I told you, I said he was involved."

Crane laughed and said, "It's Daddy."

The dark-haired woman snapped at Crane, telling him to shut up, and Crane frowned.

"Dad," said Lithgow, "this woman killed Steve Hammond. She murdered him. I saw her shoot him."

"I didn't," she said. "I only wounded him. Then we hung him, alive, over Kea's ashes and cut open his throat. And we watched him bleed to death."

The hairs on Lithgow's nape stood on end. Beside him, Murray gasped, and he sensed her shivering. Richard Murray said, "Jesus Christ."

And then McCall said, "You turned my daughter into a monster."

"That was Fraser and his pills," said the woman.

"No – no, please," said Lithgow.

"I'll kill you if I get the chance," said McCall, glaring at Lithgow.

His dad looked at him and said, "You were such a disappointment to me, Fraser. But this seemed like an opportunity to redeem yourself."

"What are you talking about?" said Lithgow, his voice a whine.

"You did what was expected of you, but then" – his dad shook his head and furrowed his brow – "you did something quite unexpected.

You took responsibility. It was surprising, to say the least."

Lithgow said, "I-I don't understand."

"You betrayed us," said McCall.

Lithgow turned to the Murrays, to McCall, and he saw disgust in their faces. He said, "Honestly, I didn't – I didn't know."

Then Murray said, "It's okay, Fraser, I believe you."

"I don't," said McCall.

Murray said, "You surprised me, too. You've been really brave, and this isn't your fault."

Lithgow looked at her, his eyes blurred with tears. His dad started to laugh, and then so did the heavies and Crane. Only the woman kept a straight face, staring at him with her purple eyes.

His dad, letting his laughter die down, said, "This is mightily sweet, I must say, but we have to come to the point."

"The point?" said Murray.

"Yes. The point," said Lithgow's dad. "The point being, Fraser, do you want to live or die? Which do you prefer?"

Lithgow said, "What?" barely getting the word out.

"You have a choice," said his dad. "You see, despite your rapscallion ways, you are, in fact, the progeny of a great family. Your lineage is royal." His dad looked him up and down and said, "Surprising, I know, to look at you. But there it is."

Lithgow shook his head, confused, so many things spinning about in his brain.

"So," said his dad, "You can die with these" – he flapped a hand and made a face at the Murrays and McCall – "people, or join me."

Lithgow gathered himself. His mind cleared. He looked his father in the eye and tried to remember anything good the older man had done for him. Apart from getting him off drugs charges, he could think of nothing; nothing that ever showed Bernard Lithgow loved his son. Lithgow glanced at Murray, then faced his father again: "I'll stay with them," he said.

Crane said, "Ha! Told you."

Murray said, "Fraser, it's all right – "

"No," said Lithgow, "I'm not a coward. I'm not a scumbag, and I'm not useless like you think I am, Dad. I'll stay with them."

His dad stared at him for a few seconds. And then he said, "All right."

Lithgow's blood turned cold, and he thought he'd piss his pants.

"It appears," said his dad, "that I'm going to have to make a decision on your behalf again, you fool."

Lithgow frowned.

"Keatch," said his dad, and the heavy with a blonde buzz-cut came forward, "bring him along," and Keatch seized Lithgow.

Lithgow shouted. McCall tried to go to his aid, but the other heavies beat him off again.

Lithgow screamed and struggled, but Keatch was bear-strong. Lithgow's dad opened the door, walked out. Keatch hauled Lithgow out the door and said, "Say bye to your buddies."

CHAPTER 93.
PROTECT THE HUMAN.

DR. AFDAL Haddad sat in his wheelchair, surrounded by boxes. The boxes contained his laboratory, the scientific bric-a-brac he'd collected over the decades. He sighed, relief sweeping over him. It had taken him a lifetime of learning, of experimenting, to achieve what he'd achieved: to create a pill containing particles of Kea that would spread the plague of vampirism through a population.

Since their arrival at Religion, the chemist had been holed away in a fourth floor room, producing a final batch of Skarlet before this evening's ceremony that would bring about Kea's rebirth.

An aluminium briefcase sat on Haddad's lap. He opened it. Two clay pots lay in the case's foam lining. The pots contained the ashes of Kakash and Kasdeja.

A vampire scuttled into the room and sniffed. The creature had been a boy once, aged fifteen or sixteen, Haddad guessed. The chemist put on his trilby, touching the band of red skin clipped to the hat. The vampire curled its top lip back and bared its fangs. Haddad knew it was hungry.

Desperate to sink its teeth into my throat, thought the old man.

But it couldn't. Not while the fragment of demon attached to the hat protected Haddad. It was the cloth of the trinity. The remains of Kea, Kakash, and Kasdeja. It grew from their shoulders like wings, like capes; it fell from their bellies as loincloths; it fanned from their heads like hair.

Those rags, those pieces of skin, had been stored in a chest beneath his father's house for years. After those soldiers killed his brothers and stole the spear and the remains, the boy Haddad returned to the house in the morning. His brothers' bodies were gone, but the chest remained, buried safely from prying eyes. He dragged it to his uncle's house where it stayed.

A year later, the young Haddad was sent to Britain. His uncle died in the 1940s. Haddad returned to Iraq for the funeral, but the chest had gone.

It took him forty years, but he found it in the house of Constantin Friniuc.

How it got to Romania, he didn't know; he didn't care. The family still had the remains, and in 1983 Haddad was ready to repossess them.

The vampires smelled their origin on those fragments of skin, and it spoke to their instincts. It said, *Don't touch; this is not food.*

"Come on," he said to the vampire, "wheel me to the lighting booth."

The vampire came up behind Haddad and started to push his wheelchair. Haddad felt the hairs on his nape rise – he had his back to a creature that could rip out his throat without a second thought.

The vampire rolled him out into the corridor.

"I was a boy when they stole these vases," said Haddad, "and it took me a lifetime to find them again." He shut the briefcase. "Kakash and Kasdeja, soon to join Kea. For the first time since the days of Alexander, the vampire trinity will reign. And London will be their Babylon."

"Doctor," said the boy, "what will happen to us? And to humans?"

"What was your name before?"

"My name, it was Jed."

"Jed, I am a descendent of Nebuchadnezzar. I have a covenant with these gods, with your makers. My fellows and myself, we shall serve them and enjoy their protection. Our task will be to harvest humans for them, producing food. Of course, you and your kind, the vampire legions, will go hunting, and make more vampires. But we must make sure the human doesn't die out completely." Haddad smiled. "We – they – will become a protected species. There will be controlled culls. There will be fenced off areas, farms, if you like." He glanced over his shoulder at the boy vampire. "You never thought, six months ago, when you were running around the streets of north London stealing cars and mugging old women that you'd be here, today, serving a great empire."

"It – it feels weird; like that was someone else doing those things I did."

Haddad's neck hurt, so he looked ahead again. They trundled along the corridors. "It was you, Jed. Back then you thought you were immortal. Now, you are."

"I am," said Jed.

"You will feed every night like a king. You will have women, if you want them. You can have anything."

"Yes, I can – I'm hungry, now."

Haddad heard the vampire sniff. He knew the creature could smell his blood. The old man said, "You can wait. You'll sate your hunger later."

"I'm hungry now," said Jed, and Haddad heard the boy's tongue lash over his lips, heard him salivate.

Haddad's fingers dug into the wheelchair's arms. "Control yourself or I'll have you thrown out into the sun."

The boy hissed. "You think I'm a slave, an animal."

"That *is* what you are, Jed: an animal. There is a hierarchy." He held his hand out flat, level with his face and said, "Here, we have the trinity, then" – his hand moved down to chest height – "we have the human descendents of Nebuchadnezzar, and finally" – his hand dropped to be level with his crotch – "down here, you – the foot soldiers." He rested his hand in his lap. "Of course, there is one species below you, underfoot, in the dirt."

"Humans," said the boy.

"Humans."

CHAPTER 94.
FAMILY REUNION.

THEY handcuffed Murray, Richard, and McCall and led them down into the bowels of Religion. The damp smell of decay hit Murray as they rumbled down in the old-fashioned elevator. The lights in the lift flickered. The car jolted from side to side. It clattered at the bottom of its run and stopped.

The door creaked open and the heavies shoved them out into a cavern. Murray and the others looked around, their gaze lifting to the wood-panelled ceiling, over the moss-covered walls, and down to the rocky floor. A crossbar ran across a hole in the ground. Figures clustered in the shadows. They appeared piled on top of each other, and sometimes they shuffled about.

Then a voice, piercing the silence, said, "Mum! Dad!"

Adrenalin flooded Murray's heart. Her gaze whipped from side to side. "David! David!" and she heard Richard say, "Son, son where are you?"

She raced towards the voice, breaking from the line, sensing Richard next to her. Her son, her youngest boy, reached out through the bars of a cage, and her heart almost burst. Michael stood at David's shoulder, reaching, now, too. And they called for their mother and father, and their mother and father stumbled towards them.

Her cuffed hands reached out and grasped the boys' hands and she cried, and the boys cried. Murray fell to her knees, no strength in her limbs, all her senses focused on her children's touch.

"My babies, my babies," she said, weeping, and they were saying, "Mum, mum," and crying too, and then Richard next to her, touching his sons, the boys saying, "Dad, dad," and Richard crying, shaking.

"How sweet," said Nadia Radu at Murray's shoulder, "a family reunion. Get them away."

Heavy hands grabbed at Murray's shoulders and dragged her away, Michael and David's hands slipping from hers. Murray reached out as the void between them grew. *No, no,* she was saying, the thug hauling her away. Another man heaved Richard from his sons, Richard swearing and threatening, begging these people to take him and let his children go free.

And then Murray saying, "Let my boys go, you've got me. They're kids."

The heavy threw her to her knees in front of the woman Murray guessed was Nadia Radu.

They were near the edge of the pit and Murray started to be aware of a terrible odour coming from the trench. She could still hear David and Michael calling for her, calling for Richard, and it froze her heart.

Radu scowled and said, "You'll be with your children, soon, the both of you. Your family will be part of a great moment in history. Look down there" – and she pointed into the pit – "and see the future of England rise from the blood and ashes."

Murray stared down into the pit.

She saw Sassie, and her stomach turned.

Sassie and another woman huddled together in the corner of the trench. They were asleep. A human shape, but longer, wider than a normal human, seemed to be forming in the blood and soil and slime.

"What's going on?" said Murray.

"Resurrection," said Radu, "that's what's going on. Bring me one of her boys."

"No," said Murray. Her skin crawled with fear. She watched as a heavy with a Celtic cross tattooed on his muscled forearm pulled David from the cage and dragged him over like he was a rag doll.

A pair of thugs held Murray and Richard back as Radu grabbed David. She held the boy against her, embracing him. Then she drew out a knife and traced it across David's throat. She stroked his chest, and he wriggled in her arms.

Murray found it vile the way this woman was touching her son and she said, "You let him go, you sick perverted bitch, or I'll kill you, I'll – kill you."

Radu grabbed David's hair, twisting his head to the side. She licked his throat. She said, "Wetting him for the vampires, Mrs. Murray."

Murray thrashed and ground her teeth, but a thug held her fast.

Next to her, Richard begged Radu to release his son, trying to get at David. But a curly-haired thug had his arms wrapped around him.

Radu's arm tightened around David's neck and she pulled him against her. She put the tip of the knife near his eye and said, "As revenge for my brother, I'll cut pieces from your son's body and make you eat them."

David cried and asked for his mum, and Murray, feeling sick, told him it would be all right, to be brave. Her heart raced, and sweat poured off her body. All her strength had gone. She said, "Leave him alone, please, he's only a child."

Crane, scuttling up to stand beside Radu, said through his broken teeth, "Go on, Nadia, cut off an ear."

Murray said, "I'll kill you, Crane, I'll kill you."

Crane laughed, showing his ruined mouth.

An alarm buzzed.

Murray flinched.

Radu's gaze skimmed the cavern.

"What's that?" said Crane.

"Guests arriving," said Radu.

She tossed David into the pit.

Murray screamed.

CHAPTER 95.
THE SKIN OF GODS.

LITHGOW'S father said, "I blame myself," and then he paused before saying, "very rarely. But then I think: Who else is there to shoulder the responsibility? Your mother, she's with me on this. There isn't anyone else."

Lithgow, forced to sit in a chair – the only piece of furniture in the room – with Keatch's hand pressing down on his shoulder, said, "Dad, what's going on?"

His dad said, "Don't you think the world is a terrible place, Fraser?"

"It is at the moment, yeah."

"Oh, this is the purge. After the purge, things will settle down."

"The purge? What d'you mean the purge, man?"

His dad looked at him with a sad face. And then, gaze still fixed on Lithgow, he spoke to the heavy: "Keatch, give us a few moments."

The heavy left the room.

They'd marched up two flights of stairs to get here. His dad had led the way with Lithgow behind him, being shoved by Keatch. The corridors were narrow and plain, paint peeling, damp patches here and there. This room, a box room, had no window. A single light bulb hung from the ceiling. Dust coated the wooden floor, and the room smelled musty. Keatch had plonked the chair in the middle of the room, forced Lithgow into it.

Now, with Keatch gone, Lithgow said, "Can I stand up, stretch my legs?"

His dad said, "Your legs don't need stretching, Fraser, sit still. Time you listened to me."

"I've always listened to you."

His dad, anger on his face, said, "You never have. That's the problem, isn't it. Had you listened, did as you were told, we wouldn't be here. Me having to pull out all the stops to save your life."

"Save my life?"

"Those interfering friends of yours, they're going to die, Fraser. Did you want to die with them?"

"I – I don't want to die – "

"No – "

"But I don't want them to die, either."

"Well," said his dad, "that's not a choice you're able to make."

"Dad, what the fuck is going on?"

"Change, Fraser, that's what's going on." His dad's face was red. The tendons in his throat corded and his eyes glistened. He said, "The old world is dying and a new one coming."

"And that means killing people."

"Yes, it does. Wiping away the scum, Fraser. Can't you see how awful this country is?"

Lithgow, feeling tears in his eyes, said, "Might be. But it's my country, and I happen to like it."

His dad sneered and said, "You like it because it allows you to be a layabout. It allows you to sell your drugs. It allows you to waste your life away on parties and – and foolishness. And who's always had to clear up your messes, eh?"

Lithgow's cheeks warmed. "Yeah, well, what are dads for?"

"Dads are for guiding, that's what dads are for. And now I'm going to guide you."

Lithgow blew air out of his cheeks. "Nothing new there, then."

"There is. I've not done it properly in the past. I've let you get away with things. Not now. If you don't listen to me, now, you'll die, Fraser. You'll be swept away with the rest of the scum. Swept away or – or farmed – "

"Farmed?"

"Yes. Don't you know what's happening?"

"No, I don't, but I'm really scared that you do."

"Nothing to be scared of. Do you know what they're doing downstairs?"

Lithgow shook his head then put his face in his hands.

His dad said, "They're resurrecting a god."

Fraser looked up, stared into his father's wide eyes.

His dad went on:

"And when that god is risen, we shall raise up his brothers, and the three shall be our new religion. And we, Fraser, we who have kept their names for thousands of years will rise up to rule this country." His dad was shaking, spit spraying from his mouth, his face red and sweaty. "With an army of vampires serving us, with a trinity of gods watching over us, we'll begin a golden age – just like Nebuchadnezzar did in Babylon. When Britain is strong, we'll grow our empire once more, we'll make the maps red again."

Lithgow watched his dad pant, the sermon taking a lot out of him.

And then Lithgow said, "You're mad."

His dad's shoulders slumped. "Is that what you think?"

"Who are these people, dad? How'd you get stuck with them?"

"Stuck with them?" His dad paused, gaze drifting off somewhere. And after a few seconds he said, "Twenty-five years ago I was a CPS solicitor prosecuting lowlifes, these lowlifes going through the system, being regurgitated, vomited back on the streets to begin the process all over again. Such an ugly country. Even with Thatcher at the helm." His dad leaned back, squaring his shoulders. "One day," he said, "this gentlemen, foreign, late middle-aged, a trilby perched on his head, came into the office. We looked him up and down, you know. We were all still a bit racist back then. And here's this Paki-looking fellow with a little hat strolling into the office. What the hell does he want? Well, this gentlemen asks for me, and throws this red rag on my desk."

"Christine Murray saw it on your wall, framed," said Lithgow.

His dad whipped out the cloth from his jacket's breast pocket. "Here with me, now. Keeps me safe. You know what it is?"

Lithgow shook his head, his throat dry. His dad tossed the cloth towards him. Lithgow handled it. It wasn't cloth – it was leathery. He smelled it, furrowing his brow, the odour recognizable.

"It's skin, Fraser," said his dad.

Lithgow flinched, and tossed the rag aside.

His dad picked it up, held it in his hands saying, "The skin of gods. The remains of immortals destroyed by Alexander the Great. Their bodies turned to ash, but this" – crushing the skin in his fist – "this survived, and this is what that gentleman, Dr. Haddad, threw on my desk."

"That's sick – skin – Jesus, man."

His dad ignored him and went on:

"Haddad told me everything, told me that my family – our family, Fraser – was one of many descended from the clan who served the immortals in Babylon. He told me our time had come again, that we'd be returned to power."

"And you accept this crap?"

"It gave me something to believe in, Fraser, something to trust in a broken world."

"You're a *Daily Mail* reader, dad, that's all. Bring back the birch and kick out the immigrants. And you're justifying mass murder because of those beliefs."

His dad's shoulders slumped. "I wanted you to believe it too, Fraser."

"I believe it, man – it's just I don't like it."

"You're descended from the same ancestors."

"I'm descended from apes, man, and I like that just fine."

His dad lunged forward, rage in his expression again: "You're a fool, Fraser, a fool. This is your last chance, boy. Do you want to die?"

"No, I don't."

"You're honoured, can't you see? We're honoured. Our family. Our bloodline goes back thousands of years. Back to royalty. To kings. And great kings, Fraser. Not these tree-loving hippies ruling over us these days. Kings who led their armies; kings who died on the frontline; kings who built cities of gold."

Lithgow said nothing. He waited for his father's fury to cool. And then he said, "I was ten, you remember? And you forced the school to put me in the football team, in goal. I hated football. I was shit. But you thought it would toughen me up, play sport. So you made the P.E. teacher – I don't know how you made him – but you made the P.E. teacher put me in the team."

"Yes, I remember. It was easy, really: accusations of kiddie fiddling were made against him, but we agreed not to prosecute. He owed us some favours."

"That's nice. Let a kiddie fiddler teach ten-year-olds. Well, he never fiddled with me, but he put me in goal that day. That was fucking abuse as far as I was concerned."

His dad nodded.

Lithgow said, "And the other team, they scored sixteen fucking goals in the first half. You remember? I sat in the penalty box, crying – crying for you to come and save me. You marched on the pitch and dragged me off, screaming at me, calling me a coward, a weakling."

"Well – "

"Yeah, well."

"You needed to be taught a lesson."

"Didn't work, did it," said Lithgow. He stood up, squared up to his dad.

"No, it didn't work."

"I didn't want a king, did I. I didn't want power. I wanted a dad."

His dad shook his head. "You don't understand – "

Lithgow craned his neck out, face in his dad's face, and said, "No, I don't. And I never want to."

"I'm doing this for you, Fraser. You don't see it – you never did – but I'm doing this for you."

Lithgow turned his back, stepped away. "You told them to give me the drugs, didn't you."

"A task for you, to get you involved."

"Yeah, great, thanks."

"We didn't approach you directly, of course. We used that Hammond character. I had Ion query him about dealers who'd be willing to deliver the drug. I knew of your acquaintance with Mr. Hammond, and that Hammond and yourself had profited together from the sale of drugs. Hence, the situation we are in."

Lithgow wheeled round, faced his dad, saying, "Fuck hence and fuck you. Hammond's dead, now."

His dad made a face. "Who cares? He wasn't important. Fodder, that's all. You shouldn't have broken in, should you. A stupid thing to do, Fraser. Had you not, he might still be alive."

"Blaming me, now?"

"Certainly."

"Typical."

"So," said his dad, "you played your part – a significant part – in the birth of this new age. You, Fraser, you spread the good news, you see," and he chuckled at that, adding: "Like a messiah – but not really." And he laughed again. "You distributed death, Fraser. You were the enabler. You killed those people so they could rise again. You were the spark that ignited new life on earth." He folded his arms, looked at his son. "Feel proud?"

Lithgow glared at his dad. He felt empty, drained. He knew he'd started this, had been responsible for this carnage. They'd played on his greed, his dad probably saying, *My son, he'll sell Skarlet if he thinks he can make money out of it.*

And, true to form, Lithgow did just that.

I've let everyone down, he thought.

So what was new?

His dad said, "You should feel proud. It's the one worthwhile thing you've ever done."

Yeah, thanks, thought Lithgow.

"So," his dad said, coming towards him, "will you join us?"

CHAPTER 96.
WAKING UP.

THE vampires stirred. They groaned and stretched. They came out of the shadows. The light fell on their pale faces, their blank eyes.

Murray saw them and she shuddered. There were dozens and dozens of them, appearing from the gloom as if from nowhere.

Nadia Radu said, "They can sense a sundown. Remarkable, isn't it? They know when it's time to feed – when it's safe to hunt."

McCall went, "Jesus H. Christ," his voice a rasp.

Crane said, "Impressive, isn't it."

Murray called her sons' names. David responded from the pit. Michael shouted from the cage. And their voices tore at Murray's heart.

Radu said, "Pick her up, so" – and a thug with blonde dreadlocks hauled Murray to her feet – "she can see the show."

Vampires crawled up a ladder that was pinned to the cavern wall, a stream of creatures clambering upwards. Some of the vampires stopped now and then, turned and sniffed the air. They were climbing towards an attic-type door in the ceiling. Murray watched as they started to slip through the door.

"They get out into the streets through there," said Radu.

Murray felt cold. She thought about them spreading over London, thought about them attacking people.

Then a voice went, "Jenna! Jenna!" and Murray jumped. She looked around and saw McCall stumbling towards a cluster of vampires. He was still calling that name: "Jenna! Jenna!"

A female vampire turned and scuttled forward. She bared her teeth, and Murray saw her fangs. The girl cocked her head to one side, studying McCall. Dreadlock chased after McCall, dragging him back. McCall struggled, desperate to get to the girl, saying, "Jenna, it's me, it's Dad."

Jenna McCall.

The sight of her chilled Murray's blood.

"That's her," said Richard, "that's Jenna, his daughter. She's dead and now she's — "

McCall, hauled away by Dreadlock, wept. He begged his daughter to come to him. He looked up at Radu, his face red and damp and creased, and said, "Let her go."

Radu said, "I can't let her go. She's not mine to let go. She's a vampire. A night creature. She's not your daughter anymore." And Radu turned to the vampire and said, "Are you hungry?"

The vampire hissed and then said, "Starving."

Radu faced McCall again. She gestured at the dreadlocked thug holding him to step back, and the thug obeyed.

Murray's throat clicked. Her guts turned cold. She tried to speak, tried to say McCall's name to warn him. But her voice came out as a rasp and carried no weight.

Radu said, "Feed, then," and Ed Crane, through his broken mouth, said, "Suck your daddy, go on," and he laughed.

And the vampire who was once Jenna McCall sprang through the air towards the man who was still her father.

McCall stared up at the creature falling towards him. He screamed Jenna's name and Jenna piled into him, shoving him on his back. She straddled him, and the sight of it made Murray sick. McCall struggled, his hands cuffed behind his back not helping. He kicked and shouted. Jenna bent her head to his throat.

Murray heard teeth chewing through flesh.

McCall arched his back and stiffened.

And his daughter drank the blood from his veins.

CHAPTER 97.
THE APPROACH.

LAWTON said, "The sun's going down."

"Guess that means we're in shit," said Rabbit.

"The deepest kind. We'd better hurry."

The sun dropped behind the horizon. Dusk washed over London. They moved into the alley at the side of Religion. Unused warehouses pressed in around them. Shadows spread over the streets as the light died. The club loomed over them and the alley was dark.

Lawton shivered as they stood near the back door, just out of reach of the CCTV camera. He clenched his teeth, fighting the fear.

He'd have to re-discover that "do it anyway" attitude a soldier needs in combat.

"What are we going to do about that?" said Rabbit, gesturing up at the camera.

"They know we're here, so it doesn't matter," said Lawton.

Lawton looked up at the sky. It was like lead; night falling. Milo and Rabbit were shapes in the gloom. Milo peered at the security device. The unit glowed green in the darkness. Milo flipped open the cover. He took a penlight from his overall breast pocket, clicked it on, and shone it on the box.

A shuffling noise further down the alley, in the pitch black, made the hairs stand up on the back of Lawton's neck.

Rabbit said, "Hear that?"

"Oh yeah," said Lawton. And then he said to Milo, "You stay here."

"Why? What's –?"

Lawton stuck a finger in the air, indicating that Milo shut his mouth. He gestured for Rabbit to follow him into the deep darkness.

They moved down into the alley's throat, colder here, darker, a smell of decay washing out to meet them. Lawton unhooked a torch from his belt and unsheathed the spear. Rabbit armed himself with two wooden stakes, one in each hand.

Lawton switched on the torch. Light flared in the alley. It looked like a dead end, the passage ending with a brick wall and a pile of bin bags. Lawton smelled them: rotten food, decay, getting thicker.

The shuffling noises grew. There was something there, but he couldn't make out where the noise was coming from – it was a dead end.

"No, it's fucking not," he said to himself.

"What?" said Rabbit from behind him.

"There's a passageway that goes around the back of the building. It's not a dead end. Fuck, there's someone there."

They crept forward, weapons brandished, sweat making Lawton's grip on the torch and the spear slippery. He tried to swallow, but his throat was dry. Coldness spread across his chest, and his legs grew weaker with every step.

A scuttling noise came from around the corner. Lawton heard groans and grunts from the darkness.

As they got closer to the far end of the alley, the torchlight showed an edge to the wall. There was another passage around the corner, much narrower than this one – possibly the width of a man.

Lawton pressed himself against the wall. He heard feet, and someone was moving up the alley. Scratching came from the darkness, above his head.

"Ready?"

"Ready," said Rabbit.

Lawton leaned against the wall, peered around the corner into the narrow walkway. He brought up the torch, threw its light into the darkness.

The light showed vampires cascading down the alley towards him. Their eyes glittered in the torchlight.

Lawton jerked, held his breath. He cast the flash lamp around. The beam showed something crawling along the wall above his head.

"Back," he said, "back, Rabbit, back – "

The creatures filed up the alley, scaled the wall, crawled along the masonry towards Lawton, Lawton stumbling away, warning Rabbit.

A vampire shot out of the passage, over their heads. It rebounded off the warehouse wall opposite and fell on Rabbit's shoulders, the vampire and Rabbit ploughing into the bin bags.

CHAPTER 98.
SECRET PANELS.

NADIA Radu gazed upwards and yelled: "Now, Dr. Haddad."

The building rumbled. The walls shuddered and groaned. Murray ducked down, and her gaze skimmed around the cavern. Dust and debris coughed from the rocks. The ceiling creaked.

"What – what's going on?" said Richard, cowering next to Murray.

"If you want to live," said Radu, "stay where you are and don't move."

Murray almost lost her balance when the floor started to rise. The noise was deafening. Creaking wood and squealing metal and hissing hydraulics. Murray gasped, her gaze lifted upwards: the ceiling rolled away to reveal the rafters of the nightclub above.

The wooden floor shuddered and rose. The panelled wood flooring, which included the pit and the cage, was moving.

"What's happening?" said Murray, swaying, holding on to her husband as the ground under them lifted. "What are you doing?"

Radu said nothing. Ed Crane laughed.

Jenna dragged her father's dead body off the rising deck. Murray looked down at the ground below. They'd risen about ten feet. She could see the void underneath the rising platform. It went down and down into pitch black, and dust rained into the darkness. Steam belched from the depths. A pillar rose up out of the steam, pushing them upwards. A scissor lift encased the pillar, and it opened slowly, creaking, as it helped lift the deck.

"A hydraulic arm, run on steam," said Radu. "Built here in Victorian times by our ancestors – by the believers who knew that this day would come."

The panelled floor ground upwards. Murray's legs buckled. The hydraulics hissed and belched out steam. The podium rose. They were thirty feet above ground, passing through into Religion. Murray stared up at the balcony. Figures lurked in the gloom, up in the balconies. She couldn't tell if they were human or vampire.

The platform stuttered. Richard stumbled and teetered at the edge. His face blanched. Murray grabbed his sleeve and pulled him to safety.

Radu said, "Stop the machinery, Dr. Haddad," and a screech filled the club before silence fell. Dust powdered down from the podium into the cavern from where it had risen.

The lights came on. Murray blinked, eyes adjusting, and scanned the balconies. Jacqueline Burrows stood up there, looking down at them. And she saw Phil Birch, who smirked at her and gave a casual wave.

Fraser, she thought; where was Fraser? What had they done with him? Was he part of this, a spy planted by these people?

Radu said, "Ladies and gentlemen, brothers and sisters – " and her voice echoed around Religion. She went on:

"We have waited three-thousand years for this night. Our generation is honoured to witness this resurrection. Many have sacrificed themselves for this day. Among them, my brother."

A gasp went through the crowd in the balcony and after it settled, Radu continued:

"He was killed by the soldier, Jake Lawton, and these" – she swept a hand in the Murrays' direction – "friends of his shall pay for Ion's murder."

"Mum," said Michael from the cage, "mum."

Radu turned and frowned. "Shut him up," she said to the thug with the Celtic cross tattoo.

Murray said, "No, leave him alone – don't you touch him or I'll kill you, kill you and your bloody god."

A chuckle rippled through the audience. Tattoo clanked a baton against the cage. The children inside recoiled.

Radu said, "Dr. Haddad," and swept an arm up to the balcony. Eyes turned in the direction she indicated, "has been our guide in this miracle, and we are all so delighted that he has lived long enough to witness this great occasion."

There was applause.

Murray scanned the audience. She identified other well-known faces, too: an England footballer, an Army general, a few MPs – from all the political parties. She quickly counted three-dozen or so people up there.

She glanced over the edge of the podium, down into the basement.

Vampires craned their necks, staring upwards. Others clung to the wall, and some hung off the ladder. They were all waiting for this creature, this shape of blood and sinew in the pit with David and Sassie, to rise up.

"Bring one," said Radu, and when Tattoo opened the cage and made a grab for Michael, she said, "No, not him – he'll be the last one."

Tattoo dragged a girl aged around nineteen, in a mini skirt and crop top, out of the cage. She kicked and screamed and scratched. Tattoo clubbed her across the head, and she sagged in his arms.

He bound the girl's ankles with a leather belt. A hook dangled from the belt. Dreadlock came over to help, and together he and Tattoo hoisted her up and fastened the hook on the rail that crossbarred the pit. The girl hung upside down.

Dreadlock handed Radu a knife. The woman took the blade and looked at Murray, saying, "Watch this and see how your first born will die."

Radu crossed to the pit. She grabbed the girl's hair and exposed the throat.

Cold fear washed over Murray. Richard sobbed beside her, saying, "Oh my heaven, oh my heaven, they're going to kill her, they're going to – "

Radu slid the knife across the girl's throat. Blood gushed from the wound. The girl twitched. The blood spilled into the pit and splashed over the creature growing in the grave. The blood drenched Sassie, David, and the dark-skinned woman.

Murray felt light-headed. She retched, but had nothing to throw up.

Radu held the knife up and light splintered off the blade. "Many of you," she said, "have never seen a sacrifice before, and it might have shocked you. But blood has to flow. For life to begin, there must be death."

Radu's face burned with passion. Her eyes were wide and filled with anger. Madness seemed to pulse through her.

Murray looked up at the balcony and said, "Make her stop. Can't you see this is madness? Birch, stop this now. You're a police officer. This is murder. Mrs. Burrows, for goodness' sake, you're a politician – you should be protecting the people, not conspiring to murder them. These are children. She's murdering children. You're murdering children – do you hear? Birch, do something."

And Richard went, "Please – please – save them, save our children."

But Phil Birch, Jacqueline Burrows, and the rest glared at them and said nothing.

Murray bowed her head and started to cry. And when Radu said, "Bring me another one," Murray knew she could do nothing to save her children and would have to watch them being murdered. And all she could hear was Ed Crane's laughter.

CHAPTER 99.
BREATH.

SASSIE, drenched in blood, held David. Aaliyah shielded them, wrapping her long arms around the woman and the boy as they cowered in the corner.

The smell of blood and meat was overwhelming.

Sassie looked up. A thug with dreadlocks took the girl's body off the rail and appeared to toss it away. Sassie knew they'd risen off the ground – was aware of it as the ceiling slid away and the nightclub's rafters drew closer.

She hadn't been sure how high they were until she heard the girl's body thud on the basement's floor a few seconds after the guard had pitched it over the edge of the platform.

The two heavies fastened another figure to the rail. The youth, his baseball cap staying on his head despite him being upside down, stared down into the pit and started screaming. Radu appeared. She pulled his cap off and tossed it away. She pulled back on his spiked hair, and he screeched.

Sassie shut her eyes. She knew what was coming next: the hiss of blood leaving the veins, the splash of it on her skin. A gasp filled the auditorium. Sassie knew they had an audience after hearing Radu speak to them, hearing their applause.

She wondered if Ed Crane was up there, come to watch her die?

After the blood stopped flowing, Sassie opened her eyes.

Aaliyah said, "Oh shit, shit."

"What?" said Sassie.

And she saw.

Terror flapped in her breast, as if something had come loose in there.

The figure in the grave pulsed. Its chest rose and fell. A vein throbbed at its temple.

David whimpered in Sassie's arms. Blood glossed the boy's body, making him slippery in her embrace.

"My God," she said, her voice a whisper, "it's becoming alive, it's – " but her voice went and for a moment she thought her mind would follow.

★ ★ ★ ★

"Get the fucking thing off me, get it off me," said Rabbit, thrashing about under the vampire.

Lawton, standing at the mouth of the passageway as the lead vampire charged towards him, said, "Milo – over here."

The vampire lunged. Lawton kicked the creature in the chest.

The vampire reeled backwards, stumbling into the others that were flooding up the alleyway. But they clambered over him, crushing him underfoot.

Another vampire sprang forward. Lawton swung the rucksack, smacked the creature across the head. It pinballed from one wall to the other in the narrow passage.

Milo dragged the vampire off Rabbit's shoulders, slammed it against a wall. The thing's head cracked against the bricks.

"Stake," said Lawton, "stake it in the chest."

The vampire sprang at Milo. Rabbit leaped to his feet, stake in hand. He drove the pike into the vampire's solar plexus, lifting the creature off its feet. The vampire screeched. Lawton smelled burning flesh. The vampire flared, fire bursting from its body. And then it fragmented into ashes, the ashes wheeling about in the breeze.

"Fuck," said Rabbit, "fuck, I can't believe it – I can't – "

"Plenty of opportunities for you to have another go, Rabbit," said Lawton, stabbing a vampire through the chest with the two-tusked spear.

Vampires poured out of the passageway, into the alley. They clambered over each other, trying to get at Lawton, Rabbit, and Milo.

Lawton said, "Get back," and backed away. The vampires flew after them.

"The door, get to the door," said Lawton.

The vampires stalked him. He counted eight, then ten, a dozen, fifteen, now. And they were filling the alley, pouring out of the passageway.

Lawton backed up. He said, "Milo, get working on that door."

"I've got your back," said Rabbit at his shoulder.

"Milo, we need to get that door open very, very quickly," said Lawton as they came level with Milo, working on the security unit.

"Okay, nearly there – it's fucking seven-digits – not that easy to remember, you know."

"Remember it, mate. These things are going to – "

The vampires attacked, rushing forward, leaping through the air.

Lawton shouted, stumbled backwards. He tripped over Rabbit. He threw out his arms to steady himself. The spear fell from his grasp. A vampire hung in the air above him, another one springing up behind it. He felt a hand grip his collar.

They're behind us, he thought, *we're cornered, we're –*

CHAPTER 100.
THEIR CHILDREN SHALL DIE.

VAMPIRES wailed in the cavern below.

Their calls echoed around Religion.

Radu said, "They know he's breathing – they can feel it – they come from him – they feel their creator's presence."

Radu's hair whipped about her head. Her eyes gaped and burned, and mascara ran down her face.

Murray peered over the edge of the platform. Vampires gazed up Murray saw McCall's body, and the carcasses of both youngsters Radu had murdered and the thugs had thrown off the deck.

Dreadlock and Tattoo slung another screaming youth on the rail, and slashed his throat – and the air thickened with the odour of blood and methane.

Screams came from the pit. A voice saying, "It's moving, it's moving."

Crane was looking down into the grave. He wore a mad grin on his wounded face.

Radu gestured to Dreadlock, and he grabbed Murray's collar and Richard's collar, dragging them forward.

Radu said, "Let them see their son's future."

Dreadlock forced Murray's head over the edge of the pit. She cried, seeing David terrified and covered in blood. Richard called his son's name.

David looked up and cried up to his parents from Sassie's arms, and Sassie looked up too, saying, "Christine," her voice desperate.

The other woman, tall and lithe, stood between Sassie and David and the monster growing out of the blood and guts and dust.

The creature was almost seven feet tall. Slimy webbing cocooned its huge frame. Its body rippled, breath moving through it, blood coursing along its veins. Its mouth opened and closed, showing the creature's serpent-like fangs. A white fluid oozed from the jaws.

"What are you doing?" said Murray, glaring up at Radu.

"That's Kea – coming to life. Your son'll be among the Lord's first victims. Your son will be immortal. He'll live forever and feed off the living. He'll be like an Adam in a new Genesis for the world."

Crane, his voice a whisper, said, "He's amazing."

Murray said, "You're mad."

Radu frowned. "Yes, I am. I am mad. I'm raging, burning with anger. My brother's dead, and I wanted him, more than anyone, to witness this."

"You're killing people," said Richard.

"Yes we are," said Radu, "bring another – bring their son – their children shall die."

Murray screamed, struggled to her feet. She stumbled towards the cage as Tattoo dragged Michael out. Dreadlock pulled Murray away. She kicked and thrashed and begged Radu to let her child go, but Radu turned away and watched as Tattoo lifted Michael and latched the boy's feet to the rail over-hanging the trench.

Murray struggled against Dreadlock, but he was too strong. There was a thud, then she fell out of his grip. She looked over her shoulder. Richard lay on top of the guard. He'd charged into Dreadlock and shoved him away. Dreadlock looked dazed. Richard drove his head into the thug's face, headbutting him, screaming as he pummelled the man's nose.

Radu whipped out the knife. Michael cried for his mother. Crane told the boy to shut up and take his death like a man.

Murray got up. She heard warnings echo around the club, people saying, "Take care," and, "Nadia, she's on her feet."

Tattoo had finished strapping Michael to the rail, and his eyes showed confusion when he turned round: should he help Dreadlock, or protect Radu?

Murray, ignoring the tattooed thug, charged at Radu as the woman stretched out her arm to cut open Michael's throat. The knife brushed his skin and he screamed.

Radu, finally reacting to the alerts from the balcony, wheeled around, her face showing disbelief. Murray rammed into her and both women plunged into the pit.

CHAPTER 101.
INTO RELIGION.

MILO grabbed Lawton by the collar, choking him. He dragged Lawton through the door saying, "Come on, come on for Christ's sake."

Lawton, reaching out, saying, "The spear – need the spear."

Milo got him inside. A vampire lunged at the doorway. Milo booted the creature in the head, its skull cracking. Rabbit, swinging his rucksack, forging a path through the vampires, and he picked up the spear.

The vampires circled him, closing in. He tossed the spear towards Lawton saying, "You go, sarge, you go," and the vampires mobbed him.

Lawton said, "No," as Milo kicked the door shut and it became pitch black, Lawton struggling and saying, "No, I'm not – "

Milo yanked him to his feet, took him by the scruff of the neck, and said, "He's dead. He told you to go, Jake. He's dead. He's gone."

"I'm not leaving Rabbit."

Lawton picked up the spear and opened the door. Vampires clawed at Rabbit. Rabbit kicked and punched and screamed. Jaws clamped to his arms and legs. They were drinking his blood. Lawton ploughed into the creatures, scattering them. He stabbed two with the opposite ends of the weapon – left, right – and they disintegrated. He slashed at the creatures with the spear, he kicked out, the rage burning in his chest.

Milo rushed out, ramming through four vampires, sending them reeling.

"Get him in," said Milo, and Lawton hauled Rabbit into the club. Milo tried to shut the door, but a vampire got his arm through. Milo gritted his teeth, pushed against the door, the tendons in his neck like ropes. He slammed his shoulder into the door. The vampire screeched. The metal door crushed the creature's arm and sliced through white flesh. Black fluid sprayed from the wound. Milo roared, one last heave. The door jerked shut hacking through bone, the arm on the floor, fingers still clawing.

"You should've left me," said Rabbit. "I'm bitten; I'm going to change."

"No you won't," said Lawton. "I've been bitten, too. You don't change unless they kill you, unless they drain you of blood."

"You've been bitten?" said Milo.

"Yes, Jenna; Jenna bit me. Took blood."

"She bit you?" said Milo, "and you didn't say? You might be infected, or something. You might be – one of them already. You might – "

Lawton frowned. He said, "I might be, I don't know. I might die, but I won't change. Whatever happens, for now I'm still me."

Milo said, "Oh, and you're an expert on vampires all of a sudden. We don't know anything about them – only what some old legends say."

"And Hollywood," said Rabbit, getting to his feet.

Milo ignored him and said, "For all I know, both of you could be, like, double agents or something – half vampire, half-human, leading me to fuck knows what."

Lawton stared at him. "You want to open that door and go home, be my guest. I'm not leading you anywhere you don't want to go."

"Out there?" Milo gestured at the door. Vampires hammered against it. It shook on its hinges. "You're fucking joking."

"Okay. Seems you're caught between vampires and half-vampires then – "

Milo backed away. "You – you *are* half-vampires – "

"No, you pillock," said Lawton, "I'm only taking part in your fucking game. I'm fine; Rabbit'll be fine. We give him some antibiotics, and he'll be fine."

Lawton treated Rabbit's wounds with iodine, bandaging the worst of them. Milo shone a torch on the injuries while Lawton worked.

And then Lawton said to Milo, "Now, are you coming or going?"

"Don't have much choice."

They hurried along a corridor that brought them to a stairwell. The torch's beams made shadows, and the shadows gave Lawton a jolt, heightened his senses. Voices carried from inside the club. They sounded frantic, screams and shouts.

"It's all go in there tonight," said Milo.

Lawton threw the light towards Rabbit and said, "You all right?"

A pale, shaky-looking Rabbit gave Lawton the thumbs-up.

Lawton nodded and said, "So you know what you're doing, where you're going?"

"I do, sarge."

"Up to the fourth floor, the lighting booth. The desk. You know where everything is?"

Rabbit nodded.

Lawton said, "Take care. We need you to get there in one piece."

"I'll get there. Not in one piece, maybe, but I'll get there," said Rabbit, and made his way upstairs.

"Fourth floor, third on the right," said Lawton.

"I know, I know," said Rabbit, the gloom swallowing him.

Lawton listened to Rabbit's staggered footsteps for a moment, and then turned to Milo:

"You ready, big man?"

"No."

"Good. Let's go."

Lawton opened the door that led to the second-floor balcony over-looking the dancefloor. The smell of death made him flinch. The noise grew louder. Figures leaned over the balcony, waving their fists and shouting.

He glanced at Milo, and Milo stared at the crowd. Lawton entered the balcony area, and a man turned to look over his shoulder.

Lawton froze.

The man wheeled around, pulled a pistol from a holster at his ribs, and aimed the gun at Lawton.

Lawton said, "Birch."

Birch, pointing the pistol, said, "I've been chasing you for days. Good of you to drop by."

★ ★ ★ ★

Murray and Radu hit the floor of the pit. The knife fell from Radu's grasp. Sassie shoved David aside, went for the knife, crawling through the slime.

She reached out, seizing the knife. Radu, recovering, slammed her heel down on Sassie's hand. Sassie screeched, pain shooting up her arm. Radu made a grab for the knife.

Aaliyah said, "No way, bitch," and kneed Radu in the ribs, and Radu lurched away.

Sassie cradled her hand. It looked broken, the knuckles crushed. Tears filled her eyes. She bit her lip, trying to keep the pain at bay.

Aaliyah grabbed the knife, went for Radu. The women wrestled. They screamed and snarled, fighting over the weapon.

Sassie looked for David and saw that he was with his mother. She went to them and checked on Murray, asking her if she was all right.

Murray nodded. "Can you get me free of these handcuffs?"

"Can you pull your wrists through? It'll tear your skin, but you should be able to."

"Okay, help me," said Murray, and then to her son: "David, help Sassie."

Murray narrowed her fingers and Sassie tried to wrench the handcuffs over her wrists. The metal chewed into her flesh. Murray grimaced. Sassie dragged them over her wrist.

Aaliyah and Radu fought. They tore at each other, clawing faces, scratching and biting. They were coated in gore.

And the creature groaned.

Sassie, panic making her shake, gave one last tug at the cuffs and they slid off Murray's left hand, breaking the skin.

Sassie grabbed David and scuttled back against the wall. Murray tried to reach up for Michael, hanging from the rail above the trench, Michael shouting for his mother.

A voice from above, a dreadlocked guard staring down into the grave, said, "He's waking up, he's moving."

Aaliyah and Radu stopped fighting.

The cocoon of flesh rippled. The skin was transparent, and Sassie could see what lurked under it. And it made her shake and whine.

An arm split the cocoon, bursting through. Fluid, warm and viscous, splashed over Sassie, but she didn't flinch: terror had her in a vice-grip. The arm was red, and the muscles along it were thick like branches.

The hand, like a spade, opened and closed, the fingers flexing to show the yellow talons. Blue veins coursed along the scarlet flesh.

Murray inched away from the creature, joining Sassie and David. They huddled together, pressed against the side of the pit.

Radu crawled towards the monster, and Sassie thought the woman's expression showed rapture: this was religious for Radu.

Aaliyah came over and said, "We've got to get out of here, that thing's waking up – whatever it is."

Another arm shot from the slime, spraying Radu with blood and pus. She roared with laughter, licked the stuff off her face and wiped it into her skin.

She craned her neck. "He's rising, he's rising. Lord Kea's rising." Her voice lifted from the hole and carried into the rafters and swept around Religion.

And in the pit, they heard the crowd's response: a roar, applause, cheers.

Murray said, "The choker," her voice a whisper.

Sassie said, "What?"

"The choker – the choker around her neck. Get the choker off her. Just do it, Sassie."

Sassie crept towards Radu. The clamour in the club grew. There seemed to be panic as well as celebration and joy up there. But Sassie ignored the noise. She moved towards Radu, her eyes fixed on the red choker around the woman's throat. Radu was on her knees, her arms held out. Sassie reached for the collar. Her fingers slid between material and skin. Radu screeched and lashed out.

The cocoon burst, spewing a thick, gluey substance over both women. Sassie got a mouthful, and the sour taste made her retch.

The creature sat up, tearing through the cocoon.

Radu bellowed and rolled away. Sassie ripped the choker from the woman's throat and fell face first in the slime. She raised her head, her nose and mouth filled with blood and flesh. She smelled heat coming from the creature, heard its breathing. But she couldn't see it yet, just sensed its presence.

Silence filled the auditorium above as Dreadlock said, "He's rising – he's rising – sitting up."

Radu stared, her mouth open.

Michael screamed and thrashed about, the crossbar creaking.

Behind Sassie, Murray and Aaliyah cried and cursed. What had they

390

seen? Could she look? She felt the vile breath on her neck. She rolled over and froze.

The creature stared down at her. Gashes trenched the red skin of its forehead. The eyes were blood-red, the lips curled back to reveal the fangs. A fan of muscle grew from beneath the monster's ears down to the shoulders, giving it a neck that was as thick as a tree trunk. These trapezium muscles were a darker red than the rest of the body; a red similar in shade and texture to the choker Sassie held in her hand. The creature raised its arms, trying to pull itself up, and the skin that grew out of the underside of its arms to form a cape was also the same.

Sassie looked from choker to vampire, seeing the similarities.

The creature roared, and saliva sprayed from its mouth, raining over Sassie. She didn't budge; she was too scared.

Then, in response to the monster's roar, vampires whined from somewhere, calling to their maker.

Kea rose up from the cocoon, which split and spilled fluid all over the pit.

Sassie, her bladder cold and heavy, stared as the monster towered above her. Red, leathery skin grew from its abdomen and fell over its crotch and down its legs to fashion a loincloth. The monster loomed over Sassie and stared down. Sassie looked Kea in the eye and rubbed the leathery choker between her fingers.

And then Radu said, "Kill them, Lord Kea. Drink their blood."

Kea snapped its head towards the voice. Radu knelt in the mess of the pit. Blood and birth dripped off her body and face. She held out her hands to the creature. Her eyes showed adoration.

Radu said, "I'm your servant, Lord Kea, your servant," and it moved across the pit towards her, unsteady on its feet.

Radu reached for her throat and said, "I have the — "

And her face changed.

The smile turned to a frown, the eyes flashed with fear. She scrabbled at her throat for the choker, gasping for breath, saying, "No, no, no."

Sassie, holding the choker up, said, "Is this what you're looking for?"

Radu screamed and went to crawl towards Sassie. But Kea bellowed and scooped her up.

Radu screamed as the monster shook her like a rag doll. Kea brought her up face-to-face and shrieked at her, Radu's hair fanning out in the gust of his breath.

Radu screamed.

Kea bit into her throat. Blood splashed from the wound. Her face blanched. She thrashed about, kicking and scratching at the monster.

As Kea drank, its skin turned a deeper red, its veins pulsed blue.

The creature snapped its head away, ripping flesh from Radu's throat. It tossed her aside and turned to face Sassie.

Sassie held out the necklace. She said, "N – No, no you – mustn't – I – I, look – I have – have this," but had no idea if it would work or not.

Kea looked beyond her. Towards Murray, Aaliyah, and David. And it inched towards them, Sassie trying to stand in its way, saying, "No, no".

And then Kea stopped. The vampire sniffed and looked up.

A few feet above its head, easily within reach, hung Michael.

The creature reached up, its huge hand cupping Michael's skull, the talons digging into the boy's temples.

CHAPTER 102.
LEAP OF FAITH.

BIRCH glanced over his shoulder when the beast bellowed from the trench, and Lawton shot forward. He grabbed Birch's wrist and headbutted him. Birch's nose burst, blood splashing. He reeled away, Lawton taking the gun from his weakened grasp.

People nearby turned.

A woman's voice said, "Get him," and a man darted forward, mean and muscled.

Lawton pistol-whipped him, cracking the guy's skull. Two more have-a-go morons hurtled towards him. Milo clotheslined one of them, whipping his thick arm across the man's throat. Lawton thought, *Fuck it;* and shot the other man in the chest.

The crowd screamed.

Vampires shrieked.

Lawton rushed to the edge of the balcony. He looked up towards the lighting booth. The strip of light up in the dark rafters showed an old man in a hat staring down at him. Lawton looked down into the club. He saw the platform, and he saw the drop down into a cavern below. Two heavies, one with dreadlocks, and that shit Ed Crane stared into a trench at the centre of the platform. Richard Murray lay a few yards away, blood on his face.

"Crane," said Lawton.

"What?" said Milo, next to him.

"Crane – that means – I'm going down." He stepped up onto the railing.

393

Milo said, "Jake, what the –?"

And Lawton leaped.

Milo saying, "Lawton, you lunatic," faded behind him and he flew down towards the platform.

He held his breath.

He saw the edge of the platform.

He saw the drop down to the cavern.

His body went cold, thinking he was going to miss the deck and plunge into those vampires down there in the basement.

He gritted his teeth, bicycled his legs.

His toes hit the platform. He teetered and said, "Shit," and saw Crane glare at him and say, "Kill him."

A guy with tattoos raced forward.

Lawton flapped his arms, trying to get his balance. He hovered on the edge, gravity tugging at him. His legs felt like paper, and his head was spinning.

Tattoo charged, dipping his shoulder. He was going to propel Lawton over the edge. The heavy roared, picked up speed, coming in hard.

Lawton pirouetted, one leg hanging over a fifty-foot drop.

Tattoo clipped Lawton's hip. And realized he'd fucked up. He screamed, going headfirst off the platform.

Lawton fell backwards on to the deck. He heard the thug's body hit the floor down below.

Then he heard: "Get the bastard," and looked up to see Crane's swollen face sneer at him.

Dreadlock, clenching his fists, creasing his brow, strode towards Lawton. Lawton felt dizzy. He didn't think he could get up in time to defend himself. He tried, but swayed, head spinning. Dreadlock, seeing him struggle, smirked. Lawton sat back down, felt Birch's gun jab into his backside. He reached for the gun. Dreadlock's face changed. Lawton shot him in the knee. Dreadlock screamed, his leg buckling. He stumbled, blood spouting from his knee. He got too close to the edge and fell, his wail ending in a thump as his body hit the ground.

Lawton got to his feet. He looked around. Up in the balconies, the crowd panicked. He saw the boy hanging upside down from a rail over the pit and a hand, too large and too red to be a human hand, clasped around the boy's skull.

He smelled death, too. He knew what that smelled like, and it was strong here.

He went to help the boy and then saw Crane. Lawton aimed the gun at Crane and the man backed away, putting his hands up, offering a smile. "N-now, now, Mr. Lawton, let's not be rash."

"I'm feeling very rash, Crane. Where's Sassie, where's Christine and –? "

A scream stopped him. And then a voice, screeching, said, "Kill it, Jake! Kill it, for God's sake!"

It was Sassie.

He went to the pit where the boy was hanging. He stared down and saw the monster, and something came apart in Lawton's belly and he almost lost all his strength and toppled into the trench.

But he steeled himself, swore at the monster because it made him feel better, and shot it in the head.

Black liquid spurted from the creature's scalp and it let go of the boy, staggering backwards. The boy screamed for his mother and Lawton realized he was Murray's son.

The creature glared up at Lawton and Lawton felt the courage drizzle out of him. He'd looked a lot of men in the eye and never felt fear, but he recognized it now.

The creature rose out of the pit, floated up like it was on wires.

The crowd gasped and chants of, "Kea, Kea," swept through Religion.

The vampires shrieked from the cavern below.

Kea towered above Lawton.

"Kill him, my Lord Kea," said Crane, "Kill the piece of shit."

Lawton, eyes fixed on Kea, said to Crane: "I'm going to put this gun in your mouth and blow the back of your head off after I'm done with this thing."

Crane said, "You're fucked, soldier boy."

The creature stretched out its arms, and the red cape of skin flapped.

"Jesus, you're a fucking ugly bastard," said Lawton, looking up at the monster, giving it all that but feeling shit scared.

The monster shrieked and the vampires responded – dozens of them, clambering up the walls, up the scissor lift, making the platform jolt.

And Lawton said, "Rabbit, I really need you to be where you're going." He whipped the spear out of its scabbard. "This is a new trick I've learned today," he said – and he pulled the spear apart, the centre shaft splitting in two, Lawton now holding the pieces like two short swords in either hand.

Kea tensed and took a backward step. Lawton saw the beast flinch and it gave him a spurt of confidence.

He scanned the club, taking in the arena. The audience leaned over the railings, to get a look at their god – the creature they'd waited centuries to see. Milo tussled with a few, easily overcoming them. But Lawton needed him down here, to help him fight the vampires that were tearing up the walls, up the scissor lift, and on to the platform.

CHAPTER 103.
TIME TO ESCAPE.

JACQUELINE Burrows watched the vampires leap up on to the platform and clamber to the balcony. She backed away, reaching into her pocket for the cloth that would keep her safe. She fished it out of her jacket and flapped it in front of her face. Others around her did the same with their marks, holding them up in whatever form they took to keep the vampires at bay.

The vampires lined the balcony, staring down at the platform. They wailed, calling to their creator. Burrows's eyes fixed on Kea. He was magnificent. A glorious beast that made the soldier Lawton look puny.

Something caught her eye. A fight in the shadows. A large man who'd come in with the soldier smashed his way through the people here, tossing them aside, throwing punches and kicks.

"The drapes, Milo," said Lawton from below, his voice echoing, "drag down those drapes – Rabbit, I need you, now – now."

The one called Milo tugged at the nearest drape. The red velvet snapped from the rail high above. The material cascaded down. People screamed as it poured over them. Streetlight filtered through the strip of pebbled glass.

The one called Milo elbowed his way through the crowd to reach the next drape. He dragged that one down, too, trapping people under the heavy material.

A voice at Burrows's shoulder said, "We've got to get out of here, Mrs. Burrows."

She wheeled, stared into Phil Birch's wide, wet eyes. His nose was red, and dried blood smeared his face. He said, "Things are going a bit crazy."

"Kea's risen," she said, "it'll be fine – won't it?"

"Mrs. Radu's dead. Lawton's causing trouble. If the police arrive – "

"You *are* the police, Mr. Birch."

He scurried over to a couch. He said, "I mean the real police, the proper ones." Birch got on his knees, reached under the couch, brought out a shotgun. He stood and held up the gun. "My 'you-never-know' weapon," he said. "And this is a 'you-never-know' moment, I'd say. We've got to go."

She shook her head. "I'm a Home Office minister, I can do – " And she faltered, her mouth open, her eyes staring into space while she thought about the situation. She looked at Birch and said, "You're right. Where's Dr. Haddad? He has Kakash and Kasdeja. We'll need them. There'll be another day."

"This way," said Birch, as screams filled the auditorium.

★ ★ ★ ★

Haddad stared down at the chaos. He leaned on the control panels. His legs felt weak and he wanted to slump back into his wheelchair, but he was frozen with terror.

Jed had wheeled him here to the lighting booth and Haddad pressed the controls that raised the platform. He'd settled back to watch Lord Kea's resurrection. He saw the figures in the balcony, the lost family he'd found and gathered over the years: the descendents of Nebuchadnezzar.

He was seven when the Fuads brought him to Britain. They were the bookkeepers, the branch of the family that held all the information. Their musty, damp cellar contained miles of shelving and filed there were family trees and histories of Nebuchadnezzar's line. Haddad spent hours in the dark, dank cavern learning the names of all the people he would trace. He pledged to bring them together one day, and they'd watch the re-birth of their gods.

And here was that day.

But everything was going wrong.

Nadia had been killed – by the very god she'd served. And that damned soldier slashed away at the vampires on the platform. He was armed with the Abrahamspear, now divided to make two swords – he'd found it; found it where Ion had failed months ago, where so many had failed since those men stole it from Haddad's home.

Haddad cried out. Another invader was tearing down the drapes that covered Religion's windows. It was no problem, now, but unless they were out of here by dawn, the sun would spill through those windows, killing the vampires.

Panic spread through the watching crowd.

"We'll have to get out before sunrise," Haddad said to Jed, cowering behind him near the door. Haddad grabbed his hat.

"I'm scared," said Jed, baring his fangs, "I can – smell fear. I don't – don't want to burn – I, I, I know how it feels. How can I know how it feels to burn in the sun?"

"You have a common heritage," said Haddad, watching the havoc through the soundproofed window of the booth. "All those who've gone before you, you share a bond with them, boy. You know what a stake through the heart feels like, what burning in the sun feels like."

The door crashed open. Haddad spun around and pain surged through his body. He leaned against the control desk to steady himself. A lean, shaven-headed man, his body all sharp edges, stumbled into the booth. The man's boiler suit was pulled down to reveal his torso. He smelled of iodine. Blood oozed from bandaged wounds in his neck, his arms, and the wounds were stained yellow. He looked pale and weak, but he wielded a stake.

"Hello, granddad," said the wounded man, "I'm Rabbit – and you're in my headlights," and he staggered forwards.

Haddad's gaze flitted to Jed, hiding behind the door. The man called Rabbit hadn't seen him. But he saw Haddad's eyes. And the Rabbit turned, following Haddad's gaze, as the vampire sprang forward.

CHAPTER 104.
THE RING.

LAWTON kicked a vampire off the platform.

"Too many of them," said Crane. "Give it up, Lawton, you've no chance."

Vampires circled Lawton. He held out the tusks. Kea towered over all the figures on the platform. Saliva oozed down the creature's chin, and it opened and closed its mouth as if flexing the jaw muscle.

Lawton's gaze darted about, looking for an escape route. "Rabbit," he said, his voice rising above to cacophony, "Rabbit, hit that switch, for Christ's sake."

"There's no switch that'll save you, now," said Crane.

The vampires closed. Then one of them stepped out from the circle and Lawton held his breath, looking into the creature's eyes. "Hello, Jake," said Jenna, her smile showing bloodied fangs. "Do you want to dance? We are in a club."

Lawton said, "Not really. You know me. Haven't got the moves." He backed away as she moved forward.

"Come on," said the vampire Jenna. "Let me finish it. Let me make it so that we're together forever. I've done Dad already. He'll be moaning at me for the rest of time, now."

"I'll kill you, Jenna."

"I'm already dead."

"Then I'll kill you again."

"You can't. You can't stab me with those things, you just can't."

"Go on," said Crane, "take him, take him down and let me watch him squirm."

A voice pierced the chaos saying, "His ring, Jake, his ring."

He turned and saw Sassie, bloodied and stained, clamber out of the pit. She held a piece of red material in her hand. The vampires turned on her and Lawton went to shout for her to take care. But the creatures, once they'd seen her, seemed indifferent, backing off. Lawton frowned.

Jenna said, "Your new girl, is she? Pity we can't kill her too. Pity she's untouchable, or you could go together."

And Lawton thought, *Why is she untouchable?*

"The ring," said Sassie again.

Crane said, "You bitch, Sassie. That mark doesn't mean *I* can't kill you," and he rushed forward.

Jenna pounced. Lawton thrust with one of his swords. The weapon pierced Jenna's chest and cracked her ribs. She screamed, tossing back her head. He grunted, driving the tusk deeper, lifting her off her feet.

Impaled on the bone, she dug her nails into Lawton's shoulders. He grimaced, the pain shooting through him. She fought against him, growling and tearing at Lawton.

The vampires wailed. Kea roared. The building trembled. The vampires came forward. From the corner of his eye, Lawton saw Crane tussle with Sassie. And then he glimpsed Murray crawl out of the pit and grab Crane's leg.

The sword sunk deeper into her chest. She stared down at him, tears of blood running from her eyes. "Jake," she said, her voice a whine, "Jake, how could you hurt me? How could you do this to me?" And for a second he felt the rage drizzle out of him. But then:

"Easy," he said, jamming the bone into Jenna's chest, right up to the hilt, till he felt the point exit through her back. She shrieked and flailed. The smell of burning filled Lawton's nostrils. He swung her around, swatting other vampires away with her body. Her skin charred. Veins of fire pulsed along her scorched flesh. Her tongue withered and her hair shrivelled.

She said his name and crumbled, her remains raining over him and powdering his clothes and his skin and his hair, and showering across the podium.

He tucked the swords under his armpits and looked at his hands. Jenna's ashes coated his skin. He stared at his palms for a moment, and

401

then turned them over to study his knuckles and his fingernails. Then he clapped his hands, scattering her residue, washing it off him.

He armed himself again, and was under attack immediately.

Murray and Sassie fought with Crane. He was lashing out at the women. Lawton kept a vampire at bay with the bone-swords. He thrust one of the tusks into the creature's chest. Like Jenna, it fragmented.

Richard Murray shouted his name, his voice desperate. Lawton spun round. Two vampires closed in on the grounded man. He struggled against his handcuffs.

Lawton raced across the platform, keeping an eye on Kea.

The creature seemed to be surveying. Lawton guessed it could step into the skirmish at any time, and put an end to it. But Kea seemed to be gauging its enemy. Maybe being awake after sleeping for three thousand years took some getting used to, and the vampire god needed to reacclimatize.

Lawton booted the vampire attacking Richard over the edge of the platform. The other creature wheeled, bared its fangs. Lawton slashed it across the face with his sword. Black liquid spurted from the wound. He kicked the vampire off the podium, and he went to Richard.

"Get me out of these things – my wife – my sons – " said Richard.

"Stick your arms out behind you."

Richard did and Lawton shot through the chain linking the cuffs. The bullet shattered the link. Richard screamed, leaped to his feet. He stormed over to get Michael down from the rail, and then stared down into the pit and said David's name.

Lawton went to Sassie and Murray's aid, his gaze darting around the club as he raced over to them. Vampires still clambered up the platform, and he sent a couple plunging back into the cavern as he crossed the deck. The audience cowered towards the back of the balcony. Lawton smelled smoke, and he saw it billowing. Someone said, "Fire! Fire!" and people started to stream out of the gallery. Milo had started to burn the drapes.

"Drag them down so if we're still in a fight come dawn, those bastards'll burn," Lawton had told him. "And set them alight. We'll raze that fucking house of devils to the ground, take all the bastards with us if we have to."

Screams and cries filled Religion.

Lawton's gaze roved the balcony.

And he saw Milo.

Lawton said, "Jesus."

Milo had the RPG pressed into his shoulder.

Lawton, fifty feet away, stared into the barrel.

"Duck," said Milo.

Lawton ducked. Milo fired. A wooden stake shot out of the RPG, tailed by white smoke. It whizzed over Lawton's head and thudded into the chest of a vampire that had just stood after climbing on to the platform. The force of the blow sent the vampire flying off the platform, the stake buried in its chest. The creature smashed into the DJ's booth and exploded into dust.

Lawton stared up at Milo and gave him the thumbs up. Milo reloaded and started popping vampires, laughing like a loon as he blew them to pieces with his new toy. Smoke was building up behind him, and now Lawton could see flames too, licking at the walls.

Lawton glanced up towards the lighting booth. Where the fuck was Rabbit? He felt a chill in his gut. He cast the fear aside, crossed to Sassie and Murray and grabbed Crane by the collar. He tossed the man aside. Crane got up, snarling. "I'll tear your eyes out, you bastard."

Lawton looked at the man like he was shit.

Crane hurtled towards him. Lawton cracked him across the jaw with one of his bone-swords. Crane stumbled away, swaying across the platform.

Sassie comforted Murray, who bled from the nose.

Lawton pounced on Crane. He grabbed the tottering man's hand. He tried to pull the ring off his finger but it wouldn't come.

Lawton took out the gun, shot a vampire through the head as it came for him. It staggered away but then regained its balance. It came again. Something hissed, struck the vampire. And it flew off the deck with one of Milo's rocket-propelled stakes pinned to its chest.

Lawton struggled with Crane, trying to rip the ring off the professor's finger. Lawton got out his knife. Crane said, "No, no, for Christ's sake." He decked Crane with an elbow to the temple. Crane sagged. Lawton went down with him.

And he sliced off Crane's finger.

Crane screamed.

Lawton stepped away. A vampire came for him. He held out the bloody stump with the ring on it. The vampire flinched and shot away.

Crane leaped to his feet and jumped about, screeching. Blood pulsed from his hand. Lawton shoved him backwards. He stumbled and bumped into Kea.

Crane froze.

Kea looked down.

Crane glanced back over his shoulder. Terror stretched his face as he looked up into the monster's eyes.

Kea rammed its talons into Crane's chest. The nails dug into flesh. Crane shrieked. Kea opened him up as if he were helping Crane off with his coat.

Blood gushed out of Crane's mouth. A terrible sound came from his throat, high-pitched and inhuman. His torso had been ripped open. His insides spooled out. His ribs showed and his heart throbbed behind the barrier of bones. Sassie fainted. Lawton took a step back, his eyes fixed on the man who'd been pulled open. Crane's eyes blinked and his mouth was open, a gurgling noise coming from his throat.

Vampires rushed forward and buried their faces in his open chest. They tore at his ribs to get to the heart and lungs, and the crack of bone jarred Lawton. A press of vampires covered Crane's remains, and Lawton heard them dismember him.

A dark-skinned woman climbed from the pit with a boy – David, he guessed – in tow. Richard helped them out.

Lawton went over to them, helped Sassie to her feet. He asked her if she was all right, and she said, in a light voice, that she was.

Vampires still clambered up the platform.

"There's hundreds of them," said Murray.

Lawton slid the ring off the severed finger and tossed the digit away. He gave Sassie the ring.

"What about you?" she said.

"I'll be fine."

Rocket-propelled stakes still whizzed around, knocking vampires off the podium. The fire crackled and the smoke thickened.

A bellow shook the building, and Lawton and the others flinched. He turned. Kea glared at them with fire in his eyes. The monster roared again, pointing a deadly looking talon in Lawton's direction.

Lawton, throat dry, his body wracked with wounds, stepped forward. He squared up to the giant vampire, brandishing the ancient swords made of fuck-knows-whose bones. He didn't give a shit. The only question in his mind was: would they kill this made-in-hell monstrosity?

Lawton, sneering at Kea, said, "Want to fight?"

Kea roared in his face, and Lawton smelled thousands of years of decay in that breath.

"Jake," said Sassie. "Jake, please," her voice a squeal of terror.

He glanced over his shoulder. Vampires crowded the platform. There were too many for Milo to pick off, although he kept firing. Lawton looked up to the balcony. Vampires closed in on Milo and Lawton said, "Look out for yourself, Cal," but Milo was surrounded.

Sassie and Murray screamed as the vampires closed in. The ring and the choker protected them, and they formed a circle around David and Michael. Sassie gave Aaliyah the choker, gave Murray the ring. Lawton said, *No*, but there were only two protective trinkets.

Richard Murray armed himself with a couple of RPG stakes that lay on the platform. With fury in his eyes and rage bellowing from his throat, he attacked a group of vampires, thrusting his stakes into chests, faces, any flesh he could find.

Kea bounded towards Lawton. The creature towered above him. The vampires circled, predators waiting to pounce on their prey.

Milo shouted from the balcony, saying, "I'm done, Lawton, I'm done, I'm – " and the smoke enveloping him.

And Lawton thought, *Rabbit, run with me* –

Sassie screamed. Lawton turned. Vampires had dragged her from the protective group, Murray trying her best to hold on to Sassie's arm, but the vampires were too strong and too many.

Lawton called Sassie's name, watched her being hauled away, Murray screaming, *No, no, no*.

Lawton went to go for her, but nails dug into his scalp. He glanced up. Kea's hand was clamped on his head, those talons tearing into his skin. His head felt like it was on fire. Lawton lashed out. He thought the creature would scalp him, tear the skin and hair from his skull.

Sassie screamed again.

Lawton said, "Sassie, no, no," and looked her in the eye as vampires bit into her body.

CHAPTER 105.
CAUGHT IN THE
HEADLIGHTS.

LITHGOW said to his dad, "Where are we going?"

"We're going to watch the show."

"What show?" said Lithgow.

Keatch gave him a shove.

His dad said, "All right, Mr. Keatch."

Keatch said, "We need to get a move on. I don't like what I'm hearing down there in the club. Sounds like things aren't going quite to plan."

Lithgow glanced over his shoulder, saw his dad bite his lip, his eyes half-closed like he was concentrating. Lithgow thought, *If things aren't going to plan, maybe Lawton's stuck his oar in; maybe he's here.*

The thought of Lawton gave Lithgow a jolt of hope.

Everything *might* be all right.

Lithgow in front, Keatch behind him, and his dad taking the rear, they were striding down a third floor corridor. Earlier, in that box room with his dad and Keatch, Lithgow had heard a grinding noise and the building seemed to shudder. That was when his dad said, "It's starting," and Keatch shoved Lithgow through the door saying, "Get moving." As they walked, the commotion in the club had grown. Lithgow sensed panic in the muffled shouts of whoever had gathered here. And his dad's face showed anxiety.

Now Keatch said, "What's going on down there?"

Lithgow's dad said, "Let's hurry up, Mr. Keatch."

"I was hurrying up; gave him a shove and you told me to lay off."

"I didn't tell you to 'lay off,' Mr. Keatch, I was merely suggesting —" His dad faltered and gave a sigh. Then he said, "Please, we must hurry. Things don't sound right to me."

They don't sound right, thought Lithgow; *that* had *to mean Lawton was here.* He said, "My mate's here, and he's brought his Army pals – you're fucked, Dad; you and your sick friends."

Keatch shoved him, and Lithgow stumbled forward. He lost his footing, starting to go headfirst, his arms flailing. Lithgow staggered around the corner, hit the floor, skin scraping off his hands, his knees jarring. Getting up on all fours, he grimaced, looked up.

Down the corridor walked a red-haired woman he recognized from somewhere. And striding beside her was a man with a bloody face and a shotgun.

★ ★ ★ ★

Rabbit reached behind him, grabbed the vampire's hair and yanked him over his shoulder, slamming him to the floor. Rabbit, the strength seeping out of him, stood on his unsteady legs. He took in the room: the control desk, the window looking down over the club, the old man, and –

The vampire lunged.

Rabbit ducked and rugby-tackled the thing around the waist. He rammed the vampire into the desk, and Rabbit felt the air rush from the creature's body. He yanked a stake from his belt. He went to stab the creature, raising the stake, but the old man said, "No, no, don't."

Rabbit faltered, glanced at the old man.

And the old man sneered at him.

Rabbit felt cold fear rush through his veins.

The vampire clawed his face and Rabbit stumbled backwards. The vampire came after him.

The old man cackled, said, "Pitiful, pitiful man – you are going to die and live again and feel hunger for the rest of time."

Rabbit threw his arms above his head, protecting himself from the vampire's attack.

Teeth bared, the creature pounced.

Rabbit slashed with his stake. He felt the point cut through skin and the vampire whined.

Rabbit gave himself room, dancing like a boxer around the lighting booth. The vampire swivelled, losing his balance, black blood spouting from its face wound.

Rabbit thrust forward, the stake sinking into the vampire's chest. The creature grimaced, and a hiss escaped its throat. It locked eyes with Rabbit and Rabbit saw the hate and the ugliness in the thing's face.

The vampire clawed at Rabbit saying, "I don't want to die."

"Tough titty," said Rabbit, and he drove the weapon deeper into the creature's chest.

The old man yelled and grabbed a metal briefcase. "Help! Help!" The old man threw his voice towards the open door. "Help! Help!" He scrabbled to his feet, sat in his wheelchair.

★ ★ ★ ★

When the voice shouted "Help! Help!" the red-haired woman and the armed man picked up their pace, racing down the corridor in Lithgow's direction.

The shout for help came from a room about twenty yards away.

Lithgow glanced over his shoulder. His dad and Keatch hurried round the corner, Keatch going, "What the hell was that?" and his dad saying, "It sounded like Dr. Haddad to me."

Haddad, thought Lithgow; *Haddad in trouble*. Could that mean Lawton's mate was in that room? So that was the lighting suite. That's where the UV controls were. That was Lawton's plan, what he'd told Lithgow in that last phone call.

Adrenalin flushed Lithgow's heart. He took a look at his dad and Keatch, their eyes fixed ahead, ignoring Lithgow.

Keatch was right behind him. He kicked out like a mule and caught Keatch just under the knee. All Lithgow's strength went into that kick, and it bent Keatch's leg back in a way it shouldn't bend. The thug screamed. Lithgow's dad ran into him, pushing Keatch over, Keatch grabbing his knee, bellowing. Lithgow's dad tripped over the lout, hitting the floor hands first.

Lithgow sprang to his feet.

The red-haired woman and the armed man were close, heading for the lighting suite, the red-haired woman throwing a glance Lithgow's way.

Lithgow faltered, fear sapping his strength.

What was he thinking? He wasn't Lawton, wasn't a soldier.

What was he going to do?

He looked back at his dad and Keatch. Keatch groaned, a sound like, "Broken my – my – broken – fucking leg," coming from him. His dad tried to get to his feet.

Lithgow went to him. He said, "Dad?" and his dad looked up.

His dad said, "Son."

Lithgow kicked him in the face.

★ ★ ★ ★

The vampire screeched. Rabbit stared at the dying creature. It was a boy, about seventeen, Rabbit guessed, younger maybe.

But not for long.

Arteries of fire threaded under the pale skin of the vampire's face. The thing's eyes filled with blood and its flesh withered. Unleashing a last shriek, the vampire shrivelled and collapsed into dust, leaving Rabbit standing there with the stake thrust into space.

Rabbit looked at the old man trying to take the brake off his wheelchair. He watched him for a few seconds and thought, *Fuck him, do what the sarge sent me here to do.*

He turned to the desk.

He saw lines of knobs and switches everywhere. Rabbit's eyes narrowed, his head spinning.

Which one is it? he thought.

He glanced through the window.

"Oh, shit," he said, seeing Lawton in the monster's claws, Lawton thrashing about. Vampires scaling the scissor lift around the piston. "Oh, shit."

His eyes roved the desk.

Which ones?

Lawton had said, *It'll be there somewhere.*

And then he saw and he gasped, and his skin goosepimpled.

The selection of sliders had a sticker above them saying UV. The sliders were divided into groups marked xenon, mercury, arc lights, and some words that had been smudged.

"Jam all the sliders right up to the highest level," Lawton had said. "Flick every fucking switch. Make sure every single UV light on that desk is on full blast. And then wreck the fucking thing so no bastard can switch them off."

Rabbit reached out.

A gun fired.

He grimaced, feeling as if someone had punched him in the back. Then numbness spread through his chest. He grew cold, turned to see a bald guy with glasses and blood on his face aiming a shotgun at him. A red-haired woman stood next to the shooter. She grinned at Rabbit and started to wheel the old man out of the booth.

The old man cackled, clutching the silver case.

"Shoot him again, Birch," said the woman. "And let's get the hell out of here."

Rabbit's vision blurred. Pain spread through his chest. His throat clogged up with blood. His legs felt like paper and he knew they couldn't bear his weight for too long.

Sarge, he thought, *sarge –*

The shotgun blasted. Rabbit's ears popped. The spray slammed into his chest, ramming him back against the desk. His vision blurred. Air hissed out of his lungs and his chest grew tighter and tighter.

He heard the old man cackling in his head.

He reached for the switch, flailing hopelessly.

I've let you down, sarge, was the thought swimming in his head; *I've let you down.*

And then a face appeared above him saying, "There, it's those – oh, shit – hit the fucking things – all of them – "

CHAPTER 106.
THE FALL.

KEA raised Lawton off his feet, the talons digging into his skull. Blood washed over his ears, down his neck. He fought the pain, but he thought he'd pass out. The monster twisted Lawton round, bringing them face-to-face. Lawton glimpsed Sassie, her eyes pleading, her mouth making the shape of his name. Vampires bit into her throat, dragging her towards the pit, her feet kicking.

Lawton forced out a shout: "No!" and anger boiled his blood, knowing Sassie was lost to him. She shrieked as the vampires pulled her down into the trench, her feet scrabbling at the edge of the trench, the last part of her to disappear.

It felt like Lawton's heart was being wrenched out.

But the rage blinded him, immunized him from the pain in his skull. He raised the swords. The creature opened his mouth, bared its fangs. Lawton stared into the purple and red maw, saw the forked tongue and the teeth. The jaw, like a snake's, dislocated to enable the monster to open its mouth wider than seemed possible.

Lawton roared and drove one of his bone-swords into the demon's mouth.

Kea's eyes bulged. The weapon stabbed through the back of its mouth, piercing the creature's skull. Lawton felt the weapon's slice through bone and flesh and muscle.

Kea unleashed a terrible shriek, spraying blood into Lawton's face.

The monster let Lawton go, but Lawton held on to the weapon, and then drove the other one into the soft flesh inches above Kea's collarbone. The demon shuddered and moaned. Lawton's weight dragged the creature's head down. He hung on to the bone-swords, his arms starting to tire, his feet dangling.

He started to kick Kea's crotch. Kea clawed at Lawton, ripping through the boiler suit, tearing away the skin of his chest.

Lawton knew he couldn't let go. But the wounds in its mouth and shoulder wouldn't kill Kea. And unless he did something, Lawton knew this monster would kill him.

The ancient bone had to be driven through Kea's heart.

Lawton shook the bone-sword buried in the vampire's mouth. A mewling came from Kea's throat. The creature thrashed about, trying to toss Lawton off the weapon.

And then the vampire started to pull the tusk out of its mouth. A shriek came from its throat, the vampire god spinning now in a bid to dislodge Lawton. Blood sprayed again. As he was spun, Lawton caught glimpses of what was going on around him:

Murray and her children cowering at the edge of the platform, holding up a ragged piece of cloth. Richard fighting off vampires, finding strength from somewhere. The dark-skinned woman, Crane's ring on her finger, going at vampires like a banshee. Smoke filling Religion, fire crackling, tearing through the club.

And vampires crawling from the pit where Sassie had been dragged.

His eyes welled with tears. Grief tore at his heart. He knew she was gone. His rage swelled again. Kea yanked the bone-sword free of its throat. Lawton let go of the other weapon, left it buried in Kea's shoulder.

Lawton dropped to the platform. The vampire god staggered. He lowered his head, glared down at Lawton. A beam of light came through the hole in the back of its head, down along its mouth. Lawton drove the bone-sword into Kea's chest. The vampire vomited black blood.

And then another light, strong and white, flashed and blinded Lawton for a second.

Religion flared.

Blinding white light.

Lawton blinked, his vision blurred. Stars danced in front of his face.

Vampires started to mewl.

412

Rabbit had found the ultraviolet switch.

The reek of burning flesh filled the air.

Smoke rose from a vampire crawling out of the trench. The creatures started to claw at their bodies as fire ignited on their skins, scorching them. Up in the balcony, flaming vampires lit up the gloom, leaping like balls of fire out of the smoke that roiled and swarmed up in the gallery.

Smoke billowed from Kea's flesh.

But the monster eyed Lawton with rage. It paid no attention to the heat, to the light destroying its offspring. Kea bore down on him and Lawton backed away, unarmed now, both his bone-swords buried in Kea's body.

Around him, vampires burned to ashes. Their dying screams deafened him. Their bodies flaming balls, plummeting off the balcony, off the platform.

The UV light was blinding.

Kea lurched forward, its skin starting to char, the red flesh turning black.

But the monster still gave off a sense of power.

It attacked.

Lawton braced himself. He felt weak and thought he couldn't take much more. But he had to stand his ground. He yelled, racing forward to face, head-on, Kea's charge. He leaped at the monster and the monster swatted him away. But Lawton grasped for the bone-sword in the beast's shoulder and yanked, the weapon sliding out of the flesh.

Kea shrieked. Smoke belched from the wound.

Lawton sprang to his feet, armed again.

Kea came again, flying at Lawton, smoke tailing off its body.

Lawton braced himself, squatting down. He sprang at Kea, bone-sword held out. They clashed. Kea bear-hugged Lawton, Lawton driving the sword into the monster's chest next to the other weapon, both horns now buried in the demon's heart.

Kea's momentum forced them backwards, sent them tumbling over the edge of the platform.

Kea bit into Lawton's shoulder as they he fell. Lawton yelled out. The bite was like acid on his skin. His chin rested on the monster's shoulder. Lawton saw the points of the bone-swords sticking out of Kea's back.

They plummeted, the breath rushing out of Lawton.

Lawton struggled, trapped by the monster's bear hug, its arms like tree trunks wrapped around him.

Heat came from Kea, now, its body burning up. The vampire opened its arms, flapping them as if to slow its fall, and Lawton came free.

They drew apart, Lawton holding on to the hilts of the bone-swords, Lawton on his back and Kea above him. He'd be crushed under the vampire's body when they hit the cavern floor.

Smoke swelled from Kea's flesh. The skin scorched and flames ignited on its arms, its legs, its scalp.

Lawton struggled to breathe.

He tugged out one of the bone-swords from Kea's chest, skewered it back into the vampire's heart. The monster shrieked and flailed. It tried to shake itself loose. Its violent thrashing caused them to roll through the air. Lawton felt as if he were being ripped apart. He couldn't breathe, his lungs somewhere in the back of his throat by now. The ground hurtled towards him.

Kea started to disintegrate, ashes whipping off its body, smoke swirling.

Lawton yelled for his life.

PART FIVE.
AFTERMATH.

CHAPTER 107.
ENEMIES OF THE STATE.

THE Home Secretary said, "Eighteen bodies were recovered from the ruins of Religion. The fire last Monday destroyed the building and caused devastating damage to nearby structures. That area of Soho will be shut to the public until further notice."

The Home Secretary coughed and continued:

"Among the bodies discovered were, as reported in the newspapers, John Petrou, a well-respected High Court judge, and the admired QC, Bernard Lithgow. The body of a former King's Regiment soldier, Richard Andrew Bittle, was also discovered. We believe, at this time, that Mr. Bittle may have started the fire."

The reporters who'd gathered for the news conference shuffled. Cameras clicked and flashed. The Home Secretary frowned, providing the photographers and cameraman with a serious image.

"Mr. Bittle," said the Home Secretary, "served in Basra with Jake Lawton, who had been questioned by police in connection with the deaths of twenty-eight people at Religion on February the sixth, 2008. Now, as we all know, you gentlemen and ladies of the press" – a murmur went through the room – "made a number of bizarre allegations after the bodies of those twenty-eight victims went missing.

416

You made bizarre allegations when a vicious drugs war broke out in London, which resulted in the deaths of many innocent people. I am not going to confirm or deny any of those allegations. They are, to be honest, not worthy of comment. They are speculation at best, lies at worst."

Hands shot up among the reporters. The Home Secretary raised an arm and went on:

"There will be time for a few questions at the end, but let me finish."

The reporters dropped their hands.

"The police still wish," said the Home Secretary, "to question Jake Lawton. He was known to have entered Religion on the night of the fire, but no trace of him has been found. Police wish to question him about his involvement in the fire, and continue to seek his help in the inquiry surrounding the deaths of the twenty-eight people at the club on February the sixth. If you glance up at the screen behind me" – the Home Secretary heard the hum of the screen – "you will note the images of three people police wish to question. They are, as you've noted, Jake Lawton, Christine Murray – one of you, I hasten to add, who has disappeared with her husband, Richard, and her sons, David and Michael – and Aaliyah Sinclair."

Cameras flashed again, and reporters scribbled in their notebooks. Whispers swept through the press pack. The Home Secretary coughed again and continued:

"We advise the public not to approach these individuals if they are spotted, but to contact the police immediately. Certainly, Mr. Lawton is a dangerous individual. He has been, in the past, accused of a crime while serving as a British soldier in Iraq – a crime that brought shame to all the brave men and women who are fighting for the freedoms of the Iraqi people and the security of the free West."

The Home Secretary nodded her head to indicate the speech had ended.

Reporters peppered questions at the podium. Arms shot up and voices crisscrossed. It was bedlam, and a Home Office press officer stood to calm the throng.

"Ladies and gentlemen," he said, "ladies and gentlemen – "

The Home Secretary took the rag of scarlet skin from her jacket pocket and held it to her nose for a moment. She sniffed, drawing in the ancient odours, the musky stench.

417

The press officer said, "Mrs. Burrows will gladly answer your questions about her recent promotion and the present situation, and the newly promoted Detective *Chief* Superintendent Phil Birch from the Met's Homicide and Serious Crime Command" – he gestured to the bespectacled man holding a clipboard – "can also respond to any queries you might have with regards these incidents."

Reporters shouted, raising their arms, thrusting their microphones forward, shouting Jacqueline Burrows's name. Her eyes scanned the crowd, and she pointed to the Sky News correspondent bobbing up and down in the front row.

CHAPTER 108.
EXILES.

CHRISTINE Murray, standing in the shadows of the pine trees, gazed out towards the sea. She couldn't see the water, but heard its swish as it came in. The sand stretched for miles. Dunes crested the beach. She watched the stick figures of David and Michael running from the water.

"It's like being the last people on earth," she said.

"One day we might be just that," said Richard, his arm around his wife's shoulder.

They were silent.

Then Murray said, "No sign of Lawton or Aaliyah – or Sassie."

Richard shook his head. "I'm sorry."

Murray said, "Jake Lawton walks at night. That's what they say, isn't it? A ghost."

"Who says?" Richard sounded irritated. He didn't like rumours, speculation; he liked facts.

"The forums, the bloggers. They say he never sleeps."

"He never did. He was insomniac."

"He kills in the dark, that's what they say. Walks at night, kills in the dark. If he is alive, I think he might have gone after the Fuad brothers."

Richard said, "I'm sure he'll be in touch, soon."

"But I'm not absolutely sure he made it out of Religion alive. No one saw him; we've not heard a thing. Just these rumours. And as for Sassie — "

"She's one of them, Chrissie, you know that."

Murray said nothing.

"I hope the boys will be all right," said Richard. "They saw terrible things. I don't think Michael is really coping."

"I've been an awful mother."

"It's all right," he said.

She shivered against him and he pulled her closer. She felt alone, though. Lost to the world. But they were exiles, after all. Banished from society. The authorities considered Lawton Public Enemy No.1. And anyone consorting with him would be held to account, too.

"They're re-grouping, aren't they. Burrows is Home Secretary, now," said Murray. "She's got more power. She'll protect Haddad; she'll protect them all. Let's hope Fraser's doing some good. I've not heard from him in weeks."

"Where was he the last you heard?"

"Some festival in Manchester."

"Any drugs?" said Richard.

She shook her head. "Not the kind we were looking for. But it's only a matter of time. They'll lie low, then start again. And they've got more of a power base, now. Burrows almost at Number Ten."

"You don't think —?"

"Why not, Richard? Why wouldn't she want the top job? That's what they're after: power. They want an empire and they'll stop at nothing."

Murray listened to the sea and to the wind whistle through the pines and silver birches, thick behind them.

Richard said, "Do you think there are many out there still? The vampires?"

"Yes, I think so. I think they're still feeding, but picking off people that won't be missed. They'll rise again when they hear that call. When Haddad gets his act together. That's all he's lived for. Kakash is next for him. And lord knows what that thing's going to be like."

"Shall we go back to the caravan?"

Murray nodded, got up and held out a hand to her husband.

Richard called the boys, and the stick figures quickened their pace.

They made their way back through the trees. A twig snapped to her right, and Murray jerked her head round to see. She tightened her grip on Richard's hand.

"What is it?" he said.

Murray shook her head, gave a weary smile. She didn't say anything; didn't want to scare the boys. But as they all headed back to the caravan park, Murray knew they were being watched.

★ ★ ★ ★

Romford, Essex – 11.15 a.m., April 2, 2008

Lithgow said, "A quarter of Black Death, please," and eyed the rows of jars lining the shelves while the blonde woman poured out his sweets into the scales.

He'd spotted the Mr Simms Olde Sweet Shoppe, and all his worries seemed to get rinsed away.

He was here to visit a club called Scandals that night. He'd told Murray, "I've heard that there's a new drug on the go down here. This lad I met, he says it's red with a 'K' on it – but then he said it might be a 'J' – he wasn't sure, but I thought it's worth checking."

And Murray said, "It's worth checking, Fraser."

After the fire at Religion, after he'd got out, Fraser went back to his flat and flushed the Skarlet pills he'd kept in the jewelled box down the loo – what he should've done that Thursday morning after those people died. He'd packed a bag and disappeared, phoning Murray with his new mobile phone number – and only Murray. Since then, she'd been his sole contact.

"Have you heard from Lawton?" he'd asked her.

She said she hadn't.

Where was he, then? Lithgow had saved his life, after all; saved them all. Reached the ultraviolet switch after Rabbit died. But now he'd been abandoned. Lawton had gone underground, some said. But Murray wasn't sure he'd even got out of Religion. The last she saw of him, he was falling off the platform with that monster. Lithgow didn't believe in God, but he prayed that Lawton had made it out alive. Because without Lawton, Lithgow knew they were doomed.

The woman scooped the sweets into a bag and handed them to Fraser with a smile. He paid and smiled back, although he found it hard these days.

He strolled into the high street and sat on a bench. He stared into the bag of sweets. His mind drifted to his childhood, to his mum taking him to sweet shops behind his dad's back and buying him all kinds of treats.

"Don't tell your dad," mum would say, "or I'll get into trouble – we'll both get into trouble."

He felt empty. He had no father, now. No mother. He just had these friends he never saw.

He picked out a sweet. He held it up and rolled it around between finger and thumb. Black, coated in sugar. He popped it into his mouth, and the sourness singed him. He puckered his face and sucked on the sweet. It was the most powerful sweet he'd ever tasted. He swore, and an elderly woman glanced at him as she passed.

Fraser sucked on the sweet and shuddered.

He'd licked off the sugary coating and now it was a smooth ball in his mouth. But still the sourness oozed out of its core. He waited for the bite, for the crunch. His eyes were half-closed, unaware of his surroundings, his mind back in childhood.

A girl said, "You all right? Look like you've been stung by a wasp."

Fraser jolted and opened his eyes. He wrapped up the bag of sweets in his hand.

"Don't I get one?" she said, glancing at the sweets in the bag, then back up to Fraser's face.

"They're strong," he said. "Acquired taste."

"Show me."

He looked at her. She had short dark hair. She was about twenty, pretty and frail, wearing a vest-top and jeans. He opened the bag and showed her. The girl made a face and pulled out her tongue.

"Ugh, Black Death, I've heard of those," she said. "They're really strong. Only for tough guys."

"Acquired taste," he said again.

She nodded, looked him in the eye. "I've got something that's an acquired taste, too."

"Oh yeah?"

"Yeah," and she put something in Fraser's hand. She leaned into him and he smelled her sweat. She said, "If you like it, come to Scandals tonight. I'll be there," and she walked away.

Fraser watched the crowd swallow her. Then he opened his hand and stared at the pill.

He grinned.

CHAPTER 109.
BORN AGAIN.

DIXIE said, "So where the fuck's Perry got to? I ain't seen him since last night."

"He was with some Christians," said Chuck, "telling 'em that the Bible says that 'grass is good' so justifies smoking pot."

"Aw, he's a fucking wanker. They'll mush his brain, man," said Dixie, rolling a joint. "They got brainwashing techniques, those Christians, brainwashing techniques Perry can't cope with."

Chuck said, "I told him. I said, 'Perry, get the fuck away, they are evil, man, evil.' But he wasn't having it, Dixie. They were like, 'We've got the best drug in the world, and it can cleanse your soul,' and Perry goes, 'Can I smoke it?' And then they go, 'No, man, it's Jesus Christ, and he's your saviour,' and Perry's there, Dixie, he's there giving it all that."

"Aw, man," said Dixie, popping the roach in the joint's backside, "they'll twist everything and he'll get involved again. Like he did with those Buddhists last year, man."

"And those jugglers the year before that – he thought juggling could bring world peace."

Dixie, eighteen, had been coming to Glastonbury on his own – well, with his mates and without his parents – for four years. His mum and dad first brought him and Perry here when Dixie was ten and Perry was seven. This was Perry's second Glastonbury without his mum and dad tagging along. They were here somewhere; they were always here. But at least they weren't in Dixie and Perry's faces.

Dixie said, "He's always getting caught up in things, man, we got to keep an eye on him," and he lit the joint. The flame glowed orange in the gloom of the tent. They were camped near the Other Stage where they'd watched the Super Furry Animals play earlier that night. Now, Chemical Brothers' tunes wafted across the campsite, and Dixie nodded his head to the distant rhythm as he belched out a plume of smoke.

Chuck, a schoolmate of Dixie, had been given the job of chaperoning Perry this year. But he was crap at the job, really. And he let the fifteen year old wander off. Nothing wrong in that — if the fifteen year old had any sense of where he was and who he was. But Perry was fucked in the head. Probably all the drugs their mum and dad smoked when he and Dixie were growing up.

"You got to go look for him, man," said Dixie, drawing more smoke into his lungs. His head swam.

"No way, Dixie, no way. He's your brother, man."

"Yeah, and we voted you nanny this year."

"No way — give me a pull — " And he snatched the joint from Dixie, sticking it between his lips. His cheeks hollowed as he drew the fumes into his throat.

Dixie said, "Aw, man, I can't fucking lose him."

He took the spliff back and smoked it. The cigarette paper crackled as the flame ate into it. A tail of smoke plumed from the end of the joint. The tent flap opened and, through the veil of smoke, Dixie saw his brother's blurry face.

Dixie flinched and blinked. His eyes adjusted to the faint light inside the tent. His brother looked —

"You look weird, man," said Chuck. "Those Christians give you a pill, yeah?"

"Yeah, man," said Perry, his voice a hiss, and when he opened his mouth Dixie saw —

"Hey, where d'you get those fangs, man?" said Chuck.

Dixie's insides turned cold. He creased his brow and watched his brother crawl into the tent. Perry looked at him and Dixie stared into his eyes and Dixie said, "What's wrong with your eyes, man?"

Perry had green eyes. Everyone called them beautiful — "Oh, you got beautiful eyes, Perry, man." But now they were tinged with red; they looked dirty. Like there was blood in them.

"Nothing, man," said Perry, on all fours, "I'm cool. Been asleep all night and all day. And now I've just woken up – and I'm hungry."

"Hungry?" said Chuck. "We got beans."

"Yeah," said Dixie, his throat dry. He was shaking, and nausea washed over him. Something was really wrong, and he wanted Perry to leave.

"Beans?" said Perry, looking at Chuck. His skin was pale, and pale was one thing Perry had never been – they called him "ruddy-faced" when he was a kid.

But he's still a kid, thought Dixie – *he'll always be a kid.*

And Perry said, "I don't want beans."

"Okay – what – " but before Chuck could finish, Perry lunged at him and bit into neck, and Chuck grunted and he gawped.

And Dixie, fear gripping him, watched as Perry drank blood from Chuck's throat.

END.

The Vampire Babylon trilogy
continues with **Krimson**. . .

ABOUT THE AUTHOR.

Thomas Emson is the pen-name of an author whose first novel *Maneater* was published by Snowbooks in April 2008. He is Welsh, but now lives in Kent with his wife. He is currently writing a sequel to *Maneater*, and planning *Krimson*, the second installment of the Vampire Trinity.

For more information, visit his blog at www.thomasemson.com or see his author page at www.snowbooks.com.

ACKNOWLEDGMENTS

Thanks to Emma and Anna at Snowbooks, who are so supportive and always provide encouragement. It's a joy to be published by Snowbooks. Thank you to everyone who bought or borrowed this book, and to those of you who loved it, and loved *Maneater* before it. Thanks to Marnie, who is everything.

turn the page for...

AN EXCERPT FROM
THOMAS EMSON'S

${\mathcal M}$ANEATER

AVAILABLE NOW
FROM SNOWBOOKS

CHAPTER 1.
EASY MEAT.

CANAL ST, MANCHESTER – JUNE 7, 1999

"SHE'LL eat you alive."

"She's only human," said Matt, gaze fixed on the girl.

"She's out of your league."

"I'm up for promotion."

Dan laughed, then said, "She'll chew you up and spit you out."

"No way. Look at her. She's easy meat."

He considered the girl for a moment. Then, swigging his Budweiser, he thought, *Yeah, I'm right: she is easy meat.*

The music throbbed up into Matt's chest. The lights flash-gunned as bodies jerked on the dance floor below. He leaned over to Dan, whose eyes roved the club in search of other prey. "I'm making my move," he said, his stare never leaving the girl at the bar.

He swaggered towards her. She crossed her legs, and Matt's gaze drifted to the darkness beneath her silver dress. The glimpse stirred something in his balls. He groaned in appreciation, heat shuttling through him. The girl sipped from the straw sticking out of the watermelon Bacardi Breezer. She swept a hand through her pitch-black hair.

He said, "I'll get you another one of those."

She snared him in her gaze. Her autumn-coloured eyes fixed on him, and a shiver creeped down his back. Matt flashed the smile, all teeth and dimples.

"Would you like one?" he said.

She said nothing. Her nostrils flared as if she was sniffing him. Her eyes were locked on Matt, and he felt the confidence drain out of him. *Look away, babe,* he thought, *like you're not interested because you really are. Smile. Frown. Shake your head. Do something.*

Matt leaned forward. Her perfume saturated his nostrils. "What's your name?" he said, hoping the noise would hide the trembling in his voice.

"Laura Greenacre."

"Matt Grundy." He offered a hand. She didn't take it. "There's no need to be like that."

"Like what?"

"Rude."

"I'm not interested. That's all."

"But we've only just met."

"Well, nice to meet you. Bye."

Shit, he thought, *lesbian.*

Dan and Matt guessed the gay club would be brimming with straight girls. Straight girls liked gay men, didn't they? Felt safe in their company. No complications. So for straight guys like them, the odds of pulling were high. Or should have been. Just his luck the hottest babe on the block was a butch. They never considered that a gay nightspot would pull in the lesbian crowd. Didn't they have their own clubs?

"Hey, I'm sorry." Matt held up his hands up in surrender. "No hard feelings. You're just the most gorgeous girl here. I didn't know you were...you know...I'm sorry. Can I buy you a drink anyw–"

"Didn't know I was what?"

"You know, that you like...girls."

She laughed and shook her head. Her long, dark hair swished over her bare shoulders. Then she said, "I don't. I mean, I'm not like that. I'm just not interested in you." She laughed again.

It was like a punch in the guts.

"Okay." He could feel his face flush. "Don't take the piss."

"I'm not taking the piss." Her laugh drifted away into the babel of music and voices. "It's just you thought I was lesbian because I didn't fancy you. How sad's that?"

He didn't know where the rage came from, but it came, and it was blinding. He flipped the beer bottle towards her, spilling it across her breasts. She sprang to her feet and stared down at her Budweiser-soaked dress.

The fury left Matt's head like it came: in a spark. He gawped at the girl, a coldness sweeping over him.

He tried to say *sorry* but no words came out, only a bumbling sound. He shook his head like a man rejecting an impossible vision. He didn't see her arm lash out, but he felt the nails dig through his shirt and into his chest. A flash of agony surged into his brain. He dropped the beer bottle, and it shattered. He grabbed the girl's arm, squeezing. It was so slender he thought it would snap in his fists.

It didn't.

It raised him off his feet.

Clubbers turned to ogle as the girl forced him upwards, the pain in his chest searing as her nails dug into his skin.

Matt looked down at her. She looked up at him. Her eyes were yellow. Animal eyes. The pupils were black slits. Matt's scream pierced the cacophony.

He felt his neck jerk as the girl tossed him away. The air rushed out of him. As he spiraled, clutching at nothingness, he glimpsed the whirlpool of faces watching him fall.

Their shrieks rattled his eardrums as he soared over the balcony and plunged into a lake of dancers. The dancers parted, and the floor hurtled towards him. The audience gasped as he crash-landed. As unconsciousness swept over Matt, he saw those yellow animal eyes: the eyes of the girl Dan warned would eat him alive.

★ ★ ★

Elena McIntyre saw the girl push her way through the crowd.

Ice water rushed through Elena's veins.

It can't be, she thought.

It's impossible.

Light drowned the club. The music died. Shouts and screams criss-crossed. Revellers babbled and thronged to the balcony to see where the man had smashed into the floor. Clubbers shoved past Elena as they dashed to secure the best spot.

It can't be her, Elena told herself, staring at the girl who was using her arms to hack a path through the forest of bodies.

434

It *is* her.

The girl had her back to Elena. They were ten feet apart. But Elena could see it on the younger woman's shoulder, nestling below the scapula.

It's you.

For Elena, the recognition was like being switched on. She started pushing through the crowd. Black shirted bouncers did the same. They were headed for the girl.

"Run!" The racket swallowed her shout. But the girl heard, and she turned to face the warning. She bolted, forging a path through the bodies. A have-a-go headcase lunged at the fleeing girl. She swatted him away as if he were an insect.

Elena followed her as the bouncers shoved through the crowd. She watched the girl bound the stairs three at a time.

The girl crashed through a door marked BOYS. Three boys spilled out, tripping over each other.

Elena reached the door. She heard glass shatter from the inside. She rushed into the toilet. Cool air brushed her cheeks. She went to the window and leaned out, careful not to wound herself on the jagged edges of glass spouting from the frame.

"I know who you are," she said as the girl got to her feet three floors below. No street lights illuminated the alley, but the younger woman was held by the moon's glare. She gazed upwards to the voice.

Elena shouted again. "I know who you are. I know *what* you are."

The toilet door crashed open and Elena turned. Three bouncers stumbled into the toilet. Elena leaned out of the window to shout an alert. The warning locked in her throat. The girl was gone.

CHAPTER 2.
KILLER.

THE blow shattered the rottweiler's ribcage.

The dog was in mid-flight, pouncing on its prey, when the monster burst from the thicket. The crack of bone snapped at the night.

The rottweiler yelped as the impact hurled it off course. The animal crashed into undergrowth.

The dog squealed and struggled and shat as teeth and claws ripped through its fur and flesh, tearing it to shreds.

The other two dogs stood statue still. They were no longer interested in chasing the prowler who had activated the alarm, which got them freed from their cage. The dogs' hesitation gave the intruder time to escape the grounds by scaling the ten-foot perimeter wall.

But something else lurked in dark, tangled undergrowth. Something huge and terrifying and lethal.

The rottweilers locked eyes with the gloom that had swallowed their pack leader. They sniffed. The scent was fat with blood and danger.

One dog whimpered. It barked a warning, stepped forward. Then it faltered.

It stepped back.

It turned and bolted, and its companion followed.

Ears back, tails between their legs, the dogs fled.

And something pursued them, bearing down on its prey.

* * *

The alarm wailed. John Thorn raced from the house. He yanked the Browning automatic from its holster.

Security lights flooded the front lawn. Thorn hurtled through the glowing pool created by the light, his heart punching at his chest.

Lucky he switched the alarm system back on after the fool who was supposed to be responsible forgot. Thorn pledged to report the guy to the security firm.

He headed for the woods at the far end of the lawn.

His grip on the gun tightened.

Thorn stopped at the edge of the lake of light and crouched. His breathing was steady, drawing the August air into his lungs. He squinted, forcing his eyes to grow accustomed to the dark. It seemed thicker, darker in the trees.

He shouted into the dark. "Armed police. If you've got a weapon, put it on the ground and step out with your hands above your head. Now."

Silence and darkness.

Voices babbled from the house two hundred yards behind him. Thorn glanced over his shoulder and clenched his teeth. A cluster of guests had gathered at the front entrance.

Get them inside, he thought.

Tuxedoed security men tried to herd the flock back into the mansion, but Sir Adam Templeton's guests scented action. They wanted to see what tripped the alarms and the security lights, what had made the dogs bark and howl.

The guests were business leaders, politicians, family, and friends of Sir Adam, formerly a Northern Ireland minister during the Thatcher regime. They were launching a venture that promised to create hundreds of jobs. Thorn had no idea what kind of jobs, or if they'd ever materialise. He didn't let that worry him. The police sergeant was focused on his job: protecting Sir Adam.

He stared into the knot of beeches and oaks. A shiver seeped through him.

Seconded to the ex-MP eighteen months earlier, Thorn had two months left before returning to duties with the Northumbria force at their HQ in Ponteland. He craved it. Wished he could fold the calendar and make those eight weeks disappear. Accompanying the insular and sullen Sir Adam to functions and meetings had been tedious; ensuring the former minister's arrogant son, Michael, kept out of trouble had been wearisome.

This latter function was secondary and unofficial, but Thorn felt it part of his responsibilities to protect the whole clan. With a host of Templetons at that evening's do, Thorn felt his duties had multiplied. The burden was a heavy one.

He whistled, hoping the dogs would react. Nothing moved in the trees. His palms were sweaty on the Browning. The gun had been unholstered only once before, but never fired in action.

Right, in you go, Johnny-boy.

He glanced over his shoulder again. The guests were being penned into Templeton Hall's Georgian structure. Two security guards hired for the night jogged down the lawn towards Thorn. With back up on the way, relief brushed away some of Thorn's tension.

He stared back into the woods.

Dark and still and silent.

He straightened and moved forward.

His feet crunched on the gravel path that circled the house and lawn. Crossing into the blackness of the trees, he felt the atmosphere tighten. The pleasing temperatures that August nights brought with them turned clammy. The beeches lurched above him. Leaves rustled and twigs cracked beneath his feet as he treaded deeper into the maw.

Swallowed by darkness, Thorn gazed upwards. Summer made the trees thick and he could only glimpse a hint of sky, a sliver of moonshine above him.

"Shit."

Thorn's legs felt like hundredweights. His bladder became heavy. His eyes watered as they fought to penetrate the blackness.

He spun round as the ground shook, twigs cracking, heavy shoes crunching through the undergrowth.

"You couldn't make any *more* noise, could you?"

The two security men who followed him from the house halted. They glanced at each other like schoolboys caught smoking.

"Found anything?" said Finch, built like an oak tree with a bushy goatee.

"Found anything? I can't *see* anything." Thorn wished them away, but he felt safer with some muscle.

The skinhead named Norton, who played rugby for the Newcastle Falcons' second eleven, drifted off to the left.

"Stay close," said Thorn. "It...whatever...they might still be out here."

Finch said, "'It'? What do you mean 'it'?"

"The dogs are dead, Finch."

"I thought you hadn't found anything."

"That's why I think they're dead."

"You called them?"

Thorn nodded, wanting to end the conversation and delve deeper into the trees. "And I heard them make a right fucking racket," he said. "Something was killing them."

Finch seemed to tense. His gaze flitted from side to side. "You think we should get some more men? Some guns?"

Thorn waved his Browning. "I've got a gun."

"Jesus Christ. Thorn. Come look at this."

It was Norton. Panic pinched his voice into a higher pitch.

Thorn's heart lunged at his ribcage. "Where are you, Norton?" He hurried through the darkness, Finch at his heels, the security man's breathing as heavy as his footfalls. "Keep talking. We can't see you."

"Here. Over here. Christ. Hurry. It must still be out here."

Thorn could hear the panic in Norton's voice.

It must still be out here.

Thorn could see the skinhead standing like a mourner at a grave. The sergeant kicked on through the undergrowth. A stench struck at his nose: a coppery smell, heavy and warm.

"There's fucking blood everywhere, man." Norton's voice was a whine.

Thorn wanted to puke. His throat locked, dry like sandpaper. Behind him, Finch coughed and spluttered and swore at the sight.

"What the fuck did that?" said Norton, as if hoping someone would make sense of the carnage.

Thorn's stare fixed on the two heads. Torn away from the bodies, the black fur on both was matted in blood. The eyes were white and empty, and the mouths gaping. The pink tongues lolled like giant slugs over the jaws.

The animals' remains were scattered about the undergrowth: a paw, a flank, a leg, bones, guts, blood.

Steam rose from the meat. Thorn felt it cling to his skin, creep up his nostrils. The hairs on his nape stiffened, and he shivered.

It must still be out here.

"Get back to the house. Call the police," said Thorn.

"Should we tell Sir Adam?" said Norton as he turned his back on the carnage. Finch had already skulked into the darkness.

"No. Don't say anything."

Finch and Norton threaded their way out of the woods. Thorn listened until their footsteps faded. He gazed at the rottweilers' remains. He still had to find the other dog. Thorn knew it would be in a similar state of dismemberment.

But whatever killed it, and these two...

His grip on the Browning tightened. Sweat leaked from his armpits. A chill leached through his bones. His eyes roved the darkness.

...could still be in here.

He stalked backwards, watching the blackness about him as best he could. If an animal (what kind of *animal* could do this?) lay in wait in the murk, it could see him. It had an advantage. A voice in Thorn's head urged him to run. But his nerves held firm against the flight instinct. A dash would only trigger an attack. He'd probably get one shot off before being downed.

Thorn kept moving. The only sounds were his breathing and the crunching of twigs as he stepped away from the bloody scene. His eyes searched for danger signs. The lights of Templeton Hall shimmered through the bulk of the beeches. It would be good to get inside; sink a brandy to temper his shakes. It would be good to –

It crashed from the thicket to his left.

He spun to face it, eyes half-closed to take the blow, gun hand ready to fire.

But it was too close.

He thrust up an arm to protect his face. The figure smacked into him. He heard a crack, and his elbow jolted. He staggered away, swiping at the darkness. Thorn gasped, ready for the attack.

It never came.

He leaned against the trunk of a tree, the bark rough against his skull. His stomach muscles knotted, and his belly lurched.

The girl lay on the ground. She was naked. Her dark hair fanned around her head and shoulders. She wiped what looked liked blood

from her mouth and chin. Her cheeks were streaked pink. A bruise
cupped her left eye.

CHAPTER 3.
TERRITORIAL.

"IS that your blood, pet?" asked PC Susan Pendle, struggling to twist her bulky frame in the passenger seat of the police car. "How did you hurt yourself?"

The girl said nothing.

"How's she doing?" asked Sergeant Ken Travis. He glanced in the rear view mirror at the suspect. He winced at her swollen eye. That's where John Thorn's elbow cracked her, he thought.

Seated in the back, she was wrapped in a blanket.

Pendle turned to face the front and shook her head. "She looks in shock to me, Sarge."

"We'll get her looked at. Get those arms patched up. Dogs gave her a good going over."

"And something returned the favour. What do you think did that? Butchered the poor animals."

Travis shook his head. "Let's look after this young lassie before we do anything else."

The five-mile drive from Templeton Hall took them through open country. Up ahead, Travis saw the Abbey dominate the dark blue skyline. Everything felt better when that building came into view. The Abbey was founded in 674AD, and loomed high in the town of Hexham. Seeing it made Travis feel he was home. Born and raised here, he was proud to serve as a sergeant in the local police station. The joy that filled him on his wedding day, and on the birth of his two sons, also filled Travis whenever he saw the Abbey. He loved the embrace of a homecoming. Even the stress of having this feral stranger in the back seat was tempered when the monument came into view.

The girl had been found naked and caked in blood at Templeton Hall. Was it her blood, as Pendle inquired, or blood from Sir Adam's mutilated guard dogs?

"What were you doing on Templeton land, pet?" said the policewoman, huffing again as she turned to face the prisoner.

Travis heard a guttural noise.

He said, "What did she say?"

Pendle faced front once more. Travis glanced across at her. The policewoman's face was pale.

"Nowt, Sarge. She growled."

"Better leave her be for now."

But Pendle persisted. She spoke into the rear view mirror this time. "You've got to tell us your name, you know. Sir Adam may want to prosecute you for trespassing. Do you understand what I'm saying, pet?"

"Do you speak English? Can you understand?" said Travis, guiding the patrol car into the town. He'd be glad to get this girl out of range. He couldn't see how such a frail little thing could have killed the Templeton dogs. But she was found in the vicinity, and that made her a suspect. Travis watched the RSPCA guys scrape up what was left of the rottweilers. He didn't like the idea of being near anyone linked to such violence. The smell of the dogs' remains had been stomach churning, and its trace remained with the girl in the back, an invisible passenger. He wanted to get home to Joanna, to a beer, and the Thai curry she'd promised him that afternoon as he left for his shift.

Travis steered the car into Hexham General Hospital's car park on Corbridge Road.

Then the girl spoke. "What are we doing here?"

Travis jammed the breaks and the safety belt bit into his chest. Pendle gasped. They twisted in their seats to face the girl.

"You *do* understand," said Pendle, glowering at the younger woman.

The girl said, "Why are we at the hospital?"

But she didn't wait for an answer. She grabbed the door handle and rattled it, whining at its refusal to budge.

"Calm down," said Travis as Pendle reached over and held the girl by the shoulders.

The girl snapped back into her seat and scowled at the officers. Strands of raven-black hair threaded over her face. Her eyes were autumn leaf crescents, deep and dark. Travis could sink into those eyes...

He sensed his flushing cheeks and coughed, turning away from the girl. "We're...we're going to have your arms looked at. Get you checked out. Then we're going to have to have a chat down at the station."

"I could kill you both, you know," said the girl, her voice calm.

But it shook Travis.

Pendle jabbed a finger at the girl. "Are you threatening us, young lady? I'm warning you—"

The girl said nothing. She stared defiantly at Pendle, then hitched her feet on to the seat and squatted there.

"Oh, my God," said Pendle.

"What is she doing?" said Travis, gawping into the rear view mirror.

"Oh, my God," said Pendle again, hand covering her mouth.

Travis heard the hiss as liquid struck the carpet, and a sour stench filled the car.

CHAPTER 4.
THE TEMPLETONS.

GUNFIRE barked and zombies groaned as Michael Templeton destroyed the undead.

This was Michael's domain. Locked in the games room, he could drown out the dullness of life at the Hall. The centrepiece of the oak-panelled room was the full-size billiard table. Skirting the walls were arcade-type games. He was playing The House Of The Dead on one of the machines. In one corner a 61-inch TV boasted a DreamCast logo, the console itself perched on a beanbag where the player would lounge. A rack of shelves on one wall brimmed with games, arranged alphabetically by Michael. A considerable stereo system was stacked at the front wall next to the door.

John Thorn sat on a stool at the bar that was set into the back wall.

Like a landlord, Sir Adam Templeton stood behind the bar, a brandy glass in his hand. The room reeked of polish and tobacco, the nicotine a clue to last night's party. Thorn guessed that Michael and the Templeton clan's young turks spent the evening in the games room, scheming and drinking and snorting.

Sir Adam's grey eyes stared into the tumbler as if he were reading the booze like a fortuneteller reads tealeaves. He said, "How old would you say she was, John?"

"Difficult to tell. She was a mess. But I'd say early to mid-twenties."

Michael was killing zombies. He grunted as another green-skinned monster exploded under a rain of bullets.

Thorn glanced at the young man and clenched his teeth. *Stop your fucking playing you little git,* he thought.

Michael's black ponytail bobbed as he squeezed the console's trigger.

"Did you get a good look at her tits?" The younger Templeton spoke into the screen as another of the walking dead was sent to video game hell.

"What?"

"Come on, John." Michael spun to face his father and the sergeant. Behind him a zombie filled the screen. The screen turned red. "She was naked. Out cold. You must've had a look."

"Enough, Michael." Sir Adam's eyes were still fixed on the brandy.

"Dad's a bit worried, you see, sergeant. He thinks the past's come back to haunt—"

"Enough, Michael." Face turning red, the older man stabbed a look at his son.

Thorn wondered what Michael meant. But he left it. He didn't like to get involved in their father-son arguments. There were too many to recall, and they all concluded with Michael storming out of the house in a blaze of threats.

Michael leaned against the arcade machine and folded his arms. His face muscles danced in anger as he clenched his mouth shut, holding back the battery of abuse he wanted to fire at his father.

"I don't want her charged," said Sir Adam. He gulped at the brandy.

Michael stepped forward. "You've got to." He crossed to the bar and slammed his hands flat on the counter. He glared at Thorn. "Father," he said, eyes still locked on the sergeant. "Father, we should discuss this. Alone."

Thorn didn't budge. He held Michael's gaze.

"Alone," said Michael more forcefully.

Thorn looked away. His gaze dropped to a copy of The Journal, the local morning newspaper, which lay on the bar. He scanned the front page. The splash told of the bid by Sir Adam and his partners to bring hundreds of jobs into the area. Next to it, a picture of Alan Shearer celebrating a hat-trick in Newcastle United's 3-0 win over Everton. "Full story: Back Page," offered the caption. A single column story to the right of the picture was headlined: "Masked rapist's third victim." He turned the paper over and read the first few paragraphs of the

Newcastle United story.

Sir Adam poured himself another brandy. He asked Thorn, "Can you let your colleagues know I've no intention of taking action against her?"

The officer nodded. "If that's what you want."

Michael huffed, and pushed himself away from the bar. "This is madness. She...she killed the dogs."

"She was about five-foot-four, weighed not much more than eight-and-a-half stone, and carried no weapons." Thorn directed his words to Sir Adam. "There's no way—"

"What the fuck do you know?"

Thorn glared at Michael.

The younger man's cheeks reddened, and his brow furrowed. He was so like his father: the wide-set eyes, the Roman nose, thin lips, sharp chin. You're daddy's boy, all right, thought Thorn, quelling the urge to smack Michael in the face, but you'll never be your father's son.

"Do not use foul language in my house," said Sir Adam.

"Then tell this beat cop to mind his own business." Michael jabbed a finger in Thorn's direction. "Tell him he doesn't know what he's talking about. Or just *tell* him."

Silence fell on the room.

Thorn had to speak to the girl. Sir Adam and Michael appeared to know her, and why she'd been there. Did she know the Templetons? Sir Adam wasn't willing to tell. Thorn didn't want Michael to tell. The younger Templeton's voice grated. It made Thorn think violent thoughts.

"Could you leave us, John?" said Sir Adam. "Thank you for tonight."

Thorn headed for his room, pacing through a corridor lined with portraits of long-dead Templetons. Voices blared behind him. The words were muffled, but father and son spat vitriol, he was sure of that.

Thorn paused at his door and glanced at the portrait staring down at him. The Templeton features were vivid, framed by snow-white hair and thick sideburns. The brass plate on the frame read: Sir Richard Templeton, MP: 1835-1902.

Slipping into his room, Thorn thought about the past and if it could come back to haunt.